WITNESS AGAINST THE BEAST

To
David Erdman

WITNESS AGAINST THE BEAST

*William Blake and
the Moral Law*

E. P. THOMPSON

'Christ died as an Unbeliever'
WILLIAM BLAKE

THE NEW PRESS

The New Press, New York

Published in the United States by The New Press, New York
Distributed by W. W. Norton & Company, Inc.
500 Fifth Avenue, New York, NY 10110

Library of Congress cataloging-in-publication data

Thompson, E. P. (Edward Palmer), 1924–1993
Witness against the beast: William Blake and the moral law / by
E. P. Thompson
p. cm.
ISBN 1-56584-099-2
1. Blake, William, 1757–1827 – Political and social views.
2. Dissenters, Religious – England – History – 18th century.
3. Radicalism – England – History – 18th century.   4. Blake, William,
1757–1827 – Religion.   5. Blake, William, 1757–1827 – Ethics.
6. Ethics, Modern – 18th century.   7. Radicalism in literature.
8. Ethics in literature.   I. Title.
PR4148.P6T47   1993b
821'.7 – dc20   92–50819 CIP

Established in 1990 as a major alternative to the large,
commercial publishing houses, The New Press is the first
full-scale nonprofit American book publisher outside of
the university presses. The Press is operated editorially in
the public interest, rather than for private gain; it is
committed to publishing in innovative ways works of
educational, cultural, and community value, which despite
their intellectual merits might not normally be
"commercially" viable. The New Press's editorial offices
are located at the City University of New York.

Printed in the United States of America

10 9 8 7 6 5 4 3 2 1

Contents

Contents

Illustrations

(Between pages 106 and 107. All pictures are by William Blake.)

1   *Eve Tempted by the Serpent*. Tempera, painted for Thomas Butts, *c.*1799–1800 (courtesy of the Victoria & Albert Museum)

2   *Satan Exulting over Eve*. Pencil, pen and black ink and watercolour over colour print, 1795 (courtesy of the J. Paul Getty Museum)

3   *The Temptation and Fall of Eve*, from Nine Illustrations to *Paradise Lost*. Pen and watercolour on paper, 1808 (gift by subscription; courtesy of Museum of Fine Arts, Boston)

4   *Job's Evil Dreams*, Plate 11 of *Illustrations to the Book of Job*, 1821 (courtesy of the Pierpont Morgan Library, New York)

5   *Moses Erecting the Brazen Serpent*. Pen and watercolour on paper, *c.*1805 (purchased 1890; courtesy of Museum of Fine Arts, Boston)

6   Title page to *Europe*, 1794 (copy G; courtesy of the Pierpont Morgan Library, New York. PML 77235)

7   *Elohim Creating Adam*. Colour print finished in pen, from the Thomas Butts Collection, 1795 (courtesy of the Tate Gallery)

8   *Michael Foretells the Crucifixion*, from Nine Illustrations to *Paradise Lost*. Pen and watercolour on paper, 1808 (gift by subscription; courtesy of Museum of Fine Arts, Boston)

9   *The Nativity*. Tempera on copper, from the Thomas Butts Collection, *c.*1799 (courtesy of the Philadelphia Museum of Art, Gift of Mrs William T. Tonner)

10 'The Garden of Love', from *Songs of Experience*, 1794 (King's College, Cambridge. Print supplied by the Syndics of Cambridge University Library)

11 'London', from *Songs of Experience*, *c.*1794 (King's College, Cambridge. Print supplied by the Syndics of Cambridge University Library)

vii

Preface

This study has its origin in the Alexander Lectures delivered in the University of Toronto in 1978. I am very much remiss in delaying publication for so long, and I offer my apologies to the University. (The demands of the peace movement and, subsequently, illness contributed to the delay.) Although this text has greatly expanded from the Lectures, the book still carries their shape: that is, in Lecture 1 I somehow covered the themes in Part I of this book, and in Lectures 2 and 3 the themes in Part II. I must once again thank the University for its encouragement and hospitality.

I have had generous help from many persons: from Jean Barsley (formerly Mrs Noakes); from John and Susan Beattie and their family for their hospitality while I was in Toronto; from G.E. Bentley Jr, Katy Ellsworth, James Epstein, Michael Ferber, Heather Glen, P.M. Grams, J.F.C. Harrison, Christopher Hill, Peter Lineham, Günther Lottes, Iain McCalman, Hans Medick, Jon Mee, A.J. Morley, the late Philip Noakes, Morton D. Paley, Michael Phillips, Mary Thale, Sir Keith Thomas, Malcolm Thomas and John Walsh. Eveline King has transformed my untidy manuscript into accomplished typing. Dorothy Thompson, once more, has given me every kind of support.

I have dedicated the book to David Erdman, the great Blake scholar, even though the dedication may prove to be an embarrassment to him, since (as I know) he disagrees with several of my suggestions. He is the most generous and helpful scholar that I have known, and we have had rich exchanges – rich at least on his part – over the past thirty years. In 1968 we jointly taught a graduate course on Blake at New York University, and I have been warmly entertained by David and his wife, Virginia, at their house on Long Island. It has been a privilege to work alongside such a superb authority on the Romantics.

ix

I also owe thanks to the libraries and institutions which I used during my research. These included the British Library, the Public Record Office, Westminster Library, the Bodleian, Birmingham University Library and Dr Williams's Library. Particular thanks must go to the Librarian and staff at the premises of the Swedenborg Society, who assisted me in many enquiries and who enabled me to consult Conference papers and Minutes, although they knew that I was not a receiver. My critical account of the early years of the Church is poor repayment, although accounts no less critical are endorsed in subsequent Swedenborgian scholarship. I must also thank Manchester University, whose award of a Simon Senior Fellowship in 1988–9 enabled me to catch up on my research, and to those graduate seminars (at Brown University, Dartmouth College, Queen's University, Ontario, and at Rutgers) which discussed these ideas with me and contributed their own thoughts. And my very warm thanks go to those who have, from time to time, given me material assistance to pursue my research: W.H. and Carol Terry, Mr and Mrs Kenneth F. Montgomery, James and Virginia Newmyer, and the Newby Trust.

My thanks must also go to those institutions which have given permission to me to reproduce pictures. (They are listed in the List of illustrations.) The chapter on 'London' is a slightly modified version of the same in *Interpreting Blake*, ed. Michael Phillips (Cambridge, 1978).

I use few abbreviations, and these are obvious ones. The exceptions are: in text and notes E stands for *The Poetry and Prose of William Blake* (New York, 1965), ed. David Erdman, with commentary by Harold Bloom. N refers to *The Notebook of William Blake*, ed. David Erdman (Oxford, 1973).

Introduction

I should explain at once what kind of a book this, and why I have been foolhardy enough to add yet one more volume to the overfull shelves of studies of William Blake. And, first of all, what this book is not. This is not another introduction to the poet and his works: excellent ones already exist. Nor is this a general interpretive study of William Blake as a whole, of his life, his writing, his art, his mythology, his thought. I will not even attempt a close engagement with the very substantial output of expert Blake studies in the past half-century. So that what I offer in this book must be, in some sense, a view from outside the world of Blake scholarship.

Can such a view be of any value? This will be for readers to judge. But I have been emboldened by a growing conviction that there are problems inside the world of Blake scholarship which might helpfully be commented upon by a historian from without. For while the scholarship advances, I am not certain that agreement about the man, or his ideas, or even about individual poems, advances in step. On the one hand, we have a multitude of individual studies, each adding some minute particulars to the sum. On the other hand, the intelligent reader, coming new to Blake, faces real difficulties in understanding what this sum may be. For there are now a great many William Blakes on offer, and while some of these are very much more convincing than others, most of them have some plausibility. Northrop Frye remarked many years ago that 'it has been said of Boehme that his books are like a picnic to which the author brings the words and the reader the meaning'. This remark, Frye continues, 'may have been intended as a sneer at Boehme, but it is an exact description of all works of literary art without exception'.

This has always seemed to me to be a wise comment; and yet it is a partial one, and one that leaves me uneasy. For there are so

many picnics going on today – each one of them licensed by some
words of Blake – and in so many different places. In 1965 Harold
Bloom was able to write, with his customary confidence, that Blake
'was not an antiquarian, a mystic, an occultist or theosophist, and
not much of a scholar of any writings beyond the Bible and other
poetry insofar as it resembled the Bible'. I think that his judgement
is more or less right, if we use the term 'scholar' in a modern,
academic sense. And yet, both before and after that judgement,
we have seen the publication of volumes, of some scholarly weight,
to show Blake the neo-Platonist, the mason and illuminist, the
profound initiate in hermetic learning, the proto-Marxist, the
euhemerist, the Druid . . . And if more cautious scholars avoid
such direct identifications, they offer us instead William Blake as
a syncretic polymath – a man aware of all these positions and
traditions, as well as others, moving freely through some remarkably well-stocked library, replete with ancient, Eastern, Hebrew
and arcane, as well as modern, sources, and combining elements
from all of these at will.

A historian has one difficulty with this. Blake's library – which
by some accounts must have been costly and immense – has never
been identified. I will return to this point, since I think we may
be able to surmise one or two curious libraries, as well as his own
private collection, to which he had access (see pp. 41–3). But even
as we ask this mundane question (which library?), we are forced
to ask ulterior questions. Who was Blake? Where do we place him
in the intellectual and social life of London between 1780 and 1820?
What particular traditions were at work within his mind? I have
written this book in the hope that a historian's view, in this matter
of placing, may prove to be helpful.

The problem today is to bring all of Frye's 'picnic parties'
together. By all means let each of us bring our own meanings, but
let us at least picnic in the same place. It is a curious consequence
of the abundant Blake scholarship of the past few years that this
has actually become more difficult than it used to be. Over a hundred years ago there was some consensus as to what kind of a man
Blake was; the oral traditions and records resumed in Alexander
Gilchrist's first major biography (1863) gave us a confident picture
of a 'visionary', eccentric genius of robust 'Jacobinical' convictions.
This placing was refined, but not substantially challenged, in
Mona Wilson's *Life* of 1927; it was given a nudge to the 'Left'

by Jacob Bronowski (*A Man without a Mask*, 1944), who perhaps over-stated the artisanal situation of Blake as an engraver; and this over-statement has been redressed by the learned studies, over a lifetime, of Sir Geoffrey Keynes, and of David Erdman, G.E. Bentley and many others, who have clearly identified Blake's familiarity with the community of London's artists.

Erdman's major study (*Blake: Prophet against Empire*, 1954, revised editions, 1965, 1969 and 1977) succeeded also in placing Blake's thought within the political and cultural context of his times. On the directly political themes I have (no doubt to the surprise of some readers) little to add. In my own placing of Blake I have learned very much from Erdman and I am greatly in his debt. All that his reconstruction of Blake lacks, in my view, is the thrust of a particular intellectual tradition: antinomianism. In brief, it is Blake's unique notation of Christian belief, and not his 'Jacobin' political sympathies, which still stands in need of examination. Despite Jon Mee's recent recovery of many possible contemporary influences upon Blake (*Dangerous Enthusiasm*, 1992) this still remains true.

This is not to say that the matter has gone unnoticed. As long ago as 1958 A.L. Morton published *The Everlasting Gospel: A Study in the Sources of William Blake*, and these insights were much enlarged in *The World of the Ranters* (1970) and by Christopher Hill in *The World Turned Upside Down* (1972). My debt to these scholars will be evident. But while Morton showed many suggestive parallels between 'Ranter' rhetoric and imagery and those of Blake, he could not identify any vectors between the 1650s and Blake's time. I cannot say that I have found with certainty any such vectors, but I have searched somewhat further, and I have also attended more closely to antinomian beliefs and their possible situation in the eighteenth-century intellectual culture. (If any readers are uncertain as to the meanings of antinomianism I must beg them to be patient: these will be explained.)

Despite every precaution, we have a continuing difficulty in our approach to Blake, which derives from our tendency to make overly academic assumptions as to his learning and mode of thought. It takes a large effort to rid ourselves of these assumptions, because they lie at an inaccessible level within our own intellectual culture – indeed, they belong to the very institutions and disciplines with which we construct that culture. That is, we tend to find that a

man is either 'educated' or 'uneducated', or is educated to certain
levels (within a relatively homogeneous hierarchy of attainments);
and this education involves submission to certain institutionally
defined disciplines, with their own hierarchies of accomplishment
and authority.

Blake's mind was formed within a very different intellectual tradition. In the nineteenth century we sometimes call this, a little
patronisingly, the tradition of the autodidact. This calls to mind
the radical or Chartist journalist, lecturer or poet, attaining by his
own efforts to a knowledge of 'the classics'. This is not right for
Blake. For a great deal of the most notable intellectual energies of
the eighteenth century lay outside of formal academic channelling.
This was manifestly so in the natural sciences and in the *praxis* of
the early industrial revolution; and it was equally so in important
areas of theology and of political thought.

The formal, classical intellectual culture (which I will call 'the
polite culture'), whose summits were attained at Oxford and Cambridge, was offered to only a small elite, and was, in theory, further
limited by the need for students and fellows to conform to the
doctrinal orthodoxy of the Church of England. Much of the
(strongly intellectual) traditions of Dissent lay outside these doors.
But alternative centres of intellectual culture can be seen not only
at the level of such institutions as the Dissenting Academies. They
exist also in stubborn minority traditions of many kinds.

Not only political and economic history can be seen as 'the pro-
paganda of the victors': this is true also of intellectual history.
Looking back from the nineteenth century, the victors appeared to
be rationalism, political economy, utilitarianism, science, liberal-
ism. And tracing the ancestry of these victors, it was possible to see
eighteenth-century thought as the progression of 'enlightenment',
sometimes working its way out through the churches, as rational
Dissent passed through unitarianism to deism. It is only recently
that historians have attended more closely to very vigorous alternative – and sometimes explicitly *counter*-enlightenment – impulses:
the Rosicrucians, Philadelphians, Behmenists: or the elaborate
theological and scientific theories of the Hutchinsonians, who were
polemically anti-Newtonian, and who had both academic expo-
nents and a more humble visionary following. In London in the
1780s – and, indeed, in Western Europe very generally – there was
something like an explosion of anti-rationalism, taking the forms

of illuminism, masonic rituals, animal magnetism, millenarian speculation, astrology (and even a small revival in alchemy), and of mystic and Swedenborgian circles.

Alternative intellectual traditions existed also – and especially in London – at the level of family traditions, and obscure intellectual currents surfacing, submerging and then surfacing again in little periodicals, or in chapels which fractured into several petty chapels, which invited new ministers or gathered around new voices, which knit up ideas and unravelled them and knit them up again throughout the eighteenth century. And we have to learn to see the minds of these men and women, formed in these kinds of collisions and voluntary associations, with more humility than patronage. Out of such an 'education', of informal traditions and collisions, came many original minds: Franklin, Paine, Wollstone-craft, Bewick, Cobbett, Thomas Spence, Robert Owen. And it is in this kind of tradition that we must place Blake.

In this tradition experience is laid directly alongside learning, and the two test each other. There is nothing of our present academic specialisation: thought may be borrowed, like imagery, from any source available. There is, in this tradition, a strong, and sometimes an excessive, self-confidence. And there is an insistent impulse towards individual system-building: the authority of the Church, demystified in the seventeenth century, had not yet been replaced by the authority of an academic hierarchy or of public 'experts'. In Blake's dissenting London of the 1780s and 1790s this impulse was at its height. Men and women did not only join the groups on offer, the Church of the New Jerusalem, the Universalists, the Muggletonians, the followers of William Huntington and of Richard Brothers (the self-proclaimed 'nephew' of the Almighty), they argued amidst these groups, they fractured them, took a point from one and a point from another, conceived their own heresies, and all the time struggled to define their own sense of system.

Of course, this has been recognised, and for a long time, by Blake scholars. I do not mean to read a lesson to those many scholars who have already done so much to place Blake's work in context. But historians have not yet done as much as might be done to help them, by recovering the obscure traditions of London Dissent, and in the absence of this work there is an ever-present tendency for criticism to slide into a de-contextual history of ideas.

And for this there might seem to be a licence afforded by Frederick Tatham, a friend of William and Catherine Blake in their last years, and an early biographer. Writing in 1832, Tatham said: 'His mental acquirements were incredible, he had read almost every thing in whatsoever language, which language he always taught himself.' And more than thirty years later he repeated this claim: Blake 'had a most consummate knowledge of all the great writers in all languages . . . I have possessed books well thumbed and dirtied by his graving hands, in Latin, Greek, Hebrew, French and Italian, besides a large collection of works of the mystical writers, Jacob Behmen, Swedenborg, and others.'

But if we set out to read 'almost everything in whatsoever language' we may end up, not with Blake, but with an academic exercise. And from 'all the great writers in all languages' we are at liberty to make our own selective construction of Blake's 'tradition', a construction which will actually distract us from William Blake. If I must name names, then let me name Miss Kathleen Raine, although her work (*Blake and Tradition*, 1968) is only one of the most formidable of other works which offer to place Blake in relation to Behmenist, hermetic, neo-Platonist and Kabbalistic thought. In Raine's notion of 'the tradition' we are pointed towards Porphyry or Proclus or Thomas Taylor (the neo-Platonist contemporary of Blake), and often suggestions are made which are helpful and sometimes probable. But although Raine stands at an obtuse angle to the reigning academicism, her notion of 'tradition' remains academic to the core. Why is this so?

It is partly because we have become habituated to reading in an academic way. Our books are not 'thumbed by graving hands'. We learn of an influence, we are directed to a book or to a 'reputable' intellectual tradition, we set this book beside that book, we compare and cross-refer. But Blake had a different way of reading. He would look into a book with a directness which we might find to be naïve or unbearable, challenging each one of its arguments against his own experience and his own 'system'. This is at once apparent from his surviving annotations – to Lavater, Swedenborg, Berkeley, Bacon, Bishop Watson or Thornton.

He took each author (even the Old Testament prophets) as his equal, or as something less. And he acknowledged as between them, no received judgements as to their worth, no hierarchy of accepted 'reputability'. For Blake, a neighbour, or a fellow-reader of a periodical, or his friend and patron, Thomas Butts, were quite as likely to hold opinions of central importance as was any man of recognised learning. Certainly, his reading was extensive; nothing should astonish us; and whatever libraries he used, he entered some odd and unfamiliar corners.

My own answer to the problem of what guided his reading will become apparent in this book. But, in brief, I suppose that his learning was both more eccentric and more eclectic – even, at times, more shallow – than is sometimes suggested. It was eccentric, in the sense that he did have some access to an almost-underground tradition of mystic and antinomian tracts, some of these derived from the seventeenth century. Eclectic (and sometimes casual or shallow), in the sense that, whereas some scholars have found in him a profound student of comparative religion and myth, I think it possible that Blake's imagination was sufficiently supplied with images of ancient and alien religious rites and beliefs from readily available secondary sources, such as William Hurd's popular compendium, *A New Universal History of the Religious Rites, Ceremonies, and Customs of the Whole World* (1788) – a work which employed a number of his fellow-engravers. And even when we enter firmer territory, such as the acknowledged Swedenborgian influence upon Blake, I will attempt to show that certain of Blake's ideas owed less to a reading of Swedenborg's writings than to an obscure little magazine published from a barber's shop in Hoxton, or to his reactions to some execrable hymns written by a zealous Swedenborgian minister, Joseph Proud. Or, when he wrestled with deist thought, I will suggest that he was less influenced by acknowledged thinkers of the Enlightenment than by Volney's *Ruins of Empire*, which the cognoscenti of the London Corresponding Society – master craftsmen, shopkeepers, engravers, hosiers, printers – carried around with them in their pockets. And, finally, when he denounced the Tree of Mystery, he certainly operated within a wide field of intellectual reference; but he was also stung to fury by a certain Robert Hindmarsh, who was introducing ceremonial forms and priestly ordinances into the nascent Church of the New Jerusalem.

Ideas happen in this kind of way. But they happen most of all in this kind of way within the tradition which Blake inhabited and extended. We must confront Miss Raine's notion of 'the tradition' and ask *which* tradition? The answer should not come to rest in a simple either/or, as in Robert Redfield's notion of a 'great' (or polite) and a 'little' (or popular) tradition of culture. Blake inhabited both of these at will. But he took with him, into both of them, a mind and sensibility formed within a different, and a particular, tradition again: a particular current within bourgeois (and, often, artisan) Dissent. Much of Raine's 'tradition' appears, at first sight, to say some of the things that Blake is saying, but it is saying them in a different way. It is genteel, other-worldly, elusive, whereas Blake – whether in poetic or in visual image – has a certain literalness of expression, robustness and concretion. Again, Raine's 'tradition', except where it draws upon Boehme, lacks altogether the radical edge or bite of Blake's expression. And (Boehme again excepted) it lacks the conscious posture of hostility to the polite learning of the Schools, *including* the polite neo-Platonist or hermetic speculations of gentry and professional men.

This is a point of importance. I will not delay to document it now. Any reader of Blake knows that it is so, and this book will keep an eye upon that point. Blake's hostility to academicism is often expressed with superb vigour, and very often within the field – the visual arts – to which he might be said, in a contemporary sense, to have submitted to an orthodox training: turn, for example, to his annotations to Sir Joshua Reynolds. At times this hostility to academicism and to polite learning assumes the tones of class war:

Rouze up O Young Men of the New Age! set your foreheads against the ignorant Hirelings! For we have Hirelings in the Camp, the Court & the University: who would if they could, for ever depress Mental & prolong Corporeal War. Painters! on you I call! Sculptors! Architects! . . . believe Christ & his Apostles that there is a Class of Men whose whole delight is in Destroying. We do not want either Greek or Roman Models if we are but just & true to our own Imaginations, those Worlds of Eternity in which we shall live for ever; in Jesus our Lord. (E94)

This is not only a war of the Imagination against the artifice and fashion of the polite culture; it is also a war of faith against a class of destroyers, and of the patronised practitioners of the creative arts against the hirelings of camp, court and university who are their patrons. This conscious posture of hostility to the polite culture, this radical stance, is not some quaint but inessential extra, added on to his tradition. It *is* his tradition, it defines his stance, it directs and colours his judgement. At times in his later years (as in passages of his 'Descriptive Catalogue' (1809) or in his unpublished 'Public Address' on his painting of the Canterbury Pilgrims (*c.*1810), this stance becomes wilful and plainly cantankerous.

I have tried to explain the intention, and also the limitations, of this book. This is not, I repeat, an introduction to William Blake, nor a general interpretive study. Nor is it, in the sense of adding 'background' or social and political context, a sketch of the 'historical' Blake. It is an intervention of a different kind. I am pursuing an enquiry into the structure of Blake's thought and the character of his sensibility.

My object is to identify, once again, Blake's tradition, his particular situation within it, and the repeated evidences, motifs and nodal points of conflict, which indicate his stance and the way his mind meets the world. To do this involves some historical recovery, and attention to sources external to Blake – sources which, very often, he may not have been aware of himself. For it is necessary to define, first of all, an obscure antinomian tradition; and then to define Blake's very unusual, and probably unique, position within it. And we cannot understand, or shuffle around, Blake's ideas until we have defined these in relation to contrary or adjacent ideas. For example, we will be in no position to judge, with Donald Davie in *A Gathered Church*, whether Blake's religious insights were or were not 'beneath contempt' unless we have understood something of the doctrines of justification by faith, imputed righteousness and atonement, as they were understood by certain of his contemporaries, and as they were revised, or rejected, by him.

Very certainly, Blake's ideas undergo important changes, but even so he returns to certain elementary affirmations and constant preoccupations. I have indicated these places, from every part of his work, as evidence of the continuity of this structure but not in order to suggest consistency in his conclusions. My central study is more strictly limited, and falls chiefly within the years 1788 and 1794. This enables me to approach three themes. First, the antinomian tradition, the possible ways in which it could have been received by Blake, and his own unique notations. This is the theme of Part I. Second, the moment of the founding of the Church of the New Jerusalem, and Blake's situation within the controversies surrounding this. Third, the moment of confluence of antinomian and of 'Jacobinical' and deist influences, and the continuing argument to which this confluence gave rise in Blake's mind and art. These are the themes of Part II.

These three moments, in my view, give us an understanding of Blake: they show us who he was. By 1794 the structure of his ideas has been laid down, and we have in our hand the clues which lead forward to the later writings. But if I succeed in identifying this structure, I by no means wish to reduce all that Blake wrote or thought to this structure. From this antinomian/deist argument there is a radiation, an exploration outwards, some of which is ambivalent, much of which I do not understand, and none of which I wish to enclose or to bring back to these primary elements.

Finally, a word of encouragement to any readers who have been attracted to Blake but who feel themselves to be beginners. They are welcome on board and I hope that they will enjoy the voyage. I have tried to explain myself as I go along: indeed, readers already learned in Blake studies (whom I welcome aboard with more trepidation) may be impatient at the care with which I explain antinomianism or Jacob Boehme. But I cannot overcome all difficulties and I must assume at times a greater familiarity with Blake's writings than beginners may have. They are urged to have an edition of Blake's complete poems beside them and to explore it as an antidote to me. For the rest Part I of this book is concerned in the main with the transmission of certain highly unorthodox or heretical Christian ideas from the mid-seventeenth century to Blake's time, and it is not closely concerned with Blake himself, although an eye is kept upon possible parallels in his own thought, tropes and visual images. It is necesary only to know that Blake was born in 1757 into a hosier's family with (it is probable) a strong radical anti-Court tradition, served his apprenticeship as an engraver, studied (and exhibited) at the Royal Academy, published his first collection, *Poetical Sketches*, in 1783, formed friendships with several notable artists, including John Flaxman and Henry Fuseli, but left little other evidence of his vigorous interior life or beliefs until 1788, on the eve of the French Revolution. His exciting output then, in his early thirties, between 1788 and 1794, which included the *Songs of Innocence and Experience* and *The Marriage of Heaven and Hell*, entitles him in the view of one historian (A.L. Morton) to be known as England's last and greatest antinomian. That is the place which I started from and in 1968 I gave an early lecture on Blake at Columbia University (in New York City), at a time of excitement when some sort of campus revolution against the Moral Law was going on, and I startled the audience by acclaiming William Blake as 'the founder of the obscure sect to which I myself belong, the Muggletonian Marxists'. Instantly I found that many fellow-sectaries were in the room. As the years have gone by I have become less certain of both parts of the combination. But that is still the general area in which this book falls. In a brief introduction to Part II I try to explain myself further.

PART I

Inheritance

CHAPTER I

Works or faith?

When Christians unto Carnal Men give ear,
Out of their way they go, and pay for't dear;
For Master *Worldly Wiseman* can but shew
A Saint the way to Bondage and to Wo.

In this verse, John Bunyan sought to enforce the lesson of Christian's first severe temptation in *Pilgrim's Progress*. After crossing the *Slough of Despond*, Christian had met with Mr Worldly Wiseman, who dwelt in the town of *Carnal Policy*. Mr Wiseman was full of good advice, and he told Christian that 'in yonder Village (the Village is named *Morality*) there dwells a Gentleman whose name is *Legality*, a very judicious man'. *Legality* could certainly help Christian to lift the burden from his shoulders, and if the old gentleman was not at home, then certainly the 'pretty young man', his son, 'whose name is *Civility*', would be able to do it as well as his father. And then, Mr Worldly Wiseman urged, Christian could send for his wife and children and settle in the village of *Morality*: 'there thou shalt live by honest neighbours, in credit and good fashion'.

The temptation was so severe that Christian succumbed to it. He turned aside from the straight and narrow path to the wicket-gate of faith, and set off for *Legality*'s house, which stood on a high and threatening hill. Beneath this hill he might well have perished, had not *Evangelist* come up with him again. *Evangelist* turned Christian back into the path, rebuking him ('the just shall live by the faith . . . be not faithless, but believing'), and instructing him as to the abhorrent creed of Mr Worldly Wiseman: 'he savoureth only the doctrine of this world (therefore he always goes to the Town of *Morality* to church)' and 'he loveth that doctrine best, for it

Note: The place of publication in the works cited is London, unless otherwise stated.

3

saveth him from the Cross'. As for *Legality*, he is 'the Son of the Bond-woman', and 'she with her children are in bondage':

This *Legality* therefore is not able to set thee free from thy Burden. No man was as yet ever rid of his Burden by him; no, nor ever is like to be: ye cannot be justified by the Works of the Law; for by the deeds of the Law no man living can be rid of his Burden: therefore, Mr *Worldly Wiseman* is an alien, and Mr *Legality* a cheat; and for his son *Civility*, notwithstanding his simpering looks, he is but an hypocrite and cannot help thee. . .

At this, *Evangelist* called aloud to the Heavens for confirmation, and words and fire came out of the mountain under which they stood, declaring: '*As many as are of the works of the Law are under the curse. . .*'

So Christian set out on a journey which was to take him from the seventeenth century to the eighteenth century and beyond, and through the hearts of hundreds of thousands of readers. But the twentieth-century reader has more difficulty in understanding the severity of this temptation. Why did Christian not just stop, and put his burden down? Or, if the reading is somewhat less crass, then certain tones of social or class conflict are noted: the humble dissenting Christian is tempted by the forms and compromises of carnal policy, and of the Established Church – but why should the doctrines of Morality be at odds with the gospel of the Cross, and, if the straight and narrow path of faith has nothing to do with Legality, or Morality, or Works, then how is it marked out and to what gate does it lead? I think it very probable that the eyes of many readers today traverse such passages in a benevolent haze of suspended attention.

I will argue, however, that such passages demand our full response. Their implications may be very radical indeed. In this episode, Bunyan is marking out a path which leads directly to antinomian conclusions, and which takes us, equally directly, into the structure of Blake's thought. We will not delay now to enquire how far John Bunyan endorsed these conclusions, or how far he hedged around his antinomian premises with doctrinal reservations.[1] We will note only that this episode of temptation carries us into a characteristic diagram of oppositions:

[1] In fact Bunyan was strongly critical of antinomianism, perhaps the more so because his own doctrines 'often skirted' it: see Christopher Hill, *A Turbulent, Seditious and Factious People: John Bunyan and his Church, 1628–1688* (Oxford, 1988), chapter 17, and p. 86.

Works	*versus*	Faith
Morality		The Cross
Legality		The Gospel of Forgiveness of Sins
Bondage		Freedom

And, if the path of *Legality* be taken, then it leads on to formalism, carnal policy, opportunism and, finally, to mere simpering *Civility*.

I will also argue that the doctrine of justification by faith, in its antinomian inflexion, was one of the most radical and potentially subversive of the vectors which carried the ideas of seventeenth-century Levellers and Ranters through to the next century. Since I can hear a scandalised snort from the Marxist–structuralist corner, I must ask the less committed readers to excuse me for a moment while I chastise my more brutish comrades. What (they are asking in that corner) can this odd-looking doctrine of justification by faith have to do with enlightenment and rigorous rationality? Surely it is no more than one more form of indulgent self-mystification within the otiose religiosity which was the sole inheritance of the English Revolution? And, if we are to make allowance for this religiose ideological formation, surely it is equally clear that the only socially effective Christian doctrine capable of motivating a radical practice must have rested upon a doctrine of Works – a zealous and this-worldly emphasis upon affirmative moral actions?

The answer is that there are persons and places for which this last proposition is valid. But that, for much of the eighteenth century, the doctrine of justification by faith was – and was seen to be – the more 'dangerous' heresy. And this was because it could – although it need not – challenge very radically the authority of the ruling ideology and the cultural hegemony of Church, Schools, Law and even of 'common-sense' Morality. In its essence it was exactly that: *anti*-hegemonic. It displaced the authority of institutions and of received worldly wisdom with that of the individual's inner light – faith, conscience, personal understanding of the scriptures or (for Blake) 'the Poetic Genius' – and allowed to the individual a stubborn scepticism in the face of the established culture, a fortitude in the face of its seductions or persecutions sufficient to support Christian in the face of the State or of polite learning. This fortitude need not necessarily be accompanied by evangelistic zeal or affirmative social action; it might equally well be defensive, and protect the quietism of a private faith, or the introverted spiritual pride of a petty sect. But it could also nourish (and protect) a more active faith which rested upon a confidence in spiritual 'freedom', liberated from the 'bondage' of Morality and Legality.

That the language of Christian's temptation continues with undiminished vigour may be seen if we traverse abruptly across more than one hundred years, from *Pilgrim's Progress* (1678) to London in the 1790s. One of the large, self-appointed noises in plebeian London at that time was William Huntington, S.S. The 'S.S.' stood for 'Sinner Saved'. Born in 1745 in a labourer's family (he was proud to proclaim that he had once been a coal-heaver), Huntington had come, by way of a small Baptist congregation in Thames Ditton and an Independent church in Woking, to London in 1782. Here he ministered at first to Baptists, but, by the 1790s, he was his own evangelist and prophet, ministering throughout the decade from Providence Chapel, Great Titchfield Street.[2] There came from his pen, throughout the 1790s, a torrent of pamphlets, sermons, admonitions and expostulations, of a loud and windy nature.

The wind blew from an antinomian quarter – indeed, from much the same quarter as exemplified by Christian's temptation by Mr Worldly Wiseman. In the 1780s he was warning his congregation lest *'legality* . . . entangle and govern their consciences'. In contrast to mere 'workmongers', the Saved must know that 'the Saviour's laws are written within us'.[3] In the early 1790s the antinomian wind blew most fiercely, and Huntington's rhetoric moved through the familiar oppositions between ceremonial, formal law, and established forms on the one hand (all these were 'a yoke of bondage') and faith and free grace on the other.

We may sample the rhetoric from *The Child of Liberty in Legal Bondage* (1794). Huntington, a self-called evangelist, decried 'legal preachers, who handle the law unlawfully . . . While they entangle the sheep of Christ, themselves are nothing but *thorns and briars.*' Established religious forms were no more than 'the old vail of the

---

[2] Ebenezer Hooper, *The Celebrated Coalheaver, or Reminiscences of the Reverend William Huntington, S.S.* (1871); Thomas Wright, *Life of William Huntington, S.S.* (1909). See also Jon Mee, 'Is there an Antinomian in the House: William Blake and the After-Life of a Heresy' in S. Clarke and D. Worrall (eds.), *Historicizing Blake* (forthcoming); and *Dangerous Enthusiasm: William Blake and the Culture of Radicalism in the 1790s* (Oxford, 1992), pp. 62–5.

[3] William Huntington, *A Sermon on the Dimensions of Eternal Love* (1784), pp. 5, 9.

law, under which the gospel is hid'. Faith must always take priority to form. When not illustrated by faith–

The law, when reflected on the mind of man, is *blackness and darkness*, and the spirit of it is darkness, fear, bondage, wrath, death, and furious jealousy still.

This, and much more of the same kind, between 1792 and 1795, when the winds of political liberty blew strongly in London. Huntington himself was no political reformer: he was a High Tory and an admirer of Pitt. But his flock was strongly disposed towards the reforming cause, and he had great difficulty in governing it: 'there was a knot of young wise men among us, who were great readers and admirers of Tom Paine. . .' These clamoured against his discourses in the House of God, but fortunately six of them soon exposed themselves by becoming given up to the sin of adultery. Presumably their partners in sin were found among those women who–

Young and old, are breathing out *slaughter* against the ruling powers. Tom Paine and Satan have stuffed their heads full of politics.[4]

In 1795 Huntington had great difficulty in holding back his flock from running after Richard Brothers, the most notable of the millenarial prophets of the New Jerusalem, while others of his flock seceded towards Winchester and the Universalists.[5] Some of his following (he implies) were, during the general repression of reformers in the mid-1790s, 'bereaved of their houses and goods', became emigrants, were imprisoned, transported or even hanged.[6] Others–

Who had some sound notions of the gospel, and some good views, and who were capable of sound speech which could not be condemned, were given up to the devil and Tom Paine, that they even sucked in the rebellion, blasphemy, and carnal logic of that man. . .

---

[4] William Huntington, *A Watchword and Warning from the Walls of Zion* (1798), pp. 76, 2–3. Huntington thought the women 'had better guide the houses, teach their children to read, and take in a little plain work'.

[5] Huntington attacked Richard Brothers in *The Lying Prophet Examined* (1795), Elhanan Winchester and the Universalists in *Discoveries and Cautions from the Streets of Zion* (1798) and elsewhere. Jon Mee, 'Is there an Antinomian in the House', discusses the breach between Huntington and Garnet Terry, who adopted more radical positions, somewhat closer to Blake.

[6] William Huntington, *Discoveries and Cautions from the Streets of Zion* (1798). These allegations probably testify to Huntington's monomania.

Others promised themselves 'from week to week French liberty by
the Sword of France and by the destruction of their own country'.[7]
As if to outbid the Painites and the millenarial prophets, Huntington bent the boughs of his rhetoric low with the imagery of the
New Jerusalem:

> Coming to God with the judge of all under his teaching, and to Jesus,
> the mediator of the new covenant by faith, and to the saints in heartfelt
> love and affection, is coming to the heavenly Jerusalem; for all believers
> *are fellow-citizens with the saints, and of the household of God.* To let Jerusalem
> come into our mind, in the language of the New Testament, is *to love one
> another. . .*

For those who had received this gospel, 'Gospel Jerusalem is now
with us.'[8]

Huntington is an unimportant figure and he is scarcely relevant
to my theme. What relevance he has lies in his *un*importance. With
his flock pulled hither and thither, to Paine, to Brothers, to the
Universalists, to the ultra-Jacobins, he is like evangelising flotsam
floating upon the culture of radical Dissent. But he can keep afloat
only by inflating his raft with the rhetoric which blows all around
him. We approach too often the 'mind of the age' through the
language of the rational or humanist Enlightenment: through
Paley, Priestley, Price, Wedgwood, Erasmus Darwin or through
genteel Behmenists. But stick your foot, or your library ticket, into
the sea of pamphlets and sermons of Dissent and of Methodist
breakaways, and we are back in 'the Tradition' indeed; but the
tradition is that of seventeenth-century Anabaptists and Ranters,
of Ezra and Isaiah, of John Bunyan, of the New Jerusalem, of
watchwords from the walls of Zion, of the Land of Beulah, of
ancient prophecies, of blood on the walls of palaces, lambs
entangled in thorns and briar and of 'the old vail of the law, under
which the gospel is hid'.

It is, of course, a rhetoric very much closer to the language of
Blake than is the rhetoric of the Enlightenment. Inattention to this
Londonish rhetoric has led us to see Blake as a more isolated figure
than he was. But while it brings us very close to Blake's language
and imagery, the fit is not exact; and when we shift our attention
from the vocabulary to the structure of ideas, then the gap becomes
manifest.

---

[7] *Ibid.*, pp. 14–15.   [8] *A Watchword and Warning from the Walls of Zion*, pp. 64–5.

The fit between the ideas of Huntington and of Blake is suggested by the title (but not the contents) of a tract of 1792: *The Moral Law not Injured by the Everlasting Gospel*. These terms were perfectly familiar to the disputatious London Dissenter of that time. But if Blake had written such a tract, then its title would have been, not reversed, but inverted: *The Everlasting Gospel Injured by the Moral Law*. It is not only that Blake stands within the antinomian tradition. He stands at a precise, if obscure, point within it, and his writings contain the purest, most lucid and most persuasive statements that issued from that tradition in any voice and at any time: 'The Gospel is Forgiveness of Sins & has No Moral Precepts these belong to Plato & Seneca & Nero', or:

> When Satan first the black bow bent
> And the Moral Law from the Gospel rent
> He forgd the Law into a Sword
> And spilld the blood of mercys Lord.   (E200)

The difficulty of such statements (if any remains) arises only if we try to tease their meanings into something else. If we take them to mean exactly what they say – that the Moral Law is the direct antagonist of the Gospel of Mercy – then they may present problems to us, but they have the simplicity of stone.

A precise, if obscure point within the antinomian tradition . . . I will attempt a reconstruction of this tradition, and consider the ways in which it may have been extended to Blake. I have no unexpected disclosures to offer. I must commence with conjectures, and conclude with some firmer evidence, out of which further conjectures will arise.

CHAPTER 2

Antinomianisms

'Antinomian' was, in the eighteenth century, as often a term of abuse as of precision. The orthodox hurled the accusation of Antinomianism at their opponents, very much as, in other times and places, accusations might be hurled of heresy, anarchism, terrorism or libertinism. And the objects of such abuse often turn out to be innocent of any such subversive intentions. They may be (as in Wesley's *Journals*) members of the flock who neglect attendances and who pride themselves too far on their own purity of heart; or, with some writers, a stern theological eye may fall upon a humble fornicator for whom the pursuit of a *doctrine* has never entered his thoughts. The term 'αντί νομος means, after all, *against the law*; and most men and women may, at one time or another, fall under that imputation.

I do not mean to search back into antiquity for the origin of this heresy. I am more concerned with a cluster of ideas present in late eighteenth-century England, and with their derivation from seventeenth-century sources. In this tradition antinomian doctrine was founded most commonly upon passages in St Paul's epistles to the Romans and to the Galatians. These passages, which originated in St Paul's polemics against the slavish observance of Jewish ceremonial and ritual regulations, were taken to have a very much wider significance. The Mosaic Law was seen, not only in its ceremonial edicts but also in its moral commandments, to be the necessary rules of government imposed upon a faithless and unregenerate people:

The law was our schoolmaster to bring us unto Christ, that we might be justified by faith.
But after that faith is come, we are no longer under a schoolmaster. (Galatians 3. 24–5)

Christ, by his sacrifice upon the Cross, in fulfilment of God's ancient covenant with man, 'hath redeemed us from the curse of the law' (Galatians 3. 13). Thereafter it is not by 'the works of the law' but by 'the hearing of faith' that believers may be justified (Galatians 2 and 3, *passim*). Believers within the church 'are become dead to the law by the body of Christ' (Romans 7. 4), they are 'delivered from the law' (Romans 7. 6):

There is therefore now no condemnation to them which are in Christ Jesus, who walk not after the flesh, but after the Spirit.

For the law of the Spirit of life in Christ Jesus hath made me free from the law of sin and death. . . (Romans 8. 1 and 2)

This is not all that St Paul said, nor is it without ambiguity. But such passages as these were commonly taken as texts by Puritan divines who inclined towards antinomian tenets. Thus James Barry, whose sermons were reprinted by William Huntington, cited such texts and concluded: 'There remains, now, no condemnation in force against that man or woman who believes in the Son of God.'

Neither did the Son of God flinch or shrink in the contest, till he had vanquished and overcome the condemning power of the law; leaving it, and all the other enemies of his elect, nailed to the cross; having, by his death on the cross, put to death the damnatory sentence of God's righteous law against God's elect. . .[1]

This is close also to Michael's doctrine in Book XII of *Paradise Lost*: 'Law can discover sin, but not remove. . .'

> So Law appears imperfect, and but giv'n
> With purpose to resign them in full time
> Up to a better Cov'nant. . .

Christ, by his sacrifice, fulfilled the old Mosaic Law, delivered mankind from its curse, and–

> . . . to the Cross he nailes thy Enemies,
> The Law that is against thee, and the sins
> Of all mankinde, with him there crucifi'd,
> Never to hurt them more who rightly trust
> In this his satisfaction. . .

---

[1] James Barry, *The Only Refuge of a Troubled Soul in Times of Affliction . . . or the Mystery of the Apple Tree* (two sermons revised and published by W. Huntington, 2nd edn, 1802), p. 80.

Henceforward those who are justified by faith (but not by 'legal works') enter upon a state of grace, subject to no laws save 'what the Spirit within/ Shall on the heart engrave'.[2] Thus those two markedly antinomian divines, James Barry and Milton's Michael. But neither would have *acknowledged* themselves to be such. Indeed, Barry actually complained:

If we preach up justification by the alone righteousness of the Son of God, freely imputed by God's act of free and Sovereign Grace, without any thing of the sinner's own qualifications joined, as con-causes there-with; then we are accounted Antinomians, we preach Free Grace, Free Grace. . .[3]

If we situate ourselves in the late eighteenth century, then we may distinguish between three positions which were described as – and which sometimes were accepted by their professors as – antino-mian. The first is inseparable from Calvinist or determinist presup-positions. Indeed, it may be the doctrine of election taken to its own *reductio ad absurdam*; or, in its social expression, it may be seen as 'Calvinism's lower-class alter ego'.[4] If one knew, as a certainty, that one was elected to be saved – and that this was God's will – then it could follow that one would be saved whatever one did: the 'saints' might live henceforth outside 'the moral law'. It might seem that this logic must lead on to scandalous conclusions. How-ever, the antinomian teacher found ways of hedging around the way to such conclusions by many thickets of apologetics. In the main, these turned on Michael's theme of the inner law of con-science: 'what the Spirit within/Shall on the heart engrave'. The elect might dispense with the moral law since they had a surer guide in conscience; and if a 'saint' led a scandalous life, then this was evidence that he or she was none of the elect. However, we need enquire into this position little further, since it offered little to William Blake. He was not troubled by Calvinist determinism, and even the concealed pre-destinarianism which he detected in Swedenborg gave him instant offence.

A second position commonly inveighed against in eighteenth-century apologetics was, in the main, a position dreamed up by main-line Protestant orthodoxy, much as Stalinist orthodoxy had

---

[2] Christopher Hill discusses Milton's proximity to antinomianism in *Milton and the English Revolution* (1977), see esp. p. 106 and chapter 24.
[3] Barry, *The Only Refuge*, p. 113.
[4] Christopher Hill, *The World Turned Upside Down* (1972), p. 130.

always to position itself between a Right and a Left deviation. On
the Right there stood an excessive belief in justification by works,
or forms; on the Left there was Antinomianism, or an excessive
belief in justification by faith, or free grace or pureness of heart,
which led on to a carelessness towards all forms or works or observances and even to a light-heartedness towards sin, supported by
over-confidence in the universality of divine mercy. Antinomians
(in the eyes of the orthodox)–

Are *against* the law . . . Some are against it in *principle*, others in *practice*,
and some in *both*. The name is most commonly applied to those who are,
in pretence at least, mighty advocates of free grace; and object to the law
as the *rule* of the good man's life.

Such persons might neglect observances, attend stage plays, music
and dancing, and break the Sabbath; others might 'take liberty to
sin, from the saving freedom, the abounding riches of divine grace'.
And from this we pass to the ritual condemnation:

In a word, an Antinomian is a living libel on Christianity; a scandal to
religion; a compound of iniquity and impudence; a nuisance, a very pest
to society; an enemy to God, to man, and to himself; Christ's opponent,
the devil's respondent. . .[5]

Thus the orthodox view. But the positions in fact avowed by the
advocates of grace could be more cogent than this, and also more
various. We will not examine these now, since, although we are
moving closer to a possible influence upon Blake, we can move
closer still. The third position attributed to Antinomians consists
in carrying to an extreme the advocacy of grace, and bringing the
gospel of Christ into direct *antagonism* to the 'covenant of deeds' or
the 'moral law'. That is, in the view of critics, there is not just too
much emphasis upon grace and faith, too little upon moral law:
the two are seen as being radically opposed to each other. This is
a meaning which observers increasingly assign to Antinomianism
in the turbulent 1790s. They believe (a critic writes)

That the Law of Moses, commonly called the Moral Law, contained in
the Ten Commandments, ought not to be preached as a rule of conduct
to believers of the Gospel, but by so doing, you should bring them again
under the Law as a Covenant of Works.[6]

[5] Anon., *Antinomianism Explained and Exploded; in a Letter to a Friend* (Coventry, n.d.), pp. 9,
15.
[6] 'A Friend to the Gospel of Christ', *A Looking-Glass for the Antinomians* (Shrewsbury, 1796),
p. 10.

It is no longer a question, as with Milton's Michael, of the Law being 'imperfect' – perhaps a necessary schoolmaster to the unregenerate – nor a criticism of the Law's limitations: 'Law can discover sin, but not remove...' The Ten Commandments and the Gospel of Jesus stand directly opposed to each other: the first is a code of repression and prohibition, the second a gospel of forgiveness and love. The two might have flowed from the minds of opposing gods. And if this is married – and when such a doctrine has gathered social force it usually has been so married – to political radicalism and to the outlook of the oppressed, then the doctrine acquires a new force again. For the Moral Law is *their* Law, the law of 'God & his Priest & King/Who make up a heaven of our misery', while the Gospel is the affirmation, in the face of all the Schools and Orthodoxies, of the truths of the pure-in-heart and the oppressed.

We are now close enough to Blake to touch some of his lines. Which we will do again in a moment. But we will first delay over one issue which has, perhaps, served to confuse a little the question of the derivation of Blake's thought from the antinomian tradition. Very commonly, because of the weight of seventeenth-century precedent – as well as specific doctrinal signatures – Antinomianism has been discussed as a distinctively Calvinist heresy.[7] That is, the emphasis has been upon the doctrine of election carried through to the extremity that the elect *must* be saved, do what they may. This may be a proper emphasis until the 1630s, but when we come to the next decades the emphasis may change.[8] Not all Ranters necessarily held themselves to be elected 'saints', and Milton's Michael was scarcely a Calvinist divine. And when we move into the eighteenth century, any necessary connection between Calvinist doctrines of election and antinomian tenets can no longer be expected.

For Pauline premises, to which Luther gave emphasis, could lead to identical conclusions. Those with a nicely discriminating theological palate might classify these as 'solifidian' rather than antinomian.[9] The solifidian premise rested particularly upon Romans 3:

[7] See Peter Toon, *The Emergence of Hyper-Calvinism* (1967).
[8] Hill in *The World Turned Upside Down* tends to emphasise antinomianism's Calvinist character, whereas A.L. Morton in *The World of the Ranters* (1970), pp. 50–1, 72, 117, 129, gives more emphasis to Lutheran heresies. See also G. Huehns, *Antinomianism in English History* (1951), pp. 13–15, 40–3.
[9] F.L. Cross (ed.), *The Oxford Dictionary of the Christian Church* (Oxford, 1974).

For all have sinned, and come short of the glory of God;

Being justified freely by his grace through the redemption that is in Christ Jesus;

Whom God hath sent forth to be a propitiation through faith in his blood. . .

Therefore we conclude that a man is justified by faith without the deeds of the law. (Romans 3. 23–5, 28)

The doctrine of justification by faith invited the further doctrine of 'imputed righteousness', which was a contentious issue in the early Swedenborgian milieu, and which we will discuss later (pp. 162–4). The point now is that the zealous life of theological private enterprise which was thrown open by the English Civil Wars allowed hundreds of humble experimenters in doctrine to fashion eclectic systems, now drawing upon Calvin and now upon Luther, now upon Joachim of Fiore and now upon Boehme. These combined in the brief climax of the Ranters (1649–51), when antinomianism in one form or another assumed epidemic proportions.[10] In this moment, the doctrine of 'free grace', derivative from St Paul and Luther, seems to me to be more significant than the Calvinist doctrine of election. John Saltmarsh's *Free Grace: or the Flowing of Christs Blood to Sinners* (1645) had a profound influence on the Ranter movement that succeeded. The emphasis is upon, not election, but belief. The free grace of Christ's blood was shed for all mankind, and all the sins of believers were 'done away on the Crosse':

The Spirit of Christ sets a *beleever* as *free* from *Hell*, the *Law*, and *Bondage*, as if he was in *Heaven*, nor wants he anything to make him *so*, but to make him *believe* that he is so.

The Gospel is 'a *perfect law* of life and *righteousnesse*, of *grace* and *truth*; and therefore I wonder at any that should contend for the ministry of the *Law* or *Ten Commandments* under Moses'. In the next year Thomas Edwards in *Gangraena* was denouncing those who held,

[10] These questions have been obscured by J.C. Davis, *Fear, Myth and History: The Ranters and the Historians* (Cambridge, 1986). Davis constructs, for the purpose of his own arguments, a somewhat narrow definition of antinomianism (pp. 21–5), with heavy emphasis on the supposed 'practical' antinomianism of sexual libertinism, and inattention to theological variants: see my 'On the Rant', *London Review of Books*, 9 July 1987. Debate as to the existence of the Ranters, initiated by Davis, of course continues: see Christopher Hill, 'Abolishing the Ranters' in *A Nation of Change and Novelty* (1990); Symposium of Comments in *Past & Present*, forthcoming (1993).

That by Christs death, all the sins of all men in the world, Turks, Pagans, as well as Christians committed against the moral Law and the first covenant, are actually pardoned and forgiven, and this is the everlasting gospel.

It was as a preacher of 'free grace' that Laurence Clarkson – later to be called the 'Captain of the Rant' – first made his mark, and William Erbery, who was to become a leading Seeker, first caught the eye of Thomas Edwards when 'he declared himself for general Redemption, that no man was punished for Adam's sin, that Christ died for all. . .' James Nayler, who is often taken as the leader of the Ranting tendency in early Quakerism, defended also 'the universal free grace of God to all mankind'.

The teaching of 'free grace' need not necessarily lead on to antinomian conclusions. In Blake's London of the 1790s this teaching was vigorously revived by several groups: by William Huntington, and by Elhanan Winchester and the Universalists, who held that Christ's blood had removed from all the curse of eternal punishment (pp. 226–7): groups which refused, with equal vigour, the antinomian resolution. But logically the solifidian premise ('faith without the deeds of the law') could pass easily, as it had done with the Ranters, to an antinomian destination (crudely, faith *against* the law). One may observe, throughout the eighteenth century, preachers, sects and churches, struggling to find some doctrinal foothold half-way down this logical slope. The visionary or pietistic sect might impose (as the Moravians did) a severe discipline upon its own members, while keeping itself at a great distance from the legalism and forms of State and Church. Or a dual standard might be employed, by which the Moral Law (both ceremonial and real) was abrogated for those within the true faith, whereas for those *without* faith the Moral Law remained binding.[11] And if this position were chosen, then it need not be held that the faithful were predestined to be so, and hence were everlastingly secured from the pains of transgression. For a believer might always fall away from the faith, and hence fall within the rule of the Law once more.

Early Methodism had a surfeit of these problems, and nearly choked upon them. The doctrine of justification by faith – a moment of 'immediate and mysterious relationship of the individual soul with the Deity',[12] coming as the free gift of God in an

[11] See William Cudworth, *The Truth Defended* (1746).
[12] E. Halevy, *The Birth of Methodism in England* (Chicago, 1971), p. 33.

experience of conversion in the heart of the receptive sinner – both brought the Wesleys and George Whitefield together, and then flung them apart in Calvinist and Arminian directions. John Wesley's Arminian resolution (an 'eclecticism which logic may call inadmissible')[13] denied predestination and denied also the irresistible power of God's free grace: the sinner must first be receptive and prepared. Only 'he that believeth' shall be saved, but it remained possible – and, as time went on, it proved to be only too possible – that believers should 'backslide'. Hence, with increasing and dismal emphasis, the doctrine of works could be brought to supplement the doctrine of faith and grace, for works were both a sign of continuing grace and an insurance against backsliding. But the antinomian heresy continued to harass the early history of Methodism. Whitefield's former fellow-preachers, William Cudworth and James Relly, might, in the view of observers, be called 'properly Antinomians', even though they themselves rejected the 'scandalous name'.[14] Cudworth, indeed, was well versed in the work of seventeenth-century antinomian divines, and reprinted a number of their tracts and sermons.[15] Cudworth and Relly denounced their critics as 'Legalists'. In the view of a later observer, the Antinomians of the 1790s had largely been recruited from those 'we commonly call Irregular Methodists'.[16] In the early years of the next century, the Primitive Methodists were often referred to as Ranters.

In this case the thrust of such Antinomianism as can be found came from a Calvinist quarter – from those who seceded from Whitefield: the notion of the abrogation of the law and the notion of elected 'sainthood' tended to go together. This is true also of another antinomian sect, the Muggletonians, whose beliefs we shall interrogate later: their doctrine of 'the Two Seeds' was inexorably predestinarian, although founded upon a materialist historical explanation of alternative conceptions (pp. 75–6). This is true also

---

[13] Ibid., p. 50.
[14] See William Cudworth, *A Dialogue between a Preacher of Inherent Righteousness and a Preacher of God's Righteousness, Revealed from Faith to Faith* (1745); W. Mason, *Antinomian Heresy Exploded, in an Appeal to the Christian World* (n.d.); James Relly, *Anti-Christ Resisted, in a Reply to . . . W. Mason* (1761); William Hurd, *A New Universal History of the Religions, Rites, Ceremonies, and Customs of the Whole World* (Blackburn, 1799 edn), p. 767. On Relly, see also Jon Mee, *Dangerous Enthusiasm*, p. 160.
[15] W. Cudworth in *Christ Alone Exalted* (1747).
[16] W. Hurd, *New Universal History*, p. 641.

of such idiosyncratic little groups as a Church of Christ in Spitalfields, which surface from time to time in eighteenth-century
London, and which may perhaps be survivals from earlier
'Ranters'. This church held that all its members were justified in
Christ and their sins blotted out – 'so that they are now holy and
unblameable and unreprovable in the eye of his justice, and are
made the righteousness of God in him. . .' But, also, all such had
been elected and 'ordained to eternal life before the world began'.[17]

There is a disposition, then, for antinomian and Calvinist tenets
to be found as a couple. But this was not *necessarily* so. It was
possible to hold that Christ had abolished the Moral Law for all
mankind, and hence for sinners as well as saved: 'the whole work
of salvation was accomplished by Jesus Christ on the cross. Christ's
blood and our sins went away together. . .' All that then remained
for the sinner to do was to attain to faith or belief. So long as he
or she remained in a state of belief, the Moral Law had no force.[18]
It was just as possible for an Antinomian to play at the game of
equivocation as it was for John Wesley.

I have said that, in the third position sketched above, we are
close enough to William Blake to touch some of his lines. But this
is so only if we discard the expectation of any notion of election:

> Thus wept they in Beulah over the Four Regions of Albion
> But many doubted & despaird & imputed Sin & Righteousness
> To Individuals & not to States, and these slept in Ulro
>
> (E169)

These are the concluding lines of chapter 1 of *Jerusalem*. The
imputation of sin and righteousness to individuals entails the doctrine of election, or predestination, which was abhorrent to Blake.
The imputation of these to 'states' is Blake's own resolution. I
cannot say that this resolution is easily explained.

What must, however, be insisted upon is the ubiquity and
centrality of antinomian tenets to Blake's thinking, to his writing

[17] *Declaration of the Faith, and Practice of a Church of Christ, meeting in Black and Grey-Eagle Street, Spitalfields; and Peter's yard in Castle Street, near Leicester Fields, and at the French Chapel in New Hermitage-street, Wapping* (n.d., but bound in with British Library copy of W. Cudworth, *Christ Alone Exalted* (1747)). For the 'French Prophets' who created a millenarian sensation in London in the first decades of the eighteenth century, see D.P. Walker, *The Decline of Hell* (1964), pp. 253–63; Halevy, *The Birth of Methodism*, pp. 52–3; Hillel Schwartz, *The French Prophets* (Berkeley, 1980); J.F.C. Harrison, *The Second Coming: Popular Millenarianism, 1780–1850* (1979), pp. 25–9.
[18] Hurd, *New Universal History*, p. 638.

and to his painting. Throughout his work there will be found this radical disassociation and opposition between the Moral Law and that gospel of Christ which is known – as often in the antinomian tradition – as 'the Everlasting Gospel'. We will encounter this throughout this study, and I will be content now with a blunt set of assertions. The signatures of this antinomian sensibility will be found, not at two or three points only in Blake's work, but along the whole length of his work, at least from 1790 until his death. They are manifest in the *Songs*. *The Marriage of Heaven and Hell* is an antinomian squib thrown among Swedenborgians. In the early prophecies, Urizen is the author of the Moral Law; in the major prophetic books the argument between law and love, repression and regeneration, is intrinsic to their structure. In Blake's annotations to several authors – notably to Watson, Bacon and Thornton – there are unequivocal and unqualified antinomian affirmations. Such affirmations recur in the conversations of his last years, recorded by Crabb Robinson. (Some statements were, very probably, so explicit and so shocking in their heresy that Frederick Tatham felt it necessary to destroy them.)[19] These statements, first offered as the voice of the 'devil' in Plate 23 of *The Marriage of Heaven and Hell* (1790–3) – 'I tell you no virtue can exist without breaking these ten commandments . . . Jesus was all virtue, and acted from impulse, not from rules' – were re-worked once more, in affirmative terms, in the late, unpublished, *The Everlasting Gospel* (c.818):

> It was when Jesus said to Me,
> 'Thy Sins are all forgiven thee.'
> The Christian trumpets loud proclaim
> Thro' all the World in Jesus' name
> Mutual forgiveness of each Vice,
> And oped the Gates of Paradise.
> The Moral Virtues in Great fear
> Formed the Cross & Nails & Spear,
> And the Accuser standing by
> Cried out, 'Crucify! Crucify!. . .'   (E793)

I am not the first to comment on the pressure of this tradition

---

[19] Tatham may have destroyed some of Blake's manuscripts, under the conviction that Blake had been inspired by Satan! See G.E. Bentley, *Blake Records* (Oxford, 1969), pp. 417–18, and, for Tatham's comment on Blake's 'Extravagant and rebellious thoughts', see his 'Life of Blake', in *ibid.*, p. 530.

in Blake;[20] nor do I suppose that very much has been settled if we
hang up his work on a hook marked 'antinomian' and think that
then we have put it in place. Antinomianism, indeed, is not a
place at all, but a way of breaking out from received wisdom and
moralism, and entering upon new possibilities. The particular
attack of Blake's thought and feeling is unique, and it cannot be
understood without reference to adjacent ideas and symbols –
although some of these (the mistrust of 'reason', the acceptance of
'energy' and of sexuality) have often come together in a cluster in
the antinomian tradition. Moreover, the fact that these characteristic oppositions recur throughout Blake's mature work does not
mean that they recur in the same way.

Even so, I am not saying nothing. I am arguing that these ideas
are intrinsic and central to the structure of Blake's thought, and
that they remain so, even when he passes from revolutionary enthusiasm to more quietist conclusions, and equally when he is subject
to very strong Deist and atheistic influences and when he has
become reconciled to a (highly unorthodox and idiosyncratic)
Christian faith. And I am arguing also that even those critics who
have noted the antinomian influence have rarely noted its structural centrality; and that, in general, extensive critical attention
has been paid to quite secondary, or even trivial, influences upon
Blake, while this major and continuing influence has remained
little examined. And, finally, I am arguing that there are readers
of Blake who still refuse to read what he plainly says, or who
dismiss as a *jeu d'esprit* a statement as flat and as challenging as
that Christ

> His Seventy Disciples sent
> Against Religion & Government   (E794)

For a certain kind of scholar, these two lines offer room for a textual
commentary upon why (from what obscure source) Blake should
have chosen the number *seventy*. If he looks at what is actually being
said in those two lines, then it seems altogether too disturbing: it
is either wrong, or mad, or it requires the rewriting of history.
Blake requires the latter.

We cannot reduce Blake's thought and art to a few antinomian
propositions. Within the field of possibility which these proposi-

---

[20] See, for example, Michael Ferber, *The Social Vision of William Blake* (Princeton, 1985), pp.
116–26, and Jon Mee, *Dangerous Enthusiasm*, pp. 57ff.

tions opened to him, a multitude of other themes are disclosed. But these themes are often governed, they are controlled and assigned their significance, by the antinomian verb. Yet, as we close in upon Blake, we find that it is necessary to disengage once more, and to interrogate a prior history of ideas. Because, however original Blake's use of the antinomian vocabulary may be, it is impossible to argue that he re-invented it *ab novo*. The terms employed – the Moral Law, the Everlasting Gospel, the New Jerusalem – are more specific and more radical than the mainstream Puritan tradition. We have therefore to enquire by what routes this tradition came down to Blake. This will help us to understand the terms which he employed, even if it cannot tell us what he did with those terms.

CHAPTER 3

The 'ranting' impulse

There is a robustness and a radical political attack – the direct
equation of the Moral Law with State and Church – as well as a
clustering of related themes in Blake's writing which takes us back
instantly to the imagery and to the intellectual world of Diggers,
Ranters, Behmenists, hermeticists and heresiarchs of the Interreg-
num. The resemblance was shown in A.L. Morton's *The Everlasting
Gospel* (1958), and the reminiscences cannot fail to strike the reader
in page after page of Morton's *The World of the Ranters* (1970) and
Christopher Hill's *The World Turned Upside Down* (1972). What
these authors and others have already recovered so expertly it is
unnecessary for me to repeat. Here I will only offer a reminder as
to certain of the ideas then in currency. If my selection appears to
be arbitrary, it has been made with an eye, not to the understanding of the seventeenth century, but to anticipations of ideas which
recur in the 1790s, either in Blake's own work or in Swedenborgian
and adjacent circles.

Notoriously the apocalyptic vision bursts forth in each period of
social disturbance. This is a time when not only the political world
but also the worlds of intellect and value are turned upside down.
Here we have the exuberant revolutionary milieu – egalitarians,
the Family of Love, Fifth Monarchy Men, Ranters; here also we
have the conjunction of the Behmenist and hermetic traditions with
a radical social constituency; here, again, we have the inspired
prophets and the pretenders to actual divinity.

Throughout this milieu there is an utter repudiation of the outward forms of religion (including, for some, the forms of marriage),
and a counterposing to these of the inner light of faith, inspiration
or prophecy. For the Digger leader, Winstanley, the God of magistrates, property-owners and the Church was 'the God Devil'
(sometimes 'the right Devil'). When the soldiers of the New Model

22

Army sang their marching song, they identified their enemy with
Antichrist or the Beast:

> For God begins to honour us,
>   The Saintes are marching on;
> The sword is sharp, the arrows swift
>   To destroy Babylon.
> Against the kingdome of the beast
>   Wee witnesses do rise. . .

Throughout the 1640s the language of the battle of the godly
against Antichrist spread out into every area of political and social,
as well as spiritual, life.[1]

The defeat of the Leveller soldiers at Burford in 1649 served as
a sharp check to the temporal political hopes of the more advanced
democrats. Like a gymnast on a trampoline, the democratic faith
which met its check at Burford, soared back into the air once more
in 1649–51, somersaulting and displaying itself in the brief Ranter
climax. For a moment the revolutionary spirit, which had met a
set-back in realistic political objectives, leapt to even more outra-
geous heights of utopian ideals and visionary teachings. *The Power
of Love* had already been a favourite theme of antinomian divines;
it was advocated with force and with practical demonstration by
Gerrard Winstanley; and the quiet and rational theorist of the
Levellers, William Walwyn, was to write in 1649:

I, through God's goodnesse, had long before been established in that part
of doctrine (called then, Antinomian) of free justification by Christ alone;
and so my heart was at much more ease and freedom, than others, who
were entangled with those yokes of bondage, unto which Sermons and
Doctrines mixt of Law and Gospel, do subject distressed consciences.

And he declared himself to be 'not a preacher of the law, but of
the gospell', the gospel of love.[2]

The abrogation of the Moral Law did not leave a vacuum, for
Law was driven out by Love. This gospel (love against law) was
sometimes known, by shorthand, as the Everlasting Gospel. In
longhand, the notion of the everlasting gospel derived from the
twelfth-century Calabrian abbot, Joachim of Fiore, and proposed
three successive Ages or Commissions: the Age of Fear and

---

[1] *Thurloe State Papers*, III, p. 137. For the 'liberation of Dissent' see M. Watts, *The Dissenters*
(Oxford, 1978; 1985), pp. 179–86.
[2] *The Power of Love* was written by Walwyn in 1643. The passage cited is from Walwyn's
Just Defence, 1649, p. 8, see Morton, *World of the Ranters*, pp. 146–7.

Servitude, which ended with the birth of Christ, and which followers might see as the Age of the Old Testament and the Moral
Law; the Age of Faith and Filial Obedience (the Age of the New
Testament and the apostolic succession); and the Age of Spiritual
Liberty for the Children of God, in which the scriptures would
appear in a wholly new light – a New Age, now imminent, and
perhaps to be announced by new prophets or Commissions of the
Spirit.[3] We do not know by exactly which routes this teaching had
reached the antinomian divines (such as Tobias Crisp and John
Saltmarsh) – to be transmitted by them to the most flamboyant of
all the Ranters, Abiezer Coppe – but by the 1640s it often came
down through the misty and suggestive filter of Jacob Boehme,
with his successive Ages of the Nettle, the Rose and the Lily.[4]

Thus the notion of the Everlasting Gospel had, by the late 1640s,
become part of the available vocabulary of radical heresy. For
Winstanley, in 1648, the time was expected when the authority of
apostles and prophets would give way to the time when 'the Lord
himself, who is the everlasting Gospell, doth manifest himself to
rule in the flesh of sonnes and daughters'. Winstanley came to see
this New Age as an Age of Reason.[5] And many joined this imagery
of the New Age to that of 'the New Jerusalem', when Babylon (or
Rome) was finally destroyed, and – in the words of the Welsh
Seeker, William Erbery, 'after the fall of *Rome*, there shall be the
new *Jerusalem*, and then the Church shall be one, one street in that
city and no more'.[6]

The Ranters, soaring from the trampoline in 1649–51, carried
the gospel of love further than Winstanley, Walwyn or Erbury were
prepared to follow. Disclaiming 'digging-levelling and sword-
levelling', Coppe proclaimed in a torrent of rhetoric a gospel of
spiritual Levelling which is 'Universall Love . . . who is putting
down the mighty from their seats; and exalting them of low degree'.
Breaking from the constraints of a Puritan upbringing, some
Ranters were said to have found relief in obscenities, swearing,
grotesque inversions of sanctified themes and divine jests, the

---

[3] See Marjorie Reeves and Warwick Gould, *Joachim of Fiore and the Myth of the Eternal Evangel*
(Oxford, 1987). The authors, however, are severely critical of any notion of a direct line
of transmission of Joachimite doctrines to Boehme, the Ranters or to Blake. But what we
should be looking for is a characteristic rhetoric and the trope of the everlasting gospel.

[4] See Morton, *World of the Ranters*, pp. 126–7; Hill, *The World Turned Upside Down*, p. 118,
note 187.

[5] Morton, p. 127; Hill, pp. 118–19, 315–16.   [6] Morton, p. 129.

exhibition of nakedness and in sexual licence. This last, together with expressions of primitive communism, naturally attracted the attention of critics most of all. For Alexander Ross Ranters was 'a sort of beasts', and, for them, 'Christian liberty . . . consists in community of all things, and among the rest, of women; which they paint over with an expression called *the enjoyment of the fellow-creature*.'[7] Going beyond the old opposition, Moral Law/Gospel, they were held to believe that 'all the commandments of God, both in the Old and New Testaments, are the fruits of the curse'. Nor can all the stories of Ranter excesses be turned away as the lampoons of prurient critics: Laurence Clarkson, in his remarkably self-revelatory auto-critique, *The Lost Sheep Found*, described how he came to the conviction that 'none can be free from sin, till in purity it be acted as no sin. . .'; and when he was 'Captain of the Rant' in London, 'I had most of the principal women came to my lodging for knowledge' until 'at last it became a trade so common, that all the froth and scum broke forth into the height of this wickedness, yea began to be a publick reproach'.[8]

As so often in a moment of political confusion and extremist – and sometimes exhibitionist – excitement, the quieter and more persevering voices are drowned in the loud noises of the self-appointed prophets. And when these prophets apostasised, they were inclined to accuse all their fellows of excesses which in fact had been specialties of their own. We have seen this very often, and we go on seeing it still. Innumerable ears attended to the roar of those called Ranters and incorporated some of their tenets into more stubborn and less self-dramatising beliefs. This can be seen, for example, in the records of several small Baptist churches in East Anglia, whose members repeatedly in the 1650s 'spake many things which savoured of Rantism', such as that they 'did not desire to be in such bondage' as to observe 'outward, ceremonial and

---

[7] This 'yellowpress' on supposed Ranters is discussed by J.C. Davis, *Fear, Myth and History*, *passim*, and Morton, *World of the Ranters, passim*. See also N. Cohn, *Pursuit of the Millenin* (1957), Appendix. Alexander Ross, *A View of all Religions* originated in 1640 and went through several revised editions. J.C. Davis, p. 124, consulting a 1653 edition, says that Ross 'saw fit not to mention' the Ranters, and he adduces this as one more proof that the Ranters did not exist; but in the (undated) edition which I consulted they are given an uncomplimentary place at pp. 256–7, as cited: also 1655 edn, pp. 387–8.

[8] For Clarkson, or Claxton, see Morton, chapter 5; Barry Reay in Hill, Reay and Lamont, *The World of the Muggletonians* (1983), chapter 6. J.C. Davis, pp. 58–75, attempts to throw doubts on Clarkson's association with any actual Ranters, in an unpersuasive display of special pleading.

carnal ordinances'.[9] Among such notions were the denial that there
was such a thing as sin, or, in Bauthumley's words, 'sin is properly
the dark side of God which is a meere privation of light'; and that
Hell had no real existence save in 'an accusing Conscience which
is Hell. . .'[10] Most important, for our purposes, was a radical, quasi-
pantheist redefinition of the notion of God and of Christ. John
Holland, one of the most sober critics of the Ranters, affirmed that
'they maintain that God is essentially in every creature, and that
there is as much of God in one creature, as in another, though he
doth not manifest himself so much in one as in another'. This is
confirmed by Jacob Bauthumley's *The Light and Dark sides of God,
Or a plain and brief Discourse of The Light side (God, Heaven and Earth)
The dark side (Devill, Sin, and Hell)* (1650), which was perhaps Holland's source:

Nay, I see that God is in all Creatures, Man and Beast, Fish and Fowle,
and every green thing, from the highest Cedar to the Ivey on the wall;
and that God is the life and being of them all, and that God doth really
dwell, and if you will personally . . . in them all, and hath his Being no
where else out of the Creatures.[11]

This has been described, by the historian of the Ranters, as 'the
central Ranter doctrine, from which all else logically flows'.[12] But
what may flow from it may depend upon different exercises of logic.
A general dispersed pantheism may flow logically into mortalism
or even materialism, in which all life returns to a common source
as streams to a sea. Or, in a more literal and intense variant, the
essential presence of God is to be found only in men and women
(his presence in nature is felt only dimly); hence these *are* God,
and, in consequence, 'man cannot either know God, or beleeve in
God, or pray to God, but it is God in man that knoweth himself,
believes in himself and prayeth to himself'.[13] As Morton concludes,
the identification of God with man and with the natural universe
might have 'two apparently opposite consequences. It might lead
to a mysticism which found God in everyone: equally it might
lead to a virtual materialism which in practice dispensed with him
altogether.'[14] It might also, one must add, lead to strange con-

[9] Hill, *The World Turned Upside Down*, p. 184.
[10] Cohn, *Pursuit of the Millenin*, pp. 338–9.
[11] *Ibid.*, pp. 336–7. John Holland, *The Smoke of the Bottomless Pit* (1657), is cited in Morton, *World of the Ranters*, p. 73.
[12] Morton, p. 73.   [13] *Ibid.*, p. 73, citing Holland.   [14] *Ibid.*, p. 74.

sequences in the unbalanced mind, for whom the very notion of 'God' was inflated with the most powerful symbolism and invested with expectations of omnipotence: for if a humble believer decided that he *was* God, or had more of the essence of God within him than his crabbed and jealous neighbours, then he might easily conceive of himself as a prophet or a pretender to God's throne.

The Ranters did not conceive of themselves as a church or a congregation: they may have used instead the term 'my one flesh',[15] for they were in fact the flesh within which dwelt the spirit of God, they were 'fellow-creatures' in Christ. This is the cluster of ideas which most concerns us, and we need not delay over other ideas which were sometimes attendant: chiliastic notions of the Second Coming, or of the rule of the Saints, various competing notions of the Resurrection, or of the enhancement of sensual joys and sexual powers in Heaven. What should be added is the influence of Jacob Boehme, whose writing was being translated at this time, and whose influence upon the Ranters may be felt – as in Bauthumley's *Light and Dark sides of God* – in a somewhat-qualified dialectic of the co-existence within God of good and evil principles. God (in Coppe's words) is both 'a jealous God, and the Father of Mercies; in him (I say) the Lyon and the Lamb, Servant and Lord, Peace and War, Joy and Jealousie, Wrath and Love, etc. are reconciled and all complicated in Unity'.[16] And this, one must add, must have been a complicating unity indeed when God had his being only in 'my one flesh'.

For by 1651 the Ranters had fallen back upon the trampoline once more with a heavy thud. Their descent was hastened in 1650 by the Blasphemy Act, and the subsequent imprisonment of several of their supposed leaders. In the less exhilarating ambience of prison, these were swift to recant, showing a lack of fortitude which would have been despised by their Lollard and Puritan forebears. And then, in a final rebound, the tumbler of the radical spirit rose into the air once more.

This time it arose, not as Ranting, but as prophetic dogma and as sectarian organising zeal. In this moment there is a scatter of competing prophets, and the consolidation of sectarian doctrines: Quakers, Fifth Monarchists, Muggletonians. And here and there thinkers of more intellectual rigour (Erbery, Pordage) retired to

---

[15] Hill, *The World Turned Upside Down*, p. 165.   [16] Cited in Morton, p. 75.

meditate more coherent systems. It was this moment, rather than
the climax of the Ranters, which found ways of transmitting itself,
by way of Baptists, Quakers, Philadelphians, Behmenists, Muggletonians and others into the next century, although much was to
be softened and transformed in the transmission.

This moment can be seen as both an extension of Ranting into
new forms and as a reaction against Ranting: what was extended
was, in the same moment, limited and controlled. The reaction
was sometimes general, sometimes very specific. The first commission given by God to John Reeve and Ludowick Muggleton was
to visit the Ranting prophets, John Robins and Thomas Tany, and
pronounce upon them a sentence of eternal damnation. (Laurence
Clarkson was later to renounce his Ranter faith and join the
Muggletonians.) A more general form of reaction is to be seen in
the increasing withdrawal from temporal objectives and expectations, so that old tenets were redefined in a more spiritual or quietist sense. Not only George Fox but also John Reeve placed in the
forefront of their teaching the prohibition of the 'sword of steel'; it
is the portion of true Christians in this world (John Reeve said)
'to suffer all kind of wrong from all men, and to return mercy and
forgiveness. . .'[17] Millenarial expectations tended – except with the
Fifth Monarchists – to be indefinitely postponed, or to be redefined
in an 'internal' sense: the New Jerusalem was an image of spiritual
community, and was perhaps already in existence among the
faithful.

Robins and Tany were two of the most bizarre voices of the
Ranting climax. Both appear to have suffered delusions of personal
divinity. Robins was sometimes known as 'the Ranter's god' or
'the Shakers' god'; his wife announced that she was pregnant with
a Messiah; Robins, who claimed that he had risen from the dead,
started to enlist and train volunteers for a crusade to the Holy
Land. When Reeve (a former disciple) visited him in the New
Bridewell and uttered his sentence of damnation, Robins collapsed
and recanted. For years afterwards Muggleton was to claim this
as a victory over Antichrist, and to taunt the Quakers with being
led and guided by the spirit of Robins.[18] Tany is more interesting,

---

[17] *A Transcendent Spiritual Treatise*, sometimes attributed to John Reeve and Ludowick Muggleton, and sometimes to Reeve alone: chapter 3, 'Of the Unlawfulness for a Spiritual
Christian to war with a Sword of Steel'.
[18] Alexander Gordon, *The Origin of the Muggletonians* (1869), pp. 16–17, and the same author's
excellent entry on Robins in DNB. L. Muggleton, *Acts of the Witnesses of the Spirit* (1699:

and might, just possibly, be more relevant to Blake. For Muggleton, Tany was 'the Head of ... the Atheistical Ranters and Quakers Principle'. A goldsmith in the Strand, he read some of Boehme's work, and, in 1650, announced that it had been revealed to him that he was 'a Jew of the tribe of Reuben' and that he must change his name to Theaurau John: he announced the return of the Jews to the Holy Land, and prepared to follow Robins with 'bow and spear'. As a necessary preparation, he circumcised himself. He was undismayed by Reeve's sentence of damnation, busied himself with other projects, claimed first the throne of England and then the throne of France, had an armed affray at the houses of parliament, and finally seems to have disappeared, perhaps in 1655, perhaps later, sailing in a home-made boat in the Channel, crying 'Ho, for the Holy Wars'.[19]

Tany, unlike Robins, left some writings behind: they are compounded of wilful eccentricity, delusion and passages of transparent intensity. His *Theauraujohn His Theousori Apokolipikal* (1651) was dedicated 'to the Army and the risen people in all Lands'. The soul of man is the divine breath of God 'inclosed within the circumference of the body': 'this is the Image of God in Man', the 'living life of our Spirit', which at death returns to a common fountain. 'Man is Christ, and Christ is God ... both one, the product are we.'

Christ in the head is a lye, without being in the heart ... Brethren, till ye be doers, ye are a lye, and ... your Religion is of the devil; for ye name Jesus to effect another end, but love is Jesus acting, by a living distributing life, to his members.

To know Hell is truly to know Heaven, for 'Hell is a separation from happiness; Hell is the restraint from injoyment.' Tany was as curt with the authority of the Scriptures as he was with that of the churches: the New Testament 'is but a name of dead letters set together with much interweaving of man's invention'.[20] We also find some passages of Behmenist dialectic:

1764 edn), pp. 20–2, 45–8; *A Transcendent Spiritual Treatise*, chapter 2; Muggleton, *The Neck of the Quakers Broken* (1756 edn), pp. 16–17; Muggleton, *A Looking-Glass for George Fox* (1756 edn), pp. 98–9.

[19] Gordon, *The Origin of the Muggletonians*, pp. 18–19, and also his entry on Tany in DNB. Hill, *The World Turned Upside Down*, pp. 181–2; Hill, *Antichrist*, p. 115; Muggleton, *Acts of the Witnesses*, pp. 20, 43–5; *A Looking-Glass for George Fox*, p. 99.

[20] In 1654 Tany in Lambeth threw a bible, along with a saddle, pistols and sword, into a great bonfire, upon which 'the people were ready to stone him'.

Take notice there is two alls, a light all, and a dark all, and God but one all to them two alls; Light and darkness to him are one . . . Love is that great day that shall burn as an oven, for love is fire. . .

And we also find the Everlasting Gospel:

This is the everlasting Gospel that should be preached, which is God dwelling with men, by a divine Evangelical living in them, they in it, here lies the mystery. . .

The heart lives in God when God lives wholly in the heart:

Now here is the mystery. Thus God lives in us, he cannot live out of us. . .

The essence creative in us is good, for 'tis God's image, but our dissenting from that living life in us, causes the evil in us. . .

It is difficult to say how much of this came to Tany through the Familist tradition, how much from Boehme ('God must become man, man must become God . . . the earth must be turned to heaven'[21]), how much from the general radical and Ranting milieu, how much was his own variation upon all these themes. In a continuation of the same work, in 1653, the Everlasting Gospel was defined simply as Love:

> Now know that can be no Gospel,
> That must be upheld by a humane Law;
> But it is the Lye in the whole earth:
> For the Gospel is Love, and then no Law. . .

Among much unloving invective against the established churches ('the *Bishops are gone*, and I Theauraujohn say, that the *Cleargy* shall not long stand'), and more Kabbalistical, Hebraic and Arabic juggling of terms, he returned often to this central theme, expressed in what had become, by now, fairly commonplace antinomian terms: those who are justified not by Works of the Law but by faith 'are risen with Christ, they act in love', and 'love is the new *Jerusalem* that is above':

God is love, and he that acteth in love, acteth in God, for them the spirit hath taken that man or woman into itself.

These were Tany's most lucid tracts, and they are not as lucid as they may appear in my extracts. Later he issued *Theauraujohn*

---

[21] Boehme, *The Signature of All Things*, cited in Hill, *Milton*, p. 312. Boehme also asserted that 'God dwells in all Things'.

High Priest to the Jewes his Disputive challenge to the Universities of Oxford and Cambridge, and the whole Hirarch of Roms Clargical Priests (1655). In this he remarked that he had 'taken my Degrees' in the two 'Colleges' of Newgate and King's Bench: 'the Prisons were alwayes the Prophets Schools, we read true Lectures in the empty walls'. Neither Oxford nor Cambridge have been able to answer his disputive challenge yet.

I beg the impatient Blake reader to favour me with at least a temporary suspension of disbelief. I am not simply rambling on, wherever curiosity may lead me. I am engaged in a complex operation, teasing out strands which may lead on to other strands across 150 years. The Ranting strand leads directly into early Quakerism, within which it was said that some former Ranters were swept up. The degree to which Ranters and early Quakers shared common attributes is another difficult question, and one which must be handled with a certain delicacy to this day, since some part of the evidence may appear to belie the sober testimony of George Fox. But the interpenetration of Ranting and Quaker notions is incontrovertible.[22] I am interested not in continuing vagaries of exhibitionist and enthusiastic behaviour among early Friends, or the ecstatic 'witchcraft-fits' (howling and groaning, foaming at the mouth, speaking with 'tongues') which Muggleton was to make much of in his polemics.[23] What is more significant is the continuity of Ranting doctrine into Quakerism, a continuity which can be easily overlooked because of the very evident Quaker reaction *against* Ranting – a reaction, above all, against the Ranter excesses in personal and sexual conduct – a reaction expressed in sobriety of life, dress and manners.

The continuity is found, in part, in a common Behmenist influence;[24] and, with this, in the literalism with which many early Friends held themselves to be vectors of the divine spirit. Reeve and Muggleton were not guilty of hyperbole when they said that the Quakers were still guided by the spirits of Robins and Tany:

The Quakers Principle is but the Ranters refined into a more civil Kind

---

[22] See Hill, *The World Turned Upside Down*, chapter 10; Morton, *World of the Ranters*, pp. 91–2; Frank McGregor, 'Ranterism and the Development of Early Quakerism', *Journal of Religious History* (Sydney, 1978), pp. 349–63.

[23] *A Looking-Glass for George Fox*, pp. 44–6.

[24] *Ibid.*, p. 10: 'I suppose *Jacob Behmont*'s Books were the chief Books that the Quakers bought, for there is the Principle or Foundation of their Religion.'

of Life. For the Ranters were so grossly rude in their Lives, that spoiled their high Language, and made People weary of them; but the Quakers that were upon the Rant are the best able to maintain the Quakers Principles of Christ within them.[25]

For many early Quakers, God was 'an infinite Spirit, that fills Heaven and Earth, and all Places, and all things', whereas 'as touching Christ's Flesh, we are Bone of his Bone, and Flesh of his Flesh, and we have the Mind of Christ'.[26] However George Fox interpreted these beliefs, contemporary observers insisted that many Quakers held to them in the most literal sense. The believers, like the Ranters, were still 'my one flesh'. They say 'some of them are Christ, some God himself, and some equal with God, because they have the same spirit in them which is in God', 'Christ hath no other body but his church'. Some inveighed against all learning (the fruit of the Tree of the Knowledge of Good and Evil). They held that they were justified by their own inherent righteousness, and that 'many of them cannot sin'; that the more othodox churches were Antichristian; 'that Christ came to destroy all property; and that therefore all things ought to be common . . . and that one man ought not to have power over another'. Thus a critical observer in 1653.[27] And there is independent confirmation that some early Quakers held most of these tenets.[28]

In this selective account we have at length reached the year 1653. And there are still a dozen or more decades to traverse before we can come up to William Blake. Is there any reason to suppose that Blake was aware of this early moment of antinomianism, or that tenets and tropes could have been conveyed to him across these decades in any form? What possible vectors could have carried this tradition from 1650 to 1790?

[25] *Ibid.*, p. 55. Cf. Ephraim Pagitt, 'the *Ranter* is . . . much of the same make with our *Quakers* . . . only the *Ranter* is less severe'; and Baxter, 'Quakers . . . were but the Ranters turned from horrid Prophaneness and Blasphemy, to a Life of extreme Austerity on the other side. Their Doctrines were mostly the same with the Ranters': Morton, *World of the Ranters*, p. 91.

[26] Muggleton, *The Neck of the Quakers Broken*, pp. 9, 23.

[27] Alexander Ross, *A View of all Religions* (1653), pp. 252–7. This account continued to be reprinted in the eighteenth century, but subsequent editors added an Appendix, pp. 322–3, noting that 'considerable alterations' had taken place among the Quakers, who were now noted for 'probity and uprightness in their dealings', frugality, simplicity, &c.

[28] See Hill, *The World Turned Upside Down*, chapter 10; J.F. McGregor, 'Ranterism and the Development of Early Quakerism', *Journal of Religious History*, 9 (1977); Barry Reay, *The Quakers and the English Revolution* (1985), chapter 2.

CHAPTER 4

The polite witnesses

We are back once more in the argument indicated in my Introduction: Blake and *which* tradition? It is an extraordinarily complex argument, and very different answers have been offered, with great confidence. For convenience we may put the answers into three groups: (1) The strongest influence upon Blake comes from one major source – the Bible – but the Bible read in a particular way, influenced by Milton and by radical Dissent; (2) To this may be added suggestions of more specific vectors – the Moravians, Baptists, Philadelphians and Behmenists, the Rosicrucians and masons, and thence to the Swedenborgians – which it is argued claimed Blake's allegiance; (3) While the influence of the first two vectors is not discounted, it is suggested that the weight of influence upon Blake is literary and scholarly: that Blake's ideas and images were derived primarily from his reading: that he was an omnivorous reader in an extraordinarily diverse (and often obscure) range of classical, neo-Platonist, Kabbalistic, hermetic and Behmenist sources. Scholars have suggested either that Blake drew upon these influences eclectically, or that his work should be placed firmly within 'The Tradition' of neo-Platonic and hermetic thought (G.M. Harper, Kathleen Raine).[1]

The answers may shade into each other. But, in the end, there is a real divergence of emphasis between (1) and (3). To make the matter more difficult, one answer may be adequate for 1788–93 but less adequate for any time after 1793 (or 1800). For it is probable that Blake, in his later years, read widely in both classical

---

[1] G.M. Harper, *The Neoplatonism of William Blake* (Chapel Hill, N.C., 1961); Kathleen Raine, *Blake and Tradition* (Princeton, 1968), 2 vols. For the possible influence of the Cambridge Platonist, Henry More, see S. Foster Daman, *William Blake: his Philosophy and Symbols* (Gloucester, Mass., 1958).

and 'mystic' sources, and, as he did so, his field of reference
enlarged and any kind of allusion is possible.

My own answer is compounded of (1) and (2), and I will propose
a new possible vector coming through to Blake in his childhood.
But when we come to the later prophetic books, then we must
attend with respect to the influences suggested in (3).

The best way into this very complex argument may be to look
at the strongest candidates offered as a line of transmission from
the late seventeenth century to Blake: the Behmenists and Philadelphians. But a search for possible influences may take us back a
great deal further: indeed to the Gnostic Christian heresy in the
first and second centuries AD. In several of the Gnostic sects there
were some quite startling pre-figurations of ideas and symbols
which recur in Blake. Gnostic dualism which proposed a second
God or demiurge as Creator of matter and the world could sometimes take the demiurge to be an evil power acting in hostility to
the Supreme Power. The Naasenes and some of the Gnostic sect
of Ophites venerated the serpent, and interpreted its role in the
Fall as a benefaction, since it first raised human beings to higher
knowledge. (This reverence for the serpent persisted in the later
heresy of Manichaeism.) The Gnostic sect of Cainites (if they ever
existed) held the God of the Old Testament to be an evil being,
and Cain and Abel to be the 'offspring of antagonistic spiritual
powers'.[2] We will find such ideas cropping up in Blake. Indeed,
Crabb Robinson, a friend of the Romantic poets and a voluminous
diarist, who recorded some fascinating conversations with Blake in
his last years, instantly recognised some of his ideas as Gnostic.
Blake had told him that 'Nature is the work of the Devil.' When
Crabb Robinson objected (in the authority of Genesis) that 'God
created the Heaven & the Earth . . . I was triumphantly told that
this God was not Jehovah, but the Elohim, & the doctrine of the
Gnostics repeated with sufficient consistency to silence one so
unlearned as myself.'[3]

Nearly all of what the eighteenth century knew about Gnosticism
came from hostile and heresy-hunting sources, such as Irenaeus,
a bishop of Lyons in the second century.[4] Blake could have picked

[2] H.L. Mansel, *The Gnostic Heresies of the First and Second Centuries* (1875), pp. 96, 101–2.
[3] G.E. Bentley, *Blake Records*, p. 545.
[4] Giovanni Filoramo, *A History of Gnosticism* (Oxford, 1990), pp. 3–4. The discovery of

up some notion of Gnostic beliefs from several second-hand
sources: even Gibbon gave a sketchy account of Gnostic dualism:
'in the system of the Gnostics, the Jehovah of Israel, the Creator
of this lower world, was a rebellious, or at least an ignorant spirit'.[5]
But it is unlikely that Blake would have directly consulted Gnostic
'sources', even such unreliable accounts as those of Irenaeus. For
a historian of Gnosticism affirms that 'we see a veritable efflores-
cence of Gnostic mythology in Jacob Boehme'.[6] The influence of
Boehme upon Blake is undoubted (and was acknowledged) and he
could have derived any Gnostic notions through this source.[7]

Jacob Boehme (1575–1624) was a prosperous shoemaker from
Gorlitz on the Bohemian border, who discussed mystic, Kabbalistic, Gnostic, alchemical (Paracelsian) and other unorthodox ideas
in a circle of merchants, intellectuals, tradesmen and one or two
noblemen, and who worked out his own theosophical system which
he published in a succession of tracts in his last years. His reputation travelled rapidly to an England which was in a state of spiritual enquiry, and by the 1640s his ideas were already circulating
among enthusiasts. The followers of Boehme were often known as
'Behmenists', but the case for a direct line of Behmenist transmission to Blake – a case sometimes suggested by those who propose
a Great Tradition of Christian and neo-Platonist mysticism – is
hazardous. I will rehearse the hypothesis briefly, since anyone who
puts together the engaging account in Désirée Hirst (*Hidden Riches*)

Gnostic works in Coptic in a jar at Nag Hammadi in Egypt in 1945 has, of course,
transformed subsequent understanding of Gnosticism.

[5] Edward Gibbon, *The Decline and Fall of the Roman Empire*, chapter XLVII (II). Secondary
accounts of Gnosticism which were possibly available to Blake include Nathaniel Lard-
ner's *History of Heretics* and *Credibility of the Gospel History* in *Works* (1788), J.L. von Mosh-
eim, *An Ecclesiastical History, Ancient and Modern* (1765), and several works by his contemporary, Joseph Priestley, especially *An History of the Corruptions of Christianity* (Birmingham,
1782). See also Stuart Curran, 'Blake and the Gnostic Hyle', *Blake Studies*, Vol. 4 no. 2,
Spring 1972. But note also the warning of G.E. Bentley: 'It is much easier to find parallels
to Blakean myth in Boehme's system than in the fragmentary accounts of Gnosticism
available to him': G.E. Bentley, 'William Blake and the Alchemical Philosophers', B.Litt.
thesis, Oxford, 1954, p. 185. Unfortunately this thesis, which is the closest examination
of the relation of Boehme's ideas to Blake's known to me, has never been published.

[6] G. Filoramo, *A History of Gnosticism*, p. xvi.

[7] In *The Marriage of Heaven and Hell* Blake wrote: 'Any man of mechanical talents may,
from the writings of Paracelsus or Jacob Behmen, produce ten thousand volumes of equal
value with Swedenborg's, and from those of Dante or Shakespeare an infinite number.'
The evidence that Blake used William Law's edition of *The Works of Jacob Behmen* (1764,
1772 and 1781) comes from his late years, when he praised Freher's plates to Henry
Crabb Robinson: see Bentley, *Blake Records*, p. 313 and note.

with works by D.P. Walker, Walton, Thune, Hutin and (with some caution) G.M. Harper and Kathleen Raine, can decipher it there.[8]

The story commences in the vortex of 'The World Turned Upside Down', when Behmenist influence was profound both upon some scholars and some Commonwealth sects. Dr John Pordage, ejected for Behmenist and other heresies from his living in 1654, returns to view in 1681, when Mrs Jane Lead, author of *The Everlasting Gospel Message*, adopts his teaching, publishes many volumes of visionary and trance-like writing, and becomes the centre of a small group of Philadelphians:

> From thy dark Cell now great Bohemine rise;
> Tutor to Sages; Mad to th' Worldly Wise.
> Wisdom's first distant Phosphor, to whose Sight
> Internal Nature's Ground, all naked bright
> Unveils, all Worlds appear, Heavens spread their Light. . .
>
> The Glorious Aera *Now, Now, Now* begins.
> *Now, Now* the Great Angelick Trumpet sings:
> A Now in ev'ry Blast, Love's *Everlasting Gospel* Rings.[9]

These ecstatic Philadelphians take us forward into the eighteenth century, when there is a brief moment of confluence and argument with the Camisards or 'French Prophets'. From this point we may find lesser and eccentric figures: Francis Lee, a disciple of Jane Lead, the advocate of an 'Enochian life on earth', 'a transcendentally exalted spiritual renovation and illumination';[10] Francis Okeley, at one time ministering to the Moravians, author of the *Dawnings of the Everlasting Gospel-Light* (1775); and Richard Clarke, a late exemplar of the tradition, a contemporary of Blake in London, much preoccupied with the symbolism of the 'New Jerusalem' and of *Revelation*.

Alongside, but standing a little apart from, this tradition we have the most articulate and cogent of the English eighteenth-century Behmenists, the Anglican clergyman, William Law (1686–1761). He is best known today for his evangelical influence upon John Wesley. But Law's nineteenth-century disciple, Christopher

---

[8] Désirée Hirst, *Hidden Riches: Traditional Symbolism from the Renaissance to Blake* (1964); D.P. Walker, *The Decline of Hell* (Chicago, 1964); Nils Thune, *The Behmenists and the Philadelphians* (Uppsala, 1948); S. Hutin, *Les Disciples Anglais de Jacob Boehme* (Paris, 1960); A.G. Debus, *The English Paracelsians* (1965). Also Francis Yates, *The Rosicrucian Enlightenment* (1972).

[9] Jane Lead, *A Fountain of Gardens*, 3 vols. (1696–1700), sig. E.2.

[10] Francis Lee, *Dissertations* (1752), p. 640.

Walton, saw him as having two aspects – the one 'Elias-like', or evangelical, the other 'Enochian' or prophetic. In his Enochian aspect Law's work runs closely parallel to the Philadelphians. Deism he saw as 'the religion of *human reason*, set up in opposition to the Gospel'. The laws of Moses were a matter of mere 'carnal ordinances', 'a temporary provisional Help'. '*Reasoning* instead of Faith brought about the first Fall', and–

To live by *Faith* is to be truly and fully in Covenant with God; to live by Reasoning, is to be merely and solely in compact with ourselves, with our own vanity and blindness.[11]

However oddly it assorts with his evangelical writings, there is a kind of spiritualised antinomian pressure in Enochian William Law.

These, then, may be traditions germane to Blake. From these the Swedenborgians were to make some early converts.[12] But, as so often, the evidence is elusive. We have no proof that Blake read any of them, although we can show the probability in certain cases. Such correspondence of this circle as survives in the late eighteenth century shows no known associates of Blake.[13] And if we look back to Mrs Jane Lead, early in the century, we can see some of the difficulties. Very certainly, Jane Lead, in her visionary writings, employs a vocabulary which seems to flash signals forward to Blake. The 'Everlasting Gospel' and the 'New Jerusalem' apart (which will be found in many different places), we also have references to the 'Pure Humanity of Christ' and to 'Christ's perfect Deity in his Eternal Humanity', to the Last Vintage and Harvest, to the 'secret gate' of the spirit, to 'states' and to 'golden chains', and (perhaps even more striking) recommendations to enter in 'to a Self-Annihilation'.[14]

Nor is this all. If we potter around in the writings of Lead, Pordage and Philadelphians we will stumble repeatedly upon 'Blakean' themes. To Jane Lead this world is 'under the government of that Great Monarch Reason, to whose Scepter all must

[11] William Law, *A Short but Sufficient Confutation of the Reverend Dr Warburton's Projected Defence of Christianity in his Divine Legation of Moses* ... (1757), pp. 63, 76–7; C. Walton, *Notes and Materials for a Biography of William Law* (1854), p. 522; Désirée Hirst, *Hidden Riches*, chapter 7.
[12] One was Thomas Hartley, author of *Paradise Restored: or a Testimony to the Doctrines of the Blessed Millenium* (1764).
[13] In Dr Williams's Library, MS 1.1.43 (Walton Papers).
[14] See, e.g., *A Fountain of Gardens*, p. 14; *Theosophical Transactions of the Philadelphian Society*, no. 1, 1697.

bow that live in the Sensitive Animal Life'.[15] This Monarch is sometimes seen as a Serpent. The title of one of Pordage's works was *The Angelickal World: or, a Treatise concerning the Angelical Principle, with the Inhabitants thereof, and God in this Principle. The Dark Fire World: or Treatise concerning the Hellish Principle, with the Inhabitants, and Wonders, and God manifesting himself in this Principle.*[16] Jane Lead is always speculating on the Seven Churches of Asia, and on four-fold, or five- or six-fold, sensual, intellectual, visionary, prophetic and mystical states. Pordage's circle also defined four degrees of revelation: (1) Vison, (2) Illumination, (3) Transportation or Translation, (4) Revelation; and as early as 1683 one was bitterly attacking 'Natural Religion':

The *Rational*, which the confounding Jesuit wold mak the *pure Religionist beleev* to be Mechanism (*the Diana of this inquisitiv Age*) and the whole Encyclopoede of Arts and Sciences but a brisk circulation of the Blood, and all thinking and reasoning Power a mere local motion, and that too tumultuous. . .[17]

(It will be seen that our author, like Tany before him and Thomas Spence after him, was a spelling reformer.) 'There is no use of *Reason* but in the Babylonish principle, and the kingdom of the beast', wrote Pordage, referring to the authority of Boehme.[18] 'All Formal Worships set up by Men, and constituted by Rational Inventions, as a Shadow must pass away', prophesied Jane Lead.[19] They would give way to the ministration of the Everlasting Gospel 'which is all Love, Grace, Mercy and Peace'.[20] And in the *Theosophical Transactions* of the Philadelphian Society – a journal conducted for five numbers in 1697 – contributors sent in Paracelsian, hermetic and Kabbalistic lucubrations replete with 'emanations' and magic numbers, and sometimes uncomfortably close to the machinery of Blake's prophetic books:

[15] *Ibid.*, p. 37.
[16] This is advertised in *A Fountain of Gardens*, but I have not found an English edition. Several of Pordage's works were never published in England, but in Amsterdam, etc., in German: see D.P. Walker, *The Decline of Hell*; Thune, *The Behmenists*, pp. 99–100. For John Pordage and his son, Samuel, see Hill, *The Experience of Defeat*, chapter 8; and Hirst, *Hidden Riches*, pp. 105–9, 168–72.
[17] J.P., M.D. (John Pordage), *Theologia Mystica* (1683), pp. 65–9, 98, 101–3. This curious work is edited by J.L. (Jane Lead) and E.H. (Edward Hooker) and carries a vigorous and witty 100-page introduction, perhaps from Hooker's pen.
[18] A Gentleman Retired from Business, *A Compendious View of the Grounds of the Teutonick Philosophy* (1770), p. 41.
[19] Jane Lead, *The Tree of Faith; or the Tree of Life* (1696), p. 1.
[20] Lead, *A Fountain of Gardens*, p. 210.

Now by these manifold Emanations, and Circular Returns or Reverbera-
tions and Extractions from the dark Waters of Nature in the Abyss and
void Chaos; as by so many Coitions and Copulations of the Male with
the Female, were brought forth all the foresaid Circular Globes and
Worlds, fill'd with all Sorts of Creatures and Inhabitants; distinguish'd
into their several Sphears and Regions of Modified Light and Darkness,
Higher and Lower . . . the inferiour Female Nature always Breathing and
Aspiring upward, as with a Divine Lust, to be impregnated with the
Influence and Immanations of the Superiour Divine Male.[21]

As a result of all these divine copulations 'thus . . . have Good and
Evil grown up together, from one Original in the Beginning of
Creation'.

It is instructive to note parallels with Blake's ideas and symbolism. But exactly what instruction do these bring? We are reminded,
perhaps, that notions which scholars confidently attribute to
Blake's reading of Proclus, Fludd or Thomas Taylor, could equally
have come through reading of this kind. We are also prompted to
reflect that notions or symbols which appear to be grand or profound when presented as part of a 'Great Tradition' of hermetic
and neo-Platonist thought need not always be handled with such
reverence. Philadelphian and Behmenist thought has a significance
as a counter-Enlightenment impulse, as a reaction against the
mechanistic philosophy of the time, and hence as a potential
resource for alternative positions. But it can scarcely be argued
that it articulated such positions. Some part of the continuing 'Tradition' was little more than an arcane vocabulary and ecstatic
visionary rhetoric, in which circulated a repetitious symbolism of
matter/spirit. And some considerable part of the 'Tradition' was
claptrap (which also, now and then, was gathered up by Blake).

Moreover, we can make few attributions of influence with any
confidence. Let us take the state of Beulah, which Blake offers as
a moony paradise, sometimes a garden of repose, sometimes marriage or sexual love, sometimes as 'a place where Contrarieties are
equally True'. Scholars at first supposed Blake found the name in
a rather non-committal reference in Isaiah: then it was noted that
he could have found it also in *Pilgrim's Progress*, in a more suggestive
passage. To put these two together, one perceptive critic has
argued, is one of Blake's 'more clever pieces of symbolic align-

---

[21] *Theosophical Transactions* (Philadelphia Society, 1697), pp. 277, 289.

ment'.[22] How much more clever, then, to put these two together
with Mrs Jane Lead's *A Fountain of Gardens* (1696):

Know then that there is a secret hidden Garden, within that Land called
Beulah, in which grow all Physical Plants, which the River *Pison* doth
Water. It is a temperate Climate, neither too Hot, nor too Cold: and the
Sun never goeth down there. For there is no Night, but one perpetual
Day in the borders of this Blessed and Beautiful Land. And here do grow
all sorts of Herbs, that have such a vigorous Seed of Life in them, that
their Life never doth fade. Here also groweth every Kind of Spicy Trees,
which through the Exhaling Sun, through the rest of the Divine Plants,
do produce a mighty Frangrancy; insomuch that none into this Place can
come, but Seraphical Ones; who are used to this pure Climate. Here are
hid within the Bowels of this Holy Ground, the Veins of pure Gold, with
all Oriental Pretious Stones.[23]

But before we claim this as a third source, or *the* source, of Blake's
Beulah, we have to ask how far the name was part of the common
currency of eighteenth-century radical Dissent, as the name for a
peaceful and fertile paradise. Certainly, it was well enough understood to Morgan John Rhees, a fervent Welsh Baptist, who, when
he founded with utopian hopes a town in Western Pennsylvania
in 1796, called it Beula.[24]

It is my impression that Beulah often came up in the rhetoric
of eighteenth-century Dissenting circles (especially Baptist). We
are dealing, not with a Great Tradition of a few scholars and
mystics, but with several little traditions, some with literary attainments and some without, all of which employed a vocabulary of
symbolism familiar to Blake.

Even attributions of influence from the scholarly tradition are
exceedingly hazardous. Let us take the Philadelphians again.
Behind them stood Boehme. Behind Boehme stood much else –
influences from Paracelsus, the Kabbala, millenarial impulses,
even gnosticism. But Boehme's influence came through to the Philadelphians by way of seventeenth-century translators and scholars,
Ranters and Antinomians (in her youth Mrs Jane Lead had sat at

[22] John Beer, *Blake's Visionary Universe* (Manchester, 1969), p. 27. Also Northrop Frye, *Fearful Symmetry* (Princeton, 1947: Boston, 1962), *passim*: Paley, p. 130; Masashi Suzuki, ' "Archi-tecture", "Foot", and "Beulah": Visionary Gate' in *Milton, English and English–American Literature*, No. 24, 1989 (Tokyo).
[23] Lead, *A Fountain of Gardens*, p. 105. Hirst also briefly notices this passage, *Hidden Riches*, pp. 303–4.
[24] See Gwyn A. Williams, 'Morgan John Rhees and his Beula', *Welsh History Review*, Vol. III, 1966–7, pp. 441–72.

the feet of Tobias Crisp, the antinomian divine[25]), and by way of Dr John Pordage, an associate of the Commonwealth radicals and visionaries. Blake may or may not have read Jane Lead or Pordage, but fellow Swedenborgians, with whom he may have argued, certainly did (below, p. 43). Moreover, there is good evidence that Swedenborg himself was influenced in his youth by the writings of English Philadelphians, as these had filtered through to Sweden by way of German pietism (pp. 133–4n). And, finally, the great influence of Milton, who himself had been touched by the Ranting and Behmenist milieu, worked continually upon Blake.[26] How are we to say, with any confidence, how a given symbol, common to all this tangled inheritance, ended up in Blake's mind?

Another way of approaching the problem is to ask the mundane question: *could* Blake have read in the various sources discussed so far? So far as I know, no scholar has yet identified any 'public' or subscription library of which Blake was a member. But most of such libraries would have been unlikely to hold stocks of 'mystic' writings. If we look, rather, at what was available in recent editions, and at the skimpy evidence as to what was to be found in private collections, the answer is remarkable. Blake *could* have found in London, in the 1790s, copies of almost every work that we have discussed. The scarcest and most inaccessible works will have been those which Miss Raine cites as central to her notion of The Tradition. If Blake consulted these, then he could only have done so in editions published in the Civil War and Commonwealth vortex: translations of *The Divine Pomander* of Hermes Trismegistus (1650), of Agrippa's *Occult Philosophy* (1651), all the englished versions of Paracelsus, all the works of Thomas Vaughan, Fludd's *Mosaicall Philosophy* (1659). And in whatever collections Blake found these (if he did) he would be likely to have found them cheek by jowl with the works of Antinomians, Ranters and Seekers, with the works of such men as Crisp, Everard, Erbery, Webster, Bauthumley or Pordage. Miss Raine always gives us the transcendental cheek and neglects to mention the antinomian and millenarian jowl.

---

[25] Nils Thune, *The Behmeniste*, p. 70. For Tobias Crisp see Christopher Hill, *Religion and Politics in 17th Century England* (1986).

[26] The major discussion of this is in Hill, *Milton*. The claims once put forward for Boehme's direct influence on Milton – see Margaret L. Bailey, *Milton and Jakob Boehme* (New York, 1914) – tend now to be discounted by scholars, including Hill.

It is in fact the more radical seventeenth-century thought which seems to have been more readily available in Blake's time. Of the Antinomians and Ranters (and their milieu) works by Tobias Crisp were republished in 1791,[27] by John Saltmarsh in 1811 and 1814,[28] by John Simpson and John Eaton in 1747,[29] by Richard Coppin in 1763, 1764 and 1768,[30] by John Everard in 1757 and 1817[31] and by John Pordage in 1776.[32] Works of Boehme remained available in several editions.[33] Virtually all of the works of John Reeve and Ludowick Muggleton were kept in print throughout the century (p. 69).[34]

The extensive range of works from these traditions which could be gathered by an eighteenth-century collector is exemplified by the private library of John Byrom (1692–1763), now in the Cheetham's Library, Manchester. A similar library may have been in the possession of a contemporary and possible acquaintance of Blake's, Henry Peckitt. Peckitt, a retired apothecary, was an ardent Swedenborgian, the first President of the Theosophical Society in London, a student of Hebrew and Arabic, an antiquarian and astronomer (perhaps dabbling in astrology?). His library consisted of many thousands of volumes 'in every branch of science' and 'a rare collection of mystical books, to which he was known to be very partial'. In the 1780s he lived in Old Compton Street, Soho, five minutes' walk from Blake: we cannot show that the two men were acquainted, but if Blake ever attended meetings of the Theosophical Society or the Reverend Duché's gatherings at Lambeth, then they would have met.[35] Prior to his adhesion to the Sweden-

---

[27] *Christ Alone Exalted* (1791).

[28] *Free Grace* (1814). Saltmarsh's *Holy Discoveries and Flames* and *Sparkles of Glory* were republished by William Huntington in 1811.

[29] Reprinted by William Cudworth, in 1747, along with Crisp in a compilation, *Christ Alone Exalted*.

[30] *The Advancement of All Things in Christ* (1763); *A Blow at the Serpent* (1764); *Truth's Testimony* (1768). For Coppin, see Hill, *The World Turned Upside Down*, pp. 177–9 *et passim*; Hill, *The Experience of Defeat*, pp. 45–6; Davis, *Fear, Myth and History*, pp. 36–40. See also below, pp. 55–6.

[31] John Everard, *Some Gospel Treasures* (Germantown, 1757). A MS note in the British Library copy says that a London edition was also printed by 'I.O.' at the 'Bible and Heart', Little Britain. *The Rending of the Vail* (1817).

[32] Anon. [Pordage] *A Compendious View of the Grounds of the Teutonick Philosophy* (1776).

[33] See the bibliography in S. Hutin, *Les Disciples Anglais*.

[34] Gerard Winstanley may have disappeared from view, although not from that of Thomas Spence, who reprinted a tract in the Digger tradition, *A Plea for a Commonwealth*, 1659, in *Pigsmeat*, Vol. III (1795).

[35] See David V. Erdman, *William Blake: Prophet against Empire* (Princeton, 3rd edn, 1976), pp. 11–12, note 19.

borgians (*c.*1783), Peckitt was a follower of Boehme, Madame Guyon 'and others of that class'. In 1785 his library ('a full waggon-load') was utterly destroyed by fire, and only a few manuscripts survived.[36] Among these – and an indication of what may have been lost – was a rare Philadelphian manuscript[37] and a copy of Tany's *Theauraujohn His Theousori Apokolipikal* (1651). At the end of the manuscript, Peckitt has made a note: 'I, H.P., cannot rely upon this Mans declarations, as I do upon the honerable Emanuel Swedenborg's writings.'[38]

That books and manuscripts from these traditions were circulating in London in the 1780s and 1790s can be confirmed from other snatches of evidence. The Muggletonian church preserved its own archives, including late manuscripts by Laurence Clarkson (See Appendix 1). A Muggletonian family of painters, the Pickersgills, owned manuscripts by the Muggletonian, Thomas Tomkinson.[39] There was something of a revival of interest in Jane Lead. Three of her works, now in the British Library, carry the stamp of Philip de Loutherbourg the painter, an acquaintance of Blake, a member of the Theosophical Society in the 1780s and a follower of the millenarial prophet, Richard Brothers, in the 1790s.[40] The Swedenborgian, Benedict Chastanier, a friend of Henry Peckitt, was also well versed in Jane Lead's writings.[41] There is preserved in Dr Williams's Library some voluble correspondence from Mrs Pratt in 1791–2, a lady who repudiated the views of her Swedenborgian husband, and who was searching for inspiration in alternative visionary traditions. She found in William Erbery, the seventeenth-century Seeker, 'a very choice author'. 'I have read manuscripts

---

[36] H.L. Tafel, *Documents concerning the Life and Character of Emanuel Swedenborg* (1877), Vol. II, part 2, pp. 1191–2; Robert Hindmarsh, *Rise and Progress of the New Jerusalem Church* (1861), p. 15.

[37] 'A faithful account of the last Hours of Mrs Jane Lead, by one who was a witness of her dying words', MS in archives of Swedenborg Society, A/25. According to Hutin, *Les Disciples Anglais*, p. 256, note 49, there was no English edition of this account (by Francis Lee), and only a German edition (Amsterdam, 1705).

[38] Archives of Swedenborg Society, MS A/25. Another remarkable library of 'scarce valuable mystical and alchymical books' was collected by John Dennis, the publisher of the *New Jerusalem Magazine*: see James Lackington, *Memoirs* (1830), p. 212; G.E. Bentley, 'William Blake and the Alchemical Philosophers', p. 113.

[39] A note on Tomkinson MSS in the Muggletonian archive shows that these were bought by the Church from the Pickersgill family, *c.*1843.

[40] The following carry the stamp of P.J. de Loutherbourg: Jane Lead, *A Message to the Philadelphian Society* (1696); *The Signs of the Times* (1699) – stamped '1796' – and *A Fountain of Gardens* (1696).

[41] [B. Chastanier], *Tableau Analytique et Raisoné de la Doctrine Céleste de l'Église de la Nouvelle Jerusalem* (1786), p. 40.

and many (almost all) Hermetic books.' Her more specific references are to Mme Guyon, Bourignon, Poiret, Boehme, Roach and
Philadelphians. At length the seventh seal was opened to her and
(following in the tradition of Jane Lead) she had her own ecstatic
visions in 'the supercelestial life'. We will encounter her again.[42]

The evidence is sketchy, but it is sufficient to show that the
books, private collections and some manuscripts were available at
that time, and in circles proximate to Blake. And yet, how far
should we be looking, in this literal way, for *books*? Or, indeed, for
these books? For there are difficulties, which some scholars pass
over too lightly, when we seek to 'derive' Blake in any direct way
from a Behmenist or Philadelphian tradition. Although Blake himself referred to Paracelsus with approval, the detectable influence
is only marginal; it may be felt, perhaps, behind some passages on
the 'poetic imagination', and in the notion of 'signatures' which
prepared Blake for Swedenborg's notion of 'correspondences': but
Blake dispensed with most of the astrological business and the
alchemical terminology of Paracelsus and Boehme. The English
Paracelsian, Robert Fludd, wrote largely and suggestively about
'the two contrarieties, or opposite natures' of which the whole
world and every creature is composed. Indeed, the essential unity
of contrary principles, light and darkness, is posed as the 'real and
onely foundation . . . of universall Philosophy and Theology'. But
a dialectic which came to influence Blake's whole stance – his
historical, moral and utopian thought – remains trapped with
Fludd, and also with Pordage and the Behmenist tradition generally, in an obscure and repetitious symbolism of creation and genesis. Why did God permit these co-existent contraries, Fludd once
asks. And his reply is a simple cop-out: 'It is too occult a Caball
to be explained by mortall capacity.' For enlightenment we must
wait till 'the seventh Seal shall be opened'.[43]

And Boehme? Undoubtedly there is a significant direct influence
here. But is it an influence central to Blake's stance? Those who
wish to place Blake firmly in the 'Great Tradition' have hurried,
with averted eyes, past some warning-signs. Thus M. Serge Hutin,
a French scholar deeply versed in Behmenist thought, has published a study of the English disciples of Boehme. In his closely

[42] Dr Williams's Library, MS 1.1.43: Mrs Pratt to Henry Brooke, 17 July 1792, 25 August
1792, 4 October 1792. See also below, pp. 138–9, and Hirst, *Hidden Riches*, pp. 26off.
[43] Robert Fludd, *Mosaical Philosophy* (1659), pp. 143–4.

argued conclusions on Blake, he notes that his writings employ the notions of 'correspondence', of the 'Grand Man' and of the primordial unity of God and the universe, but shows that there is nothing specifically Behmenist about any of these: they are current in all occultism and theosophy, and in the cosmological specula- tions of the prophetic books 'it is absolutely impossible to discover the least echo of Behmenist metaphysic'. Boehme's concept of con- traries (he agrees) had influence on Blake, but Blake translates the operation of the dialectic from metaphysical machinery to values: he has appropriated it and metamorphosised it into 'a decided antinomianism', a sort of 'gnostic antinomianism', original to Blake, pushed to extremes from which Jacob Boehme would have recoiled in horror. Blake, in Hutin's reading, was *no* disciple of Boehme, was attached to *no* previous school, but used the works of previous theosophists with complete independence of spirit.[44]

Despite Hutin's expertise, his argument is conducted at a level of generalities, and we may not be satisfied that he is a sufficiently close and perceptive critic of Blake to substantiate these conclu- sions. But another, complementary warning-sign was set up, in 1957, by Martin K. Nurmi in an excellent and close critical study of *The Marriage of Heaven and Hell*. Here Nurmi does see evidence that Blake was passing through a spiritual crisis 'in which intellec- tual affinity shifted from Swedenborg to Boehme'. But critical ana- lysis of Blake's text gives us a complex and nuanced conclusion. Blake was *not* 'a Behmenist'; in *The Marriage* he borrowed (perhaps tried out?) some ideas from Boehme 'that he had not really assimil- ated and that he was never to assimilate'. Other ideas he made 'entirely his own', but 'no ideas enter Blake's thought unchanged'. These changes were so considerable as, on occasion, to invert Boehme's meaning, and to leave us with fragments of his vocabu- lary of symbolism turned to quite different ends. And it is interest- ing to note that Nurmi and Hutin, who were working independ- ently of each other, arrive at very similar conclusions. Boehme's contraries are 'primarily cosmosgenic principles . . . they explain how creation came about more than they explain its present char- acter'. 'Blake's contraries, on the other hand, describe the vital nature of Human life, especially of ideal society. . .' 'The most important application of the doctrine of contraries' with Blake 'is

---

[44] Hutin, *Les Disciples Anglais*, chapter 8, *passim*.

the social one'. Blake's crucial distinction between active contraries and mere 'negations' owes nothing to Boehme. What Blake did was to take over some parts of the symbolic machinery of 'The Tradition' and turn it to his own purposes.

> The distinction between contraries and negations, in Blake's opinion, is a crucial one for the salvation of man. For to see the qualities of things as vital, necessary contraries is to live in a Human world of vision and imagination, whereas to see them as negations is to live in the fallen world of materialism and repressive social, religious, and political laws, a world in which the contraries are distorted and given the crude normative designations 'good' and 'evil'.[45]

To develop this theme I have had to run ahead of myself, and to assume in the readers some knowledge of the points at issue. But, short of a very long exposition, this is the only way. And it is necessary to offer this compressed critique of certain current readings of Blake if we are to propose the need for an alternative one. For Nurmi's critique implies – as Hutin's does more explicitly – that Blake has wrested the Behmenite vocabulary back into a markedly antinomian and millenarial tradition, for which Boehme himself provides only fitful, ambiguous and obscure warrant. That is, Blake's stance is very much closer to that of the seventeenth-century sectaries whom I have discussed (themselves employing some Behmenist language) than it is to the Philadelphians. This is true, most evidently, in the loss of radical attack, in the failing social content, of the theosophical tradition as it drifts (and sometimes burbles) down through the eighteenth century. The closer we are to 1650, the closer we seem to be to Blake. The fierce antinomian opposition between *our* faith and *their* reason becomes, with the Philadelphians, an opposition between mundane materialist reason and supercelestial visionary mystery. It may be true that Jane Lead was an inheritor of 'the Cromwell–Muggletonian–fanatic days',[46] but as the old century gave way to the new so that tradition was translated into an ecstatic and arcane quietism. The Philadelphians explicitly declared, in 1697, that they 'are not for turning the world upside down as some have Represented 'em'.[47]

---

[45] Martin K. Nurmi, *Blake's Marriage of Heaven and Hell* (1957; 1972 New York), esp. pp. 19–23, 30–7.

[46] As was suggested by William Law's nineteenth-century disciple, Christopher Walton, *Biography of William Law*, p. 148.

[47] *The State of the Philadelphian Society* (1697), p. 9. See Thune, *The Behmeniste*, p. 95.

Jane Lead was prophetess of a new, universal, non-sectarian New Jerusalem church; but, at the same time, the messengers of this church were to be a 'Secret Blessed Society' since 'a Philadelphian concealeth all things'.[48] And the New Jerusalem church is sometimes a 'state', and opening of 'the Soul-Centre', sometimes a 'time', when 'nothing but what is purely taught of God shall abide or stand'.[49] William Law, a much sounder scholar of Boehme, was irritated by their transports: the Philadelphians were 'great readers, and well versed in the language of J. B. [Jacob Boehme], and used to make eloquent discourses of the mystery in their meetings. Their only Thirst was after visions, openings and revelations &c. . .'[50]

Law was more true to some part of Boehme's thought, which he sought to bring within some rational exegesis. But his thought moves around the faith/reason, spirit/matter antimonies, and his emphasis upon Faith, with its concomitants, the Spirit of Prayer, Penitence, Self condemnation, Confession and Humility provides an insight into the way in which he managed to combine the prophetic (or 'mystic') and evangelical characters. It is an emphasis at the opposite pole to that of Blake, and there is scarcely any sense in which Law inhabits the older antinomian tradition: as Désirée Hirst notes, Law 'was quite out of sympathy with the radical attitude stemming from the seventeenth century Levellers and their fellows'.[51]

So we might move on through the century. Behmenist scholarship was a polite and retiring occupation. The antinomian pressure comes, not from this quarter, but, as we have seen, more often from Baptists, irregular Methodists, breakaway sects like that of William Huntington. Only the last figure on that eighteenth-century line, Richard Clarke, revives some of that radical impulse which had first impelled John Pordage. We owe the rediscovery of Clarke to Désirée Hirst, and she makes a strong case to show that he 'was a man after Blake's own heart'.[52] Very certainly she shows that Clarke, preaching and writing in London in Blake's time, employed many of the terms of the traditional vocabulary, with

---

[48] Jane Lead, *The Messenger of Universal Peace* (1698), p. 69.
[49] *A Fountain of Gardens*, p. 5.
[50] Copy of William Law to Penny, 8 April 1747, Dr Williams's Library, Walton Papers, MS 1.1.43.
[51] Hirst, *Hidden Riches*, pp. 196–9.   [52] *Ibid.*, p. 253.

emanations and Elohim and the Everlasting Gospel and covering
cherubs and much else, and with much millenarial rhetoric from
Revelation. He is a figure who straddles (as Blake also does) the
scholarly tradition of Boehme, Law and Kabbalistic studies and
the radical language of popular Dissent. But, in making this strong
case, Hirst does not allow us to see quite how eccentric, and even
cranky, this unusual man was, with his obsessive and scholastic
concern with numbers, derivations and the abracadabra of millenarianism. Nor did Clarke share Blake's kind of radical stance. Antinomians he lampooned in conventional terms as sensualists.[53] In a
compassionate passage about the poor, written in 1772, he looked
forward to a millenarial day when 'a true community of the spirit
will open a community of temporal things'.[54] But after the French
Revolution, Clarke, by now in his seventies, signalled his sense of
alarm at the new ferment within humble London radical Dissent.
The American prophet of Universal Restoration, Elhanan Winchester, had been preaching in London:

Mr Winchester is very popular for the time; he has been here: in the
doctrine of the Millenium and Restoration we agree, but no further. I
expect no Jerusalem, no Temple, no city, no land, but that the Lord
creates, and not man; the new heavens and new earth, and the new city
of the living God, and his Lamb. He expects a third city of brick and
stone, the work of the hammer and axe; if it were even of pearls, it would
not answer; for all the stone must be *living*, have life in the *heavenly materiality* of the chrystalline sea, where all Babylon, the creation in Bondage,
must be dissolved, to pass into the liberty of the glory of the Sons of God,
the true Israel.[55]

The reply of Richard Watson, the Bishop of Llandaff, to Paine's
Age of Reason, which Blake annotated with such fury, Clarke com-
mended as a 'judicious book'.[56]

I am certainly willing to accept Clarke as a spiritual kinsman to
Blake, but his degree of relationship is not within the main line of
antinomian descent. As for one other contemporary of Blake's,
whose claims have been more strenuously pressed, Thomas Taylor
the Platonist, no case for kinship can be supported. Taylor, who

[53] *Ibid.*, p. 259.
[54] *Ibid.*, p. 253.
[55] Clarke to Brooke, May/June 1790, Dr Williams's Library, Walton Papers, MS 1.1.43.
Ferber, *The Social Vision of William Blake*, pp. 190–1, suggests the Universalists and Winchester as an influence on Blake, but see pp. 226–7 below.
[56] Richard Clarke, *Jesus the Nazarus, Addressed to the Jews, Deists, and Believers* (n.d.), p. xii.

courted the reputation in the 1790s of being 'the renowned Champion of Platonic Polytheism, the modern supporter of Greek science, and lawful heir of the Genius Learning & Truth of Aristotle & Plato',[57] stands at an opposite pole to Blake. In 1792, when we know Blake's political enthusiasms were at their warmest, Taylor published his sneering *A Vindication of the Rights of Brutes*. This mean-spirited jest, embellished with neo-Platonic learning, was a scholastic *reductio ad absurdam*: if women – *any* women – were to claim equality of rights, why not also dogs and birds? Regard, for example, the independent spirit now evinced by female servants–

Who so happily rival their mistresses in dress, that excepting a little awkwardness in their carriage, and roughness in their hands, occasioned by untwisting the wide-bespattering radii of the mop, and strenuously grasping the scrubbing-brush, there is no difference between my lady and her house-maid. We may therefore reasonably hope that this amazing rage for liberty will continually increase; that mankind will shortly abolish all government as an intolerable yoke; and that they will as universally join in *vindicating the rights of brutes* as in asserting the prerogatives of man.[58]

This was compounded, in the course of a leering discussion of masturbation, with a prurient sneer at Mary Wollstonecraft.[59] And if Taylor's commonplace sexual and class prejudice and anti-Radicalism will have placed him in an opposite corner to Blake in the 1790s, so his hostility to Christianity will have done so in later years. While G.M. Harper is entitled to argue that Blake's attitude to the classical inheritance was both changing and contradictory, his final resting-point was unambiguous: 'The Greek & Roman Classics is the Antichrist' (E656). No doubt Blake read some of Taylor's works. But the influence of these upon his prophetic writings has been greatly exaggerated, and in general turns upon allusions and symbolic machinery (much of which might equally well have been drawn from other sources). It could also be argued that some of the allusions and machinery are obscurantist and regrettable. In any case, Taylor touches at no point on Blake's central stance.

The argument of the last few pages has been highly compressed and necessarily assertive. I have argued that the polite literary

---

[57] Henry Crabb Robinson to William Pattison, 31 October 1798, Pattison MSS (in private hands).
[58] [Thomas Taylor], *A Vindication of the Rights of Brutes* (1792), pp. vi–vii.
[59] *Ibid.*, pp. 81–2.

tradition (Behmenists, Philadelphians, Neo-Platonists) appears to carry some of Blake's vocabulary (including symbolic vocabulary) but that it does not prepare us for his stance nor influence the structure of his thought and art. It is a characteristic of those critics who argue most strongly for the 'Great Tradition' that they avoid discussion of stance and structure and offer Blake's thought as fragments: there is discussion of discrete symbols and myths, particular literary allusions, all of which appear to refer to a body of thought *outside* Blake's writing. And when this thought is then reconstituted, with the help of Proclus, Boehme or Fludd, it turns out to be very distant from the meanings conveyed by Blake's own text.

Blake *plays*, in his prophetic writings, with some of these symbols and myths. I could myself wish that he played with them less. But he plays in distinctive ways. In his prose, even his visionary statements have a matter-of-fact quality, totally unlike theosophical visions. He has no time for speculations about the number of the Beast or for the scholasticism of the tradition. His New Jerusalem is neither situated in an 'angelickal world' between Mount Zion and the glassy sea,[60] nor is it about to descend in some millenarial consummation[61]: 'to Labour in Knowledge is to Build up Jerusalem, and to Despise Knowledge is to Despise Jerusalem & her Builders' (E230).

If Blake read any or all of these works, he read them in his own way. He employs an inherited vocabulary to make statements directly opposed to those authorised by the 'Tradition'. He appropriates old symbols and turns them to new purposes. This is true, most of all, in the prophetic writings, where the machinery of a traditional symbolism often arouses expectations in the learned reader which are directly at odds with Blake's meaning. As John Beer has noted:

Blake's imagination has usually been at work before his reminiscence reaches the printed page: this is no passive importation of a symbol from outside but an integration into a new pattern, carrying its own associations and functions.[62]

---

[60] A Gentleman Retired from Business [John Pordage], *A Compendious View of the Ground of the Teutonick Philosophy* (1770).

[61] For an example of this kind of claptrap, see Elhanan Winchester, *A Course of Lectures on the Prophesies that Remain to be Fulfilled* (1789), in four volumes.

[62] John Beer, *Blake's Humanism* (Manchester, 1968), p. 19.

To say this may be simply to insist upon Blake's genius and originality. But if we go behind the symbols and vocabulary to the stance and structure of his thought, we may still ask whether these were wholly original, or whether he owed some part of these to other traditions. And some answer may be found by considering the various traditions of Dissent.

CHAPTER 5

Radical dissent

Let us shift our attention from the literary tradition to the vocabulary and doctrine of little churches and sects.

With the defeat of Levellers, Diggers, Ranters, and with the subsequent Restoration, the rebellious tradition of antinomianism (as its historian has written) 'curved back from all its claims'.[1] The extreme sectaries were persecuted, and some took refuge in a deliberate esotericism – a tradition of secrecy germane to Blake in his later writings. The hopes which were dashed in this world were projected into an inner world of the spirit. Here the old rhetoric lived on, but the stance of the sect towards all temporal things might now be quietist.

It is difficult for a historian to trace the record of quietist faiths. Since they do not impinge upon social or political movements, their surviving evidences are sermons, tracts, hymns, occasional internal disputes. It is even more difficult when a group makes a mystique of secrecy, like the 'Secret Blessed Society' of the Philadelphians. At the end of the eighteenth century, Philadelphians may have still had some loosely organised existence, as lecturers or preachers who gave addresses to audiences of any denomination – a sort of tiny Fabian Society, attempting to permeate the churches from within.[2]

But, as J.F.C. Harrison suggests (*The Second Coming*), Behmenist, antinomian and millenarial beliefs may have been dispersed even more widely, in the discourse of a few professional men, tradesmen and farmers, and even 'the simple and illiterate sort'. Mystical experiences were claimed by men and women 'simple and low in the world', of several denominations; a letter of 1775 survives from Ralph Mather (subsequently to become a Swedenborgian

[1] G. Huehns, *Antinomianism in English History* (1951).
[2] W. Hurd, *New Universal History*, pp. 695–6.

missionary) in which he describes many such 'poor people' up and down the country who 'love J. Behme and Wm Law'.[3]

Most difficult to identify are those who continue to be described, from time to time, as 'Ranters'. Wesley continued to meet and to argue with such people.[4] But even in the 1650s Ranting scarcely had any central organisation. In the eighteenth century 'Ranting' was little more than a term of abuse – a description of wild enthusiasm – applied with little discrimination to petty sects, or to 'irregular' Methodists.

From time to time in London little churches may be glimpsed which might (in the eyes of opponents) fit this description, like a 'Church of Christ' in New Street in 1712,[5] or a group around a 'Millennium Press' in Spitalfields who were still predicting a 'Fifth Monarchy' in 1786.[6] In the earlier part of the century, disputes between humble sectaries could still draw audiences of hundreds, at such places as 'The Magpie' in the Borough, Southwark.[7] An important stimulus for the revival of mystic and millenarial thought came with the great Huguenot immigration to London in the years following upon the revocation of the Edict of Nantes (1685) – some of the skilled tradesmen in different crafts settling in the West End, the silk weavers more thickly in the East. The neighbourhood in which William Blake grew up (the parish of St James, Westminster) shows many foreign names, some, perhaps, of Huguenot descent. Fellow electors with his father in Broad Street in 1749 include James Serzes, the minister of a 'French or Dutch Church by St James'; Philip Tuesay, a coal-merchant, born in Normandy; Dr Fevat or Fivatt, a physician; Dr Guordiant, a surgeon; and Benjamin Cusheir, an undertaker.[8]

The strong network of French Protestant churches was not, of

---

[3] J.F.C. Harrison, *The Second Coming*, pp. 21–2.
[4] See, e.g., John Wesley's encounter with antinomians in Birmingham, *Journal*, 23 April 1746.
[5] R.D., *A Description of a Gospel Church* (1712), p. 85.
[6] *Reasons from Prophecy why the Second Coming of Christ and the Commencement of the Millennium is immediately to be expected* (Millennium Press, no. 40, the corner of Dorset St, Spitalfields, 1786).
[7] Joseph Smith, *A Descriptive Bibliography of Friends' Books* (1867), Vol. I, p. 933: William Henderson, 'Truth and Reason defended against *Error* and *Burning Envy*, in a PUBLIC DISPUTE, held at the *Magpie* . . . on the 16th and 18th days of *Dec.* 1728 between John Rawlinson, a *Muggletonian*, and William Henderson, a *Quaker*, in the presence of some Hundreds of People. . .' (copy in Friends' Library); *A Conference betwixt a Muggletonian and a Baptist* (London, 1739).
[8] Pollbook of 1749 election, Westminster Reference Library.

course, antinomian or millenarian in doctrine. But around these, especially in East London, there appear to have been tremors and breakaways. A more remarkable impulse came from the Camisards or 'French prophets', who in dramatic and sometimes hysterical scenes of revivalism, *circa* 1707–10, reinvigorated the rhetoric of New Jerusalem and made many English converts, some of whom continued the tradition of prophecy and trance for several more decades.[9] There was both argument and confluence between French prophets and Philadelphians: the Camisard faith was millenarial – man should regain the perfection of Adam in communion with God, and henceforth the Law would be 'writ in every Man's Heart, so that he should have no more need to enquire of his Neighbours, but that every Man should be Priest unto himself'.[10] As the old Huguenot churches in London declined, and as the second and third generation of immigrants merged into the discourse of their fellow Londoners, it is possible (the evidence is unclear) that the more heretical among them gave adhesion to existing English sects. The most intellectual leader of the Muggletonians in the 1730s was Arden Bonel – perhaps of Huguenot extraction.[11] When William Cudworth (above, p. 17) split off from the Methodists in the 1740s his new congregations ('The Hearers and Followers of the Apostles') took over the former French church in Black and Grey Eagle Street, Spitalfields, the former French chapel in New Hermitage Street, Wapping, and the former French chapel in Castle Street, Leicester Fields.[12] Maybe these places had simply fallen vacant, or maybe – as sometimes happened when meeting-houses passed from one sect or preacher to another – some of the congregation stayed on. The 'Church of Christ' in Spitalfields certainly has a millenarial feel about it. They believed in one God, who was Christ: 'the living and true God is known no where but in Jesus Christ . . . he is God manifest in the flesh'. Their doctrine fully endorsed an antinomian notation of Free Grace and

---

9 See Hillel Schwartz, *The French Prophets*.

10 Theophilus Evans, *The History of Modern Enthusiasm* (1757, 2nd edn), pp. 100–1. Cf. Blake '. . .henceforth every man may converse with God & be a King & Priest in his own house' (E605).

11 In Dr Williams's Library, Caleb Fleming's copy of 'A.B.', *Observations on Some Articles of the Muggletonian Creed* (1735) is annotated: 'N.B. Mr Bonell was at ye head of these fanatics.' In Certificates of Denizatia (*Pubs. of the Huguenot Society*, Vol. XVIII, 1911, ed. W.A. Shaw), there are: 2 March 1681, Peter Bonnel and family; 19 August 1688, Abraham Bounel or Bonnel and family.

12 J.C. Whitebrooke, *William Cudworth and his Connexion* (1918).

the imputation of righteousness: 'God has made a deed of free gift and grant . . . which whosoever believeth, or receiveth by faith, the obedience and sufferings of Christ is imputed to them as verily as though they personally had accomplished the whole.'[13]

And what other sects lived on? It is difficult to know. A journalist in 1706 composed a kind of directory: Quakers, Muggletonians (a religion 'more talk'd of than known'), Millenaries, Sabbatarians or Seventh-Day Men, Thraskites, Adamists (whose meeting-place was 'Paradise' and whose devotions were made in nakedness), Seekers, Ranters (who condemned the Bible and called it ironically 'The Divine Legacy'), Brownists, Tryonists (vegetarians), the 'Church of the First-Born' (Behmenists), Salmonists, 'Heavenly-Father-Men' (whose whole emphasis was on Mercy) and 'Children of the New-Birth', much given to meditation and to 'Visions of Angels and Representations'. And others. The 'Sweet Singers of Israel' were 'very poetically given, turning all into Rhime, and singing all their Worship. They meet in an Ale-house and eat, drink and smoak . . . They hold that there is no Sin in them: that Eating and Drinking and Society is bles'd: That Death and Hell are a Terror only to those that fear it.' All sin is forgiven to believers, for Christ would save all by his Blood: 'the Employment of the Bles'd will be Singing of Praises to their Maker in the New Jerusalem'. There was also a 'Family of Love', described in conventionally sensational terms as holding 'a Community of Women' with sexual orgies in place of services, but who also (more soberly) maintained a stock for the poor, and believed that the soul was 'an Emanation of the Deity' which (at death) is lost 'in the Eternal Ocean of Beings': 'the greatest Sin is Doubting, or Want of Faith'.[14]

Is this just hearsay, with the seventeenth-century directories of heresy (Thomas Edwards's *Gangraena*, Alexander Ross's *Pansebia*) warmed up? It seems not: now heresies are identified, and new sects formed around old beliefs. Did all, or nearly all, of these sects die out soon after 1706? We do not know: some were probably transformed, by way of Camisards or irregular Methodists, into new sects, but others certainly lived on. Thus our author mentions the 'Copinists', who followed the associate of Ranters, Richard

---

[13] 'Declaration of the Faith, and Practice of a Church of Christ' (n.d.). See above, p. 18, and note 17.
[14] G.C. [Galton], *The Post-Boy Robb'd of his Mail* (1706), pp. 423–31.

Coppin.[15] These disbelieved in the Devil or in eternal Hell, and espoused the doctrine of Universal Restoration (a doctrine also held by Richard Clarke and Elhanan Winchester in the 1790s). Coppin had been close to some of the tenets of Thomas Tany (or Theauraujohn). Emphatically antinomian, he affirmed that the ministers of orthodox churches were 'evil angels, reserved under chains of darkness', and he distinguished between two opposed ministrations or 'contrarieties': that of the Law ('a ministration of wrath, death, the curse, hell, and condemnation') and that of the Gospel ('a ministration of love, joy, peace, life, light, heaven and salvation'). He was a firm advocate of the right of women to preach. His Universal Restoration would take in 'Heathens, Pagans, Turks, Jews, Infidels'. The true believer must pass successively through three 'states': a state of 'Nature', a state of the Kingdom of Jesus Christ in the flesh ('here man sees not God clearly but through a vail, and this vail is the flesh of Christ, which a Christian is not to stay in, but to pass through...'), and a state of the Kingdom of Jesus Christ in the spirit: 'Then will the creature, the Image of God, be reduced again into its original and divine Image.'[16] Firm evidence as to the continuity of a Coppinist sect (or group of believers) is provided by the republication of his works in the 1760s – James Relly, an 'irregular' Methodist (himself accused of antinomian heresy) complained that these publications were sold 'under my nose', and that members of his own congregation subscribed for the re-printing.[17] Philip de Loutherbourg had a copy of Coppin's *A Blow at the Serpent* (reprinted 1796) in his private library (along with the works of Jane Lead) in the 1790s.[18]

Another interesting directory of heresy was published by William Hurd at the end of the century. Once again, a good deal is hearsay, although Hurd did make some enquiries. His account suggests that the number of miniscule sects had by now diminished (but he probably did not enquire far into the East End, nor did he take notice of individual heretical preachers like William Huntington or Elhanan Winchester). There are important new arrivals in the eighteenth century: the Moravians, the Sandemanians, the

[15] For Coppin, see above, p. 42, note 30; A. Ross, *A View of all Religions*, p. 379; Richard Coppin, *Truth's Testimony* (1655; reprinted 1768), esp. pp. 58–65; *A Blow at the Serpent* (1796), *passim*; *The Advancement of All Things in Christ* (1763), p. 28.
[16] *Ibid.*, p. 58.
[17] See James Relly, *The Sadducees Detected and Refuted* (1764).
[18] Now in the British Library.

Hutchinsonians and Methodist breakaways. In each case one seems to glimpse some belief or practice which prompts a reminiscence of Blake. The Moravians were well established in London, at Nevile's Court, Fetter-lane and Chelsea; the suggestion has been made that they influenced Blake, through their antinomian emphasis upon regeneration by faith, and through the frankness of their sexual symbolism, which extended to a veneration of the genitals.[19] I do not find the suggestion convincing: regeneration by faith was common to all forms of revivalist enthusiasm (notably Methodism), Blake's employment of phallic symbolism might well have been influenced by other sources[20] or none, and there are other notable elements in Moravian symbolism (such as the obsession with the wounds of Christ) which are never to be found in Blake. The Moravian tradition seems to dilute the antinomian vocabulary; it lacks an 'intellectual' or doctrinal anti-intellectualism found in obscurer sects.

Such intellectual pretension was certainly not lacking among the Hutchinsonians. Their founder, John Hutchinson (1674–1737), offered an alternative, symbolic reading of the Scriptures, based upon an eccentric reading of Hebrew, and was a fierce opponent of Newtonianism and an even fiercer opponent of 'Natural Religion' ('The Religion of Satan'). His anti-Newtonian 'Mosaic' principles found some support in the universities, and has recently won sympathetic attention from historians of science. But Hutchinson himself would probably have been amazed to learn that he would have humble 'Hutchinsonian' followers meeting in London alehouses at the end of the century, traducing the words 'morality' and 'good works', and denouncing 'natural religion' in the name of grace.[21] Possibly Hutchinsonian arguments could have confirmed Blake in his hostility to Newton and mechanical materialism. Both this and the Moravian influence may merit further exploration.

More interesting may be Hurd's suggestion that antinomianism, in particular sectarian forms, had been pushed into oblivion by the rise of Methodism, but that it had subsequently regenerated itself from among 'irregular Methodists' and from the lapsed of other denominations. His account is worth quoting at length, since it

[19] See Jack Lindsay, *William Blake* (1978), pp. 275–6. See the sympathetic account of the Moravians in Hurd, *New Universal History*, pp. 643–68.
[20] Notably R.P. Knight, *An Account of the Remains of the Worship of Priapus* (1786).
[21] Hurd, p. 676.

carries the full comminatory tone of the times. Only two or three
meetings were now (1788?) to be found in England. Antinomians
professed a religion 'which does not inculcate morality'. They teach
that 'men may sin as much as they please; because however God
may hate sin, yet he takes pleasure in forgiving it.' They–

Discuss their religion in public houses. As morality is an unnecessary
thing, and as holiness, say they, can be no evidence of faith, so some of
them meet in a room in a public house every Sunday evening, having
before them that much despised book the Bible. Each member pays for
a pot of beer, which is drunk by the company in a social manner. Then
a text of sacred scriptures is read, and every one in his turn is called to
deliver his opinion concerning it. A great deal of jargon with no meaning
ensues, and every thing is said that can possibly be thought of against
holiness or good works. The sacred scriptures are debased to the worst
purposes, namely, to set open the flood-gates of profaneness; and youth
are corrupted under the prostituted name of religion. A few foolish, weak
and insignificant persons attend these meetings . . . They do all they
can to pervert the Scriptures, and to trample under foot every Divine
institution.[22]

The relaxed, democratic structure of the meetings is of interest,
with everyone in turn called on to speak – forerunner of a London
Corresponding Society or adult education branch. But William
Hurd was probably drawing only upon gossip. He had more
patience in expounding the doctrines of Turks, Jews, Catholics,
Moravians, Deists and the devotees of 'Numbo-Jumbo' than he
showed with these antinomians.

So – all this (and much more that is lost) was around in William
Blake's London. There had probably been, over the century, a
geographical shift in the location of sectarian Dissent, from West
to East and South London. Still, in the first half of the century,
one finds support for the old sects among professional families and
prosperous tradesmen in Westminster; at the end of the century,
the sects survive in Spitalfields (with its strong Huguenot
inheritance), Southwark or Islington, drawing support among
weavers, artisans, and petty tradesmen. Westminster and Holborn
are now the gathering-grounds for congregations which follow
more fashionable and charismatic heretical preachers, or for brand-
new sophisticated faiths like the Swedenborgian New Jerusalem
Church.

[22] *Ibid.*, p. 641.

All share some part of a vocabulary (mystic, millenarian, antinomian) which prepares us for Blake. But all lack that 'firm outline' which Blake demanded – the colours run into each other. And we should add that a major carrier of this vocabulary was simply the central tradition of radical Dissent. Milton had brushed his shoulders against antinomian doctrines, and wherever he was honoured (as Blake honoured him) some part of this inheritance might be conveyed. And if we move from doctrine to rhetoric and stance, we find the radical anti-statist tradition very much alive, and vigorously assertive in the 1790s.

We sometimes forget the total intransigence with which the eighteenth-century Dissenter (Baptist or Sandemanian or even Unitarian) could repudiate all intercourse with the Stations and Powers of this world. All saw in the Whore of Babylon not only the Roman Church but also all Erastianism: the Anglican Church *a fortiori*, and from thence all compromise between the spiritual and temporal power.

We could pick up this tradition where we will, among dissenting congregations in London and the great towns. It erupted, here and there, in fervent Old Testament rhetoric during the French Wars. And in the 1790s it also had notable intellectual representatives: for example, it is strongly marked in that group of radical Unitarians and others – William Frend, Benjamin Flower, George Dyer, Estlin, Gilbert Wakefield – with whom young Coleridge was associated.

A characteristic device of such men is to be found in an inversion, sometimes brought to the edge of blasphemy, of orthodox doctrine. Thus Estlin, in a sermon of 1795, contrasted the true gospel of Jesus 'whose first, last lesson to the world was LOVE' with orthodox religion, 'an unwieldy, cumbrous dress which has been put on the fairest form that ever was exhibited in the world'. The prophecies in *Revelation* as to the rule of Anti-Christ were now fulfilled within contemporary religious orthodoxy: they refer 'to every assumed power of decreeing rites and ceremonies and authoritatively interfering in matters of faith', as well as to 'that general corruption of morals' which prevailed among the 'professors of christianity'. All this is 'anti-christian'.[23] So it was also to George Dyer, who offered, in a pamphlet of 1799, Christ the Jacobin opposed to the Caiaphas

---

[23] John Prior Estlin, *Evidences of Revealed Religion* (Bristol, 1796), pp. 13, 41, 57.

and Pilate of Church and State: 'Christ asserted at Jerusalem liberty of thought and liberty of speech', he was 'adjudged to death
by the verdict of his own countrymen, as a seditious person, as a
libeller against church and state'.[24] Gilbert Wakefield, attacking
the apostate Bishop of Llandaff, had pointed the contrast more
savagely. The established Church he described as–

> An impious prostitution of the simplicity and sincerity of the Gospel . . .
> I regard your Archbishops, Bishops, Deans, Canons, Prebendaries, and
> all the muster-roll of ecclesiastical aristocracy as the despicable trumpery
> of priestcraft and superstition.

(One should note that the radical Dissenter could denounce
'priestcraft and kingcraft' in much the same terms as the Deist.)
'I see Religion employed as a State engine of despotism and murder
by a set of men, who are worse than heathens and infidels in their
lives.' Let *them*, he said (referring to the French War), 'fight the
battles of their Baal and their Mammon'[25]:

> I should entertain far better hopes of leading a French infidel to accept the
> pure religion of the scriptures, than a bigotted superstitious Churchman.[26]

We don't have to construe Blake into this context: he has placed
himself within it. It was in the same year – and perhaps with an
eye on the Wakefield trial – that he annotated the Bishop of Llandaff's *Apology for the Bible*: 'To defend the Bible in this year 1798
would cost a man his life. The Beast and the Whore rule without
control.' But the Bible which Blake would defend is not, of course,
that of Bishop Watson: 'Paine has not attacked Christianity.
Watson has defended Antichrist.' *Both* Paine and the Bishops were
wrong – 'The Bishops never saw the Everlasting Gospel any more
than Tom Paine.' But Paine (in Blake's view) has much the best
of the argument, since his polemics are directed, not at the Everlasting Gospel (which he does not understand) but at the Moral
Law of Antichrist:

[24] G. Dyer, *Address on the Doctrine of Libels and the Office of Jurors* (1799), pp. 109–12. The
occasion for this pamphlet was the defence of Gilbert Wakefield, himself imprisoned for
seditious libel.
[25] Cf. G. Wakefield, *The Spirit of Christianity Compared with the Spirit of the Times in Great Britain*
(1794), p. 24: 'The Worshippers of *Baal* have been always numerous, the servants of
Jehovah and his *Christ* comparatively few.'
[26] G. Wakefield, *Reply to some parts of the Bishop of Llandaff's Address to the People of Great Britain*
(2nd edn, 1798), esp. pp. 39–44. See also my 'Disenchantment or Default' in (eds. C.C.
O'Brien and W.D. Vanech) (New York, 1969), pp. 164–7.

All Penal Laws court Transgression & therefore are cruelty & Murder.
The laws of the Jews were (both ceremonial & real) the basest & most
oppressive of human codes, & being like all other codes given under
pretence of divine command were what Christ pronounced them The
Abomination that maketh desolate, i.e. State Religion, which is the source
of all Cruelty. (E607)

(In his Preface 'To the Deists' in *Jerusalem* Blake made the same
charge: 'Every Religion that Preaches Vengeance for Sin is the
Religion of the Enemy & Avenger and not of the Forgiver of Sin,
and their God is Satan, Named by the Divine Name' (E199).)
Throughout these annotations – marginal notes written under the
stress of direct responses and without thought of any audience –
Blake oscillates between two uses of 'the Bible' which are directly
opposed. He writes as one 'who loves the Bible': 'The Perversions
of Christ's words & acts are attack'd by Paine & also the perversions of the Bible; Who dare defend either the Acts of Christ or
the Bible Unperverted?' At one point he cites the authority of 'the
Bible' against Bishop Watson's apologetics; on the next page he is
stung to fury by the Bishop's complacent endorsement of the
Bible's authority for the divine justice of massacring the
Canaanites:

To me, who believe the Bible & profess myself a Christian, a defence of
the Wickedness of the Israelites in murdering so many thousands under
pretence of a command from God is altogether Abominable & Blasphemous. (E603–4)

The 'Bible' is then divided between the Gospel and the 'Jewish
Imposture . . . the Jewish Scriptures, which are only an Example
of the wickedness & deceit of the Jews & were written as an
Example of the possibility of Human Beastliness in all its
branches'. The opposition between these two is pressed to its furthest possible extent: 'Christ died as an Unbeliever & if the Bishops
had their will so would Paine.' But this is not only a simple *inversion*
of 'the Bible'–

> The Vision of Christ that thou dost see
> Is my Vision's Greatest Enemy. . .
>
> Both read the Bible day & night,
> But thou read'st black where I read white. (E516)

Nor is it a simple opposition between the Old Testament and the
New. For Blake accepts at will, not as literal truth but as a 'Poem
of probable impossibilities' whatever parts of the Bible endorse his
faith. Both Testaments provide 'Sentiments & Examples' and 'this
sense of the Bible is equally true to all & equally plain to all'. The
Bible becomes the book of Antichrist ('a State Trick') only at that
point where the Mosaic Law is 'rent' from the Gospel, and this
gospel is eternal because it exists within man's faith every day:

The Bible or Peculiar Word of God, Exclusive of Conscience or the Word
of God Universal, is that Abomination, which, like the Jewish ceremonies,
is for ever removed [i.e. by Christ's sacrifice] & henceforth every man
may converse with God & be a King & Priest in his own house.

And Blake reached, in these annotations, exactly the same conclusion as did Gilbert Wakefield in the same year: 'It appears to me
Now that Tom Paine is a better Christian than the Bishop' (E605,
609).
    This is writing which comes out of a tradition. It has a confid-
ence, an assured reference, very different from the speculations of
an eccentric or a solitary. It also assumes something like a radical
constituency, an 'us' of 'the People' or of 'every man' as against
the 'them' of the State, or of Bishops or of the servitors of 'the
Beast and the Whore'. The antinomian argument does not drift off
into transcendental essays on 'faith' versus 'works' but is pressed,
always, to a political conclusion: 'Penal Laws', 'State Religion', 'a
State Trick'. It is, as always, combative, even though at the last
moment Blake shrinks from the combat: 'I have been commanded
from Hell not to print this, as it is what our Enemies wish' (E601).
But notice '*our* Enemies': this man does not feel himself to be alone.
('Let every Christian, as much as in him lies, engage himself
openly & publicly before all the World in some Mental pursuit for
the Building up of Jerusalem' (E230).) And, as always, the language is blunt, matter-of-fact, concrete: the wicked and the faithful,
the Satanic Law and the Everlasting Gospel, are evoked as being
locked in combat in the immediate arena, in the streets, churches
and palaces of London, in a spiritual conflict which wears temporal
disguises, but which is the more real for being spiritual.
    The tradition behind Blake had become obscure by the 1790s.
Most educated men and women had long been engaged in rational
theological exegetics, in linguistic or historical criticism of the

Scriptures, in debate on the great question as to the Trinity and Christ's divinity, in arguments about miracles or about ceremonial forms, or in bolder ventures into Deism or atheism. By 1810 Blake's views had become so strange in the polite culture that Henry Crabb Robinson could comment that 'his religious convictions had brought on him the credit of being an absolute lunatic'.[27] Many years later Blake's friend, the painter John Linnell wrote, perceptively, that Blake was 'a saint amongst the infidels & a heretic with the orthodox', and, less perceptively, that 'he said many things tending to the corruption of Xtian morals' and 'outraged all common sense & rationality'.[28] But at any point between the 1640s and the 1790s there were men and women in London who would instantly have understood (and shared) Blake's reference and stance. The French prophets (and many others) had held that 'every Man should be Priest unto himself' (above, p. 54). The Coppinists (and many others) had preached the radically opposed ministrations of the Gospel and the Law (above, p. 56). A multitude of radical Dissenters saw in Church and State the Whore and Beast. I need not go on. Blake still inhabits that tradition, giving to it an unusual intransigence and purity of expression, sometimes as affirmation ('The Kingdom of Heaven is the direct Negation of Earthly domination' (E619)), sometimes as Jacobinical imprecation ('The Prince of darkness is a Gentleman & not a Man he is a Lord Chancellor' (E612)), sometimes as blasphemy, irony or jest.

And yet . . . and yet . . . How far, in the end, does this take us? It tells us what Blake was *against*, something of his stance, something of the quality of his feeling. But does it disclose certain affirmatives, certain essential and uniting ideas, recurrent images which belong to the structure rather than the ambience of this thought? Perhaps it does. Yet I remain unsatisfied. We still have not found out by what route or routes this tradition came through to Blake.

There is throughout Blake's writings an intellectual confidence and assertiveness – as of, not sentiments but *doctrines*, long-pondered and then arduously restructured and made his own, which are not 'given' in any of these sources. Of course, Blake may, through reading, conversation, the sampling of different sectarian doctrines, have made his own unique construction. Undoubtedly

---

[27] Bentley, *Blake Records*, p. 448.   [28] *Ibid.*, p. 318.

this is a major part of the answer. But I will take my sense of dissatisfaction as a licence to probe once more, and for a last time, even more deeply into one particular and obscure circle in sectarian London. It may – I have lived with this thought for many years – be a false track altogether. But it will at least bring us into very much closer proximity with the minds and voices of one group of sectaries. And if it is then considered that I have suggested the wrong group, at least we will understand more about how such groups argued, thought and passed on their faith.

CHAPTER 6

A peculiar people

There is one direct line of continuity between the antinomianism of the Civil War sects and the London of the 1790s that can be firmly established. On 3 February 1652, after the defeat of Levellers and Diggers, God spoke to John Reeve and told him: 'I have chosen thee my last Messenger for a great Work unto this bloody unbelieving World.' Joining forces with his cousin, Ludowick Muggleton (Reeve was the Messenger and Muggleton was his 'mouth'), Reeve sought to rally a following among the remnants of the Ranters. The two prophets commenced their mission by quarrelling violently with Thomas Tany; they also visited John Robins, the self-proclaimed Son of God, then in prison under sentence of death, and discovered that he was in fact the Anti-Christ. They quarrelled also with the emergent Quakers, who were competing for support in very much the same post-Ranter circles: this quarrel Muggleton kept warm long after Reeve's early death (1658) and it was repaid with equal warmth from the Quaker side. In these controversies Reeve and Muggleton discovered that they had been endowed by God with a power of the tongue, not only to bestow on their followers eternal blessing and confirmation that they were indeed of the elect, but also to curse anyone who contradicted their doctrines and sentence them to eternal damnation. These powers were used to good effect on Robins and to less effect on the Quakers.[1]

Thus the Muggletonians arose within the whitest heats of the vortex around which Ranting, Quakerism, egalitarian, Behmenist and sexual liberationist notions turned. While they quarrelled most fiercely with their most proximate neighbours, as is the way of sects, a great deal of the imagery which turned in that vortex was gathered into their doctrine. Certainly they denounced Thomas

[1] See Christopher Hill, Barry Reay and William Lamont, *The World of the Muggletonians* (1983), esp. pp. 67–9.

65

Tany and repudiated Boehme: but an intense sectarian dispute is often the signal of an *affinity*, and while Muggletonian doctrine repudiated the dispersed pantheism of the Behmenist tradition, of the Ranters ('my one flesh'), and of Tany and the Quakers,[2] and replaced it by a literal belief in a singular God/Christ in the image of man, yet in other parts of the doctrine (the nature of Creation, the origin of evil, the notion of contrarieties) Muggletonianism was grafted upon Behmenist or Ranting stock.[3] And, as if to signal this, there was gathered into the Muggletonian church Laurence Claxton, or Clarkson, who had once been known as 'the Captain of the Rant'.

We might suppose, in Muggletonianism, our missing vector. For the sect did establish itself, and it survived for over three hundred years.[4] Muggleton outlived John Reeve by forty years, enlisting 'believers in the third commission', occasionally visiting the faithful (in Cambridgeshire, Staffordshire and Derbyshire, Essex, Kent), and conducting a copious correspondence. He did not seek out followers: the faith was to be diffused by the publication of the tracts of the two prophets and a few followers (Clarkson, Sadding-ton, Tomkinson). Muggleton's funeral in 1698 was attended by 248 believers. It is probable that the church fluctuated around, or a little beneath, these numbers for the next hundred years. A count of male believers only, in 1803, showed one hundred in all England: thirty-five in London, twenty in Kent, twenty-one in Derbyshire, eleven in Norwich and the remainder diverse.[5] But the London church had recently suffered from splits and secessions, and the number of male Muggletonian believers, if heretics are taken into account, will certainly have been greater. Since women played a prominent part in the church, and since strong familial continuities can be observed, as children were inducted into the faith, we may safely double these figures.

Although its most prominent member at the commencement of the eighteenth century was a Staffordshire farmer and factor,

---

[2] *Ibid.*, pp. 47–8, 88.

[3] Muggleton argues with a correspondent influenced by Boehme in Reeve and Muggleton, *A Stream from the Tree of Life* (1758 edn), p. 33; he told another correspondent in 1661 that Boehme's 'philosophical light was above all men that does profess religion, until this commission of the Spirit came forth, which hath brought Jacob Behmen's light . . . down very low': *A Volume of Spiritual Epistles* (1820 edn), pp. 45–6; Alexander Gordon, *The Origins of the Muggletonians* (Liverpool, 1869), pp. 9–11, 19–20.

[4] See Appendix 1.

[5] Muggletonian archive.

Thomas Tomkinson, the Muggletonian church was really a London church. But for its first two hundred years it was a church without any chapel, conventicle, meeting-house or permanent home. Fiercely anti-clerical, the Muggletonians had no preachers or officers: an early attempt by Clarkson to establish himself as such ('Claxton, the onely Bishop, and true Messenger of our last Commission') was roughly brought to an end by Muggleton.[6] They met for discourse, readings and songs in each others' homes: and, ducking under the Conventicle Act, they took to meeting in public houses. Here they would hire a room for their meetings, drawing up an agreement with the publican to install a locked closet holding their books and records. To all intents and purposes they appeared as a private friendly or glee club; they sent out to the landlord for pots of beer, or for punch on their two annual ceremonial 'holidays';[7] the 'divine songs' which the members wrote were set to the popular tunes of the day ('Fanny blooming fair', 'Scots wha hae', 'Young Nancy one morn', 'The Bishop of Hereford and Robin Hood'), which no doubt disarmed the suspicions of the curious. (During the French Wars, when anti-Jacobin narks were on the look-out for seditious glee clubs, new divine songs were written to the airs of 'God save the King', 'Heart of Oak' and 'Rule, Britannia'). In 1692 we find a meeting at 'The Green Man', Holloway; in the mid-eighteenth century a 'Church of Christ' at 'The Blue Boar', Aldersgate Street; another in Barnaby Street, Southwark; then at 'The Gun', Islington, 'The Hampshire Hog' off Goswell Street, and moving from 'The Blue Boar' to 'The Nag's Head' in Aldersgate Street. This church was, like the other meeting of 'Antinomians' we have met with before (above, p. 58), 'The Little Vagabond' among the churches:

> Dear Mother Dear Mother the church is cold
> But the alehouse is healthy & pleasant & warm
> Besides I can tell where I am usd well
> Such usage in heaven makes all go to hell.[8]

---

[6] L. Claxton, *A Paradisical Dialogue betwixt Faith and Reason* (1660), p. 117. See also Reay on Clarkson in Hill, Reay and Lamont, *The World of the Muggletonians*. Also DNB (entry by Alexander Gordon) and A.L. Morton, *The World of the Ranters*, chapter 5.

[7] The holidays celebrated were 14, 15 and 16 February (to commemorate Reeve's receiving the commission from God), and 30 July (to commemorate Muggleton's release from gaol in 1677): G.C. Williamson, *Ludowick Muggleton* (1919), p. 38.

[8] This is the first version in Blake's notebook (N105). In the revised version as published in the *Songs* the last line became: 'The poor parsons with wind like a blown bladder swell.' As David Erdman notes (p. 274, note 13), this is a rare case of Blake bowdlerising one of his own poems.

There grew up early among Muggletonian believers a habit of secrecy. In the last decades of the seventeenth century they had their share of sufferings: the imprisonment and pillorying of Muggleton, fines and the seizure of goods for non-attendance at church, for refusal of parish office or of oaths of allegiance, or for blasphemy. But Muggleton advised the faithful to avoid confrontations, while Clarkson chided the Quakers for 'disturbing the peace': 'in things concerning this Government, give the Magistrates due honour. . .'[9] More painful than fines may have been ostracism and ridicule, and the accusations of obscenity and blasphemy which attached to the name. On occasion the ostracism or excommunication of the believer could take the most bitter forms: Mary Cundy, a widow in Orwell, Cambridgeshire, who died as an excommunicant, was buried in 1686 in a close next to the churchyard 'with the burial of an asse'.[10]

In self-defence, Muggletonians in the eighteenth century normally did not avow their faith publicly, unless they were directly asked. A believer wrote in 1786:

As we have no Outward Ordinances of Worship, nor bound to Meetings it is not in the power of all the Devils who govern the World to hinder our Meetings, which are, when we meet in the Streets, or in the Fields, or Change, in a House Public, or Private, or in a Vessel by Water, or on the Land, we can Mutually Edify one another.[11]

A journeyman shoemaker, migrating from London to Coventry in 1770 to find work, found himself surrounded by the suspicions of his fellow journeymen when he named his son 'Ludowick': 'Some people makes it a matter of wonder at my calling my boy after so odd a name as they stile it, and as they most of them are presbytarians, they whisper about concerning of what religion I am but canot find it out.' After some more brushes with his neighbours, 'I am Inform'd they have given me a new name, viz. Mr Odd Principle.'[12] Even some of the Muggletonian printing operations were conducted with great privacy: a master printer of the faith in Bristol wrote to the London church in 1786 offering to undertake work,

[9] L. Claxton, *The Quakers Downfall* (1659), p. 35.
[10] M. Spufford, *Contrasting Communities* (Cambridge, 1971), p. 27.
[11] Roger Gibson of New London (Connecticut) writing to the London Church: Muggletonian archive.
[12] Incomplete letter, no signature, from Coventry, 25 February 1770, to 'Loving Friend and Brother', in *ibid*.

which he promised that he could do in complete secrecy since he employed no journeymen.[13] If it was difficult to identify a Muggletonian two hundred years ago, we will find it more difficult to identify him today.

We can, however, identify some of the beliefs and practices of the church. One thing the London believers attended to with zeal and address: they succeeded in keeping in print the works of the prophets, and they even added a few new works to that number. Printing of the works of Reeve and Muggleton was going on in the 1680s and 1690s; in 1719; in the 1730s; and then, very vigorously, from 1751 to 1764, encompassing *all* the works of the prophets as well as some newly published letters – a remarkable achievement 'considering what a Handful we are, and how few of that Handful have Substance sufficient to support so great an Undertaking'.[14] The achievement did not go uncontested; Boyer Glover (the leading songwriter at that time)–

Objected against the presant subscription for printing, saying we had done sufficient already; and advised to let alone the Other for another genration, little showing his love to God or his Seed; nor Considering that Eternity is at the door, and men must be Instrements in the hand of God to fullfill his Will in divers Respects before all is finished, pertiqularly in publishing His Third Record, thereby sealing men up for that glorious yet dreadfull day.[15]

More reprinting was going on in the 1790s, and then a comprehensive programme of publication was undertaken by James and Isaac Frost (brass founders in Clerkenwell) in the 1820s. Of other publications, the most important were those of Thomas Tomkinson, published in 1695, and, posthumously, in 1721–4, 1729, 1757 and 1823.[16] The dates indicate the consistency and longevity of the enterprise, and they also are indicative of a loyal, if small, audience.

I do not intend here to recapitulate the writings of the founding prophets but rather to direct attention to some parts of the doctrine which can most clearly be seen to be alive in the eighteenth century.[17] In doing so I will attend to certain parts which suggest a possible 'fit' with William Blake. Reeve and Muggleton were seen

[13] W. Mathews, Bristol, 17 December 1786 to D. Shield: in *ibid.*

[14] Foreword by John Peat to *A Stream from the Tree of Life* (1758 edn).

[15] Unsigned and undated (but 1760s) to 'dear Friend' in Muggletonian archive.

[16] See DNB (by Alexander Gordon) for publications.

[17] An excellent summary of Reeve's doctrines is in Hill, Reay and Lamont, *The World of the Muggletonians*, pp. 74–91.

as Messengers of a Third Commission, prophets of a 'New Age'. The first age (the age of the Law and of the Old Testament) was signified by *water* (Urizen was 'prison'd on wat'ry shore'); the second age (the age of the Gospel of Jesus and of the New Testament) was signified by *blood* (one recalls the repeated motif of *Vala* in which Luvah descends in blood); the third age (the age of the Commission and of the prophetic writings of Reeve and Muggleton) was the age of *spirit*. (This possibly Joachimite notion of the 'commission' was certainly known to Blake, who told Crabb Robinson, in connection with Irving, that 'they who are sent sometimes exceed their commission'.[18]) With the Third Commission, the New Age has already commenced among the believers, with all the attendant imagery of the coming of New Jerusalem. The faithful sometimes thought of themselves as 'saints'[19] or as 'sealed' with the conviction of their redemption: 'The regenerated Children of Adam are the Church, & every believer's body is a Temple for the living God.'[20]

Muggletonian doctrine concentrated upon three areas – the problem of the first creation of matter and of the origin of evil; *Genesis* and the Fall; and *Revelation*. Both God and Matter had existed from eternity, as in Gnostic doctrine, God as an 'active omnipotent Being', matter as an 'unactive Principle' – 'inert and merely passive'. Matter was a necessary object for God to work upon, for if there had been nothing but God's own essence from eternity, 'then there was nothing for him to have Power over, or to act upon, and then he must have continued alone to all Eternity'. But while matter was 'in a Condition to be wrought upon as Clay in the Hands of the Potter', nevertheless it possessed properties different from those of God. Matter–

Was an unactive Principle from Eternity; and as it was not possible to be hid from the active omnipotent Being, he by making it active rendered it capable of producing Evil.[21]

---

[18] Bentley, *Blake Records*, p. 313.

[19] Thus Thomas Tomkinson, writing to a Friend in Ireland (1674), declares the 'effectual faith is seen in His Saints by the cheerfulness of their countenances': Letters copied by Frederick E. Noakes in Muggletonian archive.

[20] 'The Faith and Practice of the Muggletonians', 1 January 1870, in *ibid*.

[21] 'A.B.' (Arden Bonnell?), *The Principles of the Muggletonians Asserted* (1735), pp. 10–11. This was a reply to a reasonably fair pamphlet by a critic, *Observations on Some Articles of the Muggletonian Creed* (1735). Cf. a creed (undated but eighteenth century), 'I Believe God the Creator of Heaven and Earth was a Spiral Body in the form of a man from all Eternity, and that earth and water wher an Eternal Substance Distinct from the Creator.

This is an intellectually coherent view (more coherent, perhaps, than some conventional Christian apologetics), and it also brings us within hailing distance of neo-Platonist and Behmenist arguments. A similar resolution is implied in a comment of Blake's recorded by Crabb Robinson (who quizzed Blake more closely as to his theological beliefs than any other acquaintance of his last years): 'Asserted that the Devil is eternally created not by God – but by God's permission. And when I [made an] objection that permission implies power to prevent he did not seem to understand me.'[22]

Muggletonians also held to a version of Behmenist dialectic, and referred to 'God's manifesting himself by Contrarieties in Creation'.[23] But there seems to be a difficulty here. For the 'contrarieties' seem to be sometimes envisaged as an opposition between God/Nature, spirit/matter and Faith/Reason. 'The substance of earth and water were from eternity', and 'darkness, death or devil and hell lay secretly hid in that earth above this perishing Globe and in the sight of the Creator were eternally naked and bare'.[24] Creation would appear to mix, as in Manichaean doctrine, two opposing principles, one material (and evil) the other spiritual and divine. (Blake, in his last years, appears sometimes to have expressed such views: according to Crabb Robinson, 'He was continually expressing . . . his distinction between the natural & spiritual world. The natural world must be consumed.' And 'he denied that the natural world is any thing. It is all nothing and Satan's empire is the empire of nothing.'[25]) This gives us contraries, not in the Blakean sense of 'two contrary states', but as barren negations. Satan, for the Muggletonians, was the God of Reason, and–

> Reason's god is in all life,
> Human, brutal, vegetive,
> Which, at first, from nothing came,
> And must to nothing return again.[26]

(But notice also 'vegetive', so close to Blake's 'vegetate' and 'veget-

In wich Substance Lay Secretly hid the very root of Death and Darkness.' Muggletonian archive.
22 Bentley, *Blake Records*, p. 318.
23 *The Principles of the Muggletonians Asserted*, p. 21.
24 MS at back of copies of Muggleton, 'Three Records' and 'Letter to James Whitehead' in Muggletonian archive.
25 Bentley, *Blake Records*, pp. 312, 316.
26 Richard Wynne in *Divine Songs of the Muggletonians* (1829), pp. 156–8.

ative', by which he describes the material, corporeal universe of sexual generation.)

In the argument of one Muggletonian apologist, God permitted 'the root of spiritual darkness' to manifest itself since without this contrast his divinity could not have been known:

> So all contraries are manifested by contraries, as
> darkness is not known but by light, nor light but
> by the darkness; neither would any man prize his
> friends if he never met with enemies. . .
>
> Since by contraries all things are made clear,
> Without contraries nothing can appear:
> So had not God a devil sent on earth,
> We had not known his glory and his birth. . .
>
> [And] had not God permitted us to fall,
> We had not known him, nor his power at all.[27]

But equally the contraries exist within man, as Reason and Faith, and it is the *nature* of Reason to 'fight and plunder and kill':

> Roar cursed Reason roar
> You can't disturb me more
> For wrongs receiv'd
> Thy cursed Serpent Tongue
> That with Revenge is hung
> Tis what thy Nature craves.[28]

Or, as Thomas Pickersgill, a Muggletonian painter (and contemporary of Blake) wrote in a private letter in 1803:

Every thing Acts according to its Nature, Reason Acts [h]is Nature, in Going to War, to fight and kill, with Sword and Guns killing One a Nother, Army against Army, Kingdom Against Kingdom, but it is not so with faith, for no True believer . . . can make use of aney Such Weapons of Warr . . . to Slay the Image of God, our Blessed Redeemer, because faith being of a Nother Nature, which is all love, and is that peacable Kingdom of God. . .[29]

The Muggletonian version of *Genesis* was arresting:

---

[27] John Brown, a Brother to the *Saints*, and a Friend to the *Elect*, *The Saint's Triumph, and the Devil's Downfall*, &c (Norwich, n.d.), pp. 8–9.

[28] Song by Margaret Thomas, Muggletonian archive.

[29] Thomas Pickersgill to Abraham Tregone, London, 1 December 1803, Muggletonian archive.

The *Tree* of which Eve eat, called the *Tree of the Knowledge of Good and Evil*, was her being overcome by the glorious Appearance of the Devil made in the form of an Angel of Light.[30]

This Devil (or Angel of Light) appeared in the form of a glorious Serpent, who copulated with Eve. Entering within Eve's womb the Serpent transmuted himself 'into Flesh, Blood and Bone' and the offspring of this intercourse was Cain, whereas Abel and his young brother Seth (in whose generation the Devil had no part) were the offspring of the divine principle in which God had created Adam. But from the moment of the Fall, Satan disappears from the rest of the cosmos, having dissolved himself in Eve's womb and perpetuated himself in Cain and Cain's seed and only there. Hence there was implanted within the human race, at the moment of the Fall, two contrary principles, diabolic and divine: the offspring of Cain and the offspring of Seth.

In 1675 John Saddington, a sugar factor, codified with clarity forty-eight Articles of Muggletonian faith. Since the doctrine of the Two Seeds is central to these beliefs, we will resume this from the relevant Articles:

xv

I do believe that the Tree of Knowledge of good and evil was that serpent angel which GOD cast out of heaven down to this earth for his rebellion. . .

xvii

I do believe that that outcast angel or serpent-tree of knowledge of good and evil did enter into the womb of Eve, and dissolve his spiritual body into seed, which seed died and quickened again in the womb of Eve.

xviii

I do believe that Eve brought forth her first born the son of the devil, and very devil himself.

xix

I do believe that there is no other devil but man and woman; since the first devil, that serpent angel devil, became seed in the womb of Eve, and clothed himself with flesh and bone.

xx

I do believe that Cain was not the son of Adam, though he was the son of Eve.

---

[30] *Observations on Some Articles of the Muggletonian Creed*, p. 8.

XXI

I do believe that the seed of the woman and the seed of the serpent are two distinct generations of men and women in this world.

XXII

I do believe that the seed of the woman is the generation of faithful people, which proceed from the loins of blessed Seth, who was the son of Adam, who was the son of God.

XXIII

I do believe that the seed of the serpent is the generation of unbelievers or reprobate men and women, which proceed from the loins of cursed Cain, the son of the devil, and the first lying and murdering devil that ever was.[31]

The Muggletonian doctrine of the Two Seeds might seem to be inexorably predestinarian. And so, in a general interpretation, it was:

A part of Mankind are the Spawn of the Devil, or the Produce and Offspring of a carnal Knowledge the Devil had of Eve: whilst others, viz, *themselves*, are only and truly the Seed of the Woman.[32]

This was the view of a critic (in 1735), but it is a fair representation of one emphasis. But, at the same time, Muggletonians did not overlook the fact that the human race was the product of millennia of miscegenation. Hence within each man or woman two contrary principles, Satanic and divine, were implanted, struggling for dominance over each other, although in a strict view it was predestined that one only should triumph. This allowed (as with most predestinarian faiths) some laxity of interpretation. On the one hand, it was possible for the faithful to regard themselves as 'saints': the faithful, wrote Tomkinson, had the 'seal of salvation stamped in their souls. . .'[33] And at the same time, all opponents of the faithful – including, of course, kings, magistrates, priests and Quakers – could be identified unequivocally as the seed or spawn of the devil. Henry Bonel, in 1763, wrote an unloving Muggletonian song addressed to 'hypocritical priests':

[31] John Saddington, *The Articles of True Faith, depending upon the Commission of the Spirit* (1830). Written in 1675, copies were circulated in manuscript in the eighteenth-century Church.
[32] *Observations on Some Articles of the Muggletonian Creed*, p. 7.
[33] See note 19, p. 70 above.

You who by long prayers do prey on the poor,
The bread and the substance of widows devour;
Of external righteousness make a fair show,
While nothing but praise and gain's in your view;
Ye vipers, ye serpents, ye seed of the devil,
How can you escape the last great day of evil?[34]

On the other hand, it was possible to view the spiritual struggles of the uncommitted (or of backsliders) as an intense inner drama in which the divine and Satanic principles wrestled with each other for dominance. Humphry Broadbent, an early eighteenth-century believer, in a letter to a straying member of the flock, expresses this drama of pride and penitence locked in immortal combat:

It seems you through the Weakness and Luceferian Pride of thy Spirrit for promises of Silver & Gold that Perrishes have let Satan, that is thy unclean Spirrit of Reason, Captivate thy Seed of Faith . . . O! that the Allmighty God if it be his Blessed Will may open your Eyes before it be too late & that unpardonable Sin against the holy Ghost is Committed, for you know that all Manner of Sins shall be forgiven but the Sin against the Holy Ghost. . .

Since the Holy Ghost is the spirit presiding over the Third Commission of Reeve and Muggleton, this sin was defined as that of repudiating the prophet's words and backsliding from the Commission of the Spirit. But Broadbent yet had hopes that God would 'restore the strayed Sheep to his fold' before that sin was committed:

Now where your Treasure is, above in the Celistiall Heavens or below on the Teristiall perishing Earth which must stoop to Deaths Infernall Night, is best known to the Allmighty God & Your Selfe for to mee at this time it seems dubious Which.[35]

Hence Muggletonians, like other predestinarian creeds, allowed for both a determinist and voluntarist vocabulary: in the latter it was 'Uncleane Reason, the Devill' that threatened always to 'captivate the Seed of Faith'. There are certainly times when Blake also appears to play with the notion of the Two Seeds, or 'the two natures which are in man'.[36] 'Men are born with a devil & an

---

[34] *Divine Songs of the Muggletonians*, p. 159.
[35] Muggletonian archive.
[36] Thomas Tomkinson, *A System of Religion* (1857), p. 92.

angel', he told Crabb Robinson, who added: 'but this he himself
interpreted body & Soul'. And again: 'Every Man has a Devil in
himself. And the conflict between his *Self* and God is perpetually
carrying on.'[37] Nor is this simply neo-Platonist imagery, for genealogies of two seeds are offered in *Jerusalem*:

> Satan Cain Tubal Nimrod Pharoh Priam Bladud Belin
> Arthur Alfred the Norman Conqueror Richard John
> [*Edward Henry Elizabeth James Charles William George*] (*del.*)
> And all the Kings & Nobles of the Earth & all their Glories
> These are Created by Rahab & Tirzah in Ulro: but around
> These, to preserve them from Eternal Death Los Creates
> Adam Noah Abraham Moses Samuel David Ezekiel
> [*Pythagoras Socrates Euripides Virgil Dante Milton*] (*del.*)   (E226)

This version of the two seeds is turned to use to dramatise Blake's
robust republican and aesthetic sympathies, but we commence in
each case with the line of Satan/Cain and that of Adam/Seth as
sanctioned by *Genesis*. An earlier reference in *Jerusalem* (E210–11)
is more eccentric:

> I see the Maternal Line, I behold the Seed of the Woman!
> Cainah, & Ada & Zillah & Naamah Wife of Noah.
> Shuahs daughter & Tamar & Rahab the Canaanites. . .

– a line which ends with Mary: 'These are the Daughters of Vala,
Mother of the Body of death.' This notion of a 'Maternal Line'
could perhaps be sanctioned by the notion to be found among
eighteenth-century Muggletonian believers that 'the Sons of Adam,
who were called the Sons of God, intermixed in Marriage with the
Daughters of Cain, who are called the Daughters of Man. . .'[38] The
line, Cain–Adah and Zillah–Naamah is found in *Genesis* 4 verse 25
(Naamah is sister to Tubal-cain, the 'instructer of every artificer
of brass and iron' (verse 22)), where will also be found (verse 25)
authority for the line of divine seed by way of Seth. By what authority Blake married Naamah to Noah of the line of Seth (*Genesis* 5)
I do not know.

That Blake played with the notion of the Two Seeds does not
prove that he was indebted to Muggletonian doctrine. In a general
metaphorical sense the notion of the line Satan/Cain leading on to
the rulers and potentates of the earth turns up elsewhere in the

[37] Bentley, *Blake Records*, pp. 337, 547–8.
[38] *The Principles of the Muggletonians Asserted*, p. 18.

radical Christian tradition: a Digger pamphlet declared that 'Cain is still alive in all the Great Landlords'. 'Cain's brood', wrote Bunyan, were 'lord and rulers', while 'Abel and his generation have their necks under oppression'.[39] (But the *literal* notion of dual genealogies, which Blake employs, is perhaps specific to the Muggletonians.) In any case, as always, Blake does not *follow* doctrine but turns it to his own account.

I will post over that small interval between the Fall and the Annunciation. A more leisurely survey would show that Muggletonian doctrine laboured over episodes and images which also fascinated Blake, some of which were eccentric to the main concerns of Christian faith. Thus there was much attention to the cherubim with flaming swords guarding the Tree of Life (*Genesis* 3.24), identified by both Muggleton and Blake as Satanic guardians.[40] There is the same concern with the Seven Churches of Asia. Muggletonians were preoccupied with certain marginalia, such as the apocryphal Epistle of Jude and the 'Book of Enoch', which also caught the eye of Blake. But we will let these matters pass.

The story of Christ commences with the story of the Fall inverted. It was now God, and not the Serpent, who entered Mary's womb and dissolved into her conception. Eighteenth-century believers sometimes wrote creeds into their song-books or tracts. Here is one:

I believe in God the Man Christ Jeasus, in Glory who was a Spiritual Body from all Eternity Who by Virtue of his Godhead Power Entered into the narrow passage of the Blessed Virgin Mary's Womb And so Dissolved Himself into Seed and Nature as Clothed Himself with Flesh Blood and Bone as with a Garment; thereby made Capable to Suffer Death who made himself man, the Express Image of his Farther's Person And so became a Son to his own God power. He Absolutely poured out His Soul unto Death; and lay three Days Dead in the Womb of the Earth. . .[41]

(Such creeds, with their frank sexual symbolism, gave rise to accusations against Muggletonians of obscene blasphemy, and for this reason were not published.) It is important also that Muggle-

---

[39] Hill, *The World Turned Upside Down*, p. 117.
[40] See Muggleton, *A True Interpretation of the Eleventh Chapter of the Revelation of St John* (1662 and 1753), chapter xx; for Blake (and Boehme) see Raine, *Blake and Tradition*, I, pp. 329–32.
[41] MS creed in front of a copy of Muggleton, *A Transcendent Spiritual Treatise* (1822 edn) in Muggletonian archive.

tonian doctrine insisted upon the indivisibility of God, employing
the language of the Trinity only to describe differing manifestations
of the same indivisible divinity: 'I Believe God the Creator of
Heaven & Earth was a Spiritual Body in the form of a man from
all Eternity.'[42] It followed that when God 'transmuted' himself into
the infant Jesus in Mary's womb, there could then be no God in
heaven or in any other part of the cosmos – Christ, the man, was
not only divine, he was the *only* God. It followed also that between
the crucifixion and the resurrection there was no God either in
heaven or on earth: God had been killed. This must have been,
for believers, a logical, but daring and frightening, idea. In the
words of another eighteenth-century creed:

When Christ died the whole Godhead was absolutely Void of all Life
heat or Motion. Father son & Holy Ghost became Extinct in Death. The
whole Life of the Infinet power was Dead.[43]

This accentuated the dramatic sacrificial symbolism of the Cross:
God literally took on mortality and paid its penalty in order to
redeem the faithful. How he got *out* of this situation at the Resurrection was a fruitful source of dispute and dissension among subsequent believers.[44]

I want to put in a word here for the Muggletonians, who have
had a bad historical press, based often on little more than the
absurdity of the name. From a certain rational standpoint – the
single vision of literalism – all religious symbolism may appear as
absurd. The rational mind can do little more than stand outside
it and comment on its consistency or inconsistency. From this
standpoint I can see nothing more absurd in Muggletonian doctrine than in great and supposedly intellectually reputable faiths.
The story-line of *Genesis* is utterly absurd, and Muggletonians were
sometimes at pains to point out these absurdities to the orthodox:

What do you Quakers think the Tree of Knowledge of Good and Evil
was, and that Serpent that beguiled *Eve*? [Muggleton enquired with sar-

---

[42] Another creed (eighteenth century) in Muggletonian archive. Muggletonian references
to God were of a precise physical kind – in the form of an old man of about six feet
high – perhaps a figure not unlike Blake's Urizen.
[43] Muggletonian archive.
[44] In the literal version of the prophets God had the foresight to appoint vice-regents –
Moses and Elias (with whom Enoch was sometimes associated) to serve him *in absentia*
and to reclaim him from death; in the more intellectual creeds of eighteenth-century
believers, Christ was 'a Quickening Spirit', who, like grain in the earth, 'had Power to
quicken out of pale death again': Creed in Muggletonian archive.

casm]. Do you look upon it to be some Apple-tree, and the Serpent to be an ugly Snake? and so this Snake crept up the Tree, and got an Apple in his Mouth, and the Woman took the Apple out of the Snake's Mouth, and so eat of it, and gave her Husband to eat, and so brought themselves into this Misery, and all Mankind? Do you teach your Hearers this?

Or do the Quakers turn it into a mere allegory, 'so that nothing can be made of it, neither one Way nor other'?[45] And Tomkinson echoes this argument: 'The eating of an apple could not have contracted an hereditary evil, as is generally said by those who take this in the vulgar manner.'[46]

The Muggletonian doctrines of the Fall, the Two Seeds and the conception of Christ, combine literalism with a robust symbolic power. The dual impregnations of Eve and Mary give to the doctrine a certain symmetry, like a figure-of-eight, as well as intellectual consistency. And notoriously the notion of the unity of one God in the three persons of the Trinity has offered difficulties to the reason. If the Trinity is repudiated, and not merely juggled with, then we must either be led to an undivine Christ or to a Muggletonian transmutation of God into Christ. And such a translation, which follows well-authenticated natural processes, appears as no more irrational than the translation of wine and wafers into blood and flesh. I will suggest that – a few peripheral doctrines apart – Muggletonian beliefs were logical, powerful in their symbolic operation and have only been held to be 'ridiculous' because the Muggletonians were losers and because their faith was professed by 'poor enthusiasts' and not by scholars, bishops or successful evangelists.[47]

Muggletonianism also remained, throughout the eighteenth century, a faith in which believers exercised their intellectual faculties in doctrinal disputes. Hence it has a kinship with the intellectual traditions of Old Dissent rather than the raw or confessional emotionalism of Wesleyanism and the Evangelical revival. The disputes may appear as merely scholastic – do beasts partake in the Last Ascension?[48] – or even as a little sad. At a regular meeting of

---

[45] Muggleton, *A Looking-Glass for George Fox* (1761 edn), pp. 20–1.
[46] Thomas Tomkinson, *A System of Religion*, p. 93.
[47] On this (and most other matters) I am in agreement with Hill, Reay and Lamont, *The World of the Muggletonians*.
[48] The answer seems to have been 'no': see Arden Bonnell, 'A Reply to a Discourse on the Beasts Ascension Where What I formerly advanced in a Letter to Friends, against the Ascension of Beasts is further defended' (1736: MS in Muggletonian archive).

London believers in the 1760s there was a long discourse concerning the Ark:

> Whether all in it was in a spiritual Condition and eat No Food, seeing they did represant Heaven; or Whether they might not be a tipe of Heaven, notwithstanding eating or drinking, seeing they took of all Manner of Food into the Arke and it is not to be suposed the savage wild Creatures would stay to be fed by Noah after coming out of the ark, tho' Obedient to the purpose of God while in it. I shall not relate the divers Opinions as there was some on each side, but leave it to your own Judgement. . .[49]

Other issues were more significant. The doctrines were flexible enough to allow ulterior issues to be argued out in terms of its symbols. Thus the doctrine of the Two Seeds allowed for rival patriarchal and feminist emphases. Reeve and Muggleton, of course, transmitted a patriarchal orthodoxy. Sin, at the Fall, entered through the weakness of Eve, and this could happen only because Faith, in the person of Adam, was asleep, resting from his arduous toils in the Garden of Eden:

> So in the fall of Adam
> When reason Changed Condition
> Faith was asleep while he took flesh
> As says Reeves glorious Mission–

so runs a verse in a characteristically argumentative doctrinal song by James Miller (1745).[50] And Muggleton tended to invest the opposing genealogies of the Two Seeds with masculine prejudice: 'the Soul of Man doth partake of the Father's Nature, even the Seed and Nature of Faith', and so, presumably, the Seed and Nature of Reason (or the Satanic inheritance) partook of the nature of the mother.[51] According to this view, Mary's part in the conception of Christ was merely passive, as a receptacle or breeding-place for the divine seed; in neo-Platonic imagery Mary 'Clothed the Eternal spirit with a Body of flesh in her womb'.[52] So God 'Clothed Himself with Flesh Blood and Bone as with a Garment' (above, p. 77) and Mary was no more than a biological hostess to the divine donor. (It should be said, and sharply, that Blake, who is sometimes sup-

[49] *Ibid.*
[50] James Miller, 'A Spiritual Song on the two Seeds, or the Impossibility for Faith to Sinn', verse 30, MS 1772, in *ibid.*
[51] Muggleton, *The Answer to William Penn, Quaker* (n.d.), p. 82.
[52] MS eighteenth-century creed, in Muggletonian archive.

posed to have transcended gender prejudices, often was willing to employ anti-feminine imagery. That remarkable and powerful late addition to the *Songs of Experience*, 'To Tirzah', employs throughout the imagery of the feminine principle (the womb) clothing, enclosing and binding the spirit in a way which Muggletonians as well as neo-Platonists would have understood (see below, pp. 148–9). 'Christ', he told Crabb Robinson, 'took much after his Mother And in so far he was one of the worst of men.'[53]

But there were heretical Muggletonian voices who also held that Christ took somewhat after the mother, and that he was none the worse for that. Thomas Tomkinson, whose writings always contain much emphasis on the virtues of love and mercy, declared that we should say no ill of a woman, 'for though a woman was the inlet to sin, yet a woman was the outlet of sin, and the inlet of salvation':

And though the first woman compassed a man of death, hell and damnation; yet let not her after-seed by *Adam* speak ill of her: because they and her were blessed by a gracious promise of an after redemption, which was and is by this new created man compassed by a woman.[54]

Other believers pressed the argument in the eighteenth century. A paper survives which argues tenaciously (and clearly in the face of opposition) that in Mary's conception God's seed united with Eve's seed of Faith, 'and that God & man and all things that come forth of the womb receive life from the Femaile as well as the Maile'.[55] One senses that there was an active feminine presence in the tiny Muggletonian church;[56] many songs were written by women, and in the 1770s a dissident group (of both sexes) left the church under the leadership of Martha Collier, an aspirant visionary and prophetess.

One other perennial dispute had some significance. This was an attempt to break out of the severe closure imposed by Reeve and Muggleton's orthodoxy when, in their fierce opposition to the Ranters' pantheism and in their polemics against the claims of the early Quakers to divine visitation, they had repudiated any divine principle except in God/Christ. And yet the prophets were also

---

[53] Bentley, *Blake Records*, p. 548.
[54] Thomas Tomkinson, *The Harmony of the Three Commissions; or, None but Christ* (1882), pp. 52–3.
[55] Unsigned MS, n.d. but late eighteenth century, in Muggletonian archive.
[56] As also in the seventeenth-century church, see Hill, Reay and Lamont, p. 54.

responsible for implanting a contradiction in their teaching, in the doctrine of the Two Seeds. For if the Satanic principle existed nowhere in the cosmos except in the seed of Cain, might it not equally be argued that God existed nowhere but in the seed of Seth? And, again, if the founding prophets claimed divine inspiration, why might the same inspiration not come to their followers? Throughout the century believers wrestled with this, in controversies about the 'indwelling God' and 'immediate notice'.[57] The sanctified were anxious to claim at least some kinship with God: 'the same spirit that dwels in the father and in the son, the same dwels in the saints . . . and he that is joyned to Christ is one spirit, and not distinct nor seperate. . .'[58] In 1794 William Sedgwick, a leading believer, tried to find a formula to settle the dispute:

Christ is the Light that Lighteth Every man that Commeth in to the world yet none but God is Infinite. Notwithstanding tho' God the Creator virtuale [virtually] Dwells in all his Creatuers. Nothing is Capable of the Indwelling Infinite power But God alone. Why Because that wich Procedeth Cannot be Equal to that from wich it Procedeth any more than a Streem can be Equal with a Fountain. Even man in his Created Purity tho' of the very nature of the Divine Creator yet not Infinite Because it was in measuer only and so but finite. . .

In a postscript Sedgwick added that he flattered himself that if these few lines were impartially considered 'no faithfull man or woman whould Contend against it', but, in a second and more sober after-thought, he added that rather than contention should be perpetually upheld in the Church 'it whould be Best to Seperate'.[59] There were such separations, as there had been in the previous two decades, notably that of James Birch, a watch-motion maker, who claimed direct prophetic inspiration.[60] But, of course, the argument which Sedgwick attempted to resolve is one which reappears, in many forms, in quite different doctrines and churches. Sedgwick's contemporaries, the Swedenborgians of the

---

[57] Eighteenth- and nineteenth-century 'Reevonians' claimed that the denial of God's immediate notice' in human affairs was a doctrine introduced by Muggleton after Reeve's death: see W. Lamont, 'Ludowick Muggleton and "Immediate Notice"', in *ibid.*, chapter 5.

[58] Eighteenth-century MS (n.d.) of Edward Pallmer in Muggletonian archive.

[59] MS of William Sedgwick in *ibid.*

[60] For Birch see DNB (entry by Alexander Gordon) and Lamont, p. 127. Birch and W. Matthews declared themselves to be 'prophets' on the model of Reeve and Muggleton.

New Jerusalem church, were arguing it vigorously in the 1790s, in terms of 'the divine influx'.[61]

I hesitate to carry this discussion into the whole matter of *Revelation*, upon which Muggleton wrote two major commentaries and his followers wrote more. Surrounded by candlesticks, the Beast and its number, the Whore of Babylon and diverse commentaries on these, it would be foolhardy to suggest that Blake, in prophetic works or paintings, leaned more towards the Muggletonian than any other interpretation. In a few matters there may be some congruence. Muggletonians were mortalists or 'soul-sleepers'.[62] They rejected any body/soul dualism: Reeve declared 'the spirit is nothing at all without a body, and a body is nothing at all without a spirit: neither of them can live, or have a being, without the other'.[63] 'The soul of man is generated with its body,' repeated Saddington, 'therefore it liveth and dieth with the body, and is never parted from it.'[64] 'The soul is the author and cause of every action', wrote Tomkinson: 'It is that which acts and lives, thinks and perceives.' 'It is not possible to conceive, that the soul can be conscious of its existence, it cannot be sensible of itself if it center not in a body. . .'[65] Blake's 'voice of the Devil' in *The Marriage of Heaven and Hell* also exposed the error that 'Man has two real existing principles: Viz: a Body & a Soul'. 'Man has no Body distinct from his Soul; for that call'd Body is a portion of Soul in this age' (E34).

The soul, however, will be awakened dramatically from its sleep at the Last Judgement, since, although it perishes with the body like grain, there is 'an invisible principle or seed still remaining, which will spring forth'.[66] Muggletonians affirmed that all celestial creatures, including angels, were created in the form of males, but without the faculty of procreation: 'neither was there any Female created in the Celestial Heavens'.[67] As one ecstatic female believer sang:

---

[61] Muggletonians sometimes used the term 'the divine income': see, e.g., 'A copey of a Letter Origenaly written by James Birch to Joseph Coal and the Brethren in Wales' (1778) in Muggletonian archive.

[62] See Tomkinson, *A System of Religion*, p. 91.

[63] See James Hyde, 'The Muggletonians and the Document of 1729', *The New-Church Review* (Boston, Mass.), 7, 1990, pp. 215–27.

[64] John Saddington, *A Prospective Glass for Saints & Sinners* (1823), p. 104.

[65] Thomas Tomkinson, *A System of Religion*, pp. 57, 83–4.

[66] *Ibid.*, p. 120.

[67] Muggleton, *The Answer to William Penn, Quaker*, pp. 4–5.

> There is all such creatures as is here,
> But spiritual, like chrystal clear;
> All males, not made to generate,
> But live in divine happy state. . .[68]

At the Last Judgement the souls would spring forth in changed bodies; according to Tomkinson, the saints 'will have bodies, new, pure, and glorious', the reprobate will have dark spiritual bodies 'suitable to their evil nature and wicked lives',[69] but both (it would seem) translated into androgynous form.[70] Blake also employed on occasion the image of souls awakening from their graves (it was Mercy who 'changed Death into Sleep') (E30). And in the *Song* 'To Tirzah' he also borrowed, from some source, perhaps from Boehme, the notion of an androgynous resurrection:

> Whate'er is Born of Mortal Birth
> Must be consumed with the Earth
> To rise from Generation free. . .

And the engraving accompanying 'To Tirzah' is inscribed: 'It is Raised a Spiritual Body.'

I am uncertain as to how far it is helpful to define eighteenth-century Muggletonians as millenarians. They shared in the wide-spread Christian faith in a Second Coming, but had taken pains to distinguish themselves from Sectaries such as the Fifth Monarchists who believed in a literal reign of Christ on earth.[71] On the other hand, Christ's return was still expected, but only in heaven–

Those who expect a God here upon this earth, after any other manner than a personal Jesus, seated on a throne of eternal glory in the Heaven above, will never find him; and whoever looks for a God to come before the end of the world, or a God without a personal form, will find their hopes in vain.[72]

In the early years of the Church, while memories of the spiritual disturbance of the Commonwealth still kept alive expectations, the Last Judgement was sometimes felt as imminent: 'we that live now near the end of the world', wrote Tomkinson, 'are waiting for his

---

[68] Rebecca Batt, in *Divine Songs of the Muggletonians*, p. 140.
[69] Tomkinson, pp. 121–2.
[70] Reeve, *Sacred Remains* (n.d.), p. 90; Reeve and Muggleton, *Joyful News from Heaven* (n.d.), p. 56.
[71] 'Christ will come no more to reign upon this earth with his saints, as it is imagined by many. . .': Saddington, *The Articles of True Faith*, p. 19.
[72] Tomkinson, *A System of Religion*, p. 81.

second coming.[73] As the years stretched out into decades, the expectations of the faithful seem to have been postponed. One eighteenth-century Creed runs–

I Believe The same Mighty God, the man Christ Jesus in Glory, will suddenly Appear In the Clouds of heaven to Judg Both the Quick and the Dead and to make an Everlasting Sepperation Between the Elect and the reprobate world. The One will Enter into Ever Lasting happyness & the Other in Endless & Everlasting Torments to all Eternety where will be weeping & Nashing of teeth for Evermore. Amen.[74]

But there is less suggestion that these satisfactory arrangements would be fulfilled at an early date. The groups which seceded with Birch and Martha Collier in the last decades of the century expressed a renewed millenarial fervour. But the orthodox believers were millenarians only in the quieter sense that 'a New Age' (the Third Age of the Spirit) had already commenced when John Reeve received his 'Commission' in 1652. Their songs and correspondence frequently employ the symbolism of the Last Vintage, the winepress of God, the threshing-floor of the barn and the separation of the wheat from the reprobate tares – 'when the Harvest is ripe and a General seperation shall take place and be divided the *Seed* of the Woman and the *Seed* of the Serpent which is now so entangled together. . .'[75] Then at last the elect should gain their new bodies of 'bright burning glory' and 'they shall all ascend together as one body, to meet their head, the Lord Jesus, in the air'.[76]

It is a silly enough picture, but it is one which many Christians in many churches have shared. It is also one which Blake turned to his own account repeatedly in his writings and his paintings.[77] I don't mean that Blake ever used these images in exactly the same way. Muggletonians offered them as literal accounts of events to be firmly expected; for Blake, 'the Last Judgment is not Fable or Allegory but Vision' (E544), and he added in a grumpy aside: 'A Last Judgment is Necessary because Fools flourish' (E551). But what is interesting, in the present context, is that Blake's visions repeatedly return to this vocabulary of symbolism. This is a

[73] *Ibid.*, p. 80.
[74] MS in Muggletonian archive.
[75] Letter (n.d.) from John Carwithon of Derby to the London church, in Muggletonian archive.
[76] Muggleton, *A Transcendent Spiritual Treatise*, chapter xiv.
[77] See David Bindman, *Blake as an Artist* (Oxford, 1977), chapter 19.

language, a set of signs, which he knows by heart, but which he
employs as he pleases. And at certain points Blake's vocabulary
has a markedly Muggletonian accent.

I will return to this in a moment. But first we may enquire a
little further into the eighteenth-century Muggletonian Church.
How did these doctrines fare in the keeping of a small sect which
survived through decades of eighteenth-century Enlightenment?
And here we encounter a paradox within a paradox. The old seventeenth-century sects which survived into the new century faced the
choice of submission to the rationalism and civilising modes of the
time, with an accompanying upwards drift in the social status of
their following – and this was the trajectory of Old Dissent in
general, including those old opponents of the Muggletonians, the
Quakers; or else of maintaining their original doctrinal integrity
(and a diminishing familial and perhaps plebeian following) by
ever-fiercer resistance to rationalism, to the polite theology of biblical criticism and to accommodation with Newtonian physics, and
by ever-stronger insistence upon the virtues of faith, grace and
purity of heart. Such was the course followed by some minuscule
(and threatened) sects, some Baptist congregations and by some
of those swept up by Whitefield's and Wesley's early evangelism.
The impulse – the return to grace – was often explicitly 'counter-
enlightenment'; hemmed in in the first half of the century, this
impulse eventually met with its reward in the last decades of the
century, breaking out from its petty strongholds, sweeping across
the counties and multiplying into thousands of little Bethels.

This 'counter-enlightenment' resistance may very certainly be
seen in the Muggletonian Church. Where seventeenth-century
antinomians, Familists or Seekers had laboured with sweat on their
spiritual brows through forests of vivid imagery in the effort to
bring some kind of logic or system into being, most eighteenth-
century mystics and antinomians relaxed into anti-rational pos-
tures and gave up the struggle. No theme recurs more often in the
Muggletonian songs than hostility to Reason, 'the right devil'. The
faithful prided themselves on their rejection of the reasons of the
enlightened. They pitted their faith against the 'serpent reasonings'
of polite learning. In one song by Thomas Tomkinson—

> Love, what art thou that art divinely bent?
> And how cam'st thou into this continent?
> What is thy birth, and where can divines tell?
> Yes, but not such as in Cambridge do dwell.

Yet Cambridge schools know thy bare name of love
But not the nature that comes from above;
For tho' love there was born and born again.
Yet divine breath's not known by learned men. . .[78]

This active stance of resistance to the hegemony of the polite and reputable culture was enforced with a severe, even intellectual, severity. Education itself was no less than re-enacting the Fall, by eating of the Tree of the Knowledge of Good and Evil. In the front of one eighteenth-century song-book I find transcribed on the title-page (*c.*1777)–

By edducation most have been mislead
So they believe because they were so bred
The Priest continues what the Nurse began
And thus the Child imposes on the Man[79]

'There is no use in education', Blake told Crabb Robinson in 1825. 'I hold it wrong. It is the great sin. It is eating of the tree of the knowledge of good and evil. . .'[80]

Muggleton, a working tailor, had expressed particular hostility to the learned professions. His followers, in the main, were tradesmen, artisans and persons in humble circumstances. Among eighteenth-century Muggletonians I have found butchers, watch and clock-makers, a shoemaker, a painter, a musician, a printer, a master weaver, a ticket porter, a joiner, a tailor, a clerk, a pastry cook: believers are found in most parts of London, but more thickly in the City and East End (Leadenhall Street, Cripplegate, Mile End, Spitalfields, Moorfields, Whitechapel) than the South or West. Muggletonians had no priesthood or officers of any kind. They imposed few duties on each other. Perhaps the first was the accumulation of funds to keep the works of the Prophets in print. They succeeded in doing this; and from these tracts they won a few literate recruits. They were also sustained by strong traditions of familial loyalty.[81] They survived, with indomitable tenacity, the long years in the wilderness, and yet they had no share in the subsequent evangelical harvest.

This brings us to our second paradox. For the Muggletonians were not only anti-enlightenment: they were also anti-evangelical.

---

[78] *Divine Songs of the Muggletonians*, p. 372.
[79] At front of MS Song Book collected by John Peat, *c.*1777, in Muggletonian archive, Brit. Lib. Add. MSS 60211.
[80] Bentley, *Blake Records*, p. 540.
[81] Family continuities can be traced in the *Divine Songs* and Muggletonian archive.

For they had survived the rational bombardments of the century by lying low and keeping their heads down. They were quietists in the most elementary sense: they kept quiet. The fellowship of the faithful was itself a little Zion:

> Who shall in Zion's joys abide
> Where Revelations softly glide
> The man whose faithfull heart and Tongue
> Ne're strove to do his Neighbour wrong
> Nor try'd with Infamy his name
> In Reason's Kingdom to defame
> Whilst lofty Cedars, scorcht with fire
> Who dare unto the Sun aspire
> Upon the humble rose, distills
> The Spicy dew of Zion's hills.[82]

This self-confident, introverted enthusiasm contributed to the transmission, with singular purity, of the doctrines. But it left them unequipped to evangelise. If they had found great numbers turning towards them they would have been alarmed at the possibility of Satan's seed entering among them. Small numbers at least brought with them a sense of security, from which they could contemplate with equanimity the oncoming downfall of their enemies:

> The fat-gutted priest will roar for assistance;
>   The lawyer may say, he did plea for a fee;
> But unto our God they have both shewn resistance,
>   They are damn'd without mercy to eternity.[83]

It is greatly heartening to think of a small circle of friends, united in love, singing these lines in the midst of eighteenth-century London – perhaps in a private room in 'The Gun' in Islington or 'The Blue Boar' in Aldersgate Street. But this would be the limit of their formal expression. Their faith forbade them to attend any formal public worship. They held no formal services, and their meetings – apart from their two annual 'feasts' or 'holidays' – were confined to readings from the works of the Prophets and the singing, *not* of hymns, but of 'divine songs' or 'songs of grateful praise'. Even prayer they regarded as a 'mark of weakness' ('marks of weakness, marks of woe').[84] Among believers (who often referred

[82] From lines by Margaret Thomas in MS Song Book, Brit. Lib. Add. MSS 60207.
[83] From a song by John Peat (mid-eighteenth century), in *Divine Songs*, p. 441.
[84] One of John Birch's heresies was to disparage songs in favour of prayer; but prayer presumed God's 'immediate notice', the Reevonian 'heresy' which Birch espoused. For

to each other, like Quakers, as Friends) the traditions of the
Church and of former believers were cherished:

> I know John Saddington, and Claxton both
> Were strong believers; and wrote things of worth;
> John Brown; and others glorious things have pen'd,
> But farr too short of my Renowned Friend,
> Brave Tomkinson, like to a Cedar tall
> In fair Libanus that o'er topped all.[85]

(Claxton also was remembered still, in 1760, for other qualities,
one believer writing of a quarrelsome friend: 'I believe Brother
Ned is a faithfull man but a little like Clackston, full of Speritualll
Pride.'[86]) As late as the 1790s oral anecdotes of the Prophets still
circulated.[87] Although the Church had not property, funds or regular minutes in the eighteenth century, the manuscripts of the
prophets, of Saddington, Tomkinson, Bonnell, and others, and of
humble believers were carefully preserved, either in closets
installed in the pubs where they met or in private hands.

It was a highly literate Church, but small enough for all its
internal affairs to be conducted by manuscript. Believers spent
many hours in copying the works of their forebears, in circulating
doctrinal polemics, in corresponding with provincial friends and
in transcribing letters from believers in distant places (Ireland,
Wales, North America). The songs, until the 1790s, were copied
by each believer – according to his or her own selection – into a
private song-book, and it was clearly a devout ambition of each
believer to add an acceptable song to the common stock.[88] Sick,
needy and aged believers were, from time to time, on an *ad hoc*

prayer, see also G.C. Williamson, *Ludowick Muggleton*, p. 30; Alexander Gordon, *Ancient and Modern Muggletonians* (Liverpool, 1870), p. 44.

[85] Early eighteenth-century MS verses, 'Elegy on Tomkinson's death, addressed to William Hall', in Muggletonian archive.

[86] John Wright to 'Loving Brother', complaining of Edward Fever's behaviour, MS, n.d. (*c*.1760), in *ibid*.

[87] 'I have been told by an ancient Believer who now sleeps that had it from one that lived in the prophet's day that it was common for the Believers to dispute one with another in the prophet's presence, and he would sit and hear them. . .': MS letter, Hudson to Mr Collier, n.d. (but *c*.1779), in *ibid*.

[88] A collection was made in 1711 called 'A Divine Garland of Spiritual Songs and Verses for the Consolation of the Seed of Faith, written by the Believers of the Communion of the Spirit'. This remained in MS and was copied (sometimes with additions) by the faithful. The first printed collection of *Songs of Gratefull Praise* was in 1790(?), a much-enlarged *Divine Songs of the Muggletonians* was published in 1829. The MS Song Books are now in Brit. Lib. Add. MSS 60207–60230.

basis, supported by their fellows. Muggletonians were opposed to capital punishment, and, like the Quakers, they were supposed to refuse tithes and oaths, and they certainly refused the use of arms. Thomas Pickersgill wrote to a believer who worked in Chatham docks in 1803: 'My dear friend, I understand . . . that you are in greate trobles, for the power of the Nation Wants you to take up Arms againts the Common Enemy, these are great Trobles to a New born Saint. . .' No true believer could 'become a Slave to a Slave':

> On my own part I would live on one penny worth of bread per day, and drink at the clear stream, before I would use such cursed weapons as Swords & Guns, cannot you git you living no where but at Chatham. . .[89]

In response to this moment of crisis a petition was drafted to the authorities: 'we being a peculiar people redeem'd by the Lord Jesus Christ our consciences are too tender to make use of the sword of steel to slay the Image of God with'.[90] 'If you Avenge you Murder the Divine Image', wrote Blake (E792):

> The Soldier armed with Sword & Gun
> Palsied strikes the Summers Sun. . .
>
> Nought can deform the Human Race
> Like to the Armours iron brace.   (E483)

I like these Muggletonians, but it is clear that they were not among history's winners. Nor did they wish to be. It was their business to preserve and to hand down the divine vision. By the mid-eighteenth century we can see that they were a recondite sect, whose beliefs appeared to outsiders as impenetrable and esoteric (if not obscene and blasphemous), whose closet and chest of manuscripts enclosed the sleeping energies of a half-forgotten spiritual and political vocabulary, and who were highly intellectual disciples of an anti-intellectual doctrine. Here at least we have identified one possible vector of seventeenth-century traditions, both Ranting and Behmenist, whose faith holds in suspension certain key ideas and critical images which should arrest the attention of the reader of William Blake.

I have been engaged, throughout the first part of this book, in an

---

[89] Pickersgill to Tregono, 1 December 1803, Muggletonian archive.
[90] In Muggletonian archive.

exceedingly difficult argument, and I am not wholly sure myself what this argument adduces. I have directed attention to the anti-nomian tradition, and have suggested a number of sources germane to Blake's thought. I have suggested more: that the Muggletonian Church preserved a vocabulary of symbolism, a whole cluster of signs and images, which recur – but in a new form and organis-ation, and in association with others – in Blake's poetry and paint-ing. I will go further: of all the traditions touched upon, I know of none which consistently transmits so large a cluster of Blakean symbols.

This is a difficult and contestable point, and I shudder at the thought of the learning that would be required to establish it. What other sects were there, about which we know nothing and about which nothing will ever come to light? But I must argue that I have been directing attention not just to discrete symbols or tenets but to certain elements critical to the *structure* of Blake's thought and art. I will single out four such elements.

First, there is the specifically antinomian tradition, with its repu-diation of the Moral Law. This will have been apparent through-out. The tenets of Reeve and Muggleton were close to those of Milton's Michael ('law can discover sin, but not remove'), with the additional predestinarian severity of the doctrine of the Two Seeds. The moral law is inscribed in human nature to enlighten and restrain corrupted Reason;[91] its origin was in the Fall (although Moses was the first explicitly to propound its prohibitions) and it entered in through the Serpent-Angel's 'Nature of Reason' and 'so by Generation the Law comes to be written in every Man's Heart'; 'man finds it there accusing of him, but knows not how it came written there'.[92] As such the Law has a certain serviceability, in constraining those – including magistrates and temporal powers – whose corrupted Reason would otherwise be under no restraint. It may even, on occasion, protect the saints from their persecutors. But 'though the law may sometimes hinder a sin, yet it can never root out sin . . . It changeth not the heart'.[93] Christ came to fulfil the law, with his blood displacing it with the gospel of love: 'the

---

[91] See *A Stream from the Tree of Life* (1758), p. 71; Muggleton, *A True Interpretation of the Eleventh Chapter of the Revelation of St John* (1753 edn), p. 100.

[92] Reeve and Muggleton, *Acts of the Witnesses* (1764 edn), p. 124; also Muggleton, *A Letter sent to Thomas Taylor, Quaker* (1756 edn), p. 96.

[93] Tomkinson, *Truth's Triumph*, p. 294.

law was given by Moses, and grace and truth by Jesus Christ'.[94]
'The moral law was written in the nature of reason, and so had
death written in it'; by 'fulfilling' the law Christ liberated the elect
from eternal damnation.[95] Believers 'are not under the law, but
under grace', and they are 'freed from the law of sin and death':

The law is not written in the seed of faith's nature at all, but in the seed
of reason's nature only. Therefore the seed of faith is not under the law,
but is above the law. . .[96]

Whosoever hath the divine light of faith in him, that man hath no need
of man's law to be his rule, but he is a law unto himself, and lives above
all laws of mortal men, and yet is obedient to all laws.[97]

Hence we are placed within the characteristic set of antinomian
oppositions. The Law is warlike and punitive, the Gospel is merciful and pacific.[98] Law and Gospel are sometimes seen as direct
contraries. The Moral Law was promulgated by Moses. 'I declare',
wrote Reeve, 'that the Law of Moses, both moral and ceremonial
. . . did belong to the Jews only.' The gospel of Jesus made 'all
Observations of the Law of Moses . . . of no Use for ever'.[99] (Blake
held that 'the laws of the Jews were (both ceremonial & real) the
basest & most oppressive of human codes' (above, p. 61).) Envy
is the leading principle of the Law (or Reason); Love the leading
principle of the Gospel – sometimes referred to among believers as
the 'everlasting gospel'.[100]

Love lieth down at Envy's Feet to be killed of him, and slayeth Envy by
its Patience and Meekness. . .

Love is generous, and pitiful; but Envy is covetous and cruel. . .[101]

The Two Seeds are impelled either by 'pure burning love' or 'a
fiery law of unbelieving burning envy'.[102] The first are in bondage,
the second in freedom: 'We who are believers are both free-born,
and free by redemption':[103]

---

[94] *A True Interpretation*, p. 11; also *A Stream*, p. 71.
[95] *Ibid.*, p. 108.   [96] *Ibid.*, p. 10.
[97] Tomkinson, p. 288.   [98] *A True Interpretation*, p. 228.
[99] Reeve, *Sacred Remains* (n.d., but 1706), p. 74.
[100] See, e.g., *Sacred Remains* (1706), p. 78.
[101] Reeve and Muggleton, *Joyful News from Heaven* (1658), pp. 37–8.
[102] Tomkinson, *Truth's Triumph*, p. 284.
[103] Saddington, *The Articles of True Faith*, p. 54.

The law of Moses and gospel of Jesus are contrary . . . The law and sin are a cross couple, and a sad society, in that they gender to bondage, whilst faith in the free-woman genders to peace.[104]

Finally, and in the vocabulary of Christian radicalism, the Law belongs to the priests and potentates of the earth, the Gospel to believers without temporal ambitions. 'The dragon, beast, and false prophet, they by their council, power, and authority, did invite all the kings of the earth . . . to fight against the Lord Jesus, and the remnant of the seed of faith, who are the saints. . .'[105] Against these powers the faithful may employ only spiritual weapons: in a song of Thomas Tomkinson:

> Love is the fiery chariot sent from on high,
> Love mounts the saints into eternal joy,
> Love being such as I've described to be,
> Love I will love, and love, do thou love me.[106]

Against this image of the 'chariot of fire' is counterposed the image of the Law as a 'flaming sword'. 'Those cherubims which had the flaming sword which turned every way, to keep the way of the Tree of Life' Muggleton declared to be of the same nature as the Serpent, 'which had the same law of reason written in their seed'. 'And this flaming sword . . . was that very law of reason which . . . is called the moral law, or the law of Moses.'[107]

> When Satan first the black bow bent
> And the Moral Law from the Gospel rent
> He forgd the Law into a Sword
> And spilld the blood of mercys Lord.   (E200)

> I stood among my valleys of the south
> And saw a flame of fire, even as a Wheel
> Of fire surrounding all the heavens: it went
> From west to east, against the current of
> Creation, and devour'd all things in its loud
> Fury & thundering course round heaven & earth. . .

[104] Tomkinson, p. 289.
[105] *A True Interpretation*, p. 236.
[106] *Divine Songs of the Muggletonians*, p. 373.
[107] *A True Interpretation*, p. 56. The authority for this in Genesis 3, v.24: 'So he drove out the man; and he placed at the east of the garden of Eden Cherubims, and a flaming sword which turned every way, to keep the way of the Tree of Life.'

> And I asked a Watcher & a Holy-One
> Its Name; he answered: 'It is the Wheel of Religion.'
> I wept & said: 'Is this the law of Jesus,
> 'This terrible devouring sword turning every way
> He answer'd: 'Jesus died because he strove
> 'Against the current of this Wheel; its Name
> 'Is Caiaphas, the dark Preacher of Death,
> 'Of sin, of sorrow & of punishment:
> 'Opposing Nature! It is Natural Religion;
> 'But Jesus is the bright Preacher of Life
> 'Creating Nature from this fiery Law
> 'By self-denial & forgiveness of Sin. . .'   (E230)

As soon as we attend to such passages of Blake, we must see that he is writing directly in this antinomian tradition, but also that he is employing its terms in original and idiosyncratic ways not sanctioned by any part of that tradition. The suggestion of a Muggletonian derivation for Blake's vocabulary becomes more persuasive if we attend to a second element in these doctrines, the explicit and repetitive identification of 'Reason' as the Satanic principle, the fruit of the Tree of the Knowledge of Good and Evil.

No theme recurs more in Muggletonian discourse. The angels only are creatures of pure reason. Reason entered the human race through the Fall and the seduction of Eve, and temporal reason is always 'unclean' and 'corrupted'. Reason is 'the right devil',

That devil . . . that tempts men and women to all unrighteousness, it is man's spirit of unclean reason and cursed imagination.[108]

'It was the Spirit of Reason in Man that always blasphemed and fought against God, and persecuted and killed the Just and the Righteous, because God would not accept of the Devil Reason's Worship', wrote Muggleton, who had had some persecution from reasonable magistrates himself. And, by way of illustration, he discussed Pilate's 'reasons' for condemning Christ:

His Reason was, he thought better to keep the Favour of *Caesar*, and the Honour of this World, than the Peace of his Conscience and Favour with God; so his Reason and their Reason together delivered up the Just One to be crucified by reasonable Men; for the Centurion, and those that guarded him, were reasonable Men also. . .[109]

---

[108] See James Hyde, The Muggletonians.
[109] *A Looking-Glass for George Fox* (1756), pp. 62–3.

'Christ & his Apostles were Illiterate Men', wrote Blake: 'Caiaphas Pilate & Herod were Learned' (E657). 'Rational Truth is not the Truth of Christ, but of Pilate. It is the Tree of the Knowledge of Good & Evil' (E610).

If anything, the theme of Reason, the 'right devil', became more prominent in Muggletonian doctrine among believers in the eighteenth and nineteenth centuries, as they found their faith threatened on every side by rationalism. The reason got a remarkably bad press in their songs of the mid-eighteenth century. In one (by George Hermitage):

> Darkness long kept me fast bound,
> Sin and death my soul did wound,
> Reason's chains made me to groan;
> Freedom, freedom then unknown.[110]

In another (by William Miller), on the fate of the reprobate after the Last Judgement–

> Reason will here with reason lie,
> Howling to all eternity;
> A burning sand their bed will be,
> And dying, live eternally.[111]

Few themes recur with more consistency in the whole trajectory of Blake's work than Reason (often in association with the moral law) binding, constraining or corrupting life. It is suggested even in that fragment of juvenilia, 'Then She bore Pale desire' ('Reason once fairer than the light till foul in Knowledges dark Prison house' (E438)), and it is found still in those late works, 'The Gates of Paradise' ('Serpent Reasonings . . . of Good & Evil' (E265)) and the Laocoon inscriptions – where, however, Reason has become synonymous with the reasons of materialism: 'Money, which is the great Satan or Reason the Root of Good & Evil in the Accusation of Sin' (E272). Between these two points the values which Blake attributes to Reason change a good deal – Reason is the 'ratio of all we have already known' or 'the bound or outward circumference of energy' (E34) but with Urizen the repressive symbolism is enforced. In *Milton* and *Jerusalem* the 'spectre' is 'the reasoning power in every man', at enmity with poetry and imagination. Blake's note on 'A Vision of The Last Judgment' commences:

---

[110] *Divine Songs of the Muggletonians*, p. 18.   [111] *Ibid.*, p. 203.

The Last Judgment when all those are Cast away who trouble Religion with Questions concerning Good & Evil or Eating of the Tree of those Knowledges or Reasonings which hinder the Vision of God. . . (E544)

'Angels are happier than Men . . . because they are not always Prying after Good & Evil in one Another & eating the Tree of Knowledge for Satans Gratification' (E555).

These first two elements may be found in other sources than Muggletonianism, although the specific identification of Reason (rather than Pride or Lust or Disobedience) with the Serpent seems to me to be rare.[112] But when we put these together with two other elements, then the hypothesis of some Muggletonian influence upon Blake becomes persuasive. The third element is to be found in the unusual symbolism of the Fall, and of the Serpent-Angel's actual copulation with Eve and transmutation into flesh and blood in her womb.

Serpent-symbolism, of course, has a central place in Blake's work: it is even more prominent in his visual art than in his poetry. I will argue that it can be found in his poetry as early as in *An Island in the Moon* (1784), in a song which is given to the Cynic:

> When old corruption first begun
> Adornd in yellow vest
> He committed on flesh a whoredom
> O what a wicked beast
>
> From them a callow babe did spring
> And old corruption smild
> To think his race should never end
> For now he had a child. . .   (E445)

If we take 'old corruption' as the Serpent-Angel appearing as an 'angel of light' ('Adorned in yellow vest') and the whoredom committed on flesh as his copulation with Eve, then this is Muggletonian symbolic machinery, and, in the race that 'should never end' we have Cain and the Two Seeds. This imagery is manifestly present in 'I saw a chapel all of gold'

> I saw a serpent rise between
> The white pillars of the door
> And he forcd & forcd & forcd
> Down the golden hinges tore

---

[112] However, it is found in William Law: '*Reasoners* are of the Seed of the Serpent . . . to live by Reason is to be a prey of the old serpent, eating dust with him, grovelling in the mire of all earthly passions. . .': *A Short but Sufficient Confutation of the Reverend Doctor Warburton* (1757), p. 66.

It is there in *America* (1793) where Orc:

> anon a serpent folding
> Around the pillars of Urthona, and round thy dark limbs
> On the Canadian wilds I fold. . .

> I see a serpent in Canada, who courts me to his love. (E50–1)

It returns again in the *Book of Urizen* (1794), 'When Enitharmon, sick, Felt a Worm within her womb:

> All day the worm lay on her bosom
> All night within her womb
> The worm lay till it grew to a serpent
> With dolourous hissings & poisons
> Round Enitharmon's loins folding. . .

(The child was named Orc.) It continues in the convoluted couplings of serpents and females in the prophetic books; and it takes a new and powerful form (both visually and in verse) in the image of the 'mortal coil' – a literal serpent coil – which Christ sheds on the cross, shedding thus one of his two natures.

One or another form of this symbolism repeatedly recurs in his graphic art and painting. It is found in 'The Temptation of Eve' (1799–1800) (Illus. 1). David Bindman has written:

Eve's position within the coil of the serpent is apparently unprecedented in European art and although her hand reaches upward it is not towards the apple in the mouth of the serpent; she appears to be preening herself at the serpent's flattery, and the sexual overtones are confirmed by her open nakedness and her failure to make the gesture of modesty associating the fatal act with the sense of shame. . .[113]

It is true, as Bindman points out, that Blake had Milton's authority for the gorgeous presence of the upright serpent:

>   And towards Eve
> Address'd his way, not with indented wave
> Prone on the ground, as since, but on his rear,
> Circular base of rising foulds, that tour'd
> Fould above fould a surging maze, his Head
> Crested aloft, and Carbuncle his eyes;
> With burnished Neck of verdant Gold, erect
> Amidst his circling spires, that on the grass
> Floted redundant. . .

But Milton's serpent then conducts Eve, with many wily speeches, to another part of the Garden where the Tree is found. He neither

[113] Bindman, *Blake as an Artist*, p. 119.

seduces her nor himself offers her the apple. Bindman also suggests as 'unprecedented' the presence of the sleeping Adam with his spade on the ground behind Eve. But this also finds authority in Muggletonian doctrine, where, we recall, the Serpent could seduce Eve only because Faith was asleep (above, p. 80). Blake's Serpent is emphatically a Muggletonian 'Angel of Light' accomplishing a material seduction. To complicate matters further, a Muggletonian influence may have been felt upon Milton, just as the Miltonic influence is felt upon young Blake, whose 'old corruption' was 'adorned in yellow vest' after Milton's serpent 'with burnished Neck of verdant Gold'. Phallic symbol the serpent may be, and manifestly is, but we cannot avoid the additional Muggletonian identification.

I am talking about symbolic machinery, or vocabulary, not the realised effects. Even in the Cynic's song in *An Island*, Blake appropriates the vocabulary to a new purpose, passing on into a ludicrous polemic against 'Surgery'. The Serpent becomes an image of the material body, as later it sometimes becomes a symbol of Nature: 'the vast form of Nature, like a Serpent, roll'd between'. As machinery, however, the serpent often appears as ravishing the female, as in 'the chapel all of gold' (p. 171), or as giving rise to a monstrous conception, as in the *Book of Urizen*.

Eve is shown even more explicitly within the coital embrace of the serpent in 'Satan Exulting over Eve' (Illus. 2) as also in 'The Temptation and Fall of Eve' in the *Paradise Lost* series (Illus. 3), where the apple is transferred from mouth to mouth. In the extraordinary illustration to Job, 'Job's Evil Dreams', a Satanic God with cloven hoof points to the Mosaic Tables of the Law: once again he is entwined with a serpent (Illus. 4). The Satanic characters and mythical malevolent beasts in Blake's paintings nearly always have reptilian scales, most thickly around the genitals. The striking painting of 'Moses Erecting the Brazen Serpent' (Illus. 5) may carry a somewhat different symbolism: Blake was no admirer of Moses and one suspects that he was not following biblical authority (Numbers xxi, 6–9) but was taking the serpent as a symbol of the Moral Law. And Blake was delighted to borrow, probably from Stukeley, the image of organised religion as a 'serpent temple'.[114]

[114] W. Stukeley's *Stonehenge, a Temple Restored to the British Druids* (1740) and *Abury, a Temple of the British Druids* (1743) clearly had a strong influence upon Blake: see Jon Mee, *Dangerous Enthusiasm*, chapter 2: also Raine, *Blake and Tradition*, Vol. II, pp. 236–7.

But one cannot proclaim that Blake's symbols stand for one thing or for two things only. They are constantly shifting in emphasis and sometimes seem to 'mean' whatever Blake wishes at the time. Even the confident S. Foster Damon in his *Blake Dictionary* offers for serpent 'a number of overlapping meanings'. One is Hypocrisy, especially in priestly form. 'The Serpent also symbolizes the worship of Nature', as it is found on the title page of *Europe* (Illus. 6).[115] Further, the serpent may represent Nature herself: 'its coils represent its dull rounds and repetitions'.[116] One would not refuse any of these meanings, and other critics have other emphases. John Beer finds the serpent to be a symbol both of energy and of selfhood.[117] Morton Paley finds that it represents the 'energies of nature . . . and cyclical recurrence'.[118] Other uses suggest that the serpent may sometimes be Reason.[119] To complicate matters further serpent-entwined gods may be found in the iconography of Zoroastrianism and Mithraism, although it cannot be shown that Blake knew this.[120]

If we wish to examine the meaning with which Blake invests these symbols, then we cannot do it with a scatter-shot of examples: each examination must return to the context of the poems or paintings. The serpent may indeed sometimes symbolise the imprisoning selfhood, or may appear, as critics of the neo-Platonic persuasion have argued, as a symbol of constraining matter or Nature. In the famous print, 'Elohim Creating Adam' (Illus. 7) the material imprisonment of Creation is suggested by the giant worm or serpent coiled around Adam's leg. It must follow that Christ's sacrifice on the Cross expels this serpent-nature; in shuffling off the 'mortal coil' Christ resumes a spiritual uncorrupted body and

---

[115] David Erdman notes also that this serpent embodies 'energy, desire, phallic power, the fiery tongue': *The Illuminated Blake* (Oxford, 1975), p. 157.

[116] S. Foster Damon, *A Blake Dictionary* (1973 edn), pp. 365–6.

[117] John Beer, *Blake's Humanism* (Manchester, 1968), *passim*, and the same author in *Blake Newsletter*, Vol. 4, no. 4, Spring 1971, p. 145. Northrop Frye first emphasised that 'the serpent with its tail in its mouth is the perfect emblem of the Selfhood', but his analysis is confusing: *Fearful Symmetry* (Princeton, 1947), chapter 5.

[118] Morton D. Paley, *The Continuing City: William Blake's Jerusalem* (Oxford, 1983), p. 109. Blake himself claims the serpent as shut up in 'image of infinite/finite revolutions. . .'

[119] In different sketches for the title page of *Europe* Blake appears to associate the serpent, who fathers Orc upon Enitharmon, with the rational principle (emerging from the neck of Los) or with Moses–Urizen, riding upon the serpent's head and holding the tablets of the Moral Law: see Martin Butlin, *William Blake* (Tate Gallery, 1978), p. 54, figs. 70, 71: Erdman, *The Illuminated Blake*, p. 396.

[120] Mary Jackson, 'Blake and Zoroastrianism', *Blake: an Illustrated Quarterly*, Vol. II, no. 2, 1977.

promises the same to the faithful. This is forcefully expressed in
'Michael Foretelling the Crucifixion' (Illus. 8), with the serpent's
head nailed to the Cross beneath Christ's feet. For this there is
authority also in *Paradise Lost* (Book XII), Christ's sacrifice in the
same moment removing the Law and redeeming man's sin:

> But to the Cross he nailes thy Enemies,
> The Law that is against thee, and the sins
> Of all mankinde, with him there crucifi'd,
> Never to hurt them more who rightly trust
> In this his satisfaction. . .

The image was familiar in the antinomian tradition (see above,
p. 11) and is found in at least one (somewhat less memorable)
Muggletonian song:

> The writings which against me stood,
>   It was God's law, I see;
> But God has shed his precious blood,
>   And slew the law in me;
> I see it nail'd upon a cross
>   When Christ was crucified;
> And now my soul is at no loss,
>   For God for me has died.[121]

Blake handled the same theme in verse with his usual robust
assertiveness:

> And thus with wrath he did subdue
> The Serpent Bulk of Natures dross
> Till he had naild it to the Cross
> He took on Sin in the Virgins Womb
> And put it off on the Cross & Tomb
> To be Worshiped by the Church of Rome   (E515)

Once again, the congruence in symbolic vocabulary and in antinomian tenets falls short of any proof of Muggletonian influence.
The myth of the Serpent, Samael, who had relations with Eve, from
which Cain was the offspring, can be found also in Kabbalistic
writings.[122] (But I do not think that these also carry the image of

---

[121] *Divine Songs of the Muggletonians*, p. 213.
[122] See A.E. Waite, *The Holy Kabbalah* (1902; 1965), p. 286. The Muggletonians had some
notion of these traditions: Tomkinson refers to 'the Hebrew doctors' and specifically to
'Menacham, a Jewish Rabbi' for the confirmation that the seed of the Serpent was
conveyed to Eve: *The Muggletonian Principles Prevailing* (1695; 1822), p. 45. A problem in
identifying Kabbalistic, like Gnostic, sources is that they may pass through so many

the serpent-nature entering thereafter into the human race).[123] In any case, it seems to me unreasonable to suppose that Blake would have taken so vivid and persuasive a symbolic cluster from seventeenth-century hermetic sources rather than from a sect whose members were his contemporaries in London, and whose publications were also contemporaneous. And the case for some Muggletonian influence becomes even stronger when we bring these three elements together with a fourth, and final, one: the unique image of God incarnated as Jesus Christ, and having no other existence save as Christ. This theme is as important as any which we have examined. But, when considered in relation to Blake, it cannot be discussed except in conjunction with the Swedenborgian notion of the 'divine image'. And since this must involve us in a change of symbolic machinery and a whole new *dramatis personæ* I will leave it to Part II.

It is time that I was a little more plain with my readers. Where is my argument tending? And, equally, where is it *not?*

First, I am not suggesting that we can reduce any part of Blake's art to the exposition of Muggletonian doctrine. (There are, in any case, parts of that doctrine, such as the rigid predestinarian notion of the Two Seeds, which he would have found to be abhorrent.) I am suggesting that he could have been situated in some way in relation to this tradition, which made available to him certain antinomian tenets and a remarkable and coherent cluster of symbols, which he then employed (along with others) much as a painter sets the paints on his palette to work. What he did with these symbols is another question again, but I find it helpful to identify the source of the pigments.

Second, I have been emphasising that this 'vocabulary' was readily available, in the publications and discourse of believers in Blake's London. We first encounter William Blake in a precise religious context as a signatory to a document of the Swedenborg-

---

intermediaries, pre-eminent among them Jacob Boehme: see Désirée Hirst, *Hidden Riches, passim.* Sheila Spector in 'Kabbalistic Sources – Blake's and his Critics'', *Blake: an Illustrated Quarterly,* Vol. 17, no. 3, Winter 1983–4, shows what (very imperfect) accounts of Kabbala could possibly have been available to Blake, but there is no evidence that he used these.

[123] The language of the Two Seeds was employed by Boehme and by George Fox (R. M. Jones, *Spiritual Reformers in the 16th and 17th Centuries* (1914), pp. 225–6) and also more widely: see Christopher Hill, *The English Bible and the Seventeenth-Century Revolution* (1993), pp. 239–42.

ian New Jerusalem Church in 1789. We will examine this context
in the next part. But it is relevant to note now that the similarity
of certain Muggletonian and Swedenborgian tenets was remarked
upon by observers at the time.[124] It would have been strange if
there had been no exchanges between the two groups of believers,
even if these had ended in mutual repudiation.[125] And that at least
one or two members of that early New Jerusalem milieu were
versed in Muggletonian sources is confirmed by the re-printing in a
Swedenborgian magazine of 1790 of some of Thomas Tomkinson's
writing (see below, p. 160).

Third, I am not suggesting that William Blake was a member
of the Muggletonian Church. I did play half-heartedly with the
notion for some years. But I can now announce, as my only definit-
ive finding, that at any time after 1780 he was not, for I have
examined the Church's records which are comprehensive enough
after this date to warrant confidence. Nor have I identified any
known friend of Blake's. Nor have I even identified any persons
who by neighbourhood, occupation or common interests might
seem to be likely acquaintances of Blake. Nor does it seem anything
but improbable that Blake would have rubbed shoulders with the
London believers who, at the end of the 1780s, an observer wrote
off (prematurely) as 'a set of jolly fellows, who drink their pot
and smoak their tobacco', meeting on Sunday evenings 'at obscure
public-houses in the out-parts of London, and converse about those
of their sect who have gone before them'.[126] We would expect to
find Blake, in the late 1770s or 1780s, in the more sophisticated
ambience suggested by *An Island in the Moon*, or in the polite proto-

---

[124] See W.H. Reid, *The Rise and Dissolution of the Infidel Societies in the Metropolis* (1800), p. 53:
'The principal article of this self-called *New* church . . . is just as *Old* as Muggleton and
Reeves; who, after the protectorship of Oliver, were the first who published, that the
whole godhead is circumscribed in the person of Jesus Christ, still retaining the human
form in heaven. . .'

[125] The Muggletonians formed an obsessively close and hostile relation with Swedenborgians, who replaced the Quakers as the prime object of their comminations, perhaps
because of a supposed identity in their doctrine that Christ is God. In 1845 a Mr
Robinson of Camberwell, writing to a believer in New York, described the Swedenborgians as 'one of the worst Spirits in opposition to Truth': 'they say that Christ was the
Almighty God, yet they deny his being the whole and alone God'. Copy of letter in
Muggletonian archive. See also Gordon, *Ancient and Modern Muggletonians*, p. 60.

[126] Hurd, *New Universal History*, pp. 669–71. Hurd was probably not going on much more
than gossip. He alleged that the Muggletonians had 'a very pernicious effect on the
morals of the people. It has induced many of them to become Deists and practical
Atheists.'

Swedenborgian meetings held by the Reverend Jacob Duche in Lambeth.[127] We can say with some confidence that Blake at this time was an adherent of no 'sect'; his annotations show a repugnance to 'sectaries', although a sympathy with 'poor enthusiasts'.

But, even so, this does not quite conclude the matter. For the interesting question may be, not what faith Blake subsequently adopted, but in what faith he was brought up as a child. The enquiry must then be extended backwards to the 1740s to 1760s, when Blake's parents were young and were establishing their household. The suggestion that 'Blake does not belong by birth to the established church, but to a dissenting sect' – although firmer than any of the numerous subsequent hypotheses – gives us too little to go on.[128] More interesting, perhaps, is Gilchrist's information that William's matter-of-fact elder brother, James (a hosier like their father), 'had his spiritual and visionary side too; would at times *talk Swedenborg*, talking of seeing Abraham and Moses' and to outsiders seemed, like his brother, to be 'a bit mad'.[129] This is confusing – not many Swedenborgians in London had visions of 'Abraham and Moses' – and to an outsider any strange symbolic vocabulary might have been put down to 'talking Swedenborg'. What it does suggest is that both brothers shared an inherited familial vocabulary which was arcane.

Much would become clear to us if William Blake had been born into a Muggletonian family. The Church was vigorous in the mid-century, winning new converts, actively publishing the prophets' works and writing many new songs. There was also a smaller group of believers, in a 'Church of Christ' known as Reevites or Reevonians. These appear to have followed the more radical and also less aggressive and less bullying writings of John Reeve, disavowing several of Muggleton's absurdities, and at the same time avowing their ability to converse with angels and have visions of the dead (a faculty which Muggleton repudiated).[130] But next to nothing is known of the Reevonians and I doubt whether anything ever will be known. As for the orthodox Muggletonian Church, no member-

[127] Erdman, *William Blake: Prophet against Empire*, p. 12, note 19; J.F.C. Harrison, *The Second Coming*, p. 72.
[128] Bentley, *William Blake*, p. 452, translating Crabb Robinson's essay in the *Vaterländisches Museum*, 1811.
[129] Alexander Gilchrist, *Life of William Blake* (1863; 1942), p. 48.
[130] See Lamont, 'Ludowick Muggleton and "Immediate Notice"'.

ship records survive for those decades, and among the surviving correspondents and song-writers no name of any Blake appears.

There does, however, appear the name of George Hermitage, two of whose songs – which are better than the usual run – turn up in the Muggletonian *Divine Songs* and in several manuscript song-books compiled around the mid-century. From several evidences – stylistic, the air to which one song was set – one may confidently assume that George Hermitage was writing songs for believers *circa* 1750.[131] And, back-tracking from this, I have found that William Blake's mother, who had been previously known as Catherine Harmitage should more properly be known as Hermitage. She was almost certainly the widow of Thomas Hermitage, hosier, of 28 Broad Street. Soon after her first husband's death she married James Blake, also a hosier, of Glasshouse Street, uniting the two businesses at her own address. Hermitage is not a common name (nor is Harmitage), but other Hermitages can be found in the registers of the same parish of St James's, Westminster, one of whom, named George, appears in 1742 as father to a baby. So we can at least establish that there was a George Hermitage, of an age to be Catherine's brother-in-law or other kin, living in the same Westminster parish. We cannot show that he was the same George who wrote Muggletonian songs, although the dates fit well enough. The evidence for all this is set out at more length in Appendix 2.

If Catherine Hermitage had Muggletonian kin – if she came herself from a Muggletonian family – then this would explain very satisfactorily the derivation of William Blake's antinomian vocabulary. If George the songwriter was kin to Thomas, then this is plausible, for, like all sectaries, Muggletonians were by preference endogamous – and Catherine, in choosing a second husband, might have looked for someone sympathetic to her faith as well as to a convenient business alliance. By one account, Blake composed some of his earliest illuminated songs to be hung up in his mother's chamber.[132] And in the same place, this whole vocabulary of signs, the robust antinomian beliefs, and the tradition of writing 'divine songs', could have entered his formative mind.

---

[131] Hermitage's songs were copied in several eighteenth-century song books (Muggletonian archive). 'Praises to my Maker's glory' was to the air 'Stella, darling of the Muses' (Mrs Pilkington).

[132] Bentley, p. 481.

We could suppose that William Blake in his childhood was made familiar with the structure of antinomian thought and the central images of *Genesis* and *Revelation* in a Muggletonian notation; that he turned sharply away from this in his 'teens, rejecting the know-all dogmatism of the sect, and its philistinism towards all the arts (except divine songs); read widely and entered the artistic world without restraint; took stock of works of the Enlightenment; was led back towards his origins by reading Boehme and Swedenborg; and then, in his early thirties (the years of the *Songs* and the *Marriage of Heaven and Hell*) composed a symbolic world for himself in which the robust tradition of artisan and tradesman antinomianism reasserted itself, not as literal doctrines, but as a fund of imaginative possibilities and as intellectual footholds for an anti-Enlightenment stance.

This is not a large 'finding'. We are not likely to find more, since if Blake's family *had* been Muggletonian, they would have kept this to themselves and made no open testimony. I will leave it with four verses from one of George Hermitage's songs:

> When I saw the Serpent's head
> In man bruised, my sorrows fled;
> CHRIST's ascension from the grave,
> Freedom, freedom, to me gave. . .
>
> Tell me not what reason saith;
> Reason has not light of faith;
> Reason doom'd to endless woe,
> Freedom, freedom cannot know.
>
> Though he long has claim'd the field,
> The last fight shall make him yield;
> Adam's sons shall then regain
> Freedom, freedom, lost through Cain. . .
>
> Brethren, now come join with me
> In praises for your liberty,
> Till we chaunt in heavenly bowers,
> Freedom, freedom, freedom's ours.[133]

It is at least a pleasant fiction to think of Blake's mother crooning that song to baby William on her lap.

[133] *Divine Songs of the Muggletonians*, p. 19.

CHAPTER 7

Anti-hegemony

This has been a long, and perhaps strange, way into William Blake. On one matter I am impenitent. Blake can't have dreamed up a whole vocabulary of symbolism, which touches at so many points the traditions which I have discussed, for himself *ab novo*. Nor can he have put it together like mosaic from his reading. Things don't happen like that. Nor can it have arisen just from a reading of the Bible, for this presupposes the Bible, and particular passages of *Genesis*, read *in a particular way*. The author of the Prefaces to *Jerusalem* and the 'Annotations to Watson', of *The Marriage of Heaven and Hell* and *The Everlasting Gospel*, was writing within a known tradition, using terms made familiar by seven or eight generations of London sectaries.

Certainly my argument does not stand or fall upon the Muggletonian hypothesis. What this does is to give the argument concretion and indicate one possible actual context. Whether or not Blake's family, or any of them, came from this particular church is not the critical question. There were other sects and other milieux, whose records may be irrecoverable. Coppinists and 'Sweet Singers of Israel' perhaps had meetings and discourses over doctrine of a similar kind, at least until the 1740s or 1750s. The astonishing survival of these Muggletonian records shows at least that such kinds of people were about, that their faith was strong and that the seventeenth-century antinomian traditions ran strongly through to Blake's time. He must have come from some such familial context.

By 1750 or 1760 it is probable that most of the petty sects reported as existing in 1706 no longer survived in their old forms. But the vocabulary survived, and it was continually in search of new vehicles for its expression. The sects had never been hermetically sealed against each other; part of the intellectual excitement of sectarianism (then, as now) had been found in the factional

106

1 *Eve Tempted by the Serpent.* Tempera, painted for Thomas Butts, *c.*1799–1800.

2   *Satan Exulting over Eve.* Pencil, pen and black ink and watercolour over colour print, 1795.

3   *The Temptation and Fall of Eve*, from Nine Illustrations to *Paradise Lost*. Pen
and watercolour on paper, 1808.

4 *Job's Evil Dreams*, Plate 11 of *Illustrations to the Book of Job*, 1821.

5 *Moses Erecting the Brazen Serpent*. Pen and watercolour on paper, *c*.1805.

6 Title page to *Europe*, 1794.

7 *Elohim Creating Adam.* Colour print finished in pen, from the Thomas Butts Collection, 1795.

8   *Michael Foretells the Crucifixion*, from Nine Illustrations to *Paradise Lost*. Pen and watercolour on paper, 1808.

9   *The Nativity.* Tempera on copper, from the Thomas Butts Collection, *c.*1799.

10 'The Garden of Love', from *Songs of Experience*, 1794.

11 'London', from *Songs of Experience*, c.1794.

12 *The Number of the Beast is 666.* Pen and watercolour, painted for Thomas Butts,
*c.*1805.

13 *The Whore of Babylon*. Pen and watercolour, painted for Thomas Butts, c.1809.

14 'A Poison Tree', from *Songs of Experience*, 1794.

15   *Malevolence*. Watercolour drawing, 1799.

16   Title page to *The Book of Urizen*, 1794.

17 *God Writing upon the Tables of the Covenant.* Pen and watercolour, painted for Thomas Butts, *c.*1805.

18   *The Blasphemer*. Pen and watercolour, painted for Thomas Butts, *c.*1800.

19   *The Woman Taken in Adultery*. Pen and watercolour over traces of pencil on paper, painted for Thomas Butts, 1805.

20   *The Great Red Dragon and the Beast from the Sea.* Pen and ink with watercolour over graphite, painted for Thomas Butts, *c.*1803.

disputes between sects, the open debates, the struggle to convert each other's disciples. An earnest seeker might sample different sects, and move on from one to another. Such seekers were still to be found at the end of the century, like the earnest artisans, John Wright and William Bryan, who, in 1789, walked all the way to Avignon in search of spiritual revelation.[1] And the same fierce intellectual disputes continued. When the Reverend Richard Clarke came to the city in 1788 and preached universal redemption, 'the sectaries were ready to tear him out of the Pulpit; and one person called out when preaching at the Temple Church, "This man preaches false doctrine."'[2] We will do best to think of a sectarian and antinomian gathering-ground in London, where heretical tracts were cherished, where sects suffered secessions and new hierarchs arose, where Behmenists disputed with Universalists, and where seekers shopped around among preachers and little churches. If James Blake, Senior, can be shown to have been, at some moment, a Baptist or a Moravian, or if Catherine Hermitage was at one time a Muggletonian, this does not go to prove that they remained in these churches always. It is more relevant that we should see them within this general gathering-ground, with its intellectual and sometimes passionate concern for heretical doctrine. And it was from this same gathering-ground that some of the first members of the Swedenborgian New Jerusalem Church were to be drawn.

By the end of the eighteenth century this tradition of plebeian and tradesman Dissent had drifted a great distance away from the polite and rational religious culture – a culture which, with its uneasy memories of the Commonwealth, still feared 'enthusiasts'. And the derisory judgements which the learned and the accomplished then made upon these enthusiasts still imposes itself upon us today. We see them only as eccentrics or as survivors. At a casual glance it seems self-evident that those who turned their backs upon rational (and historical) biblical criticism, and who even ignored or traduced all the advancing findings of the natural sciences (as did the Philadelphians, Hutchinsonians and Muggletonians), must have been locked into a religiose fantasy-

[1] J.F.C. Harrison, *The Second Coming*, pp. 69–72. A brisk account of this episode is in Robert Southey, *Letters from England* (1807), Vol. III, chapter LXVIII.

[2] Dr Williams's Library, Walton Papers, MS 1.1.43, Langcake to Henry Brooks, 1 August 1790.

world; they are quaint historical fossils. Donald Davie, who has cast a casual and partial eye upon the 'antinomian and heretical sects' which '*effectively* influenced Blake', has concluded that 'as specifically *religious* insights, their ideas are beneath contempt'. And he asks whether we may not have, in Blake, 'a case of an imaginative genius born into a stratum of religious experience too shallow to sustain him'.[3]

In my view, the reply which Davie predicates, in the manner in which he proposes the question, is profoundly wrong, and this book is offering a different answer. But Davie is still asking a necessary and significant question.

I cannot see how an answer can be provided, by one who is not a Christian, at the level of arguments as to the rationality of particular religious beliefs. How are we to say which view is 'shallow': the doctrine of the Virgin Birth or the Muggletonian doctrine of God's transmutation in Mary's womb into Christ?

It might be more helpful to consider, not individual doctrines but the degree to which different traditions were capable of sustaining, in the vocabulary of their doctrines, a disciplined and consistent pursuit of knowledge and an enquiry into value, even when subsequent ages have come to the view that much of this vocabulary was erroneous. Where most kinds of positive knowledge are concerned (scientific, historical) then the answer would seem to be flatly on Davie's side: the mystical and antinomian sects were not only shallow, they adopted a counter-Enlightenment stance which was obscurantist. But where social or political assumptions or enquiries into value are at issue, then the answer must be very much more complex.

The danger is that we should confuse the reputability of beliefs, and the reputability of those who professed them, with depth or shallowness. I have already suggested, in discussing justification by faith, that the antinomian position was consciously anti-hegemonic. That is, if we accept the view that in most societies we can observe an intellectual as well as institutional hegemony, or dominant discourse, which imposes a structure of ideas and beliefs – deep assumptions as to social proprieties and economic process and as to the legitimacy of relations of property and power, a general 'common sense' as to what is possible and what is not, a

---

[3] Donald Davie, *A Gathered Church* (1978), p. 52.

limited horizon of moral norms and practical probabilities beyond which all must be blasphemous, seditious, insane or apocalyptic fantasy – a structure which serves to consolidate the existent social order, enforce its priorities, and which is itself enforced by rewards and penalties, by notions of 'reputability', and (in Blake's time) by liberal patronage or by its absence – if we accept this large mouthful, then we can see that these antinomian sects were hegemony's eighteenth-century opposition.[4] More than this, antinomianism's intellectual doctrines (the suspicion of 'reason', justification by faith, hostility to the Moral Law) constituted in quietest periods a defence against the reigning hegemony, in more active periods a resource for an active critique not just of policies or personalities but of the deep assumptions of the social order.

And we can take this argument a little further. For what the antinomian or Muggletonian declaimed against as 'Reason' we might today prefer to define as 'Ideology', or as the compulsive constraints of the ruling 'discourse'. Antinomian doctrine was expressive of a profound distrust of the 'reasons' of the genteel and comfortable, and of ecclesiastical and academic institutions, not so much because they produced false knowledges but because they offered specious apologetics ('serpent reasonings') for a rotten social order based, in the last resort, on violence and material self-interest. In short, the antinomian stance was not against knowledge but against the ideological assumptions which pretended to be knowledge and the ideological contamination of the rest.

I am bringing into emphasis a *resource* of antinomianism, a *stance* towards the polite culture, whose strength is most evident in the confidence which it gave to Blake. But this emphasis also enables us to put into a single place a sociological and an intellectual analysis of this minority tradition. For in cultural or intellectual terms it is significant that antinomianism is an artisan or tradesman stance. Notations of class derived from the categories of an industrial society will always be anachronistic and misleading when brought to English eighteenth-century society. In between the basic polarity of the gentry and 'the industrious sort' or 'the labouring poor' there is an immense range of different social gradations and aspirations, but we are taken little further if we try to

---

[4] In my view John Barrell's persuasive argument as to the classical character of Blake's views of art and its function takes too little account of this anti-hegemonic stance: see *The Political Theory of Painting from Reynolds to Hazlitt* (Yale University Press, 1986), chapter 3.

categorise these as 'petit-bourgeois', or 'middle class'. For what may define the consciousness of these groups more clearly will be such factors as their degree of *dependency*; that is, their dependence on or independence of the lines of interest, influence, preferment and patronage which structured that society from top to bottom. In so far as some – but by no means all – tradesmen and artisans had a degree of occupational independence from interest and patronage somewhat greater than their more affluent neighbours who were petty clergy, tutors, clerks in public office, soldiers or sailors, attorneys and even (in some cases) journalists or artists, so it was possible for a more robust, anti-Court, and sometimes republican, consciousness to be nourished in this milieu.

And to this we must add a further cultural or intellectual definition of 'class'. Everything in the age of 'reason' and 'elegance' served to emphasise the sharp distinctions between a polite and a demotic culture. Dress, style, gesture, proprieties of speech, grammar and even punctuation were resonant with the signs of class; the polite culture was an elaborated code of social inclusion and exclusion.[5] Classical learning and an accomplishment in the law stood like difficult gates-of-entry into this culture: the grammarian must show his expertise in derivations and constructions, the politician a familiarity with the models of Rome, the poet and artist a fluency in classical mythology. These accomplishments both legitimated and masked the actualities of brute property and power, interest and patronage. A grammatical or mythological solecism marked an intruder down as an outsider.

Antinomianism, and in particular Muggletonianism, can be seen as an extreme recourse open to the excluded. It challenged the entire superstructure of learning and of moral and doctrinal teaching as ideology: the Reason of the Seed of the Serpent, now embodied in the temporal rulers of the earth. If we read this as a simple opposition between reason and unreason (or blind faith) then this is self-convicted irrationalism. But if we consider the *actual* assumptions of the 'Age of Reason' then the antinomian stance acquires a new force, even a rationality. For it struck very precisely at critical positions of the hegemonic culture, the 'common sense' of the ruling groups, which today can be seen to be intellectually unsound and sometimes to be no more than ideological apologetics.

---

[5] See Olivia Smith, *The Politics of Language 1791–1819* (Oxford, 1984).

In particular, the dominant mechanistic (environmentalist or associationist) psychology with its set of stepping-stones from self-interest to rational benevolence (whose evidence is useful works) is challenged by the antinomian doctrine of the unlawed impulses of faith and love. The increasingly remote and impersonal image of God, the Newtonian prime mover of 'Natural Religion', is challenged by the personal embodied image of God/Christ. The profoundly paternalist character of the dominant social thought and moral sensibility is curtly challenged by the antinomian vocabulary of the humble saints persecuted by the temporal powers. Above all, antinomianism offered a central challenge to the Moral Law in a society whose legitimating ideology was precisely that of Law. And when we recall that this same polite and rule-governed society multiplied new prohibitions and capital offences on every side, placing the altar of Tyburn at the centre of its institutions, can we decide so easily on which side 'reason' is to be found?

This may help us also to place Blake. Blake came, very firmly, from a background of London *tradesmen*. His father and mother were hosiers (although not, it seems, enrolled in the Guild), his wife was probably a tradesman's daughter, and the same social status was maintained throughout life by his younger brother, James, who was described by Gilchrist as 'an honest, unpretending shopkeeper in an old-world style'. Blake grew up in the strongest centre of tradesman and skilled artisan *independency* in the kingdom; both his father and his mother's first husband voted for the anti-Court candidate in the face of every resource of influence and courtly pressure in the dramatic election of 1749 (see Appendix 2); and we may at the least assume that an anti-Court propensity was implanted in him in childhood. When Erdman tells us that Blake's interest in the paintings of Mortimer, Barry and Fuseli 'had aligned him with the underdog in the art community' I suspect that he has placed the cart before the horse. Blake was already disposed to take their part because 'while Sr Joshua [Reynolds] was rolling in Riches' and while 'only Portrait Painting [was] applauded & rewarded by the Rich & Great' they were deprived of fame and patronage. Blake had been taught in childhood to place a critical distance between himself and the Rich and Great. And the distance was never closed. Annotating *The Works of Joshua Reynolds* he came upon a list of members of the Literary Club which included Reynolds, Dr Johnson, Edmund Burke, Sir John Hawkins, the Hon.

Topham Beauclerk and Dr Goldsmith, and he noted: 'Oliver Goldsmith never should have known such knaves' (E629). By the late
1780s and 1790s, when perhaps we may begin to use the term
'middle class' Blake found many of his friends and associates
among artists and intellectuals from a middle-class milieu. Even
so, his relations with gentry or clergy (William Hayley, Esq., the
Reverend Dr Trusler) remained exceedingly tetchy, watchful
against any controlling gesture of patronage, full of the susceptibil-
ities of one who doubted whether he should know such knaves.

The difficulty is that, in today's received wisdom, tradesman or
shop-keeper is suggestive of conservatism and dependency: 'petty-
bourgeois' has become a term of commination. But in eighteenth-
century London the tradesmen were, exactly, where a robust, Wilk-
esite, radical independency was located. And if we suppose that
Blake's family were adherents at some time of an antinomian faith,
then this independency would have had an uncrackable doctrinal
defence, a profound cultural resource in faith, a presumption of
spiritual superiority over the Rich and Great. What most distingu-
ishes these pockets of radical Dissent among the trades is a stubborn lack of deference, both social and intellectual.

This lack of deference is the veritable signature of William Blake.
It is true that the gifted tradesman's son found entrance into the
'republic' of artists – or into what, in today's jargon, may be seen
as an upwardly mobile profession – taking him away from the
stodgy station of his brother James. It is also true that the arts are
professions with their own long historical traditions, some – but
by no means all – of which are strongly resistant to deference.
Blake's chosen masters and friends – Barry, Flaxman, Fuseli – will
have confirmed him in his anti-deferential stance, his fury against
patronage, his desire for an enlightened 'public' and an open
market for artistic talent: 'Liberality! We want not Liberality   We
want a Fair Price & Proportionate Value & a General Demand
for Art' (E626).

But the stance itself, which extends far beyond the arts and into
matters of intellectual, political and religious judgement, has got
that kind of cultural confidence and hostility to genteel hegemony
which we have found in the sectarian traditions of radical Dissent.
There is the abrupt dismissal of Bacon's *Essays* as 'Good Advice
for Satans Kingdom'; 'the Wisdom of this World is Foolishness
with God' (E609). When Bacon comments suavely that 'triumphs,

masks, feasts, weddings, funerals, capital executions, and such shews . . . are not to be neglected', Blake notes: 'Bacon supposes that the Dragon Beast & Harlot are worthy of a Place in the New Jerusalem' (E616). The oppositions proposed are between Caesar and Christ, or between Jesus and 'the Prince of darkness' who 'is a Gentleman & not a Man he is a Lord Chancellor' (E612). What belongs to Caesar is power, riches and war, and an attendant ideology which masks, apologises for and rationalises power or 'Satans Kingdom'. Hence there follows a profound and critical suspicion of classical learning, of Greek or Roman models in philosophy, politics or art, which are the innermost defences and ornaments of the polite culture. 'Moral Precepts' [i.e. the Moral Law] 'belong to Plato & Seneca & Nero' (E608); Bacon's references to Sylla, Caesar and Augustus are dismissed with the comment, 'Roman Villains' (E618); and, in his last year, annotating Thornton: 'The Greek & Roman Classics is the Antichrist' (E656). Thornton's God 'is just such a Tyrant as Augustus Caesar & is not this Good & Learned & Wise & Classical' (E658). As for the hegemonic rhetoric of his society, in terms of Constitution and Law, the judgement is explicit: 'All Penal Laws court Transgression & therefore are cruelty & Murder' (E607). And 'Satans Kingdom' is seen as of one piece, as a *systematic* order: the power and the ideology must be taken together. Those intellectuals and artists who are corrupted by patronage or who act as apologists for the *status quo* are doubly damned, for it is art's divine mission to be eternally at war with this Kingdom. On the title page of Reynold's *Works*: 'This Man was Hired to Depress Art' (E624). Blake frequently falls back upon abuse of 'hirelings' or 'Cunning Hired Knaves':

The Enquiry in England is not whether a Man has Talents. & Genius But whether he is Passive & Polite & a Virtuous Ass: & obedient to Noblemens Opinions in Art & Science. If he is; he is a Good Man: if Not he must be Starved. (E632)

But this situation is maintained also by the ideological defences of polite rational philosophy. Reynold's assertions are grounded upon Bacon, Locke, Newton and Burke, for whose works Blake feels 'Contempt & Abhorrence' since 'they mock Inspiration & Vison' (E650). This is the old antinomian antimony, but faith has been replaced (although not always) by inspiration, imagination or the poetic genius. These are engaged in eternal war with Satan's Kingdom, and that war is on every front: material, ideological, artistic, political. When Malone, introducing Reynolds, refers to England's 'unparalleled state of wealth and prosperity' (in 1798!) and ridicules the 'seditious declamations' of reformers, Blake comments: 'This Whole Book was Written to Serve Political Purposes' (E630). And, nearly thirty years later, he wrote on the title page of Thornton's new translation of the Lord's Prayer, 'I look upon this as a Most Malignant & Artful attack upon the Kingdom of Jesus By the Classical Learned' (E656).

Not many antinomians delivered such shrewd and accurate blows against the ideological defences of their society as did Blake. They preferred, in the eighteenth century, to disengage from the combat and to nurture a somewhat spiritually complacent faith. But it is their confident stance, their robust contempt for the ruling ideology, which was transmitted to Blake. And if we follow any of Blake's annotations closely, we are left in little doubt as to who is shallow. Examine the 'Annotations to Watson'. Who is shallow? Blake, or the utterly self-satisfied and intellectually complacent bishop, with his justifications for genocide ('The Word of God is in perfect harmony with his work; crying or smiling infants are subjected to death in both') and his bland composure: 'Kings and priests . . . never, I believe, did you any harm.' That the antinomian tradition had limitations is apparent; yet 'shallow' can scarcely be the right word for a tradition nurtured so long and so tenaciously, or for one so close to the impulse of John Milton and John Bunyan. By the end of the century, certainly, it was becoming cranky, esoteric or a mere family habit. Blake, himself almost certainly a child of the tradition, let his whole intellectual and imaginative genius play upon its detritus, recomposed some of its elements in new and more challenging forms, and redirected it forward to us.

The Muggletonian archive

I had been trying to track down the Muggletonian archive for a few years, when a correspondence about Muggletonian doctrine commenced in the *Times Literary Supplement* (see 7 March, 11 April, 1975). An observant and accurate historian, the Unitarian minister, the Revd Alexander Gordon, was permitted to visit the Church's reading room in 1869, and he published two valuable lectures[1] in which he described his findings. He also contributed informed entries on a number of Muggletonians to the DNB.[2] The meeting room was then in 7 New Street, Bishopsgate, where all the Church's papers and properties were kept. (The site was close to Walnut Street Yard, the Prophet's birthplace.) The trail remained warm until 1939, when it ran out. In about 1919 the meeting room was moved to 74 Worship Street (also in Bishopsgate) where a believer was installed as caretaker.[3]

The *TLS* correspondence enabled me to mention my searches and to ask readers for information. In a few days I received a message from a friend that she had been contacted by a Mr Johnson, whose father-in-law, Mr Philip Noakes, was 'the last Muggletonian'. A meeting was arranged: Mr Noakes was cautious but courteous, and an invitation to his home at Matfield near Tunbridge Wells in Kent followed, where Mr and Mrs Noakes received

---

[1] Alexander Gordon, *The Origin of the Muggletonians* (1869); *Ancient and Modern Muggletonians* (1870).

[2] Gordon's DNB entries, in addition to Muggleton and Reeve, include Birch, Claxton, Alexander Delamaine, Boyer Glover, Saddington and Tomkinson. These were among 778 entries he contributed to the DNB. Gordon was Principal of the Unitarian College, Manchester, from 1889 to 1911; H. McLachlan, *Alexander Gordon* (Manchester, 1932): private communication from the Revd F. Kenworthy, Principal of the College, 22 June 1965.

[3] Information from the late Philip Noakes. No. 7 New Street was 'destroyed by enemy action' in the Second World War, private communication from the Secretary, Bentworth (New Street) Limited, 2 June 1965.

me with warm hospitality. Mrs Noakes (while sympathetic) was not herself a believer, and it seemed that Mr Noakes was indeed the last Muggletonian.

It was a strange situation. Nr Noakes himself was the last repository of a 300-year-old tradition. He conversed with me freely about Muggletonian practices and doctrine, which had been carried down to him with a clarity (and, indeed, coherence) which reproduced their seventeenth-century origin. Mr Noakes frequently said: 'We believe' – and yet one could not point to another believer. There was absolutely nothing of the fanatic or crank in his manner. He was always quiet and concise in his explanations, and I quickly formed a respect for him. On his part he seemed to be pleased that there was a revival of interest in the faith and he did everything he could to help me.

I found out that the Church's archives had been in the upper floor of the meeting room at 74 Worship St, with the now elderly believer as caretaker. This house was fire-bombed in 1940 or 1941, and the caretaker moved out. Mr Noakes, who was a fruit farmer in Kent, and was one of the Church's three trustees, drove up to Covent Garden with a load of apples, and packed into more than eighty apple boxes all the archives of the church. He took these back to his farm, where they were again threatened by a V-bomb, and eventually the boxes were placed in storage in a Tunbridge Wells furniture depository.

However, Mr Noakes had preserved some of the most interesting documents in his own home. These included three large guard books with papers and correspondence of the London Church: (1) late seventeenth century to mid-eighteenth; (2) mid-eighteenth to early nineteenth; and (3) subsequently. With extraordinary goodwill and trust, he allowed me to carry these off for a while, to study and xerox. There were also a number of notebooks in which Muggletonian documents had been carefully transcribed by Mr Noakes and his father.[4] (Unfortunately, once transcribed, the originals were destroyed.)

The apple boxes? I did not get a chance to see these until a later visit. Mr Noakes and I spent a long afternoon in the furniture depository, where a somewhat grumpy staff had dragged all eighty-plus into view in a dimly lit store-room. We started with no. 1. It was wholly made up of nineteenth-century paper-covered reprints

---

[4] See William Lamont, 'The Muggletonian Archive' in *The World of the Muggletonians*.

of the works of Muggleton and Reeve. And so, on and on, for eighty boxes. Eventually at boxes 80–82 we struck oil. Eighteenth-century bindings appeared, and manuscripts, as well as holograph song-books. I confess that the light was so bad that, when we came to the last box, with trembling fingers I lit a match. I was rewarded by finding in front of me a manuscript by Lawrence Claxton (Clarkson). We managed to get these last three boxes back to Mr Noakes's house and to inspect them at more leisure. It seemed that all the manuscripts which Alexander Gordon had seen in the 1860s had been preserved.

My concern, of course, was to guide the archive to a national library. But here we met with a difficulty. Muggletonians eschewed evangelism unless by the printed word. It was in print that the faith must be preserved, and through which conversions might be made. Mr Noakes was willing to let the archive pass to a library, but on condition that the library housed also all the Muggletonian reprints and circulated libraries in the English-speaking world offering to supply copies. This proved to be too large a commitment for any library which I approached to accept.

I then departed for a year to teach in the United States (1976–7). On my return I learned with dismay that Mr Noakes had been seriously ill with angina: he was anxious to lodge the archive in a suitable library and was willing to forego his previous conditions. We approached the British Library which – after a little hesitation – agreed to purchase the archive.

The hesitation was about title: did Mr Noakes have title to dispose of the Church's property? It seemed that possession was nine points of the law. No other surviving member of the London church (or any other) could be found. The Church was never an incorporated body. Philip Noakes (then over seventy) was the last survivor of three Church Trustees. He himself was the descendant of well-known Muggletonian families – Noakes and Frost – Joseph and Isaac Frost being particularly active in the Church in the early nineteenth century.[5]

---

[5] Outstandingly active in the Church's affairs in the first half of the nineteenth century – scrutinising the archive, editing *Divine Songs* – Joseph and Isaac Frost were brass founders in Clerkenwell. Isaac Frost published in 1846 *Two Systems of Astronomy,* a literal portrayal of Muggletonian cosmology – a handsome example of early colour plates. The Frosts were perhaps associated with an Elias Noakes (also a Muggletonian) in their business in the early nineteenth century. James Frost's daughter, Florence Frost, married Frederick Noakes, Philip Noakes's father (Conversations with Philip Noakes, 1977).

That is how the archive came, in January 1978, to the British Library. Mr Noakes died less than two years later, and over three hundred years of direct transmission of a unique faith came to an end.

From internal evidence it seems that in 1772 the Church collected together all manuscripts and letters, as well as books, available, and from that time forward held them as Church records and library, in locked closets in the public houses where they met. In 1831 the entire collection was scrutinised very carefully by two leading Church members, Joseph and Isaac Frost, and they wrote on the covers annotations. As a result of their scrutiny a few hitherto unpublished letters of Muggleton and Reeve were published as *Supplement to the Book of Letters* (1831). The archive eventually was preserved in the reading room in 7 New Street, opened in May 1869. This was where Alexander Gordon saw it.

The British Library has arranged the archive in eighty-nine volumes, Add. MSS 60168–60256, to which some supplementary volumes of transcribed correspondence will subsequently be added. The series is divided into five parts: Letters, Add. MSS 60168–60183; Treatises, Add. MSS 60184–60206; Verse, Add. MSS 60207–60230; Accounts, 60231–60245; Printed Works, 60246–60256. In the 'Letters' will be found the contents of the three guard books which Mr Noakes loaned to me, at 60168–60170. This includes general church correspondence, including some letters exchanged with believers in Ireland, Connecticut, &c; material concerning internal church disputes, including the splits occasioned by James Birch and Martha Collier; and copies of matters of church concern. In preparing this book for the press I have in general relied on the xeroxes in my possession, but the cautious scholar will find most of my quotations in Add. MSS 60168 and 60169.

The 'Treatises' are mostly copies of works by Muggleton, Reeve, Claxton, Tomkinson, Saddington, and others: several of the works of Tomkinson and Arden Bonnell are unpublished.

The 'Verse' is made up in the main of the manuscript songbooks copied by believers in the eighteenth century. A standardised collection, dating perhaps from 1711, was entitled 'A Divine Garland of Spiritual Songs': to this subsequent believers made their additions, or compiled new selections altogether. These manuscript collections were perhaps replaced by the printed *Songs of Grateful Praise*

(?1790) – I have not seen a copy[6] – which, however, included only twenty-one songs and was replaced in 1829 by the very much fuller *Divine Songs of the Muggletonians* (228 songs collected by the industrious Joseph and Isaac Frost, which leaned heavily on mid-eighteenth-century and subsequent songs, and dropped some of the earlier ones). The manuscript collections therefore remain significant.

The 'Accounts' are accounts and include lists of members.

The 'Printed Works' include a few MS annotations of interest.

As I go through my files concerning this matter I am surprised to be reminded as to how much time and labour were expended in inspecting, recording and guiding the archive to its haven, and the formidable volume of correspondence generated. But all is sweetened by the recollection of the kindness shown to me by Mr and Mrs Noakes. It was indeed a privilege to have been taken into the confidence of 'the Last Muggletonian'.

---

[6] Its existence is recorded by Gordon, *Ancient and Modern Muggletonians*, pp. 44–5, and Joseph Smith, *Bibliotheca Anti-Quakeriana* (1873), p. 320.

William Blake's mother

According to Bentley's authoritative *Blake Records*[1] and other sources William Blake's father and mother were married in St George's chapel, Hanover Square, on 15 October 1752, as 'James Blake and Catherine Harmitage'. An inspection of the register disclosed that the entry was undoubtedly Hermitage, and not Harmitage. (Extensive searches in sundry Westminster registers and indexes in fact turned up no Harmitages.) Catherine was then about thirty and James twenty-nine.[2]

The chapel at St George's, Mayfair, was a notorious bucket-shop for marriages, and convenient for couples who did not want to tangle with the Church of England. No licence, publication of banns or consent of parents were required: 6,000 marriages were registered between 1749 and 1753, and a critic commented that it 'constructed a very bishopric of revenue' from the fees. The facilities were advertised in the papers: 'The Marriages (together with a Licence on a Five Shilling Stamp and Certificate) are carried on for a guinea, as usual' (*London Gazette*, 12 January 1749). The chapel was brought under Church control in 1753.[3] There is an unexplained cross beside the names of James and Catherine. All that one can say is that the chapel was a place where radical dissenters, outside the Church, might obtain a quick marriage.

Catherine comes into the record out of obscurity. In fact she was the widow of Thomas Hermitage of 28 Broad Street, near Golden Square.[4] The rates on this property had been paid by — Armitage

[1] G.E. Bentley, *Blake Records*, p. 2.
[2] *Ibid.*, p. 47. The name is correctly recorded as Hermitage in H.M. Margoliouth, 'William Blake's Family', *N&Q*, Vol. 192 (1947), pp. 380–1.
[3] Margoliouth; George Clinch, *Mayfair and Belgravia* (1892), pp. 56–8.
[4] This appears from the will of Thomas Armitage of the parish of St James, Westminster, haberdasher and hosier, drawn 23 July 1751 and proved 27 November 1751 in PRO. P.CC. Wills. This leaves, after several legacies, the residue of his estate to his wife, Catherine Armitage.

from 1748 to 1753,[5] and in the fiercely contested Westminster election of 1749 the poll-book shows Thomas Hermitage, of Broad Street, hosier, voting for the anti-Court candidate.[6] (Blake's father, James Blake of Glasshouse St, hosier, voted on the same side in the same poll.) Thomas Hermitage's will was proved in November 1751. The marriage of Catherine with James Blake took place eleven months later. It was a fortunate uniting of two businesses. James Blake had only recently completed his apprenticeship. The newly married couple moved into Broad Street in 1753, and (if Catherine was already there and paying the rates) perhaps earlier.

Not much can be found out about the Hermitage family, despite extensive searches.[7] Several Hermitages can be found in the parish registers of St James's, Westminster, between 1720 and 1750. It will be recalled that a George Hermitage has two songs in the *Divine Songs of the Muggletonians*, probably from the 1730s or 1740s. Could George have been Thomas's kin? George and Susannah Hermitage appear as parents of a child (Elizabeth) in the parish register in November 1742. If Muggletonians favoured endogamy Catherine's first husband, and herself, might have been of the faith?

---

[5] Bentley, *Blake Records*, pp. 551–2.
[6] Both the printed pollbook and MS poll are in Westminster Reference Library: *A Copy of the Poll for a Citizen for the City and Liberty of Westminster* (1749) and (MS) WR/PP (1749).
[7] I must thank Jean Haynes for genealogical assistance.

PART II

Human images

Introductory

In this part I will discuss some aspects of Blake's work, and the context of that work, in the years 1788 to 1794. In 1788 William and Catherine Blake were living in Central London, at 28 Poland Street (Soho), but in 1790 they moved south of the river to Hercules Buildings, Lambeth, where they stayed until 1800. Blake was busy engraving and writing. He worked as an engraver for (among others) Joseph Johnson, the bookseller and leading publisher of Radical Dissenting authors. But he did not aim at publication in the usual ways. In 1788 he commenced his 'illuminated works', in the form of relief etchings, and only a few copies of each were sold, among his patrons, friends and acquaintance. Catherine helped in the work, especially the colouring: each copy is unique, and sometimes (as with the *Songs*) the pages are in a different sequence. In 1788 also the Blakes appear to have become closely interested in the Swedenborgian New Jerusalem Church, although they soon became alienated from it. This is a theme of chapters 8, 9 and 10. In 1789 the *Songs of Innocence* were engraved and published although after 1794 they were usually issued bound together with the *Songs of Experience*. After the French Revolution Blake was probably drawn more closely into the Radical Dissenting circles which warmly supported it. In 1790 or 1791 he commenced a long poem, in prophetic mode, on *The French Revolution*, to be published by Joseph Johnson, but only the first book survives, in a set of page proofs. It presumably went unpublished and the project was discontinued. Blake did not attempt to employ normal publishing channels again.

That is a bald summary of a very active and productive life. These were also times of great excitement in London with the accelerating events in France, with the passionate debates provoked by Thomas Paine's *The Rights of Man* (part one, 1791; part two, 1792), and with the formation and rapid growth of the popular reform societies, culminating in the failed attempt of the government to convict the leaders of the London Corresponding Society for high treason in 1794.

After the Blakes broke with the Swedenborgians – the break is dramatised by the satirical and polemical critique, *The Marriage of Heaven and Hell* (published in 1793 although commenced in 1790) – it is not easy to place them in any church or group. Perhaps the experience extinguished Blake's appetite for 'joining'? There were numerous illuminist and millenarial circles in London which he could have entered, but there is no evidence to associate him with any.[1] All such circles were either swept by revolutionary enthusiasm in 1789–92, or, like the Swedenborgians or the groups around William Huntington (above, pp. 6–8), were thrown into controversy by the events in France and by Paine's *Rights of Man*.

There can be no doubt that Blake shared these enthusiasms. Alexander Gilchrist, his first biographer, who had the direct testimony of several of Blake's surviving acquaintances, had no hesitation in describing him as an ardent republican:

Down to his latest days Blake always avowed himself a 'Liberty Boy', a faithful 'Son of Liberty'[2] . . . He courageously donned the famous symbol of liberty and equality – the bonnet-rouge – in open day, and philosophically walked the streets with the same on his head.[3]

Gilchrist reports that after the days of terror in Paris in September 1792 Blake 'never wore the red cap again'. That is possible. But there was no reversal in his republican enthusiasm. This is testified by his writings and his art, as any close study shows.[4] Even Blake's trial for sedition in Sussex in 1803–4, which is sometimes treated as a literary humour, was a serious matter. No doubt the evidence

---

[1] See Iain McCalman's excellent study, 'The Infidel as Prophet: William Reid and Blakean radicalism' in *Historicising Blake*. For illuminist circles, see Clarke Garrett, *Respectable Folly: Millenarians and the French Revolution in France and England* (Baltimore, 1975), and J.F.C. Harrison, *The Second Coming*.

[2] There was in fact a 'Sons of Liberty' with a brief existence as a secession from the London Corresponding Society: see *Selections from the Papers of the London Corresponding Society*, ed. Mary Thale (Cambridge, 1983), index under 'reform societies'. But this is perhaps to take Blake's claims too literally.

[3] Alexander Gilchrist, *The Life of William Blake* (1907 edn), pp. 95–6. Gilchrist's widow, Anne, staunchly repeated this in her entry on Blake in DNB (1902). As to the *bonnet-rouge*, the normally reliable Bentley (*Blake Records*, p. 40, note 3) says 'Gilchrist got the colour wrong' and says it should have been a white hat. But the white hat was a symbol borrowed from Henry Hunt in the post-war agitations.

[4] Notably, of course, David Erdman's brilliant study, *Blake: Prophet against Empire*.

against him was perjured, with respect to the actual indictment. But it could have found its source in village gossip as to Blake's indiscretions. A careful watch was kept in these years upon reformers, especially in coastal districts, and men were jailed for utterances similar to those of which Blake was accused.[5] Blake had to thank his influential friends, like his patron, William Hayley, his excellent defence barrister, Samuel Rose, and perhaps his reputation in the village as an amiable eccentric, for his acquittal.

Undoubtedly Blake belongs with the Jacobin tendency among English reformers. He straddled two social worlds: that of intellectuals and artists, and that of tradesmen and artisans. In the first world, he was occasionally present at Joseph Johnson's weekly dinner parties, where he will have met Paine, Fuseli (already his friend), possibly Dr Priestley, no doubt Mary Wollstonecraft.[6] Yet his name has not been recorded among the active members of this circle's reform organisation, the Society for Constitutional Information. In the second world, no barrier would have prevented Blake from joining a division of the London Corresponding Society. In surviving division lists, while tradesmen and artisans are most numerous, occasional 'gentlemen' are present, as well as engravers, surgeons, booksellers, &c. Yet there is no William Blake in the lists that survive.[7] A Lambeth Association (where the Blakes lived) even rose to the dignity of having assigned to it as government spy the botanic printer to His Majesty: no doubt with such a patron he could scarcely refuse the assignment. But again there is no mention of Blake.[8]

However, it is not the intention of the present study to review the political and social associations of Blake. This has already been done by other scholars. My intention, rather, is to follow the intellectual routes by which (through Blake) the antinomian tradition

---

[5] For the trial, see Bentley, *Blake Records*, pp. 122–48. And see, for example, PRO KB11.61, Indictments 41 Geo. III, Hil. Kent; a Dartford coachmaker for saying 'Damn the King, and those who wear his livery.'

[6] For a judicious assessment of Blake's relations with Johnson and with the 'Paine set', see Erdman, *Blake: Prophet against Empire*, pp. 153–62.

[7] This is supported by my own searches in the Public Record Office, among Privy Council, Treasury Solicitor's and Home Office papers, as well as the searches of other scholars.

[8] Frederick Polydore Nadder: information, based on TS and PC records, kindly supplied by Dr Günther Lottes. Thomas Spence was a member of this Association. Dr Lottes adds (in a private communication) that if Blake had been a member this would almost certainly have been recorded, since the Association engaged in some histrionic drilling and was watched closely by government.

came to a conjunction with the Enlightenment and in particular with Jacobin thought, argued with it, and gave rise to the unique Blakean mutation.

Blake's consistently radical and antinomian stance persisted within large fluctuations in his preoccupations, in his optimism or pessimism as to the outcome of the revolutionary struggles of his own time (in France or in England), in his optimism or pessimism as to his own art, and in his relation to Painite or deist (and atheist) thought. In this relationship Blake was more influenced by the blunt, activist, iconoclastic thought of the popular reformers than he was by the thought of the *philosophes*. He was attracted by the French revolutionary and atheist thinker, C.F. Volney (see below, pp. 199–202) and repelled by Gibbon; and it would not be difficult to show that he was equally attracted by Paine and repelled by the hero of the intellectuals, the polite philosophical anarchist, William Godwin. The moment of Blake's greatest poetic achievement belonged exactly to this moment of extraordinary conjunction, at the time of the French Revolution, when that part of Enlightenment thought, represented by the blunt, humane, ultra-radicalism of Paine and Volney collided with an older antinomian tradition, co-existed fraternally in Blake's heart and argued matters out inside his head. This is the theme of chapters 11 and 12 and indeed of the whole of Part II. William Blake, the antinomian caught in the Enlightenment, should be our central thesis. Once this is understood, the rest falls into place. Moreover, the antinomian inheritance was not just some old baggage which could be discarded once he was enlightened. For it enabled Blake to question and to resist the simplicities of mechanical materialism and Lockeian epistemology, in which the revolutionary impulse was to founder. For in shedding the prohibitives of the Moral Law, Blake held fast to the affirmative: Thou Shalt Love. It is because this affirmative remains an essential need and quest of our own time that William Blake still speaks with such power to us.

CHAPTER 8

The New Jerusalem church

Until now we have been engaged in a conjectural history of ideas. In this part we can commence on firm ground at last, in April 1789, when the names of W. and C. Blake appear in a document of the Swedenborgian New Jerusalem Church. Now at last we know where to find Blake, on the eve of the French Revolution, as a Swedenborgian.

But as soon as we tread on this ground it begins to quake beneath us. David Erdman, in a rollicking polemic in 1953, utterly demolished the 'legend' of Blake's early Swedenborgianism;[1] and so effectively was it demolished that, until recently, scholars were discouraged from looking into the matter much further.[2] (They have, of course, examined, sometimes obsessively, Swedenborg's own writings for influences, sources, themes, but that is a different matter.) And much of what Erdman established cannot be controverted. It is scarcely possible that Blake's father could have been 'a Swedenborgian', Blake could not have written the song, 'The Divine Image', in 1789 while sitting in a church which was not opened until 1799, nor could his father and brother have studied books which were not published until after their deaths. But if we replace this legend within a careful context, we still may make something of it.

What we know about Blake's intellectual evolution is very little. We have his fooling passage of poetic autobiography addressed to his friend Flaxman in 1800; three of Swedenborg's works annotated by Blake; the signatures of the Blakes on the New Church docu-

---

[1] 'Blake's Early Swedenborgianism: a twentieth-century Legend', *Comparative Literature*, 5 (1953), pp. 247–57.
[2] A notable exception is the helpful article by Morton D. Paley, '"A New Heaven is Begun": Blake and Swedenborgianism', *Blake: an Illustrated Quarterly*, 1979, 12, no. 2, pp. 64–90.

ment at the General Conference, at Easter, 13–17 April 1789: and one or two scraps of reminiscence. For the rest we must interpret the poet's own writings.

When Blake offered an intellectual autobiography to his friend, the sculptor and painter John Flaxman, in 1800, his c.v. did not come to a climax with a doctorate and the publication of his first learned articles. It was that of a self-educated seeker after truth:

> Now my lot in the Heavens is this, Milton lov'd me in
>   childhood & shew'd me his face.
> Ezra came with Isaiah the Prophet, but Shakespeare in riper
>   years gave me his hand:
> Paracelsus & Behmen appear'd to me, terrors appear'd in the
>   Heavens above
> And in Hell beneath, & a mighty & awful change threatened the
>   Earth.
> The American War began. All its dark horrors passed before my
>   face
> Across the Atlantic to France. Then the French Revolution
>   commenc'd in thick clouds. . .   (E680)

This should not be read too literally. We are not to suppose that a formal education (Milton, the Old Testament, Shakespeare, Paracelsus, Boehme) was completed before the American War began. (It is difficult to detect any influence of Paracelsus or Boehme in Blake's early *Poetical Sketches* (1783) or *An Island in the Moon* (1784).) The syntax and thrust of the verse, which hurries us on, with a comma, from Behmen to 'terrors' and thence to 'horrors', suggests a preoccupation with Paracelsus and Boehme coincident with the 'mighty & awful change' signified by the passage of the American into the French Revolution. Blake is describing a single experience, made up of both spiritual and corporeal events, rather than a sequence of steps in time. And Flaxman, a Swedenborgian 'receiver', could be expected to understand the 'correspondence' by which the intellectual and historical events emblemised and echoed each other.[3]

Three of Swedenborg's works were annotated by Blake, probably in 1788–90. The annotations show a distinct modification in Blake's response to Swedenborg. His annotations to *Heaven and Hell* (1784) are desultory and languid. His annotations to *Divine Love*

---

[3] It might, however, be significant that Blake in 1800, did not include Swedenborg in his list.

and Divine Wisdom (1788) suggest a thorough-going and sympathetic scrutiny, with Swedenborg's doctrines set against Blake's own already developed and strongly formed system. His annotations to the *Divine Providence* (1790) suggest ridicule or indignant rejection.[4] There is a suggestion of a rapid passage through the Swedenborgian influence, to which, however, in later years he may have returned.[5] In the same years he annotated Lavater's *Aphorisms on Man* (1789) in great detail.

Blake appears to have liked Lavater more than he liked Swedenborg, and where he most approved its 'true Christian philosophy' was at those points where Lavater emphasised humanity's 'divine' attributes. 'Man', Blake exclaimed at one point, 'is either the ark of God or a phantom of the earth and of the water' (E585). But he gave, for the time, the benefit of the doubt to Swedenborg. The Swedish seer moves through so many convolutions, so many correspondences and self-contradictions, that it was difficult for Blake to decide. When, shortly afterwards, he annotated his *Divine Providence* he had decided very firmly *against*: 'Cursed Folly', 'Lies & Priestcraft', 'Predestination'. If one part of man was the dispersal of the divine essence, how could his end be predested? Moreover, Blake was watching like a hawk every reference to 'truth' and the 'understanding'. The Reason which Blake suspected had some affinity with what he was defining at the same time in *There is No Natural Religion* as 'natural or organic thoughts'. In opposition to Locke (and all that Blake was later to make him and Newton responsible for) Blake proposed that 'naturally' man 'is only a natural organ subject to Sense'; but 'none could have other than natural or organic thoughts if he had none but organic perceptions' (E1–3). Without divine spirit or 'poetic genius' in humanity, expressed in the affections and not in the understanding, man could never transcend his own material nature. Swedenborg's vaporous exegesis appeared at times to confirm Blake's view and won his approval: where the seer spoke of Divine Love in some higher part

---

[4] See Erdman, 'Blake's Early Swedenborgianism', pp. 139–46. Also Morton D. Paley, *Blake and Swedenborgianism*, pp. 17–21.

[5] Garth Wilkinson recorded that Blake's friend and patron, C.A. Tulk, was told by Blake that 'he had two different stages; one in which he liked Swedenborg's writings, and one in which he disliked them. The second was a state of pride in himself, and then they were distasteful to him. The first was a state of humility, in which he received and accepted Swedenborg'; James Spilling, 'Blake the Visionary', *New Church Magazine*, May 1887, p. 210.

of the hierarchy to Understanding, or where he said that it was impossible for man 'from a *merely natural* Idea' to 'comprehend that the Divine is every where', Blake underscored or wrote: 'Mark this.' But he was clearly thinking at the same time of recent disputes 'in the society', where some 'absurd' and 'perverse' members (moreover, 'mercenary & worldly' ones) were denying the possibility of visions and even asserting that 'love recieves influx through understand^g' (E596, 598).

What is apparent is that Blake has brought to both Lavater and Swedenborg an advanced and ordered system of thought. There is no conversion here: it is a strict examination. This system Blake had adopted, or evolved for himself, probably by 1788. But what about his fellow Swedenborgians? Admirers and receivers of Swedenborg had been corresponding and grouping in the 1780s. By the end of the decade several tendencies were evident. A strong tendency remained committed to working within the Church of England. A philosophically minded group gathered around the Revd Jacob Duché, and eventually evolved into the Theosophical Society, a group which Blake could have sometimes attended.[6] After failing to convince their colleagues who were dedicated to the permeation of the Established Church, Robert Hindmarsh and a group of supporters decided to go ahead and inaugurate a separatist New Jerusalem Church in May 1787.[7] This Church immediately began to enrol members. In December 1788 this group sent around 500 copies of a circular letter calling a first general conference of the New Church for the following April: the tone of the letter was welcoming:

Any person within the circle of your acquaintance, whom you know to be a Lover of the Truths contained in the Theological Writings of Emanuel Swedenborg, and friendly to the formation of a New Church . . . you are at Liberty also to invite.[8]

---

[6] Morton D. Paley, 'Blake and Swedenborgianism', p. 16; Charles Higham, 'The Reverend Jacob Duché, His Later Life and Ministry in England', *New Church Review*, 22 (1915); Robert Hindmarsh, *Rise and Progress of the New Jerusalem Church* (1861), pp. 40–1; Erdman, pp. 11–12, note 19; Clarke Garret, 'Swedenborg and the mystical enlightenment in late eighteenth-century England', *Journal of the History of Ideas*, 1984.

[7] Thomas Robinson, *A Remembrancer and Record* (Manchester, 1864), pp. 86–9. The Church was preceded by a 'Society for Promoting the Heavenly Doctrines of the New Jerusalem Church', meeting in the Middle Temple, from which a minority, led by Hindmarsh, seceded to form the New Church. This was formally named the 'New Church' in May 1788: *Minute Book of the Society* in New Church Library and Archives.

[8] Reprint of circular letter in Swedenborgian Society archive, H25.

What the attenders were called upon to endorse at the conference itself was somewhat stricter and more doctrinal than that. They were required to assent to thirty-two propositions, which included the repudiation of the Old Church, a renunciation of the Trinity (Jesus Christ is 'the only God') and various proposals as to the forms and conduct of the New Church.[9] These propositions were subscribed to by seventy-seven signatories, the attenders at the conference. There are then added eighteen further signatures, including those of W. and C. Blake. A comparison of the signatures with the Minutes of the Great Eastcheap church shows that the overwhelming majority of the seventy-seven were already admitted as church members (fifty-six or more), while not one of the subsequent eighteen had been so admitted, in the period May 1787 to April 1788. The Blakes therefore attended as sympathisers, not as members.[10] A subsequent circular letter to 'all lovers of Truth', transmitting the resolutions, claimed that there was 'not a single dissentient Voice among us'.[11] Thus we know that Blake, at Easter 1789, was willing to assent to a large mouthful of Swedenborgian doctrine.

To read through more than a few pages of Emmanuel Swedenborg's writings induces such mental tedium that few students of Blake succeed in conveying more than the same tedium in their commentaries. It is difficult to understand what a poet with an imagination so concrete could have made of a language which dissolves whatever it touches into abstractions. A more concentrated attention reveals that Blake was reading into Swedenborg opinions which he already held and which he seemed to glimpse through hazes which arose probably from similar Behmenist fires. What Swedenborg tried to do was to bring this extraordinary and contradictory group of ideas (some from Behmenist sources) within a polite and rationalised framework.[12]

---

[9] These thirty-two proposals are reproduced in the *Minutes of the First Seven Sessions of the New Church* (1885). See also Bentley, *William Blake*, pp. 35–7. However, a markedly different and doctrinally much stricter set of forty-two propositions is reproduced in P.F. Gosse, *Portefamille d'un Ancien Typographe* (Le Haye, 1824). These were perhaps sent out with the original circular letter?

[10] *Minutes.* If the Blakes formally joined the Church it will have been during the period when the pages have been cut out of the Minutes.

[11] Gosse. The circular was signed by Swedenborgian heavyweights – Augustus Nordenskjöld and C.B. Wadstrom (from Sweden), Henry Peckitt, Henry Servanté, Benedict Chastanier, J.A. Tulk, but not by Robert Hindmarsh.

[12] Swedenborg had not only read Boehme in his youth but also Pordage and Jane Lead; C.W. Schneider, *Nachricht von der so-genannten neuen Kirche, oder dem neuen Jerusalem* (Weimar,

The decline, simply in terms of literary exuberance, from the seventeenth-century antinomians is discouraging. The direct influence
of these writings upon Blake was slight, except (as in *The Marriage
of Heaven and Hell*) through opposition. At most he was confirmed
in the mental style of thinking in 'correspondences' (but this, under
other names, is of the very nature of poetry); he was encouraged
to speak of objectifying his insights as visions or as conversations
with spirits: and he was confirmed in a mode which enabled him
to read the Bible as myth or as parable. Indeed, this was singled
out for particular note at the beginning of an account of the principal doctrines of the New Church. Swedenborg–

> points out an intire and singular way of reconciling the apparent contra-
> dictions in scripture, by distinguishing between two kinds of truth,
> namely, genuine and apparent. He maintains that the holy scripture, as
> well as every thing in nature, is resolvable into one or other of these two
> kinds of truth. Thus, when it is said, that the sun rises or sets, this is
> only an apparent truth, as the genuine truth is, that the earth revolves
> around its own axis[13] . . . Just so (says Swedenborg) it is with the Scrip-
> tures . . . Thus, when it is said, that God is angry, and revengeful, that
> he punishes and casts into hell, we are to understand that it is man who
> brings punishment on himself, and casts himself into hell. . .[14]

If the Blakes were prepared to indicate support for the New
Church in 1789, this signified not only a general support for
Swedenborg's writings but also a commitment to working with
fellow Swedenborgians in promoting a new church. We have perhaps paid too much attention to the writings, too little to their
interpreters and to the notion of such a 'church'. The old seer had
spent his last months in England, where he had died at his lodgings
in 1785.[15] In addition to Swedenborg's published works which were
steadily undergoing translation into English, the seer had left a
heap of manuscripts, and these included a 'spiritual diary' in Latin,
a copy of which was brought from Sweden by C.B. Wadstrom in
1787 and left in the hands of a disciple named Benedict Chastanier,

1789), pp. 26–8. I am indebted to Dr Hans Medick for a sight of this rare item. In
addition, according to Walton, Swedenborg had read Reeve and Muggleton, as well as
William Law; C. Walton, *Notes and Materials for a Biography of William Law*, p. 158. See
also anon. [B. Chastanier], *Tableau Analytique et Raisoné de la Doctrine Céléste de L'Eglise de
la Nouvelle Jerusalem* (1786), p. 40n.
[13] Blake inverts this in *Milton*, 1 (E126, lines 15–16).
[14] *New-Jerusalem Magazine* (1790), pp. 102–3.
[15] Anon., *Remarks on the Assertions of the Author of the Memoirs of Jacobinism respecting the Character
of Swedenborg* (Philadelphia, 1800), p. 11.

a French surgeon who had emigrated to England in 1763 and who formed a centre of international communication.[16]

The Church was a gathering-ground for a miscellany of seekers after mystic experiences, Behmenists, Philadelphians, Rosicrucians, masons, enthusiasts for mesmerism and magnetism, and after the initial euphoria of the founding conference, different tendencies at once revealed themselves. What was going on in these early years has been seriously obscured in orthodox Swedenborgian apologetics, especially those which derive from Robert Hindmarsh, who was intent upon presenting an apostolic succession descending from his own mysterious derivation of the power to ordain priests as a result of a lottery. Indeed, the closer one gets to the actual record the more Hindmarsh's *Rise and Progress of the New Jerusalem Church* appears to merit as much and as little credence as Stalin's *Short History of the CPSU(B)*. If there had been a Trotsky in that small congregation in 1789 – if Blake had been that Trotsky – his name would certainly have been expunged from the record. Indeed, the critical pages for the critical period (May 1789 to April 1790) were cut out of the Minute Book of the Society (or Church) meeting in Great Eastcheap. The annual conferences continued (a federal occasion) but in 1792 two rival sets of Minutes of the conference were issued, and in 1793 rival conferences were held.[17]

The most forceful evangelist for the New Church was undoubtedly Robert Hindmarsh, the son of a Methodist minister, James, who also joined the work. A printer, he kept himself busy in both spiritual and corporeal ways. In the apt characterisation of Swedenborg's biographer, William White, 'to him the New Jeru-

[16] The spiritual diary was also known as 'Memorabilia', and Chastanier translated a few 'memorable relations' from it for the Swedenborgian journals; see below, p. 141: James Hyde, *A Bibliography of the Works of Emmanuel Swedenborg* (1906), pp. 118–19. Chastanier gives a few biographical reminiscences in an eccentric pamphlet, *A Word of Advice to a Benighted World* (1795). I am grateful to the Royal Library of Stockholm for the sight of a copy, and to Professor Morton Paley for obtaining this for me. The *Prospectus* for the *New-Jerusalem Magazine* (British Library press-mark, 823c1(3)), to be edited by Henry Servanté and Chastanier claims that one of the editors 'is the Possessor of all the Original Manuscripts of Emmanuel Swedenborg, now in Stockholm', and that he had established the legal right to these copies. See also James Hyde, 'Chastanier and the Illuminati of Avignon', *New-Church Review* (Boston, Mass.), 14, 1907, pp. 181–205.

[17] Swedenborgian scholars corrected much of the record subsequently in their journals and other publications, drawn upon below. The most substantial independent study of the early church is Peter J. Lineham, 'The English Swedenborgians, 1770–1840' (University of Sussex, Ph.D. thesis, 1978). Also Alexander J. Morley, 'The Politics of Prophecy: William Blake's early Swedenborgianism' (Queen's University, Ontario, M.A. dissertation, 1991).

salem was no mystic city, but a sort of New Clerkenwell. It was a shop for the sale of theological notions warranted fresh from Heaven.'[18]

The Church at Great Eastcheap grew rapidly. At least one hundred members were admitted (by the unanimous voice of the members) up to the point in April 1789 when the Minutes are torn out. One knows from other sources that the members included a few gentry, among them J.A. Tulk, the father of Blake's patron, C.A. Tulk, former ministers of other persuasions (like James Hindmarsh) and surgeons and professional men. In a few cases the Minutes give occupations of new members – two booksellers, two tobacconists, a carver and gilder, chemist, cooper, druggist, enameller, letter carrier, musical instrument maker, shoemaker, smith, watchmaker, and often also their wives. As Robert Southey was to note, 'Few or none of the congregation belonged to the lower classes, they seemed to be chiefly respectable tradesmen.'[19] Over the door of the Church's rented premises in Great Eastcheap was posted the words 'Nunc Licet' (It is now allowable). This presumably was founded upon Swedenborg's claim (adopted as article thirty-three on the foundation of the New Church)–

That now it is allowable to enter intellectually into the Mysteries of Faith, contrary to the ruling Maxim in the Old Church, that the Understanding is to be kept bound under Obedience to Faith.[20]

What happened next is remarkably obscure. (This is where the pages of the Minutes have gone.) There was a thundering row and probably two or three different rows. First sex and then the French Revolution reared their ugly heads. After many solemn meetings, the Church 'withdrew herself' from six members, and these six included Robert Hindmarsh himself, as well as the French emigré and long-standing receiver, Henry Servanté, and two prominent Swedish enthusiasts, Augustus Nordenskjöld and C.B. Wadstrom.[21] One issue turned upon authorised and unauthorised ver-

---

[18] William White, *Emmanuel Swedenborg* (1867), Vol. II, p. 612.

[19] Robert Southey, ('Don Manuel Alvarez Espriella'), *Letters from England* (1814), Vol. III, p. 113.

[20] P. F. Gosse, *Portefamille*, article 33. The authorities cited are Swedenborg's *True Christian Religion*, Nos. 185 & 508. The *New-Jerusalem Magazine* (1789) carried 'NUNC LICET' on its first page, and (number 2) surrounded the words in a circlet of roses.

[21] Carl T. Odhner, *Robert Hindmarsh* (Philadelphia, 1895), p. 26, drawing upon the recollections of an early Church member, the Revd Manoah Sibley, *An Address to the Society of the New Church meeting in Friar Street, near Ludgate Hill, London* (1839).

sions of the prophet's *Conjugal Love*. The authorised version of this swimmy vision of Swedenborg's, which did not appear until 1794, could not have offended the strictest Elder of the Kirk. But there had been much discussion and piecemeal publication in the previous five years. Chastanier's earlier versions had an imagery more explicit and more sexy: some passages inserted in the *New Magazine of Knowledge Concerning Heaven and Hell* (1791) described the nakedness of angels who 'in bed . . . lie copulated as they were created, and thus they sleep. . .' These passages (Chastanier commented) and the explicit sexuality of heaven gave 'offence'.[22]

The offence had been severe. For this and previous publications and debates had been the apparent occasion for the Church withdrawing itself from six leading members. I say 'apparent' because the official record of any organisation is usually the smoke and not the fire: people seize on an issue and formulate rules and resolutions as a pretext for fighting out ulterior (but often unstated) issues. Some subsequent accounts suggest that what were at issue were not theological views but sexual practices. When a version of Swedenborg's *The Delights of Wisdom respecting Conjugal Love* was published in 1790[23] it was felt necessary to preface it with cautions against 'that dangerous and Anti-Christian Doctrine of a plurality of wives, which has lately been propagated. . .' A Church veteran recalled, sixty years later, that there was advocacy of the views that bachelors might take mistresses, and those receivers with 'disharmonious' marriages whose wives rejected the New Age might dismiss their wives and take concubines. 'I forget', this aged member wrote, 'whether or not the wife was to have the same privilege.'[24] This is a familiar area of male amnesia. But our loyal veteran, Mr Hawkins, promptly continued to reassure the faithful: 'I do not recollect any case where the notion was acted on.' However, other veterans were around to question his account. Dr Bateman, who had been doctor to both Hindmarsh and Sibley, reaffirmed that 'some of the early receivers' viewed Swedenborg's doctrines 'from an unchaste ground', and Elihu Rich affirmed that it was 'well known' to members that the matter had not stopped

---

[22] Vol. II, pp. 193–6, 248. A note in the Swedenborgian Society's copy of the *New Magazine* identifies the translator of the offending passage as J.A. Tulk.

[23] This was a publication of the London Universal Society, for which see below. A copy is bound in with the *New-Jerusalem Magazine*, as a supplement, Brit. Lib. press-mark C110d.7.

[24] John Isaac Hawkins in *New Church Repository* (NY), 1853, pp. 143–4.

short at theory: such sexual evils 'really existed at a period a little later'.[25] Indeed, Augustus Nordenskjöld, the author of an ambitious plan for the establishment of the New Jerusalem – a plan which made much of these unusual doctrines on marriage[26] – was himself accused of '*unchaste* conduct during his stay in Manchester . . . such as no New Churchman could overlook'.[27] Manoah Sibley, one of the first New Church ministers, went so far as to recall, forty years later, that in 1789 'the floodgates of immorality were in danger of being thrown open'.[28]

The supposed 'heresy' was in fact no heresy, for Swedenborg at one time or another advocated most of these views and, indeed, was an arrant male chauvinist. He condoned fornication by those who 'cannot as yet enter into marriage, and, from their passion for the sex, cannot moderate their desires', so long as they 'limit the vague love of the sex to one mistress'. But not with a virgin nor a married woman, and with no promise of marriage. He did endorse separation from a wife who was a non-receiver, and engaging 'a woman in her stead as a bed associate'. And Mr Hawkins's uncertainty can be clearly answered. This indulgence was granted only to men, 'but *not under any circumstances* is a corresponding indulgence granted to women'. The reason (explained Swedenborg) is that 'with men is the love of the sex in general, but with women the love *of one of the sex*'. 'The male sex', as is well known, 'has stimulations which actually kindle and inflame, but which is not the case with the female sex.' In short, some men might be 'driven so strongly by the inborn *amor sexus* they cannot contain themselves'.[29]

The chance survival of a few letters affords us a glimpse into the other side of such a situation of marital disharmony. Mary Pratt was an earnest Philadelphian and mystic seeker, and in January 1792 she was writing to her spiritual adviser, Thomas Langcake,

My husband is a strenuous follower of the visionary Swedenborg, and as the writings of the Baron militate against the pure doctrine and experience

[25] Dr Henry Bateman, *ibid.*, pp. 144–5; Elihu Rich, *ibid.*, p. 542.
[26] For Nordenskjöld's plan, see Morton Paley, *Blake and Swedenborgianism*, pp. 22–4. In general Paley and Peter Lineham, *The English Swedenborgians*, have excellent accounts of these early disputes.
[27] R.L. Tafel, *Documents concerning The Life and Character of Emmanuel Swedenborg* (1877), Vol. II, p. 807.
[28] C.T. Odhner, *Robert Hindmarsh*, p. 26.
[29] Tafel, Vol. II, pp. 1299–1304; W. White, *Emmanuel Swedenborg* (2nd edn, 1868), pp. 559–62; Odhner, *Robert Hindmarsh*, pp. 27–30.

of God manifested in the flesh, I have no fellowship with my partner in religion; nay I have been most cruelly treated by him, for my progress in the supercelestial life.

Mr Pratt, a builder and a relative of Lord Camden, can be identified as a contributor to the *Magazine of Knowledge concerning Heaven and Hell* under the guise of 'Ignoramus'. That the vibrations of this marriage were not wholly harmonious may be inferred if we scan the lucubrations of Ignoramus on 'the Lord's Maternal Humanity'–

The Lord was absolutely born as another man, being born of a woman, consequently inherited every evil and false hereditarily from his mother . . . His conception being from the Father, the being, the esse, the life of the Lord was Jehovah; but the recipient human form was from Mary, therefore his soul being Jehovah, could not possibly have the least shadow of evil; but in the humanity he received from Mary, was the recipient form of every evil then existing. . .[30]

Such profoundly anti-feminine views (which were indeed those of Swedenborg also and which perhaps influenced Blake's strange poem 'To Tirzah' (see below, p. 149)) may have contributed towards his wife, Mary's, search for solace not only in 'the supercelestial life' but also in communion with a certain 'Mr X':

I love and esteem Mr X; indeed he is the only person I have any fellowship with; and although our experience differs, yet he is pressing after the prize in earnest, through many difficulties both inward and outward.[31]

Scholars have with good reason tried to puzzle out where the Blakes may have been during these disputes in the early Church. It might seem that Swedenborg's teachings, and Nordenskjöld's plan, gave some licence to the old antinomian heresy of 'free love'. And in any event, Blake, who had recently annotated Lavater: 'They suppose that Womans Love is Sin, in consequence all the Loves and Graces with them are Sin', and who, in two years' time, was to write the *Visions of the Daughters of Albion*, with its explicit scenes of 'happy copulation', might seem to be on the side of the sexual liberation party. And there is even an oral tradition which

---

[30] Vol. II, p. 311. Ignoramus is identified as Pratt in pencil on the end-paper to my own copy (Vol. I) of the *Magazine*.

[31] Dr Williams's Library, MS 1.1.43. Mary Pratt added (14 October 1792) 'I have a persecuting husband and an infamous son, who is allowed plenty of money, while I am dealt with like Hagar the Ismailite – kept without a shilling.'

suggests that Blake meditated the taking of a concubine, to Catherine's distress.[32]

But it may not be so simple, and I suspect that the Blakes took neither side in the dispute. For as soon as the 'heretics' were excluded it would seem that dissension broke out among themselves. Some met in August 1789 to form a new society, 'The Universal Society for Promotion of the New Jerusalem Church'. This society was clearly prosecuting the old dispute. Its first resolution declared that –

the Truths contained in the Treatise of Conjugal Love . . . ought to be regarded . . . as the chief Jewel, support and Basis of the New Church, the fundamental Love of all Celestial, Spiritual and Natural Love. . .

These truths must be 'fully received' before any Society could be formed on genuine principles. But this 'chief Jewel' (it seems) was to be understood only in its spiritual sense, for members of the Society were also strictly instructed to keep the Ten Commandments. The Society also promised a speedy and accurate translation of the Treatise on Conjugal Love.[33]

The Secretary of the Universal Society was Henry Servanté, with J.A. Tulk, Chastanier and the two Swedish enthusiasts, Nordenskjöld and Wadstrom in support. The latter two were chiefly responsible for committing the Society to a rather grand project which no doubt had an influence on Blake's imagination: the plan to establish 'a Free Community on the Coast of Africa, on the Principles of the New Church'.[34] This plan was pursued with energy, the King was petitioned for his support and protection, Sierra Leone was selected, and in 1791 Nordenskjöld died pursuing rumours of an African Swedenborgian following.[35]

It is important to note that Robert Hindmarsh was not of the Universal Society. His objective remained, steadily, the recapture of the original Society at Great Eastcheap. This is emphasised by the fact that 1790 saw the publication of two Swedenborgian journals in London. The first, *The New-Jerusalem Magazine*, was the

---

[32] Mona Wilson, *The Life of William Blake* (1971 edn), p. 72.
[33] Constitution of 'the Universal London Society for Promotion of the New-Jerusalem Church', Swedenborg Society archive, H24.
[34] *Ibid.*, resolutions 12 and 13.
[35] See Paley, 'Blake and Swedenborgianism', Appendix A.

organ of the Universal Society. It ran for only six monthly numbers, from January to June, when it folded for lack of support.[36] Its editor was Servanté, J.A. Tulk its part-owner, and Chastanier passed on to the journal some unpublished passages from Swedenborg. Against this threat to his hegemony, Hindmarsh exerted his full energies as official Printer, not only to Swedenborg but also to His Royal Highness the Prince of Wales. Expending 100 guineas in advertising, and issuing 50,000 handbills, he launched *The New Magazine of Knowledge Concerning Heaven and Hell*, in March 1790. This ran until October 1791, in twenty numbers, and Hindmarsh was the sole editor.[37] When Servanté's journal collapsed, a somewhat irritable Chastanier returned to Hindmarsh's correspondence columns.

Where in all this do we find the Blakes? There are no substantial clues. But we can at least show that Blake was probably reading both of these journals. I have a number of instances of this, which it would be tedious to set forth in detail. We must be content now with a blunt demonstration.

The New-Jerusalem Magazine. The magazine published in its first two numbers five 'memorable relations', translated from a manuscript copy 'transmitted to us from Sweden'. The translation was presumably Chastanier's. In the first memorable fancy a 'satan' suddenly appears:

All Satans are merely natural, and can reason acutely, but from the fallacies of the senses; for which reason they see falses as truths . . . This Satan, when he came in view, appeared at first with a white living face, afterwards with a dead pale face, and, lastly, with a black infernal face.

It would seem that Blake had this in mind, and was mocking it, in his last 'memorable fancy' in *The Marriage of Heaven and Hell* where an Angel is challenged by a Devil: 'The Angel hearing this became almost blue but mastering himself grew yellow, & at last white pink & smiling. . .' (Plate 23, E42). The reversal is a characteristic trick of Blake's as is the reversal of devils and angels. Swedenborg's memorable fancy was not republished for fifty

---

[36] One thousand copies monthly were printed, but only half were sold, and fewer paid for: *New-Jerusalem Magazine*, p. 255.
[37] Hindmarsh, *Rise and Progress*, pp. 108–9. When the *New Magazine* ended it was followed by a *New-Jerusalem Journal* – also a Hindmarsh production – in 1792.

years.[38] I think it is clear enough that Blake was reading this journal.

The New Magazine of Knowledge Concerning Heaven and Hell. The example here is not so conclusive, since alternative sources can be found. But if Blake was reading it he cannot have overlooked the publication in the first three numbers, in three instalments, of J.P. Foersch's 'Natural History of the BOHON-UPAS, or POISON-TREE of the Island of JAVA'. This grisly account concluded that the Poison Tree may be called 'the *Tree of Death*, originating in *Hell*'. It is not likely to have contributed anything to Blake except the title of his 'Song of Experience'.[39] More convincing evidence might be found in the general discourse of the magazine, which touched on so many of Blake's preoccupations.

Meanwhile, apart from publishing, what else was Hindmarsh doing? He was not the man to suffer tamely the humiliation of being expelled from a Church which he had founded. Defeated on a matter of spiritual doctrine, he found a corporeal means of redress. He went to the landlord of the Church's premises in Great Eastcheap, and talked him into making him the sole tenant. He then descended on the astonished congregation and announced that they must either accept his doctrines and his form of church government or leave. Most of them left, in May 1792, and found a new temporary abode for New Jerusalem in Store Street, Tottenham Court Road.[40] Soon after the torn-out pages of the Eastcheap Minute Book resume, Hindmarsh was back there with a slender and disciplined congregation.

The dissensions, on this occasion, although they turned upon formal questions of church government, had a political dimension. None of the leading church members who survived to later years to write the history of the Church were of a radical or revolutionary persuasion. Chastanier who, on other counts, might have been close to Blake's positions, could only see (in 1792) that France was distracted by 'a spirit of mad philosophy'.[41] But clearly some

[38] Chastanier also called the memorable relations Swedenborg's 'Spiritual Diary'. For the complicated bibliography, see R.L. Tafel, *Emmanuel Swedenborg*, Vol. II, pp. 807–8, 1002; James Hyde, *A Bibliography*, pp. 118–19; *New-Church Review*, 1907, p. 441.

[39] Blake changed the title to 'A Poison Tree' from the advanced draft in the notebooks where it was 'Christian Forbearance'. *The Notebook of William Blake* (Oxford, 1973), ed. David V. Erdman, p. 114 reversed.

[40] Thomas Robinson, *A Remembrancer*, pp. 95–6, 113; Walter Wilson, *History and Antiquities of Dissenting Churches*, pp. 170–1.

[41] *New-Jerusalem Journal*, 1792, Vol. I, pp. 367–70.

members of the Great Eastcheap flock were touched by the democratic upsurge of those years. Matters came to a crisis, not in terms of political issues, but on questions of Church discipline and government. One point is overwhelmingly clear: Robert Hindmarsh himself was an ultra-conservative, desperately trying to bring the movement under discipline and hierarchical control. He advocated an episcopal (indeed papal) form of government, with the power to ordain priests derivative from his own supposed authority.[42] Somehow or other he managed to dominate the Second Annual (federal) Conference of the Church in 1790, but his authority was rejected at the Third Annual Conference in April 1791. This conference accepted several priests already ordained, but insisted that in future no priests should be ordained without the recommendation of the society to which they belonged and the approbation of the General Conference. Hindmarsh and his clique of self-appointed priests insisted that the power of ordination should remain with them. In opposition to this, a resolution was passed to put the clergy 'on an equal footing' with the laity. Whether ministers would be allowed salaries was questioned.[43]

Hindmarsh returned to the offensive at the Fourth Annual Conference (1792), proposing an elaborate priestly form of government, with 'one visible Official Head' (himself or his father) rather than 'the Votes of the People at large'. Hindmarsh's opposition to more democratic forms of Church government was explicitly political: he observed the duty incumbent upon all in the 'present critical moment, when the Principles of Infidelity and Democracy was Spreading abroad' to stand forward for the Constitution and Order.[44] And he read to the conference a declaration of solemn disapprobation of republican or democratical principles. It was his big throw and he lost: the conference rejected his proposals. But the Printer to the Prince of Wales was not so easily to be beaten. He printed a rival version of the conference Minutes, enlarging

---

[42] On the Church's foundation leading members drew lots for the power to ordain: Robert Hindmarsh drew a ticket mysteriously marked 'Ordain'. Subsequently he placed his name at the head of documents and added: '*Ordained by the Divine Auspices of the Lord*', Thomas Robinson, pp. 137–8. For Hindmarsh's version, see his *Rise and Progress*, pp. 69–71.

[43] *Ibid.*, pp. 95–8; *Minutes of the First Seven Sessions of the General Conference of the New Church* (1885).

[44] On the revolutionary sympathies of some early Swedenborgians, see Lineham, *The English Swedenborgians*, pp. 268–82. C.F. Nordenskjöld translated Paine's *Rights of Man* into Swedish.

upon his own position. He repeated his objection to the appointment of ministers 'by popular Elections'. Authority is the Lord's,
and is delegated to Kings and Ministers, who 'represent the Lord,
and not the People'. Appointment to offices in Church or State 'by
the popular Voice is so much like . . . atheistical Doctrine', and it
was 'absurdity to say that the Sheep have the Right and Power of
chusing and dismissing their Shepherd'. In 1793 there were rival
annual conferences: the Fifth (meeting in Birmingham) and a rump
meeting in London under Hindmarsh. Thereafter no more conferences were held until 1897, although Hindmarsh continued for
several years to meet with a small group of devotees to his episcopalian regime.[45]

Thus the founding five years of the Church were full of dissension. And we still have not placed Blake within this. Perhaps the
nearest we may get to a comment on the whole episode, as the
permissive 'Nunc Licet' gave way to Hindmarsh's priesthood, is
in the Song of Experience, 'The Garden of Love':

> I went to the Garden of Love,
> And saw what I never had seen:
> A chapel was built in the midst,
> Where I used to play on the green.
>
> And the gates of this Chapel were shut,
> And Thou shalt not. writ over the the door;
> So I turn'd to the Garden of Love,
> That so many sweet flowers bore,
>
> And I saw it was filled with graves,
> And tomb-stones where flowers should be:
> And Priests in black gowns, were walking their rounds,
> And binding with briars, my joys & desires. (E26)

One possible link with Blake is suggested by a strange half-
serious, half-satirical proof of 1791.[46] 'Sons of Liberty, Children of
the Free-born Woman!' this commences and it offers a supposed

---

[45] Robinson, pp. 109, 115; *Minutes*, pp. 4, 7; Hindmarsh, *Rise and Progress*, pp. 145–8. On
the conservative evolution of the New Church in the 1790s, see also John Howard, 'An
Audience for *The Marriage of Heaven and Hell*', *Blake Studies*, Vol. III, no. 1, Fall 1970,
which shows that the Church placed an increasingly heavy emphasis on the decalogue:
i.e. the Moral Law.

[46] Emmanuel Swedenborg's *New-Year's Gift to his Readers for 1791*. This has been ascribed to
Benedict Chastanier: see Hyde, 'Benedict Chastanier and the Illuminati of Avignon', p.
205.

letter from the seer, indicting the fallacies of contemporary New-Churchmen, including that of 'the accursed doctrine of Predestination . . . the Cockatrice's egg'. This, of course, was also Blake's complaint in his indignant annotations to Swedenborg's *Divine Providence*. In a 'postscript' Swedenborg is made to give an enthusiastic description of 'the Lord's True Christian Church'. The Church's true members will be–

conspicuously distinguishable from all the rest of men, by their true and unaffected brotherly love, most tender regards and affections towards each other, as well indeed as by their most unbounded benevolence towards all their fellow-creatures of any nation, country, people, and language, religion, sect, or party whatsoever, and by their most indefatigable zeal in doing good to all God's creatures. Oh what a Society that will be!

Or as Blake had it more laconically, in his annotations to *Divine Love and Divine Wisdom*, 'The Whole of the New Church is in the Active Life & not in Ceremonies at all' (E595). There are other touches which suggest a Blakean association: a reference to a 'Real Devil' which cannot become an 'Angel of Light, agreeably to the system of Jacob Behmen, George Welling, Law, and most of the Hermetic Philosophers'.[47] And there is an editorial comment in which the author castigates those sects which 'fall into that unpardonable Babylonish Error, of thinking none can be saved but those who wear its own livery' and who 'naturally dwindle into that most antichristian principle of cordially hating whosoever . . . do not . . . precisely think as they do'.[48] This conforms to Blake's known dislike of 'Sectaries' (E582).

These inferences might place Blake in alliance with Chastanier, formerly of the Universal Society. But the evidence is inconclusive. And to press the suggestion too far is to lose the revolutionary and antinomian force of Blake's critique of Swedenborgianism. We have to find some other way of breaking open this problem. And the best point of entry may be with the 'divine humanity'.

---

[47] *Ibid.*, p. 27. This prompts the speculation that the author (Chastanier) might have been a possible original of the Angel in the *Marriage of Heaven and Hell* 'who is now become a Devil [and] is my particular friend; we often read the Bible together in its infernal or diabolical sense which the world shall have if they behave well'. (E43).

[48] *Ibid.*, p. 31.

CHAPTER 9

'The Divine Image'

'The Divine Image', in my view, is the axle upon which the *Songs of Innocence* turn, just as 'The Human Abstract' is the axle for the *Songs of Experience*. It is often supposed to be a profoundly Swedenborgian song, and this is what we must examine. It is certainly true that the 'Divine Human' was at the centre of Swedenborgian discourse at that time; indeed, it might be said to be the signature of the New Jerusalem church. When Robert Southey visited a congregation, he found that—

Christ is his *divine*, or in his *glorified human*, was repeatedly addressed as the only God; and the preacher laboured to show that the profane were those who worshipped three Gods. . .[1]

In shorthand the doctrine was Christ is God, and Robert Hindmarsh was astounded to find these words chalked by unknown hands on walls in and for miles round London in the early 1780s.[2]

The doctrine of Swedenborgian receivers was set forth as the first to be recorded in a 'Compendious View of the principal Doctrines of the New Church':

Contrary to Unitarians who deny, and to Trinitarians who hold, a Trinity of persons in the Godhead, they maintain, that there is a Divine Trinity in the person of Jesus Christ, consisting of Father, Son, and Holy Ghost, just like the human Trinity in every individual man, of soul, body, and operation. . .

That Jehovah God himself came down from heaven, and assumed human nature for the purpose of removing hell from man, of restoring the heavens to order, and of preparing the way for a new church upon earth; and that herein consists the true nature of redemption, which was effected solely by the omnipotence of the Lord's Divine Humanity.[3]

[1] Southey, *Letters from England*, Vol. III, p. 113.   [2] Hindmarsh, *Rise and Progress*, p. 13.
[3] *New Magazine of Knowledge concerning Heaven and Hell*, Vol. I, pp. 16–18.

146

The Liturgy of the Church required that the Minister announce to the assembly that they were gathered to 'glorify his DIVINE HUMANITY'.[4]

The 'divine humanity' lay in the assumption by an omnipotent God of human nature in Christ's person. This was done, not by splitting into a Trinity, but by God infusing His own life into Christ, through the 'divine influx'. The doctrine created difficulties for early receivers. The Reverend Joseph Proud, a General Baptist Minister in Norwich who was converted to the New Church, later recalled his troubles when a Swedenborgian introduced him to 'the doctrine of the LORD as the only God in His divine Humanity':

I could very well agree to the Lord as being the *only God*, but when he mentioned a *divine humanity* I warmly opposed him and reply'd, 'what is divine cannot be *human*, nor what is *Human*, be *divine*'.[5]

Correspondents returned to the theme in the New Church magazines. Correspondents from Keighley affirmed–

That there is a Trinity in the Lord, namely, the Divinity, the Divine Humanity, and the Divine Proceeding . . . [but] a divine Trinity may be considered to exist in one person, and so to be one God; but not in three persons.[6]

The Reverend Proud, fully converted, explained the doctrine in a discourse in a newly opened New Jerusalem temple in Birmingham to which he ministered. God was '*in one person only*':

As to his essential divinity, he is the Father – as to his divine humanity, he is the Son – and as to his divine operation, he is the Holy Spirit. . .

He took on–

our nature; in that nature subdued the powers of hell, redeemed mankind, and made salvation possible to all; . . . he glorified that humanity, made it divine, united it with his own essential divinity, and is therefore *God and man in one divine person*.[7]

With the bringing of the divine together in one person, it is not surprising that the Unitarians viewed the Swedenborgians as competitors. Joseph Priestley addressed letters to members of the

[4] *Liturgy of the New Church* (printed and sold by R. Hindmarsh, 1791).
[5] 'Memoirs of Joseph Proud', MSS in Swedenborg Society Conference Library, 1822, pp. 7–8.
[6] *New Magazine of Knowledge*, Vol. II, p. 237.
[7] J. Proud, *The Fundamental Doctrines of the New Jerusalem* (Birmingham, 1792), p. 15.

New Church, urging them to adopt the Unitarian solution and to acknowledge Christ as a man 'but that God was with him, and acted by him'. A ding-dong exchange ensued.[8] In the course of this some apologetics turned upon the contrasting sexual derivation of the divine human. Swedenborg affirmed that 'human nature cannot be transmuted into the Divine Essence, neither commixed therewith'. Therefore a distinction must be maintained in Christ's genesis between the 'human nature from the mother' and the Divine Essence from the divine influx, or from the Father (i.e. the male principle which infused his soul).[9] What Mary supplied was 'a covering, called the maternal human, or a body like our own, so that the divine human (which was eternal and infinite) dwells in the maternal human, which was finite. . .' At the resurrection Christ cast off all materiality, the maternal human. 'Hence the God we worship, is not the material human of this world, but he that ever was, is, and ever will be, the invisible *I am*. . .'[10]

Correspondents in the *New Magazine* joined the same discussion, and it is difficult not to feel that the Virgin Mary was subjected to some male animosity. A distinction is laboured between the divine principle (always male) and the *humanum maternum* or in Swedenborg's phrase the *humanum infirmum*, 'the unfixed, unsteady, infirm humanity' (from the mother).[11] 'Ignoramus', whom we have already met (above, p. 139), explained that 'by putting off the humanity from the mother, is evidently meant the conquering and expelling the evil, and by putting on the humanity from the father, is bringing the first principles of human nature, or the divine human, into the ultimates. . .'[12] Another correspondent concluded that Christ's conception (or infusion) was 'manifested in the lowest parts of human nature, and the infirm body derived from the Virgin was tainted with hereditary evil. . .'[13] Hence it must be decisively put off. Chastanier returned to the columns with yet another passage from Swedenborg from his store of manuscripts.

[8] Joseph Priestley, *Letters to the Members of the New Jerusalem Church* (Birmingham, 1791), p. 31; J. Proud, *A Candid and Impartial Reply to the Reverend Dr Priestley's Letters* (Birmingham, 1791); R. Hindmarsh, 'Letters to Dr Priestley', *Analytical Review*, 11, Appendix, p. 517, 14, pp. 190–3; J. Bellamy, *Jesus Christ the Only God* (1792), a reply to Priestley.
[9] Bellamy, p. 51, citing Swedenborg, *Arcana Coelestia*, 2655–2659.
[10] Bellamy, Letter II.
[11] Benedict Chastanier, 'On the Lord's Humanity', *New Magazine*, 2, pp. 305–9. See also 2, pp. 266–8.
[12] *Ibid.*, 2, p. 313.
[13] *Ibid.*, 2, p. 314: 'M.B.G.'

From this it appeared that on the cross 'the Lord, from the divine in himself, wholly expelled the evil which he derived from his mother. . .'[14] 'Ignoramus' returned to the attack in the *Magazine*'s final number, making a clear distinction between the Lord's masculine and feminine souls: 'there was not an evil or a false that ever existed in the world, but what the Lord inherited from the mother as to the recipient form in the feminine soul'.[15]

All this helps one to understand the late addition to the *Songs of Experience*, 'To Tirzah', which some critics have found 'obscure':[16]

> Whate'er is Born of Mortal Birth,
> Must be consumed with the Earth
> To rise from Generation free;
> Then what have I to do with thee?
>
> The Sexes sprung from Shame & Pride
> Blow'd in the morn: in evening died
> But Mercy changd Death into Sleep;
> The Sexes rose to work & weep.
>
> Thou Mother of my Mortal part
> With cruelty didst mould my Heart,
> And with false self-decieving tears,
> Didst bind my Nostrils Eyes & Ears.
>
> Didst close my Tongue in senseless clay
> And me to Mortal Life betray:
> The Death of Jesus set me free,
> Then what have I to do with thee?

This, if we set aside the enigmatic second verse, might be an expression of orthodox Swedenborgian doctrine, even according to 'Ignoramus'. The *maternum humanum* supplies only a covering to clothe the divine spirit, and Blake recalls the words of Jesus to Mary (John 2:4): 'Woman, what have I to do with thee?' To this he adds a wider mythic dimension, in the name 'Tirzah', perhaps taken from *Revelation* 1.11, the name of a city which is rival and opponent to Jerusalem and which becomes for Blake an emblem of 'worldly authority and . . . materialistic thought'.[17] The poem

[14] *Ibid.*, 2, pp. 374–6.   [15] *Ibid.*, 2, pp. 442–4.
[16] As did Sir Geoffrey Keynes in his notes to the reproduction of the *Songs* (Oxford, 1967), p. 154.
[17] David W. Lindsay, *Blake: Songs of Innocence and Experience* (Atlantic Highlands, N.J., 1989), pp. 82–3.

was not added until 1805, and perhaps later, and hence belongs
to a period in which Blake may have been becoming reconciled to
Swedenborgianism.[18] And in *Jerusalem* he wrote:

> A Vegetated Christ & a Virgin Eve, are the Hermaphroditic
> Blasphemy, by his Maternal Birth he is that Evil One
> And his Maternal Humanity must be put off Eternally (E247)

However, let us return to 1789. All this debate about the 'divine
human' does rather little to prepare us for Blake's beautiful poem,
'The Divine Image':

> To Mercy Pity Peace and Love
> All pray in their distress:
> And to these virtues of delight
> Return their thankfulness.
>
> For Mercy Pity Peace and Love,
> Is God, our father dear:
> And Mercy Pity Peace and Love,
> Is Man his child and care.
>
> For Mercy has a human heart
> Pity, a human face:
> And Love, the human form divine,
> And Peace, the human dress.
>
> Then every man, of every clime,
> That prays in his distress,
> Prays to the human form divine
> Love Mercy Pity Peace.
>
> And all must love the human form,
> In heathen, turk, or jew.
> Where Mercy, Love & Pity dwell
> There God is dwelling too.

It is a pity to argue about so transparent a poem, but this must
be done. Mr F.W. Bateson, in common with other critics, found it
to be 'a thoroughly Swedenborgian poem',[19] and Kathleen Raine
has concurred: 'There could be no more simple and orthodox state-

---

[18] Alicia Ostriker, *William Blake, The Complete Poems* (Harmondsworth, 1977), p. 889, says
that poem cannot be earlier than 1803; Erdman (E722) suggests mid-1805 or later. Blake
told Crabb Robinson in 1826 that Christ 'took much after his Mother And in so far he
was one of the worst of Men'.

[19] F.W. Bateson, *Selected Poems of William Blake* (1957).

ment of the central doctrine of the New Church.'[20] It may therefore seem surprising that the poem, immediately, in its first verse, commences with a refutation of Swedenborg. For Swedenborg had argued in *Divine Love and Divine Wisdom*:

With Respect to God, it is not possible that he can love and be reciprocally beloved by others, in whom there is . . . any Thing Divine; for if there was . . . any Thing Divine in them, then it would not be beloved by others, but it would love itself. . .

Blake, who was then in his most sympathetic state towards the seer, challenged this with 'False': 'Take it so or the contrary it comes to the same for if a thing loves it is infinite' (E593). The first verse of 'The Divine Image' could not be more explicit in its rejection of Swedenborg's doctrine, and the verses which follow consolidate this. The poem resumes 'the central doctrine of the New Church' in no way.

One can illustrate this by the means of contrast. An early convert to the New Church, whom we have met already, was the Revd Joseph Proud, aged forty-five, who had already served for some twenty-five years as minister of the General Baptists. Converted dramatically to the new faith, he had a little reputation as a poet,[21] and – shortly after visiting London from Norwich in 1789 – he was urged to prepare a volume of original hymns for the use of the public worship of the New Church.[22] He did this with expedition, writing a modest contribution of three hundred hymns in the intervals between breaking the news to his Norwich flock that he was about to leave them to become one of the first Ministers of the New Church (in Birmingham). One of his first efforts was, exactly, 'On Divine Humanity',[23] from which these verses are taken:

---

[20] Raine, *Blake and Tradition*, I, p. 20. Also Raine, 'The Human Face of God', in *Blake and Swedenborg*, ed. Harvey F. Bellin and Darrell Ruhl (Swedenborg Foundation, N.Y., 1985), pp. 88–90. Miss Raine is strongly committed to the view that there could not possibly have been any humanist influence on Blake and therefore reads 'The Divine Image' as 'deep eschatological mystery'.

[21] His dreadful poem announcing his conversion, *Jehovah's Mercy made Known to all Mankind in these Last Days* was published in 1789 by Hindmarsh. I do not think that all mankind read it. The Old Church could not have received worse references: it was '*sunk, vastated, fallen*', 'polluted' and 'to Whoredome, gross Adultery is given'.

[22] (Ed. E. Madeley), Revd Joseph Proud, *The Aged Minister's Last Legacy* (1854), p. xi; MS 'Memoir of Joseph Proud', pp. 15–16; at the General Conference, 5 April 1790, Proud announced that he had already written many hymns: *Minutes*, pp. 8–9.

[23] This hymn was singled out for special publication in the *New Magazine*, Vol. I, p. 288 (August 1790).

> . . . Lord, we come to thee,
>   And bow before thy throne;
> In thy Divine Humanity,
>   Thou art our God alone.
>
> Thy esse none can see,
>   That is beyond our sight;
> But thy Divine Humanity
>   Is seen in heavenly light.
>
> Thou art the only God,
>   The *only Man* art thou;
> And only thee our souls adore,
>   At thy bles'd feet we bow.
>
> In essence thou art one,
>   And one in person too;
> Tho' in thy essence seen by none,
>   Thy person we may view. . .

In another hymn, on the same theme, we have these verses:

> But thou art God & God alone,
>   In thy Humanity;
> Before thee, Lord, no God was known,
>   Nor shall be after thee.
>
> Thy human nature is divine,
>   Divine is human too;
> Here God and Man in one combine,
>   And not three Gods, nor two.

One begins to suspect, from a certain barren shuttling of paradoxes, that the doctrine at this point created headaches for the pastor and perhaps dissension among the flock. And this can be confirmed by two lines from a further hymn:

> Why should we fear to say or sing,
>   Our God is Man alone. . .

But the Dutch courage of Mr Proud is immediately covered by an evasive footnote: 'By man alone, understand that God is the only man, strictly speaking, as all mankind are men from him and not in themselves. . .'[24]

---

[24] Joseph Proud, *Hymns and Spiritual Songs for the Use of the Lord's New Church* (2nd edn, 1791), pp. 142, 219–21. The first edition, in 500 copies, was published in 1790.

Let us now return to Blake's poem, and attempt the painful exercise of reading it with Mr Proud's alternative still in our mind. The instant contrast is between the deference of Proud and the egalitarian humanism of Blake.[25] Without any outrage or rupture of logical or poetic structure, with the greatest quietness, we move from the acceptable (although not to Swedenborg) statement of the first verse to the heresy of the last three. There is indeed some difference in matter between Blake and Proud. Blake passes by altogether the doctrinal issue of the Trinity. And there is an absence in him of that obeisance before 'thy throne' ('Thee we adore, eternal Lord/In thy Humanity') which distances God once more ('beyond our sight'), so that the notion of God's humanity comes through not as authentic but as a metaphysical conjuring trick. 'Thy esse none can see/That is beyond our sight' – but Blake's divine esse can be seen, in human virtues, and only seen there.[26] This is what Blake's song is about, and what it is saying is not so much around the theme of 'divine humanity' as of human divinity: the poem is called 'The Divine Image'. And hence if man worships – but Blake does not use this word, he uses prayers of distress, thankfulness and love – he must worship these qualities as he finds them in himself. Blake is breaking both with the paternalist image of God which (whether a vengeful Father or an all-knowing First Cause or, as with Mr Proud, a somewhat muddled but bene-volent gentleman) occupied a position of critical importance within all eighteenth-century ideology, and he was breaking also – and as I think explicitly – with the abasement before 'Jehovah God in his GLORIFIED HUMANITY' as it was demanded by the Confes-sional of the New Church as expressed in its *Liturgy* (another Hind-marsh product):

Most merciful Lord Jesus, who in thy DIVINE HUMANITY art the Only God of Heaven and Earth, the supreme Governor of the Universe, and before whom the whole Angelic Host fall prostrate in profound Humili-ation, permit us thy sinful Creatures, Worms of the Earth, to approach thy heavenly Majesty. . .[27]

---

[25] See Heather Glen, *Vision and Disenchantment: Blake's 'Songs' and Wordsworth's Lyrical Ballads* (Cambridge, 1983), pp. 151–6.

[26] In the Hindmarsh version of the *Liturgy* it is stated in a footnote that 'the Faces of Jehovah' in Holy Scripture signify 'the Love, Mercy, Peace and Goodness of the Lord'.

[27] An *Order of Worship* was drawn up as early as January 1788; Hindmarsh, p. 60. The Liturgy was named for revision at the second Annual Conference, April 1790: *Minutes*.

Blake at all times kept his distance from the Swedenborgian doctrine of the 'divine humanity'. The problem of immanence and transcendence, identity and essence, was being worked at in different ways in the early New Church milieu. A contributor to the *New Magazine of Knowledge Concerning Heaven and Hell* tried to explain it by offering a Swedenborgian version of the Lord's Prayer:

Our Father,	O infinite eternal esse,
Who art in the heavens	Manifested in the heavens
Hallowed be thy name	Whom we adore in the existence of thy Divine Humanity
Thy Kingdom come,	Let the divine influx of wisdom
Thy will be done	And love,
As in heaven	Flowing from thee through thy new heavens
So also upon earth.	Be received with a pure affection by each member of thy New Church.
Give us this day	Give us according to our various states of want
Our daily bread. . .	That true nourishment of our souls, that will be our increasing spiritual support to eternity. . .[28]

Nor was this contributor ('Ignoramus' once more) unusual in finding exceptional difficulty in selecting proper spiritual correspondences for such corporeal terms as 'earth' and 'bread'. The characteristic movement is away from the concrete image, whereas Blake leads us back to 'heart', 'face', 'form' and 'dress'. And it is Swedenborg's own writings which are responsible for this evasive movement. 'What Person of Sound Reason', he had asked in the *Divine Love and Wisdom*, 'doth not perceive that the Divine is not divisible?' If he should say—

that it is possible there may be several infinities, Uncreates, Omnipotents and Gods, provided they have the same Essence, and that thereby there is one and the same Essence but one and the same Identity?

This passage had bothered Blake (then in his most sympathetic state towards Swedenborg) a great deal. His annotation runs:

Answer   Essence is not Identity but from Essence proceeds Identity &

---

[28] Vol. II, p. 352. Another dreadful version of the Lord's Prayer appeared in the *Order of Worship* in which 'give us this day our daily bread' is given as 'a suitable supply from thy divine human give us momentarily, according to our state of reception'.

from one Essence may proceed many Identities as from one Affection
may proceed. many thoughts
Surely this is an oversight.

That there is but one Omnipotent Uncreate & God I agree but that there
is but one Infinite I do not. for if all but God is not Infinite they shall
come to an End which God forbid.

If the Essence was the same *as the* Identity there could be but one Identity.
which is false
Heaven would upon this plan be but a Clock but one & the same Essence
is therefore Essence & not Identity. (E593)

A consideration of this important note would take us back to
Behmenist and Muggletonian notions of eternity and creation (see
above, p. 70). But in its immediate relevance it bears upon the
problem of the 'divine humanity'. Blake prefers an image which
allows 'many identities' to proceed from one 'essence', just as many
thoughts may proceed from one 'affection': this allows him to think
of the divine essence both as 'one & the same Essence' and also
as that essence expressed in the many identities of men, while still
remaining essentially divine.

   Swedenborg offered texts which were both diaphonous and contradictory, and which allowed several positions to be held. Thus
(1) – as endorsed in the principles of the New Church – it was
limited to the doctrine of God taking on mortal form in Jesus and
thus *assuming* divine humanity. As Proud warbled, 'thy esse none
can see' but 'thy Divine Humanity/Is seen in heavenly light.' But
(2) an extension of this could be proposed, in that God makes
himself known to man through heavenly inspiration, working upon
his affections (rather than upon his understanding) and hence his
'esse' enters into man as 'love'. A constant Swedenborgian image
is of the sun as the source of the influx of love, and of man's
spirit as the reflector or recipient of this influx. That part of man
enlightened by love shares in the divine esse and is in that sense
itself divine. Thus Miss Raine cites Swedenborg's *True Christian
Religion*:

A man is an organ of life, and God alone is life: God infuses his life into
the organ and all its parts; and God grants man a sense that the life in
himself is as it were his own.[29]

[29] Raine, *Blake and Tradition*, Vol. 1, p. 18.

And she concludes that Blake is 'preaching the doctrine of the New Church'. But Blake's song doesn't sound like this. He sounds as if he is saying something much blunter: there is nothing in 'The Divine Image' about God 'infusing' or 'granting' to man 'a sense' of life being 'as it were' his own. I can't find the words 'as it were' anywhere in the Blake *Concordance*. It sounds as if Blake is saying exactly what he says in *The Marriage of Heaven and Hell*: 'God only Acts & Is, in existing Beings or Men' (E39). And that, too, can be read in two different ways: that God, as some disembodied esse, only finds embodiment in existing beings or men: or that there is no God anywhere else. I suspect that Blake fluctuated between contrary states, perhaps emphasising in 1789 the first, the second in 1791–3 and at some time thereafter returning to the first.[30]

In any case, we have a clear idea of how Blake came to his poem. In 1789 when annotating the humanist, Lavater, he was delighted with certain passages. When he fell upon 'He who *hates the wisest and best of men, hates the Father of men; for, where is the Father of men to be seen but in the most perfect of his children?*' he struck out both of the 'hates' and inserted above them 'loves' and underlined the italicised phrase, adding: 'this is true worship'.[31] When Lavater wrote that 'art is nothing but the highest sagacity and exertion of human nature; *and what nature will he honour who honours not the human?*' he underlined again, and noted 'human nature is the image of God'. And, immediately above, Lavater had written: '*He, who adored an impersonal God, has none; and, without guide or rudder, launches on an immense abyss that first absorbs his powers, and next himself.*' Blake underscored the whole passage, and exclaimed: 'Most superlatively beautiful & most affectionatly Holy & pure would to God that all men would consider it' (E586). This prepares us for the annotation to Swedenborg's *Divine Love and Wisdom*, probably in the next year, especially section 11 where the seer comments that the Africans 'entertain an Idea of God as of a Man, and say that no one can have any other Idea of God'. Blake notes approvingly: 'Think of a white cloud. as being holy you cannot love it but think of a holy man within the cloud love springs up in your thoughts. for to

---

[30] As late as 1820 Blake annotated Berkeley: *Siris*: 'God is Man & exists in us & we in him.'

[31] Blake returns to this in *The Marriage of Heaven and Hell*, Plates 22–3 (E42): 'The worship of God is. Honouring his gifts in other men each according to his genius. and loving the greatest men best, those who envy or calumniate great men hate God. for there is no other God.'

think of holiness distinct from man is impossible to the affections. Thought alone can make monsters, but the affections cannot' (E592–3).

There is, of course, a pre-history to all this. The eighteenth century, as is notorious, saw a general movement among the enlightened dissenters through Arianism to Socinianism towards the resting-place of Unitarianism, which entailed the denial of the Trinity and of Christ's divinity. This was one way to a humanist Christ. But the Muggletonians, the Philadelphians and what there was of an articulate antinomian tradition, took, with variants, a different path. Positing only one God, they might see him in the pantheist tradition, as dispersed through all life, or, as did the Muggletonians, as assuming Himself, in the infant Christ, full mortality. Thus Reeve:

There is no other God but the Man Jesus . . . the eternal God, the Man of Glory, who is a distinct God in the Person of a Man . . . Therefore . . . they cannot take the Sword of Steel to slay their Brother, because they know that Man is the Image of God.[32]

Thus also Thomas Tomkinson, some of whose gentle and slightly rationalised versions of the Muggletonian faith were published posthumously. He speaks of God 'begetting himself into a Son . . . God sent forth HIMSELF to be made of a Woman, to redeem us from the Curse of the Law. . .'[33] Both the pantheist and the embodiment-of-God-as-Christ versions were found among eighteenth-century Muggletonians, and they sometimes co-existed in the same mind. I find in a letter of a believer, William Sedgwick, in 1794 the old tension between the two being held:

Christ is the Light that Lighteth Every man that Commeth into the world yet none but God is Infinite. Notwithstanding tho God the Creater virtuale Dwells in all his Creatures. Nothing is Capable of the Indwelling Infinite power But God alone . . . Even man in his Created Purety tho of the very nature of the Divine Creator yet not Infinite. . .

The argument is close to the discourse preoccupying the New Church, but the emphasis – and where the Muggletonians differed sharply from the Swedenborgians – lay upon Christ's concentrated divinity:

[32] John Reeve, *Sacred Remains* (n.d.), p. 83.
[33] *A System of Religion*, first published in 1729 from manuscripts found among Tomkinson's papers after his death, pp. 22–3.

The Eternal God Left his glorious kingdom Came Down & Enterd The Blessed virgin Mary's whomb. There Desolved his Spritual Body in to seed and Natuer & Quickend into a body of flesh Blood & Bone Like unto man in all Respects (Sins Only Excepted). . .[34]

Man is the 'Image of God' and he is also the 'ark' or 'tabernacle' of God: and God is Christ. The image of Christ is always that of the sun or of blinding light: as Richard Pickersgill, the Muggletonian painter, wrote in 1803, in heaven 'we shall behold the bright burning Glorious person'.[35] It is such a bright burning glorious infant that Blake shows us in his remarkable (and unprecedented) Nativity, with Christ springing from Mary's womb into the hands of St Elizabeth, with St John the Baptist (also an infant) looking on (Illus. 9). David Bindman finds this treatment to be 'unique in European art': the 'moment of birth is represented as a heavenly burst of radiance'.[36]

> And thine the Human Face & thine
>   The Human Hands & Feet & Breath
> Entering thro' the Gates of Birth
>   And passing thro' the Gates of Death.   (E171)

The pantheist view, which proposed God as some quantum of divine energy dispersed through all life, but more especially in the spiritual nature of men and women, and the notion of God as Christ, are difficult to combine, and perhaps intellectually impossible. Or the difficulty may only be in reconciling these two alternative versions of the same vision. I suggest that, in his later years when he had rejected deism, Blake was often preoccupied with the problem of reconciling, through imagery or myth, these seemingly contradictory visions. Perhaps we have it in *Vala*:

Then those in Great Eternity met in the Council of God As one Man, for contracting their Exalted Senses They behold Multitude or Expanding they behold as one As One Man all the Universal family & that One man They call Jesus the Christ, & they in him & he in them Live in Perfect harmony. . . (E306)

Or in his *Descriptions of the Last Judgement*:

. . . I have seen [those States] in my Imagination when distant they appear as One Man but as you approach they appear Multitudes of Nations . . . I have seen when at a distance Multitudes of Men in Har-

---

[34] British Library, Muggletonian archive.   [35] *Ibid.*
[36] Bindman, *Blake as an Artist*, pp. 121–2.

mony appear like a single Infant sometimes in the Arms of a Female (this represented the Church). (E546)

And we have it also in the splendid exchange with Crabb Robinson in December 1825:

On my asking in what light he viewed the great question concerning the Divinity of Jesus Christ, he said; '*He is the only God.*' But then he added – 'And so am I and so are you.'[37]

Crabb Robinson was floored by that, and so in a way are we, although we rejoice at Blake's triumph and have a swift sense of some revealed truth. But what we may actually be sensing is a creative contradiction. Blake is refusing to renounce 'Mercy's lord' or to reduce the gospel to the level of rational historical explanation;[38] but equally he is refusing to sublimate Jesus or his gospel into an abstraction, to tease out from this some bodiless fiction and call this 'God', or to humiliate himself before a divine essence in which all men share. The reply breaks at a bound from the net of the theological disputes of his time, between Arian, Socinian, Unitarian or Deist positions. It conveys a truth of a poetic kind, expressive of a certain equipoise and tension of values, appropriate to lyrical expression. And expressed thus, neither Urizen nor Crabb Robinson could answer it.

Obscurities can arise in the later prophetic books, not just because Blake was managing his art badly, but because he was attempting to reconcile doctrines that could not be logically reconciled. The books plunge into obscurity at exactly those points (of which the problem of the unity and the dispersal of the godhead is one) where Blake was involved in actual doctrinal or philosophical contradictions.

But a contradiction in thought, which derives from an acute tension of contrasting values, neither of which can be abandoned, can be wholly creative. If we will neither deny Christ's divinity nor elevate it above that of mortal creation which shares in the same divine essence, then we have an intense and mystic humanism. If God exists in Men and nowhere else, then the whole cosmic conflict between darkness and light, things corporeal and spiritual, must be enacted within oneself and one's fellow men and nowhere

---

[37] Bentley, *Blake Records*, p. 310.
[38] In later years he said that Swedenborg 'was wrong in endeavouring to explain to the *rational* faculty what the reason cannot comprehend', *ibid.*, p. 312.

else. This meant above all – and this was perhaps the greatest
offence of such an heresy in the eyes of a more vengeful Christian
tradition – breaking with any sense of personal conviction in original sin. There had been a Fall and a dispersal of the godhead;
the godly nature of man now struggled to repair the breach and
return to universal harmony, the family of love, Jerusalem. Were
man to be called an abject and sinful worm would be (from this
standpoint) to blaspheme against the godhead within him. 'Every
thing has as much right to Eternal Life as God who is the Servant
of Man.'[39]

I cannot see that either Lavater or Swedenborg offers to us the
vocabulary or the imagery of 'The Divine Image'. Blake's annotations to them indicate not discovery but recognition and assent, or
correction and exposition, of tenets already held. It is a poem which
with purity and lucidity holds in tension and reconciles the two
positions we have been exploring. From the first verse – and how
much is won in the first verse – we are drawn into an ascending
circle of mutuality. It was therefore with a delighted shock of recognition that I came across in the *New Magazine of Knowledge Concerning Heaven and Hell*, inserted without preliminaries or explanation, a long extract from Thomas Tomkinson's *A System of Religion*:
'That God ever was, is, and will be, in the Form of a Man':

Can righteousness and holiness act forth themselves without a body? Or
do you ever read, that righteousness and holiness were ever acted forth,
in, or by any other form but the form of a man? When God said, *Be ye
holy as I am holy*: what! must the souls run out of the bodies to be like
him? If they did, they would be nothing. Where would mercy and justice,
meekness and humility, be found? There could be no such virtues known,
or have being, were they not found to center in a body.[40]

Here are our virtues of delight, and here is our human embodiment
of the divine. It provides a clearer (and more Blakean) introduction
to 'The Divine Image' than does Swedenborg. It is a tantalising
piece of evidence. No other theological authority, apart from
Swedenborg and contemporary readers of the review, appeared in

[39] Blake's 'Annotations to Thornton', *c.*1827 (E658).
[40] The extract leads Vol. I, no. 6 of the *New Magazine* (August 1790), pp. 243–7. It is taken,
with some cutting but no alterations, from Tomkinson's *A System of Religion*, chapter 2.
The Swedenborgians continued to show an interest in Tomkinson: see James Hyde, 'The
Muggletonians and the Document of 1729', *The New-Church Review* (Boston, Mass.), 7,
1900, pp. 215–27.

the two volumes of the magazine. Whose hand brought it to the editor's attention? At least we have evidence that there was one person in that early New Church milieu conversant with Muggletonian writings. 'The Divine Image' might even be called a Tomkinsonian song.

CHAPTER 10

From innocence to experience

There were other contentious issues in the early New Church which may have concerned William Blake. For we have overlooked so far another of the principal doctrines of the church:

That the imputation of the merits and righteousness of Christ is a thing as absurd and impossible, as it would be to impute to any man the work of creation; for the merits and righteousness of Christ consist in redemption, which is as much the work of a divine and omnipotent Being, as creation itself. They maintain, however, that the imputation, which really takes place, is an imputation of good and evil; and that this is according to a man's life.[1]

Alongside this went a rejection of the doctrine of 'justification by faith alone' and of 'the notion of pardon obtained by a vicarious sacrifice or atonement' rather than repentance and reform.[2] These doctrines were associated with Calvinism, and perhaps with Calvinist antinomianism. An observer in 1788 singled out the doctrine of the imputation of the righteousness of Christ as a central doctrine of antinomians, who believe that they have no inherent righteousness, since 'the whole work of man's salvation was accomplished by Jesus Christ on the cross. Christ's blood and our sins went away together. . .' Hence works are unnecessary: belief is all that is required. 'Our righteousness is nothing but the imputation of the righteousness of Christ. A believer has no holiness in himself but in Christ only.'[3]

Thus the doctrines appear to be intended to wall out antinomianism.[4] And the church certainly had the authority of

---

[1] *New Magazine*, Vol. 1, p. 18. Also *New-Jerusalem Magazine*, p. 104.
[2] *Ibid.*   [3] W. Hurd, *New Universal History*, pp. 640–1.
[4] See 'Z.Z.', 'Thoughts on Imputed Righteousness', *New Magazine*, Vol. 1, p. 295, taking issue especially with Tobias Crisp, *Christ Alone Exalted*, which had been republished in 1791.

Swedenborg, who in *The True Christian Religion* (1781, chapter XI) denounced imputation.[5] And yet the New Church's emphasis upon the matter has a look as if to repel a heresy in its midst. And there had been one very notable poetic expression inclining towards this heresy. In Book III of *Paradise Lost* Milton's Christ intercedes for man 'as a sacrifice/Glad to be offer'd' and God accepts:

> His [Adam's] crime makes guiltie all his Sons, thy merit
> Imputed shall absolve them who renounce
> Thir own both righteous and unrighteous deeds,
> And live in thee transplanted, and from thee
> Receive new life.

This doctrine has two sides. First, it is of Christ's sacrifice and atonement (or ransom) for man before God. Second, the emphasis is more upon Christ's forgiveness of man and his intercession with God on man's behalf. As we have seen, the first aspect of the doctrine had been repudiated by Swedenborg and also by the New Church. And in this Blake almost certainly agreed. Many years later Crabb Robinson recorded: 'Speaking of the Atonement in the ordinary Calvinist sense, he said: "It is a horrible doctrine: If another pay your debt, I do not forgive it."'[6] 'But the language of 'ransom' and of man's 'redemption' by Christ's sacrifice endured within New Church apologetics,[7] and was confused only by the question of God's dual identity: if he was Christ, how did he intercede with himself?[8] Very certainly the New Church ascribed to God/Christ the role of delivering man from evil. As one of the church's principal doctrines recited:

That Jehovah God himself came down from heaven, and assumed human nature for the purpose of removing hell from man, of restoring the heavens to order, and of preparing the way for a new church upon earth; and that herein consists the true nature of redemption, which was effected solely by the omnipotence of the Lord's Divine Humanity.[9]

But this redemption 'did not consist in the passion of the cross' but was a regeneration effected more slowly by the repentance and

---

[5] See also *New-Jerusalem Magazine*, pp. 141–2.   [6] Bentley, *Blake Records*, p. 548.
[7] Yet only as translated into its 'internal' sense' Thus 'redemption by the *blood of Christ* means redemption by *divine truth* proceeding from the Lord.' &c: *New Magazine*, I, p. 320.
[8] An apologist explained that 'the true meaning of *atonement* or *expiation* is the removal of evils from man, and not the appeasing of Wrath in God, who is essential love and mercy; and . . . the removal of evil is effected solely by the Lord's Divine Humanity. . .': *ibid.*, 2, pp. 133–4.   [9] *Ibid.*, I, p. 18.

works of redeemed man.[10] Blake had no time for the language of
Christ's intercession with a wrathful God: 'Forgiveness of Sin is
only at the Judgment Seat of Jesus the Saviour where the Accuser
is cast out' (E555). And he often insisted upon using the language
of God and of Christ, but as opposed principles.[11]

Returning to Milton, whom Blake so greatly admired, we find
him presenting Christ in *Paradise Lost* (Book xi, lines 32–6) as
pleading with his unforgiving Father:

> . . . let mee
> Interpret for him, mee his Advocate
> And propitiation, all his works on mee
> Good or not good ingraft, my Merit those
> Shall perfet, and for these my Death shall pay.

Mankind redeemed will be 'Made one with mee as I with thee am
one.' And in Book xii (line 290ff.) Milton moves much closer to
the antinomian doctrine of justification by faith alone: 'Law can
discover sin, but not remove':

> Some bloud more precious must be paid for Man,
> Just for unjust, that in such righteousness
> To them by Faith imputed, they may finde
> Justification towards God, and peace
> Of Conscience, which the Law by Ceremonies
> Cannot appease, nor Man the moral part
> Perform, and not performing cannot live.
> So Law appears imperfet, and but giv'n
> With purpose to resign them in full time
> Up to a better Cov'nant. . .

Christ, by fulfilling the full rigour of the Moral Law, appeases
'high Justice' (lines 400ff.):

> The Law of God exact he shall fulfill
> Both by obedience and by love, though love
> Alone fulfill the Law. . .
> Proclaiming Life to all who shall believe
> In his redemption, and that his obedience
> Imputed becomes theirs by Faith, his merits
> To save them, not thir own, though legal works.

[10] *Ibid.*, 2, p. 333.
[11] 'He spoke of the Old Testament as if it were the evil element', recorded Crabb Robinson:
Bentley, p. 548.

> For this he shall live hated, be blasphem'd,
> Seis'd on by force, judg'd, and to death condemnd
> A shameful and accurst, naild to the Cross
> By his own Nation, slaine for bringing Life;
> But to the Cross he nailes thy Enemies,
> The Law that is against thee, and the sins
> Of all mankinde, with him there crucifi'd. . .

Thus Milton, Blake's mentor, gave outstanding expression to doctrines which the New Church repudiated. We cannot say exactly how Blake responded to this repudiation. His whole-hearted emphasis was not upon intercession or imputation but on Christ as a figure of forgiveness. As he was to write later in the *Everlasting Gospel* (1818): 'What then did Christ inculcate. Forgiveness of Sins   This alone is the Gospel & this is the Life & Immortality brought to light by Jesus': (E792)

> It was when Jesus said to Me
> Thy sins are all forgiven thee
> The Christian trumpets loud proclaim
> Thro all the World in Jesus name
> Mutual forgiveness of each Vice
> And oped the Gates of Paradise
> The Moral Virtues in Great fear
> Formed the Cross & Nails & Spear
> And the Accuser standing by
> Cried out Crucify Crucify   (E793)

He also took over with vigour the symbolism of Christ's feet nailed to the cross and also to the serpent's head, which represented his sinful and mortal part, shed at the crucifixion:

> And thus with wrath he did subdue
> The Serpent Bulk of Natures dross
> Till he had naild it to the Cross
> He took on Sin in the Virgins Womb
> And put it off on the Cross & Tomb
> To be Worshipd by the Church of Rome   (E515)

(It will be noted how this symbolism also takes in the 'Tirzah' theme: above, p. 149.) Blake also selected this theme for one of his illustrations to *Paradise Lost*. In David Bindman's words, he 'shows the Crucified Christ resting upon the bodies of Sin and Death, with the nail in His foot piercing the head of the Serpent' (see Illus.

8).[12] But is the female beneath the cross the discarded *maternum humanum*? (see above, pp. 148–9).

It will be noted that Blake's strongest statements of the pre-eminent virtues of Christ's forgiveness appear very often linked to the repudiation of the Moral Law: that is, with a markedly antino-mian inflexion. And this would have been anathema to the ruling powers in the New Church. We cannot with certainty say that Blake held these views in 1789–90 (his New Church days) although they are clearly present a year or two later in *The Marriage of Heaven and Hell*: 'Jesus was all virtue, and acted from impulse. not from rules' (E42). And there is evidence that antinomian heresy troubled the New Church in its early years. The *New Magazine* carried a contribution in September 1790 censuring 'the notion of *imputed righteousness* which prevails at this day with too many. They think that they can do nothing for themselves, therefore Christ must do all.' They discount 'repentance, self-examination, and continued watchfulness [as] legal doctrines for the carnal and unconverted':

Observe, too often, their bitter tempers, spiritual pride, and uncharitable censures; and yet these things trouble them not, because they are *justified freely without the work of the moral law*.[13]

Joseph Proud (who was very much of Hindmarsh's party in the 1790s) was haranguing his Birmingham congregation in 1791 against the 'falses' of imputed righteousness and justification by faith. It was 'generally believed' that the Lord came to abrogate or set aside the moral law. 'They say it is a *legal bondage*, a *covenant of works*, and in itself *impracticable*.' They say that Christ 'fulfilled every iota of that law on *our account*, and in *our stead*'. They accuse their critics (and accuse Proud himself?) of being 'a pharisee and a workmonger', and declare 'we are not under the law, but under grace'. And Proud added, perceptively, this is to suppose two Gods, with different natures: one of wrath, the other of mercy.[14]

Blake did not circle around the doctrines of 'imputation' and 'justification by faith', since his routes to truth were impulsive and imaginative, and not doctrinal. But it is clear that the New Church – or at least the Hindmarsh faction which effectively con-trolled the press – was censoring positions for which he had strong

---

[12] Bindman, *Blake as an Artist*, p. 189.   [13] Vol. 1, p. 295.

[14] J. Proud, *Twenty Sermons on the Doctrines and Truths of the Lord's New Church* (Birmingham, 1792), pp. 93–6.

sympathy. And the evolution of the Church's forms was in the same direction. We have noted already Hindmarsh's efforts to introduce episcopalian forms of government (see p. 143). In the Liturgy of the church (1791) were introduced prayers for the king, royal family, both Houses of Parliament and all magistrates. More remarkably, in the evening service a prayer was introduced for the bishops, priests and ministers of the old Church.[15] The Reverend Proud was especially anxious to impress his loyalty on the Birmingham populace. During the 'Priestley Riots' in 1791 (Proud recorded proudly):

> Two or three times the mob came to destroy our Temple, upon a supposition that we were against Church & King, as the unitarians were supposed to be, & the last time the Mob came by thousands, with wood under their arms, to burn our Temple. I rush'd in among the Crowd, to the Ring Leaders, explained to them that we had no connection with Dr Priestley or that Party, & that we wish'd no ill to the Church, or to the King, & putting a guinea or two into their hands . . . they went away, with *'Huzza to the New Jerusalem for ever.'*[16]

Proud became 'the model clerical priest' of Hindmarsh's order, preaching with an inner purple silken vest, outer garment of fine white linen and golden girdle.[17] Servanté, in a private letter, wrote that Proud, Sibley and Hodson were 'tinctured with some of the old Papal leaven of priestly supremacy'. James Hindmarsh, the father of Robert Hindmarsh, after his ordination at Eastcheap 'justly obtained the nick-name of Bishop of *Babylon*'.[18]

Let us resume what we know of the New Church episode, and what we may reasonably surmise. The first year or two of the Church were clouded with dissension. For the Blakes the entire Swedenborgian moment was fraught with conflict, but was nevertheless of profound significance. We cannot clearly identify Blake with any of the conflicting groups, but again and again we seem to glimpse his face, obliquely situated to a particular argument. There is his recognition of a body of visionary writing undoubtedly carrying some of the old Behmenist imagery. There is identification

---

[15] *Liturgy of the New Church* (4th edition, printed and sold by R. Hindmarsh, 1791), pp. 42, 56–7.

[16] Proud's MS 'Memoirs', p. 27.

[17] Robinson, *A Remembrancer*, p. 141. To be fair to Proud, this dress was recommended by the Annual Conference in 1791; *Minutes*. Robinson states that Proud was the only one to wear it.

[18] *Monthly Observer*, 1858, pp. 280–1, quoting Servanté to Glen, 19 October 1806.

not only with certain beliefs (Christ is man) but also with the very
notion of a New Church of regenerated humankind. There is also
some shared jargon of correspondences (chariot for doctrine, Edom
for what is natural, dragon for the 'falses' of religion). The influence
was deep, and, with *The Marriage of Heaven and Hell*, productive of
polemic. It would also seem that Blake's antinomian tenets were
resisted from the start by the orthodox within the Church.

If this is so, then 1789–90 will have been a profoundly unhappy
experience – one of exalted enthusiasm followed by disenchantment
and rejection. And the experience will have been the more cutting
if we conjecture also that the *Songs of Innocence* were Blake's own
offering to the life of the New Church. The *Songs* (apart from three
which were drafted in 1784) were written at a time (1789 and
perhaps into 1790) when we know that Blake was most closely
interested in the church. The story that Blake wrote 'The Divine
Image' in 'the New Jerusalem Church, Hatton Garden' has been
quite properly dismissed, since that 'temple' was not opened until
1797.[19] However, the source of the story is a strong one: Charles
Augustus Tulk, who said that he had been told this by Blake, was
the son of J.A. Tulk, an attender at the Theosophical Society and
a founder member (an active one) of the New Church. C.A. Tulk
was born in 1786, only three years before 'The Divine Image'
was written, and became in later years a close Swedenborgian
sympathiser and a steady patron and friend of Blake's.[20] The
temple in Hatton Gardens is the one which he will have remembered from his childhood, and if told by Blake that he had written
the song in the New Church he could well have passed on the story
with that addition.[21] Blake could have written 'The Divine Image'
in the new church, albeit in Great Eastcheap and not in Hatton
Gardens. And indeed the impulse of the church might have been
behind the conception of a group of poems around the theme of
'innocence'.

[19] James Spilling, 'William Blake, Artist and Poet', *New Church Magazine*, June 1887, p. 254,
demolished in Erdman, 'Blake's Early Swedenborgianism'.

[20] Raymond Deck, 'New Light on C.A. Tulk', *Studies in Romanticism*, 16, 1977, no. 2. J.A.
Tulk was probably the author of 'A Layman', *A Letter Containing a Few Plain Observations,
addressed to the Unbiased Members of the New Church* (n.d. but 1807?), which complained of
the 'absurdity' of attempting to 'create a New Clergy', an opinion which Blake might
have shared.

[21] The story in fact came by way of another Swedenborgian, J. Garth Wilkinson. For
Wilkinson's enthusiastic promotion of Blake's *Songs*, see Geoffrey Keynes, 'Blake, Tulk
and Garth Wilkinson', *The Library*, 4th ser., 26, 1945, and Deck, *New Light*, pp. 115–16.

In any case, we know that the early members of the church were anxious to have songs and were looking around for them. We have seen that shortly after he visited London in 1789 Joseph Proud was requested to compose a volume of hymns for the use of the New Church (above, p. 151). This was on the 'understanding that I had a turn for poetry'. 'In about three months . . . I presented them with a volume of better than 300: they were approved of, & 500 copies immediately printed.'[22] If Mr Proud could have made an offering of three hundred hymns in three months, Blake (who can never have liked Mr Proud very much) may have been stimulated to a little quiet competition. Moreover, we have evidence that the members of the church were actively concerned about the matter of songs, and that it may have been controversial. When Proud informed the 1790 Annual Conference that his hymns were ready, much satisfaction was expressed, but–

It was the unanimous request . . . that the Hymns may consist of Praises and Glorifications only, and not of Prayer and Supplication; as singing implies an *Elevation* of Mind, which is suited to an Act of *Praise*, but apparently inconsistent with the *Humiliation* requisite in Prayer.[23]

This sounds like a polite expostulation. If this was a triumph for a liberal tendency it was reversed at the next Annual Conference (1791), which was firmly controlled by Hindmarsh. This went to the trouble of rescinding even such a resolution, while forms of prayer and expressions of abject humiliation were being introduced into the *Order of Worship* and the *Liturgy* (see above, p. 153).

All these points of controversy – hymns, forms, humility – related to the central question: what was the life of the New Church to consist in? Blake's view, while he remained an enthusiast, was unequivocal: 'The Whole of the New Church is in the Active Life & not in Ceremonies at all' (E595). But the active life could include songs. It is surely more than a coincidence that Blake should have

---

[22] Proud, MS 'Memoirs', pp. 14–16. The dating of this is unclear. The hymns may have been written, discussed and approved in 1789, but not published until 1790. See also Proud, *The Aged Minister's Last Legacy*, p. xi.

[23] *Minutes*. Perhaps in response Proud claimed (falsely) that he had avoided 'whatever is *petitioning*, or *prayer wise*' as well as 'every Subject that is *improper for Praise, Thanksgiving, and Glorification*': Hymns and Spiritual Songs for the Use of the Lord's New Church (2nd edn, 1791), Preface v. But he continued the argument in a sermon, 'Humility Recommended', published the next year in *Twenty Sermons*. Blake repeatedly expressed his hostility to self-abasement and humiliation, as in the *Everlasting Gospel*, 'God wants not Man to Humble himself/This is the trick of the ancient Elf' (E511).

written the *Songs of Innocence* at exactly the same time that the New
Church was calling for songs? What kind of songs, if one was
determined to exclude all ceremonial, humiliation, prayer and
obeisance before a paternal image of God, lessons of reward and
eternal punishment, and, at the same time, the 'natural religion'
of a deist First Cause? The songs must either be such as 'The
Divine Image', or else songs of the primary affections (through
whom alone the divine 'influx' of love could come, as in 'The Little
Black Boy') – songs of innocence. And Swedenborg could have
afforded to Blake a further suggestion, in the course of various
lucubrations on the state of little children in heaven, which could
have allowed Blake to proceed to his *Songs* while still having within
his mind (as yet not fully realised, for the 'experience' was to take
forms which he did not expect) a simultaneous notion of innocence's limitations and the need for complementary and contrary
songs of experience:

Innocence is the receptacle of all heavenly good things, and therefore the
innocence of little children is the place and ground of all their affections
for good and truth, and consists in a resigned submission to the government of the Lord, and a renunciation of man's own will . . . but the
innocence of little children is not genuine innocence because void of
wisdom; for genuine innocence is wisdom. . .[24]

And so the *Songs* could have evolved: some on the primary affections and sympathies, some showing 'resigned submission' and
renunciation of will, others glimpses of human *potentia*.[25]

   This kind of offering was not what Hindmarsh, Proud and their
supporters (like 'Ignoramus') wanted for the New Church. Already
we have seen them at work to establish ceremonial, to ordain a
priesthood, to expel democracy and to establish ritual forms: the
Tree of Mystery was actually growing before Blake's eyes. The
New Church, it turned out, was almost immediately to endorse
half the forms and more than half of the ritualistic vocabulary (of
prayer and humiliation before God) of the Old, and to become a
refuge for genteel, well-heeled, *bien-pensant* spirits with an inclina-

---

[24] 'An Account of Infants or Little Children in Heaven', *New Magazine*, Vol. 1 (May 1790),
p. 111. The date is too late to have directly influenced the *Songs*. But no doubt this was
one of Chastanier's translations from his hoard of MSS, and it could have been circulated
before publication or have been read at a private gathering. Or Swedenborg (who
repeated himself copiously) may well have written this elsewhere.

[25] See Glen, *Vision and Disenchantment*, chapter 4.

tion towards artistic and visionary experience. This was the prohibitive chapel which Blake found in the midst of 'The Garden of Love', and the submissive self-abasement which he treated ironically in the *Experience* plate (see Illus. 10) of that song.

As the opposition (expelled from Great Eastcheap) fell away in disillusion, the New Church took a marked lurch to the political right, and this at a time when the radical Dissent of Price and of Priestley, under the influence of the French Revolution, was moving rapidly in the opposite direction. The Blakes went spinning off into whatever world they had come from, not (it would seem) as members of a breakaway Swedenborgian sect but with a more radical sense of disenchantment and disgust. It had been, if anything, a confirmation that 'the Active Life' perishes within 'Ceremonies'. It was no doubt after he had walked past Great Eastcheap that Blake wrote in his notebook the savage companion poem to 'The Garden of Love':

> I saw a chapel all of gold
> That none did dare to enter in
> And many weeping stood without
> Weeping mourning worshipping
>
> I saw a serpent rise between
> The white pillars of the door
> And he forcd & forcd & forcd
> Down the golden hinges tore
>
> And along the pavement sweet
> Set with pearls & rubies bright
> All his slimy length he drew
> Till upon the altar white
>
> Vomiting his poison out
> On the bread & on the wine
> So I turned into a sty
> And laid me down among the swine

The journey from the 'Garden of Love' to the sty was the journey from Innocence to Experience. Experience did not cancel out Innocence, for if innocence had been polluted by the serpent, it remained in its purity as emblematic of human potential. The sty, of course, was that of advanced radicalism (later Jacobinism) and Deism: the sty of Tom Paine, Joel Barlow, Joseph Johnson the dissenting publisher and his circle, and Mary Wollstonecraft, whose *Original Stories* for children Johnson engaged Blake to illustrate in 1791. There need be no doubt about 'the swine'. Burke's epochal and blundering vulgarity, 'the swinish multitude' was proudly and truculently adopted by the radicals as the titles of periodicals and pamphlets show – *Pig's Meat*, *Rights of Swine*, *Hog's Wash*, with contributions by 'Old Hubert' and 'Porker'. And at the same time the Hindmarsh-controlled *New-Jerusalem Journal* was denouncing–

Those who herd together like swine in *mobelo-equality*, aiming at republicanism, from which the worst infernals in hell are preserved by the pure mercy of the Lord.[26]

The exact route which Blake followed on this journey we do not know. An important staging-post was the joyfully satirical rejection of Swedenborgianism in *The Marriage of Heaven and Hell*, a work which was commenced in 1790 and completed in 1792–3 and which preceded the completed *Songs of Experience*. This includes (at Plate 23) one of his most explicit statements of antinomianism. In this 'Memorable Fancy' the Devil says:

The worship of God is: Honouring his gifts in other man each according to his genius: and loving the greatest men best, those who envy or calumniate great men hate God, for there is no other God.
The Angel hearing this became almost blue but mastering himself grew yellow, & at last white pink & smiling, and then replied,
Thou Idolater, is not God One? & is not he visible in Jesus Christ? and has not Jesus Christ given his sanction to the law of ten commandments and are not all other men fools, sinners, & nothings?
The Devil answer'd; bray a fool in a morter with wheat, yet shall not his folly be beaten out of him: if Jesus Christ is the greatest man, you ought to love him in the greatest degree; now hear how he has given his sanction to the law of ten commandments: did he not mock at the sabbath, and so mock the sabbaths God? murder those who were murderd because of him? turn away the law from the woman taken in adultery? steal the labor of others to support him? bear false witness when he omitted making a defence before Pilate? covet when he pray'd for his disciples, and when he bid them shake off the dust of their feet against such as refused to lodge them? I tell you no virtue can exist without breaking these ten commandments. (E42)

Against the argument that this is not Blake's voice but a provocat-

[26] *New-Jerusalem Journal*, 1792, p. 433.

ive voice reading Swedenborg in an 'infernal' sense – itself a jest upon Swedenborg's 'internal' sense – it should be recalled that he was to rework many of the same themes some years later and in his own voice in 'The Everlasting Gospel'.

The best way to follow Blake's route is to go direct to the *Songs*. Whether or not Blake had always envisaged some 'experience' poems as complementary to 'innocence', between 1789 and 1794, with the succession of French Revolutionary events and with the Painite excitement in London, experience had taken on an altogether more dramatic form. *Innocence*, and *Experience* were engraved and bound together, with the sub-title, 'Showing the Two Contrary States of the Human Soul'. What is evident at once is the quite new emphasis upon, and indeed validation of, 'energy',[27] – an energy often identified with revolution – as well as, both in the *Experience* songs and in *The Marriage of Heaven and Hell*, the emphatic turn to a dialectic of 'contraries', which – while present in Swedenborgianism – undoubtedly indicates that Blake was vigorously renewing his earlier interest in Behmenist (and perhaps Muggletonian) thought. Together with these important emphases there is also an explicitness in social and political criticism ('Holy Thursday', 'The Chimney Sweeper', 'The Garden of Love', 'London') which aligns the *Experience* songs with the advanced radicalism of the times.

'London' is not clearly paired with any song in *Innocence*, unless one takes as its contrary the rural song of play, repose and fulfilment, 'The Echoing Green'. Let us, then, examine it in its own right.

---

[27] See Morton D. Paley, *Energy and Imagination: A Study of the Development of Blake's Thought* (Oxford, 1970).

CHAPTER II

'London'

'London' is among the most lucid and instantly available of the
Songs of Experience. 'The poem', John Beer writes, 'is perhaps the
least controversial of all Blake's works', and 'no knowledge of his
personal vision is necessary to assist the understanding'.[1] I agree
with this: the poem does not require an interpreter since the images
are self-sufficient within the terms of the poem's own development.
Every reader can, without the help of a critic, see London simultaneously as Blake's own city, as an image of the state of English
society and as an image of the human condition. So far from requir-
ing a knowledge of Blake's personal vision it is one of those foundation poems upon which our knowledge of that vision can be built.
A close reading may confirm, but is likely to add very little to,
what a responsive reader had already experienced.

But since the poem is found in draft in Blake's notebook we are
unusually well placed to examine it not only as product but in its
process of creation. Here is the finished poem:

> I wander thro' each charter'd street,
> Near where the charter'd Thames does flow.
> And mark in every face I meet
> Marks of weakness, marks of woe.
>
> In every cry of every Man,
> In every Infants cry of fear,
> In every voice: in every ban,
> The mind-forg'd manacles I hear
>
> How the Chimney-sweepers cry
> Every blackning Church appalls,
> And the hapless Soldiers sigh,
> Runs in blood down Palace walls

[1] John Beer, *Blake's Humanism* (Manchester, 1968), p. 75.

> But most thro' midnight streets I hear
> How the youthful Harlots curse
> Blasts the new-born Infants tear
> And blights with plagues the Marriage hearse   (E26–7)

In Blake's draft the first verse was originally thus:

> I wander thro each dirty street
> Near where the dirty Thames does flow
> And see in every face I meet
> Marks of weakness marks of woe[2]

The first important change is from 'dirty' to 'charter'd'. Another fragment in the notebook helps to define this alteration:

> Why should I care for the men of thames
> Or the cheating waves of charter'd streams
> Or shrink at the little blasts of fear
> That the hireling blows into my ear
>
> Tho born on the cheating banks of Thames
> Tho his waters bathed my infant limbs
> The Ohio shall wash his stains from me
> I was born a slave but I go to be free[3]

Thus 'charter'd' arose in Blake's mind in association with 'cheating' and with the 'little blasts of fear' of the 'hireling'. The second association is an obvious political allusion. To reformers the corrupt political system was a refuge for hirelings: indeed, Dr Johnson had defined in his dictionary a 'pension' as 'In England it is generally understood to mean pay given to a state hireling for treason to his country.' David Erdman is undoubtedly right that the 'little blasts of fear' suggest the proclamations, the Paine-burnings and the political repressions of the State and of Reeves' Association for Preserving Liberty and Property against Republicans and Levellers which dominated the year in which these poems were written.[4] In

---

[2] *The Notebook of William Blake*, ed. David V. Erdman (Oxford, 1973), p. 109; hereafter cited as N.

[3] N113. The obliterated title of this fragment has been recovered by David Erdman as 'Thames'.

[4] See David Erdman, *Blake: Prophet against Empire*, which fully argues these points on pp. 272–9. These poems were 'forged in the heat of the Year One of Equality (September 1792 to 1793) and tempered in the "grey-brow'd snows" of Antijacobin alarms and proclamations'. See also A. Mitchell, 'The Association Movement of 1792–3', *Historical Journal*, 4: 1 (1961), 56–77; E.P. Thompson, *The Making of the English Working Class* (Harmondsworth, 1968), pp. 115–26; D.E. Ginter, 'The Loyalist Association Movement, 1792–3', *Historical Journal*, 4: 2 (1966), 179–90.

the revised version of 'Thames' Blake introduces the paradox
which was continually to be in the mouths of radicals and factory
reformers in the next fifty years: the slavery of the English poor.
And he points also ('I was born a slave but I go to be free') to the
first wave of emigration of reformers from the attention of Church-
and-King mobs or hirelings.

But 'charter'd' is more particularly associated with 'cheating'.
It is clearly a word to be associated with commerce: one might
think of the Chartered Companies which, increasingly drained of
function, were bastions of privilege within the government of the
city. Or, again, one might think of the monopolistic privileges of
the East India Company, whose ships were so prominent in the
commerce of the Thames, which applied in 1793 for twenty-years'
renewal of its charter, and which was under bitter attack in the
reformers' press.[5]

But 'charter'd' is, for Blake, a stronger and more complex word
than that, which he endows with more generalised symbolic power.
It has the feel of a word which Blake has recently discovered, as,
years later, he was to 'discover' the word 'golden' (which, nevertheless, he had been using for years). He is savouring it, weighing its
poetic possibilities in his hand. It is in no sense a 'new' word, but
he has found a way to use it with a new ironic inversion. For the
word is standing at an intellectual and political cross-roads. On
the one hand, it was a stale counter of the customary libertarian

---

[5] 'The cheating waves of charter'd streams' and 'the cheating banks of Thames' should
prompt one to think carefully of this as the source which first gave to Blake this use of
'charter'd'. The fullest attack from a Painite source on the East India Company did not
appear until 1794: see the editorial articles in four successive numbers of Daniel Isaac
Eaton's *Politics for the People*, 2: 8–11: 'The East India Charter Considered'. These constituted a full-blooded attack on the Company's commercial and military imperialism ('if
it be deemed expedient to *murder* half the inhabitants of India, and *rob* the remainder,
surely it is not requisite to call it *governing* them?') which carried to their furthest point
criticisms of the Company to be found in the reforming and Foxite press of 1792–3. No
social historian can be surprised to find the banks of the Thames described as 'cheating'
in the eighteenth century: every kind of fraud and racket, big, small and indifferent,
flourished around the docks. The association of the banks of Thames with commerce was
already traditional when Samuel Johnson renewed it in his 'London' (1738), especially
lines 20–30. Johnson's attitude is already ambiguous: 'Britannia's glories' ('The guard of
commerce, and the dread of Spain') are invoked retrospectively, in conventional terms:
but on Thames-side already 'all are slaves to gold,/Where looks are merchandise, and
smiles are sold'. Erdman argues that the 'golden London' and 'silver Thames' of Blake's
'King Edward the Third' have already assimilated this conventional contrast in the form
of irony: see Erdman, pp. 80–1.

rhetoric of the polite culture. Blake himself had used it in much this way in his early 'King Edward the Third':

> Let Liberty, the charter'd right of Englishmen,
> Won by our fathers in many a glorious field,
> Enerve my soldiers; let Liberty
> Blaze in each countenance, and fire the battle.
> The enemy fight in chains, invisible chains, but heavy;
> Their minds are fetter'd; then how can they be free?[6]

It would be only boring to accumulate endless examples from eighteenth-century constitutional rhetoric or poetry of the use of chartered rights, chartered liberties, magna carta: the word is at the centre of Whig ideology.

There is, however, an obvious point to be made about this tedious usage of 'charter'. A charter of liberty is, simultaneously, a denial of these liberties to others. A charter is something given or ceded; it is bestowed upon some group by some authority; it is not claimed as of right. And the liberties (or privileges) granted to this guild, company, corporation or even nation *exclude* others from the enjoyment of these liberties. A charter is, in its nature, exclusive.

We are at a cross-roads because it is exactly this exclusive and granted quality of liberties which was under challenge; and it was under challenge from the claim to universal rights. The point becomes clear when we contrast Burke's *Reflections* and Paine's *Rights of Man*. Although Burke was every inch a rhetorician he had no taste for stale rhetoric, and he used the word 'charter' lightly in the *Reflections*. 'Our oldest reformation', he wrote, 'is that of Magna Charta':

From Magna Charta to the Declaration of Right it has been the uniform policy of our constitution to claim and assert our liberties as an *entailed inheritance* derived to us from our forefathers, and to be transmitted to our posterity. . .

We have an inheritable crown, an inheritable peerage, and a House of Commons and a people inheriting privileges, franchises, and liberties from a long line of ancestors.

Burke was concerned explicitly to define this chartered, heritable set of liberties and privileges (exclusive in the sense that it is 'an

---

[6] E415. If we take the intention of this fragment to be ironic, then Blake was already regarding the word as suspect rhetoric.

estate specially belonging to the people of this kingdom') as against any general uncircumscribed notion of 'the rights of man'. It is in vain, he wrote, to talk to these democratists:

> of the practice of their ancestors, the fundamental laws of their country ... They have wrought underground a mine that will blow up, at one grand explosion, all examples of antiquity, all precedents, charters, and acts of parliament. They have 'the rights of men'. Against these there can be no prescription. . .

Liberty, for Burke, must have its 'gallery of portraits, its monumental inscriptions, its records, evidences, and titles'. The imagery, as so often, is that of the great house of the landed gentry, with its walks and statuary, its galleries and muniments' room.

For Burke, then, 'charter' and 'charter'd', while not over-laboured, remain among the best of good words. But not for Paine: 'I am contending for the rights of the *living*, and against their being willed away, and controuled and contracted for, by the manuscript assumed authority of the dead.' A charter implied not a freedom but monopoly: 'Every chartered town is an aristocratical monopoly in itself, and the qualifications of electors proceeds out of those chartered monopolies. Is this freedom? Is this what Mr Burke means by a constitution?' It was in the incorporated towns, with their charters, that the Test and Corporation Acts against Dissenters operated with most effect. Hence (Paine argued – and economic historians have often agreed with him) the vitality of the commerce of un-incorporated towns like Manchester, Birmingham and Sheffield. The Dissenters (he wrote), 'withdrew from the persecution of the chartered towns, where test laws more particularly operate, and established a sort of asylum for themselves in those places ... But the case is now changing. France and America bid all comers welcome, and initiate them into all the rights of citizenship.'

This is (for Paine) the first offence of 'chartered': it implies exclusion and limitation. Its second offence was in its imputation that anyone had the right to *grant* freedoms or privileges to other men: 'If we begin with William of Normandy, we find that the government of England was originally a tyranny, founded on an invasion and conquest of the country ... Magna Carta ... was no more than compelling the government to renounce a part of its assumptions.' Both these offences were criticised in a central passage which I argue lay somewhere in Blake's mind when he selected the word:

It is a perversion of terms to say that a charter gives rights. It operates by a contrary effect – that of taking rights away. Rights are inherently in all the inhabitants; but charters, by annulling those rights in the majority, leave the right, by exclusion, in the hands of a few . . . The only persons on whom they operate are the persons whom they exclude . . . Therefore, all charters have no other than an indirect negative operation.

Charters, he continued, 'are sources of endless contentions in the places where they exist, and they lessen the common rights of national society'. The charters of corporate towns might, he suggested, have arisen because of garrison service: 'Their refusing or granting admission to strangers, which has produced the custom of *giving, selling and buying freedom*, has more of the nature of garrison authority than civil government' (my emphasis).

Blake by now had come to share much of Paine's political outlook, although he did not share his faith in the beneficence of commerce. He thus chose 'charter'd' out of the biggest political argument that was agitating Britain in 1791–3, and he chose it with that irony which inverted the rhetoric of Burke and asserted the definitions of 'exclusion', the annulling of rights, 'negative operation' and 'giving, selling and buying freedom'. The adjectival form – charter'd – enforces the direct commercial allusion: 'the organisation of a city in terms of trade'.[7]

The other emendation to the first verse is trivial: in the third line 'And see in every face I meet' is altered to 'And mark. . .' And yet, is it as trivial as it seems? For we already have, in the fourth line, 'Marks of weakness marks of woe'. Thus Blake has chosen, with deliberation, the triple beat of 'mark'. And we respond to this, whether we are conscious of the nature of the response or whether the words beat upon us in subliminal ways: even in these biblically illiterate days we have all heard of 'the mark of the Beast'. Some of Blake's central images – his trees, and clouds, and caves, and serpents, and roots – have such a universal presence in mythology and literature that one may spend half a lifetime in the game of hunt-the-source. And sometimes the hunting is fruitful, provided that we remember always that the source (or its echo in Blake's

---

[7] Raymond Williams, *The Country and the City* (1973), p. 148.

mind) is not the same thing as what he makes of it in his own art. Miss Kathleen Raine, a Diana among hunters, has found this:

The opening lines of *London* suggest very strongly Vergil's account of the damned in Hades:

> Nor Death itself can wholly wash their Stains;
> But long-contracted Filth ev'n in the Soul remains.
> The Reliques of inveterate Vice they wear;
> And spots of Sin obscene in ev'ry Face appear.[8]

The suggestion need not be excluded; this echo, with others, could have been in Blake's mind. But if so, *what does Blake do with it?* For Blake's poem evokes pity and forgiveness – the cries, the 'hapless Soldiers sigh', 'weakness' and 'woe' – and not the self-righteous eviction to Hades of 'long-contracted Filth', 'inveterate Vice' and 'spots of Sin obscene'. Moreover, in the amendment from 'And see' to 'And mark', Blake (or the speaker of his poem) closes the gap between the censorious observer and the faces which are observed, assimilating both within a common predicament: the marker himself appears to be marked or even to be mark*ing*.[9]

But 'mark' undoubtedly came through to the reader with a much stronger, biblical resonance. The immediate allusion called to mind will most probably have been 'the mark of the Beast', as in Revelation xiii.16–17:

And he causeth all, both small and great, rich and poor, free and bond, to receive a mark in their right hand, or in their foreheads:
And that no man might buy or sell, save he that had the mark, or the name of the Beast, or the number of his name.

The mark of the Beast would seem, like 'charter'd', to have something to do with the buying and selling of human values.

This question is incapable of any final proof. The suggestion has been made[10] that Blake's allusion is not to Revelation but to Ezekiel ix.4: 'And the Lord said unto him, Go through the midst of the city, through the midst of Jerusalem, and set a mark upon the foreheads of the men that sigh and that cry for all the abominations

---

[8] Kathleen Raine, Vol. I, pp. 24–5 (citing Dryden's *Aeneid* VI. 998–1001).

[9] Heather Glen has noted that 'the sense of an inevitable and imprisoning relationship between the "facts" he sees and the way in which he sees is reinforced by the use of "mark" as both verb and object'. See 'The Poet in Society: Blake and Wordsworth on London', *Literature and History* 3 (March 1976).

[10] Among others, by Harold Bloom and David Erdman, and, with a different emphasis, by Heather Glen.

that be done in the midst thereof.' The man who is ordered to go through the city has 'a writer's inkhorn by his side'. This seems at first to fit the poem closely: in 'London' a writer goes through the city of abominations and listens to 'sighs' and 'cries'. But even a literal reading does not fit the poem's meaning. For Blake – or the 'I' of his poem – is not setting marks on foreheads, he is observing them; and the marks are those of weakness and of woe, not of lamentations over abominations. Moreover, in Ezekiel's vision the Lord then orders armed men to go through the city and to 'slay utterly old and young, both maids and little children, and women: but come not near any man upon whom is the mark. . .' Thus those who are marked are set apart and saved. Neither the intention nor the tone of Blake's poem coincides with Ezekiel's unedifying vision. Nor are we entitled to conflate the allusions to Revelation and to Ezekiel with some gesture towards an ulterior 'ambivalence' in which Blake has assimilated the damned to the elect. For if one point is incontestable about this poem it is that *every* man is marked: *all* share this human condition: whereas with Ezekiel it is the great *un*marked majority who are to be put to the sword. Such a conflation offers temptations to a critic but it would destroy the poem by introducing into its heart a direct contradiction of intention and of feeling. Ambiguities of this dimension are not fruitful multipliers of meaning.

There is, further, the question of what response the word 'mark' is most likely to have called up among Blake's contemporaries. I must assert that the allusions called first to mind will have been either to the 'mark of Cain' (Genesis iv.15)[11] or to the 'mark of the Beast' in Revelation. And the more radical the audience, the more

[11] This suggestion has been pressed by Stan Smith, 'Some Responses to Heather Glen's "The Poet in Society"', *Literature and History* 4 (Autumn 1976). The 'mark of Cain' in Genesis was sometimes assimilated in theological exegesis to the mark of the Beast. The Lord curses Cain and condemns him to be a fugitive and a vagabond. Cain complains that he will be killed as an outlaw, and the Lord replies: 'Whosoever slayeth Cain, vengeance shall be taken on him sevenfold. And the Lord set a mark upon Cain, lest any finding him should kill him.' Whether the Lord did this as an act of forgiveness or as a protraction of the punishment of ostracism and outlawry (as anthropologists would argue) is a matter of interpretation. Stan Smith certainly carries the Lord's intentions very much too far when he takes the mark as a sign of 'election'. But he is surely right to argue that the poem can carry *this* ambivalence (men are 'both agents and patients, culprits and victims'), since in Blake's Christian dialectic the mark of Cain could stand simultaneously as a sign of sin and as a sign of its forgiveness. See Blake's chapter title to the 'Genesis' fragment: 'Chapter iv How Generation & Death took possession of the Natural Man & of the Forgiveness of Sins written upon the Murderers Forehead' (E667).

preoccupied it will have been with the second. For generations radical Dissent had sermonised and pamphleteered against the Beast (Antichrist) who has had servitors 'which worshipped his image' (Revelation xvi.2): social radicalism equated these with userers, with the rich, with those successful in buying and selling. And interpreters of Revelation always fastened with fascination upon the enigmatic verse (xiii.18): 'Let him that hath understanding count the number of the Beast: for it is the number of a man' (see Illus. 12). Such interest in millennial interpretation became rife once more in the 1790s;[12] it turned above all on these chapters of Revelation with their recurrent images of the Beast and of the destruction of Babylon, and the humble were able to turn to their own account the imprecations against kings, false prophets and the rich with which these chapters are rife. We hardly need to argue that Blake, like most radical Dissenters of his time, had saturated his imagination with the imagery of Revelation: chapter xiv (the Son of Man with the sickle, and the Last Vintage) is implanted in the structure of *Vala* and of *Jerusalem*.

These considerations, which are ones of cultural context rather than of superficial verbal similarities, lead me to reject the suggested allusion to Ezekiel. What Blake's contemporaries were arguing about in the 1790s was the rule of Antichrist and the hope of the millennium: the mark seen in 'every face' is the mark of the Beast, a mark explicitly associated with commercialism. And if we require conclusive evidence that Blake was thinking, in 'London', of Revelation, he has given us this evidence himself, with unusual explicitness. For the illumination to the poem[13] appears to be an independent, but complementary, conception; and for this reason I feel entitled to discuss the poem also as an independent concep-

[12] See, e.g., Thompson, pp. 127–9, 420–6, and sources cited there; and Morton D. Paley, 'William Blake, the Prince of the Hebrews, and the Women Clothed with the Sun', in Morton D. Paley and Michael Phillips (eds.), *William Blake: Essays in Honour of Sir Geoffrey Keynes* (Oxford, 1973). Swedenborgians were much concerned with interpretation of Revelation; and the verses which I have cited ('no man might buy or sell, save he that had the mark . . . of the beast') were discussed in the *New Magazine of Knowledge Concerning Heaven and Hell*, 1 (July 1790), 209–11. When Blake's acquaintance Stedman heard the news, on 6 April 1792, that Gustavus III, the King of Sweden, had been assassinated, his mind turned in the same direction: 'despotism dies away. Witness France, whose King may be compared to the beast in Revelation, whose number is 666, and LUDOVICUS added together makes the same. One, Sutherland, lately shot himself before King George . . . Such are the times': *The Journal of John Gabriel Stedman 1744–1797*, ed. Stanbury Thompson (1962), pp. 340–1; I am indebted to Michael Phillips for this reference.

[13] See Illus. 11.

tion and within its own terms. The illumination (if I am pressed to confess my own view) adds nothing essential to the poem, but comments upon the same theme in different terms. Nor are we even certain how the poem and the illumination are united, nor why they complement each other, until we turn to *Jerusalem*, Book 4 (E241):

> I see London blind & age-bent begging thro the Streets
> Of Babylon, led by child, his tears run down his beard

In both the poem and the illumination, London's streets appear as those of Babylon of Revelation; but in the illumination it is London himself who is wandering through them.[14]

In the second verse the important change is from 'german forg'd links' to 'mind-forg'd manacles'. The reference was, of course, to the Hanoverian monarchy, and perhaps to the expectation that Hanoverian troops would be used against British reformers.[15] The change to 'mind-forg'd' both generalises and also places us again in that universe of Blakean symbolism in which we must turn from one poem to another for cumulative elucidation. In this case we have already noted that the image of the mind as 'fettered' by the invisible chains of its own unfreedom had appealed to Blake in his youthful 'King Edward the Third'. The development of the image is shown in another fragment in the notebook, 'How to know Love from Deceit':

> Love to faults is always blind
> Always is to joy inclind
> Lawless wingd & unconfind
> And breaks all chains from every mind

---

[14] One further suggestion may be offered about the mark of the Beast. The Muggletonians afford yet one more possible resonance of 'mark'. In Swedenborgian exegesis the 'mark of the Beast' was sometimes taken to signify the solifidian doctrine of justification by faith without works. But Blake can scarcely have been using 'mark' in this way, since this was precisely his own, antinomian, 'heresy'. The Muggletonians, however, offer a very different interpretation. In their meetings prayer was rejected, as a 'mark of weakness', and Muggleton wrote:

> The mark of the beast is this, when a head magistrate or chief council in a nation or kingdom, shall set up . . . a set form of worship, he or they having no commission from God so to do, and shall cause the people by their power and authority . . . to worship after this manner of worship that is set up by authority, as this beast did. . .

> Hence to receive the mark of the Beast signifies 'to worship the image set up' by established authority. L. Muggleton, *A True Interpretation of . . . the Whole Book of the Revelation of St John* (1808), pp. 174–5. This appears to take us very much closer to the universe of Blakean symbolism than do the Swedenborgian glosses.

[15] See Erdman, pp. 277–8.

> Deceit to secresy confind
> Lawful cautious & refind
> To every thing but interest blind
> And forges fetters for the mind

The 'mind-forg'd manacles', then, are those of deceit, self-interest, absence of love, of law, repression and hypocrisy.[16] They are stronger and harder to break than the manacles of the German king and his mercenaries, since they bind the minds not only of the oppressors but also of the oppressed; moreover, they are self-forged. How then are we to read 'ban'? F.W. Bateson, a confident critic, tells us 'in every execration or curse (*not* in every prohibition)'.[17] I can't share his confidence: one must be prepared for seventeen types of ambiguity in Blake, and, in any case, the distinction between a curse and a prohibition is not a large one. The 'bans' may be execrations, but the mind may be encouraged to move through further associations, from the banns before marriage, the prohibitive and possessive ethic constraining 'lawless' love (' "Thou Shalt Not" writ over the door'), to the bans of Church and State against the publications and activities of the followers of Tom Paine.[18] All these associations are gathered into the central one of a code of morality which constricts, denies, prohibits and punishes.

The third verse commenced in the notebook as:

> But most the chimney sweepers cry
> Blackens oer the churches walls

This second line was then changed to:

> Every blackning church appalls

The effect is one of concentration. Pertinacious critics have been able to invert most of Blake's meanings, and readers have even found to suppose that these two lines (in their final form) are a comment upon the awakening social conscience of the churches

---

[16] Blake was also thinking of priestcraft, as we know from 'The Human Abstract'. Nancy Bogen suggests (*Notes and Queries*, new series, 15: 1 (January 1968)) that he may have been reading Gilbert Imlay's *Topographical Description* (London, 1792): on the Ohio (where the Thames-born slave will go to be free) Imlay found freedom from priestcraft which elsewhere 'seems to have forged fetters for the human mind'. But the poem itself carries this suggestion only in so far as the manacles immediately precede the 'blackning Church'. Fetters and manacles were anyway part of a very general currency of imagery: see, e.g., Erdman, p. 129, n. 35.

[17] F.W. Bateson, *Selected Poems of William Blake* (1957), p. 126.

[18] See E.D. Hirsch, *Innocence and Experience* (New Haven, 1964), p. 264.

under the influence of the evangelical revival: the churches are appalled by the plight of the chimney-sweeping boys.[19] The meaning, of course, is the opposite; and on this point the notebook entitles us to have confidence. In the first version the churches are clearly shown as passive, while the cry of the chimney-sweepers attaches itself, with the smoke of commerce, to their walls. By revising the line Blake has simply tightened up the strings of his indignation by another notch. He has packed the meaning of 'The Chimney Sweeper' of the *Songs of Experience* (whose father and mother 'are both gone up to the church' to 'praise God & his Priest & King,/Who make up a heaven of our misery') into a single line, the adjective 'blackning' visually attaching to the Church complicity in the brutal exploitation of young childhood along with the wider consequences of the smoke of expanding commerce. 'Appalls' is used in a transitive sense familiar in Blake's time – not as 'is appalled by' but as puts to shame, puts in fear, challenges, indicts, in the same way as the dying sigh of the soldier indicts (and also threatens, with an apocalyptic image)[20] the Palace.[21] 'An ancient Proverb' in the notebook gives the three elements of a curse upon England:

[19] For an example of this confusion, see D.G. Gillham, *Blake's Contrary States* (Cambridge, 1966), p. 12: 'The Church is horrified at the evil of the sweeper's condition, but it is helpless to do much about it. . .'

[20] On this point, see Erdman, pp. 278–9. The British reformers of the 1790s were, of course, at pains to stress the identity of interests of the soldiers and the people: and also to expose military injustices, flogging, forcible recruitment ('crimping'), etc.

[21] Many examples could be given of this transitive use of 'appal': see also the OED and the last line of 'Holy Thursday' in *Experience*. Thus William Frend, who shared something of Blake's ultra-radical Christian values, wrote: 'Oh! that I had the warning voice of an ancient prophet, that I might penetrate into the innermost recesses of palaces, and appal the haranguers of senates!' Frend's 'appal' means 'throw into consternation', 'warn', 'shock'. The phrase was used in the appendix to William Frend, *Peace and Union Recommended* (St Ives, 1792): this pamphlet occasioned the celebrated case of Frend's trial before the Vice-Chancellor and his expulsion from Cambridge: see Frida Knight, *University Rebel* (1971), esp. chapter 8. The pamphlet was on sale by mid-February 1793 (William Frend, *Account of the Proceedings. . .* (Cambridge, 1793), p. 72), and the appendix caused especial outrage among loyalists, and by the first week in May the University had opened its proceedings against Frend. From the juxtaposition of ancient prophet, palaces and appal, and from the fact that Blake and Frend shared friends and sympathies (see Erdman, pp. 158–9), one could argue that Blake's line could carry an echo of this celebrated case. But this is highly unlikely: Erdman gives a terminal date for inscribing the *Experience* drafts in the notebook as October 1792 (N7) – although 'appalls' was introduced as a revision, perhaps subsequently. But it is unnecessary to argue for such direct influence. What we are really finding is a vocabulary and stock of images common to a particular group or a particular intellectual tradition, in this case that of radical Dissent. It is helpful to identify these groups and traditions, since they both place Blake and help us to unlock his meanings: but as to the actual 'source' we must maintain a steady scepticism.

> Remove away that blackning church
> Remove away that marriage hearse
> Remove away that [place: *del.*] man of blood
> You'll quite remove the ancient curse.[22]

Church, marriage and monarchy: but if he had left it at 'place',
then it could have been Tyburn (or Newgate), the place of public
execution – the altar of the 'Moral & Self-Righteous Law' of Babylon and Cruel Og, in the centre of London, whose public rituals
Blake may have witnessed.

The poem, in its first version, was to end at this point, at 'Runs
in blood down Palace walls'. But Blake was not yet satisfied: he
returned, and worked through three versions of a fourth, concluding verse, squeezing it in between other drafts already on the page.
One attempt reads:

> But most thro wintry streets I hear
> How the midnight harlots curse
> Blasts the new born infants tear
> And smites with plagues the marriage hearse.

Bateson tells us that 'the images are sometimes interpreted as a
reference to venereal disease. But this is to read Blake too literally.
The diseases that descend upon the infant and the newly married
couple are apocalyptic horrors similar to the blood that runs down
the palace walls.'[23]

It may be nice to think so. But the blood of the soldier is for
real, as well as apocalyptic, and so is the venereal disease that
blinds the new-born infant and which plagues the marriage hearse.
We need not go outside the poem to document the increased discussion of such disease in the early 1790s,[24] nor, to turn the coin over,
the indictment by Mary Wollstonecraft and her circle of marriage
without love as prostitution. The poem makes the point very literally. Blake was often a very literal-minded man.

Another fragment in the notebook is closely related to this con-

---

[22] N107.
[23] Bateson, *Selected Poems*, p. 126. See also the more elaborate (and unhelpful) argument of
Harold Bloom, *Blake's Apocalypse: A Study in Poetic Argument* (Ithaca, 1963), pp. 141–2,
which also discounts the clear meaning of the third line.
[24] As, for example, the long review of Jesse Foot, *A Complete Treatise on the Origin, Theory,
and Cure of the Lues Venerea etc.* (1792 – but based on lectures read in Dean Street, Soho,
in 1790 and 1791) in *Analytical Review*, 12 (April 1792), 399, and 13 (July 1792), 261. See
also the discussion in Grant C. Roti and Donald L. Kent, 'The Last Stanza of Blake's
London', *Blake: an Illustrated Quarterly*, 11: 1 (Summer 1977).

clusion: a verse intended as the conclusion to 'The Human
Abstract' (or so it would seem) but not used in its final version. It
does not, in fact, relate directly to the imagery of 'The Human
Abstract' and we may suppose that Blake, when he realised this,
saw also how he could transpose the concept to make a conclusion
to 'London':

> There souls of men are bought & sold
> And milk fed infancy for gold
> And youth to slaughter houses led
> And [maidens: *del.*] beauty for a bit of bread.[25]

This enables us to see, once more, that 'London' is a literal poem
and it is also an apocalyptic one; or we may say that it is a poem
whose moral realism is so searching that it is raised to the intensity
of apocalyptic vision. For the poem is not, of course, a terrible
cumulative *catalogue* of unrelated abuses and suffering. It is
organised in two ways. First, and most simply, it is organised about
the street-cries of London. In the first verse, we are placed with
Blake (if we are entitled – as I think we are – to take him as the
wandering observer) and we 'see' with his eyes. But in the second,
third and fourth verses we are *hearing,* and the passage from sight
to sound has an effect of reducing the sense of distance or of the
alienation of the observer from his object of the first verse, and of
immersing us within the human condition through which he walks.
We *see* one thing at a time, as distinct moments of perception,
although, by the end of the first verse, these perceptions become
cumulative and repetitive ('in every face . . . marks . . . marks').
We *hear* many things simultaneously. Literally, we hear the eerie,
almost animal cadence of the street-cries (and although we may
now be forgetting them, if we were to be transported somehow to
eighteenth-century London, these cries would be our first and most
astonishing impression), the cries of the children, the 'weep', 'weep'
of the chimney-sweeps, and, led on by these, we hear the more
symbolic sounds of 'bans', 'manacles' and the soldier's 'sigh'. This
second verse is all sounds and it moves through an acceleration of
generalisation towards the third. If 'charter'd' is repeated, and if
'marks' falls with a triple beat, 'every' falls upon us no less than
seven times: a single incidence in the first verse prepares for five
uses in the second and a single incidence in the third ties it into

[25] N107.

the developing structure. 'Cry' also falls three times, carrying us from the second verse to the first line of the third. But in the third verse there is a thickening of sensual perception. Until this point we have seen and heard, but now we 'sense', through the sounds (the 'cry' and the 'sigh'), the activities that these indicate: the efforts of the chimney-sweep, the blackening walls of the churches, the blood of the soldier. We are not detached from this predicament; if anything, this impression of 'hearing' giving way to 'sensing' immerses us even more deeply within it.

We have been wandering, with Blake, into an ever more dense immersion. But the opening of the fourth verse ('But most thro' midnight streets I hear') appears to set us a little apart from this once more. 'I hear' takes us back from ourselves to Blake who is a little apart from the scene and listening. Nothing in the earlier verses had prepared us for the darkness of 'midnight streets', unless perhaps the 'blackning Church': what had been suggested before was the activity of the day-time streets, the street-cries, the occasions of commerce. The verse is not knitted in tidily to the rest at the level of literal organisation: the 'Marriage hearse' is a conceit more abstract than any other in the poem, apart from 'mind-forg'd manacles'. Since we know that he had intended at first to end the poem with three verses,[26] should we say that the final verse was an afterthought tacked on after the original images had ceased to beat in his mind – imperfectly soldered to the main body and still betraying signs of a separate origin?

It is a fair question. Blake, like other poets, had afterthoughts and made revisions which were unwise. And if we were to stop short at this literal or technical organisation of the poem we could make a case against its final verse. But we must attend also to a second, symbolic, level of organisation. The immersion in sights and sounds is of a kind which forces one to generalise from London to 'the human condition'. The point is self-evident ('In every cry of every Man'). But this kind of statement, of which a certain school of commentators on Blake is over-fond, takes us only a little way, and a great deal less far than is sometimes knowingly implied. For 'the human condition', unless further qualified or disclosed, is nothing but a kind of metaphysical full stop. Or, worse than that, it is a bundle of solecisms about mortality and defeated aspiration.

[26] This is emphasised by the fact that it was the first line of verse 3 which (in the notebook draft) was to begin with 'But most. . .'; 'But most the chimney sweepers cry'.

But 'the human condition' is what poets make poetry *out of*, not what they end up with. This poem is about a *particular* human condition, which acquires, through the selection of the simplest and most archetypal examples (man, infant soldier, palace, harlot), a generalised resonance; it expresses an attitude *towards* that condition; and it offers a unitary analysis as to its character.

Two comments may be made on the attitude disclosed by Blake towards his own material. First, it is often noted that 'London' is one of the *Songs of Experience* which carries 'the voice of honest indignation'. This is true. The voice can be heard from the first 'charter'd'; it rises to full strength in the third and final verses (appalls, runs in blood, blasts, blights). But it is equally true that this voice is held in equilibrium with the voice of compassion. This is clear from the first introduction of 'mark'. If we have here (and the triple insistence enforces conviction) the 'mark of the Beast', Blake would have been entitled to pour down upon these worshippers at the shrine of false gods the full vials of his wrath:

And there followed another angel, saying, Babylon is fallen, is fallen, that great city, because she made all nations drink of the wine of the wrath of her fornication.

And the third angel followed them, saying with a loud voice, If any man worship the beast and his image, and receive his mark in his forehead, or in his hand,

The same shall drink of the wine of the wrath of God, which is poured out without mixture into the cup of his indignation; and he shall be tormented with fire and brimstone in the presence of the holy angels, and in the presence of the Lamb:

And the smoke of their torment ascendeth up for ever and ever: and they have no rest day nor night, who worship the Beast and his image, and whosoever receiveth the mark of his name.[27]

But Blake indicates 'weakness' and 'woe', and the slow rhythm of the line, checked at mid-point, suggests contemplation and pity rather than wrath. Nor is this note of grave compassion ever lost: it continues in the cries, the fear, the tear: even the soldier is 'hapless'. If 'London' is that part of that human condition which may be equally described as 'Hell', it is not a hell to which only the damned are confined, while the saved may contemplate their tor-

---

[27] Revelation xiv. 8–11. These verses immediately precede those in which the Son of Man appears with 'in his hand a sharp sickle', and which lead on to 'the great winepress of the wrath of God' (xiv. 14–20) – that vision of the last vintage which worked in Blake's imagination.

ments; nor is this Virgil's 'Hades'. This is a city of Everyman; nor
do we feel, in our increasing immersion, that we – or Blake himself – are observers from without. These are not so much our fellow-
damned as our fellow-sufferers.

The second comment upon Blake's attitude is this: his treatment
of the city departs from a strong literary convention. To establish
this point fully would take us further outside the poem than I mean
to go. But one way of handling the city, both in itself and as an
exemplar of the human condition, derived from classical (especially
Juvenalian) satire; and in this it is the city's turbulence, its theatre
of changing human passions, its fractured, accidental and episodic
life, its swift succession of discrete images of human vice, guile or
helplessness, which provided the staple of the convention. Samuel
Johnson's 'London' was the place where at one corner a 'fell attor-
ney prowls for prey' and at the next a 'female atheist talks you
dead'. And the convention was, in some part, a countryman's convention, in some part a class convention – generally both: a country
gentleman's convention. From whichever aspect, plebeian London
was seen from outside as a spectacle. Wordsworth was still able to
draw upon this convention – although with significant shifts of
emphasis – in *The Prelude*.[28]

Blake's 'London' is not seen from without as spectacle. It is seen,
or suffered, from within, by a Londoner. And what is unusual
about *this* image of the-human-condition-as-hell is that it offers the
city as a unitary experience and not as a theatre of discrete episodes. For this to be so, there must be an ulterior symbolic organisation behind the literal organisation of this street-cry following
upon that. And this symbolic organisation should now, after this
lengthy discussion, have become fully disclosed. The tone of compassion falls upon those who are in hell, the sufferers; but the tone
of indignation falls upon the institutions of repression – mind-forg'd
manacles, blackning Church, Palace, Marriage hearse. And the
symbolic organisation is within the clearly conceived and developing logic of market relations. Blake does not only list symptoms:
within the developing imagery which unites the poem he also dis-
closes their cause. From the first introduction of 'charter'd' he
never loses hold of the image of buying and selling although these
words themselves are never used. 'Charter'd' both grants from on

---

[28] See Williams, *Country and City*, chapter 14, and Glen, 'The Poet in Society'.

high and licenses and it limits and excludes; if we recall Paine it
is a 'selling and buying' of freedom. What are bought and sold in
'London' are not only goods and services but human values, affections and vitalities. From freedom we move (with 'mark') to a race
marked by buying and selling, the worshippers of the Beast and
his image. Then we move through these values in ascendant scale:
goods are bought and sold (street-cries), childhood (the
chimney-sweep), human life (the soldier) and, in the final verse,
youth, beauty and love, the source of life, is bought and sold in
the figure of the diseased harlot who, herself, is only the other side
of the 'Marriage hearse'.[29] In a series of literal, unified images of
great power Blake compresses an indictment of the acquisitive
ethic, endorsed by the institutions of State, which divides man from
man, brings him into mental and moral bondage, destroys the
sources of joy and brings, as its consequence, blindness and death.

It is now evident why the final verse is no afterthought but
appeared to Blake as the necessary conclusion to the poem. The
fragment left over from 'The Human Abstract'

> There souls of men are bought & sold
> And milk fed infancy for gold
> And youth to slaughter houses led
> And beauty for a bit of bread

is a synopsis of the argument in 'London'. As it stands it remains
as an argument, a series of assertions which would only persuade
those already persuaded. But it provided, in its last line, the image
of the harlot, whose love is bought and sold, which was necessary
to complete 'London' and make that poem 'shut like a box'. And
the harlot not only provides a culminating symbol of the reification
of values, she is also a point of junction with the parallel imagery
of religious mystification and oppression: for if this is Babylon,
then the harlot is Babylon's whore who brought about the city's

---

[29] With 'Marriage hearse' we are at the point of junction with another universe of imagery
which critics of the 'neo-Platonist' persuasion emphasise to the exclusion of all other
aspects of Blake's thought. In this universe, for the spirit to assume mortal dress is a
form of death or sleep: hence sexual generation generates death: hence (these would
argue) 'Marriage hearse'. There are times when Blake uses images in this way, although
often with more equivocation, inversion or idiosyncrasy than this kind of criticism suggests. This is not, however, one of these times. The poem is not concerned with lamenting
the constrictions of the spirit within its material 'coffin' but with the 'plagues' which
'blight' sexual love and generation.

fall 'because she made all nations drink of the wine of the wrath of her fornication'. For English radical Dissent in the eighteenth century, the whore of Babylon (see Illus. 13) was not only the 'scarlet woman' of Rome, but also *all* Erastianism, all compromise between things spiritual and the temporal powers of the State, and hence, very specifically, that extraordinary Erastian formation, the Church of England. One recalls Blake's annotations to Bishop Watson (throughout), and his polemic against 'The Abomination that maketh desolate. i.e. State Religion which is the Source of all Cruelty' (E607). Hence the harlot is able to unite in a single nexus the imagery of market relations and the imagery of ideological domination by the agency of a State Church, prostituted to the occasions of temporal power.

To tie the poem up in this way was, perhaps, to add to its pessimism. To end with the blood on the Palace walls might suggest an apocalyptic consummation, a revolutionary overthrow. To end with the diseased infant is to implant life within a cycle of defeat. And yet the poem doesn't *sound* defeated, in part because the tone of compassion or of indignation offers a challenge to the logic of its 'argument',[30] in part because the logic of the symbolic analysis of market relations proposes, at the same time, if not an alternative, at least the challenge that (in compassion and in indignation) this alternative could be found.

In any case, these pages of mine have been teasing out meanings from one poem of sixteen lines. And Blake's larger meanings lie in groupings of poems, in contraries and in cumulative insights into differing states. 'London' is not about the human condition but about a particular condition or state, and a way of seeing this. This state must be set against other states, both of experience and of innocence. Thus we must place 'London' alongside 'The Human Abstract', which shows the generation of the prohibitive Tree of Mystery, whose fruit continually regenerates man's Fall: and in this conjunction 'London' (when seen as hell) shows the condition of the Fallen who lie within the empire of property, self-interest, State religion and Mystery. And when the poem is replaced within the context of the *Songs* it is easier to see the fraternal but trans-

[30] See F.R. Leavis, 'Justifying One's Valuation of Blake', in Paley and Phillips, *Essays*, p. 80: 'the effect of the poetry [of the *Songs*] is very far from inducing an acceptance of human defeat. One can testify that the poet himself is not frightened, and, further, that there is no malevolence, no anti-human animus, no reductive bent, in his realism. . .'

formed relationship which Blake's thought at this time bears to Painite radicalism and to the deist and rationalist critique of orthodox religion. 'London' is informed throughout by the antinomian contempt for the Moral Law and the institutions of State, including monarchy and marriage, just as are 'The Garden of Love' and 'The Chimney Sweeper'. With great emphasis it is coming to conclusions very close to those of Paine and his circle. A conjunction between the old antinomian tradition and Jacobinism is taking place.

But while Blake is accepting a part of the Painite argument he is also turning it to a new account. For while 'London' is a poem which a Jacobinical Londoner might have responded to and accepted, it is scarcely one which he could have written. The average supporter of the London Corresponding Society would not have written 'mind-forg'd' (since the manacles would have been seen as wholly exterior, imposed by oppressive priestcraft and kingcraft); and the voice of indignation would probably have drowned the voice of compassion, since most Painites would have found it difficult to accept Blake's vision of humankind as being simultaneously oppressed (although by very much the same forces as those described by Paine) and in a self-victimised or Fallen state. One might seem to contradict the other. And behind this would lie ulterior differences both as to the 'cause' of this human condition and also as to its 'remedy'.

For Blake had always been decisively alienated from the mechanical materialist epistemology and psychology which he saw as derived from Newton and Locke. And he did not for a moment shed his suspicion of radicalism's indebtedness to this materialism, with its prime explanatory principle of self-love. We shall return to this. So that if Blake found congenial the Painite denunciation of the repressive institutions of State and Church, it did not follow that humanity's redemption from this state could be effected by a political reorganisation of these institutions alone. There must be some utopian leap, some human rebirth, from Mystery to renewed imaginative life. 'London' must still be made over anew as the New Jerusalem. And we can't take a full view of even this poem without recalling that Blake did not always see London in this way; it was not always to be seen as Babylon or as the city of destruction in the Apocalypse. There were other times when he saw it as the city of lost innocence:

The fields from Islington to Marybone,
To Primrose Hill and Saint Johns Wood:
Were builded over with pillars of gold,
And there Jerusalems pillars stood.

. . .

The Jews-harp-house & the Green Man;
The Ponds where Boys to bathe delight;
The Fields of Cows by Willans farm:
Shine in Jerusalems pleasant sight.

And it could also be the millennial city, of that time when the moral and self-righteous law should be overthrown, and the Multitude return to Unity:

In my Exchanges every Land
Shall walk, & mine in every Land,
Mutual shall build Jerusalem:
Both heart in heart & hand in hand.   (E170, 172)

CHAPTER 12

'The Human Abstract'

If 'London' shows the conjunction between Blake's antinomian tradition and Painite radicalism – and also the incompatibility of the two – then 'The Human Abstract' shows the conjunction with and also the incompatibility between antinomianism and deism. But before we examine the poem we should look more carefully at ways in which deism influenced Blake. (I am taking it that deism stopped short of atheism and, while rejecting with various degrees of emphasis Christianity and church organisation, still maintained a belief in a First Cause and a divine plan. That was the position where Paine stopped, while Volney probably went on to atheism.)

Blake was to preface the third chapter of *Jerusalem* with an address to the deists, who are identified somewhat loosely with the preachers of 'Natural Morality or Natural Religion'. Voltaire, Rousseau, Gibbon and Hume are singled out for mention (E198–9). In this Blake was rehearsing his unwavering commitment to his earliest illuminated plates, 'THERE is NO Natural Religion' and 'ALL RELIGIONS are ONE' (1788). These manifestos include an unqualified rejection of any epistemology derived from sense perception as well as any religion derived from natural evidences: 'if it were not for the Poetic or Prophetic character the Philosophic & Experimental would soon be at the ratio of all things, & stand still unable to do other than repeat the same dull round over again' (E1). Against 'natural' or materialist epistemology Blake asserted the power of the Poetic Genius or Imagination, and the presence of innate ideas: 'Man is Born Like a Garden ready Planted & Sown':

Innate Ideas are in Every Man, Born with him: they are truly Himself. The Man who says that we have No Innate Ideas must be a Fool & Knave. (Annotations to Reynolds: E637)

His comminations were most commonly directed against Bacon,
Locke and Newton, who

> Deny a Conscience in Man & the Communion of Saints & Angels
> Contemning the Divine Vision & Fruition, Worshiping the Deus
> Of the Heathen, The God of This World, & the Goddess Nature
> Mystery Babylon the Great, the Druid Dragon & hidden
>   Harlot. . .   (*Jerusalem*: E251)

But on occasion other names are added to the trio:

>   . . . this Newtonian Phantasm
> This Voltaire & Rousseau: this Hume & Gibbon & Bolingbroke
> This Natural Religion! this impossible absurdity
>   (*Milton*: E140)

Successive Blake scholars have helpfully explored the reasons for
Blake's antipathy to most of these, especially to Newton and
Locke.[1] But the influence of Gibbon has received less attention.
We should make the imaginative effort to read the argument of
Gibbon in Chapter xx of *Decline and Fall of the Roman Empire* as an
antinomian or radical Dissenter would have read it. Here, surely,
was a feast for the eyes of those long prepared to believe that all
State Religion was the Anti-Christ? Constantine (Gibbon leaves
the reader in no doubt) embraced Christianity for reasons of State:
he was persuaded that the faith 'would inculcate the practice of
private and public virtue' – an end which should recommend itself
to any 'prudent magistrate':

The passive and unresisting obedience which bows under the yoke of
authority or even of oppression must have appeared in the eyes of an
absolute monarch the most conspicuous and useful of the evangelical
virtues. . .

The reigning emperor (Constantine) 'though he had usurped the
sceptre by treason and murder, immediately assumed the sacred
character of vice-regent of the Deity'. Moreover, Gibbon saw Constantine's progress towards Christianity as being in inverse ratio
to his progress towards morality:

He pursued the great object of his ambition through the dark and bloody
paths of war and policy . . . As he gradually advanced in the knowledge
of truth, he proportionally declined in the practice of virtue.

The year in which he convened the Council of Nice was polluted

---

[1] See D. Ault, *Visionary Physics: Blake's Response to Newton* (New York, 1974). Also Edward
Larrissy, *William Blake* (Oxford, 1985), pp. 70–3.

by the murder of his eldest son. Moreover, the establishment of the faith as imperial orthodoxy was accompanied by the degeneration of that faith: 'the piercing eye of ambition and avarice soon discovered that the profession of Christianity might contribute to the interest of the present, as well as of a future, life. The hopes of wealth and honours, the example of an emperor, his exhortations, his irresistible smiles, diffused conviction among the venal and obsequious crowds which usually fill the apartments of a palace.'

The clearest response can be seen in Blake's later work:

> The strongest poison ever known
> Came from Caesar's laurel crown. . .

Or we find it in his Address 'To the Deists' and in the verses which immediately follow. For his most concise expression of antinomian doctrine is followed immediately by an explicit reference to Gibbon's work:

> When Satan first the black bow bent
> And the Moral Law from the Gospel rent
> He forgd the Law into a Sword
> And spilld the blood of Mercys Lord.
>
> Titus! Constantine! Charlemaine!
> O Voltaire! Rousseau! Gibbon! Vain
> Your Grecian Mocks & Roman Sword
> Against this image of his Lord!   (E200)

The reference is to Chapter XLIX in the final volume published in 1788, in which Gibbon describes the donation of Charlemagne which established the temporal dominion of the Papacy, a donation endorsed by the forged 'donation' of Constantine: 'the world beheld for the first time a Christian bishop invested with the prerogatives of a temporal prince'. But if Blake could have found in every chapter of Gibbon evidence to illustrate the opposition of the 'moral law' to the 'everlasting gospel' he would (*and for the same reasons*) have been repelled in every chapter by Gibbon's tone. For Gibbon could, and by the same arguments, justify the donation of Charlemagne and the persecution by the imperial State of the early Christians. Of the first:

In this transaction, the ambition and avarice of the popes has been severely condemned. Perhaps the humility of a Christian priest should have rejected an earthly kingdom . . . I will not absolve the pope from the reproach of treachery and falsehood. But in the rigid interpretation of the laws, every one may accept, without injury, whatever his benefactor can bestow without injustice.

Of the second, 'the ecclesiastical writers of the fourth or fifth centuries ascribed to the magistrates of Rome in previous centuries the same degree of implacable and unrelenting zeal which filled their own breasts against the heretics or idolators of their own times'. But

> . . .the greatest part of those magistrates who exercised in the provinces the authority of the emperor . . . and to whose hands alone the jurisdiction of life and death was intrusted, behaved like men of polished manners and liberal educations, who respected the rules of justice, and who were conversant with the precepts of philosophy. (Ch. xvi)

Thus the 'Grecian mocks & Roman sword', the urbane sentiments of the defenders of property and order which Blake was to see, under whatever religious forms, as 'natural religion'. As he was to write in the address 'To the Deists' which prefaced the 'Grey Monk':

> Those who Martyr others or who cause War are Deists, but never can be Forgivers of Sin. The Glory of Christianity is, To Conquer by Forgiveness. All the Destruction therefore, in Christian Europe has arisen from Deism, which is Natural Religion. (E199)

Thus in 1804. The influence of Gibbon upon Blake has been an argumentative one: he has ended up by accepting Gibbon's history, while redefining State Christianity as polity and self-interest and therefore as 'deism'. But in 1792, and perhaps for some years thereafter, Blake had been subjected to influences of a quite different order. Undoubtedly Blake was deeply interested in researches into comparative religion and mythology, which had been enlarging for the previous century.[2] This came sometimes from deist, sometimes from more orthodox Christian sources, and by the 1780s and 1790s such exercises had become a commonplace of intellectual discourse. By exactly which routes this body of knowledge and of speculation came to Blake is unclear. He certainly had a quirky interest in Druidism,[3] was fascinated by Stukeley's identification of Stonehenge as the 'serpent temple', probably knew Richard Payne

---

[2] See Frank E. Manuel, *The Eighteenth Century Confronts the Gods* (Boston, Mass., 1959), and (for Blake) Jon Mee, *Dangerous Enthusiasm*, chapter 3.

[3] See *ibid.*, chapter 2.

Knight's *A Discourse on the Worship of Priapus* (1786) and also the
recent translation of the *Bhagavad-Gita*,[4] and he could (but need
not) have consulted Jacob Bryant's *A New System: Or an Analysis of
Ancient Mythology* (3 vols., 1774–6).[5] However, I wish to press the
claims of another candidate, C.F. Volney.[6]

Volney's *Ruins* belonged decisively, not to an academic, but to
a revolutionary tradition: he pressed always his arguments to conclusions both republican and hostile to State Religion. Once published in English it was enthusiastically taken up by London radicals; extracts were circulated as fly-sheets;[7] and by the mid-1790s
every advanced member of the London Corresponding Society
could have bought a tiny cheap edition to carry around in his
pocket.[8] It was a book more positive and challenging, and perhaps
as influential, in English radical history as Paine's *Age of Reason*,
which it preceded by several years. And it is by no means a trivial
book. It is an essay in comparative mythology in a form (a 'vision')
congenial to Blake. Volney had had the chance of seeing some part
of Dupuis' twelve-volume *Religion Universelle, ou L'Origine de Tous
les Cultes*,[9] whose standpoint is succinctly expressed in the preface:
'For me, the Gods are children of men; and I think, with Hesiod,
that the earth has made Heaven.' In a sense Volney offered a
'trailer' for Dupuis in his *The Ruins; or a Survey of the Revolutions of
Empire*, published in Paris in 1791, but a passionate, polemical
trailer. Where Dupuis emphasised the emergence of all religions
from a common Mithraic origin (in Sun-worship), Volney proposed a succession of naturalistic explanations, in which human
needs or natural experiences were objectified in deities, thence

[4] *The Bhagrat-Geeta, or Dialogues of Kreeshna and Arjoon*, trans. Charles Wilkins (1785). See also Morton D. Paley, *Energy and the Imagination*, p. 139.
[5] Northrop Frye, p. 173, doubts whether Blake read this. Jerome J. McGann shows that Blake and Bryant held different views of ancient mythology: 'The Idea of an Indetermin- ate Text', *Studies in Romanticism*, 25, no. 8, Fall 1986, esp. pp. 312–14, and he offers Alexander Geddes, *Prospectus of a New Translation of the Holy Bible* (1786) as another influ- ence upon Blake. Jon Mee recovers more about Geddes in *Dangerous Enthusiasm*, chapter 4, and (on Bryant) pp. 132–3.
[6] See Brian Rigby's helpful essay, 'Volney's Rationalist Apocalypse', in Francis Barker *et al.* (eds.), *1789: Reading Writing Revolution* (University of Essex, 1982). Jon Mee pays close attention to Volney's possible influence upon Blake: *Dangerous Enthusiasm*, esp. pp. 138– 42.
[7] The confrontation between the 'distinguished class' and the 'people' was circulating as a fly-sheet perhaps as early as December 1792: in PRO, HO 42.23 fo. 631 (my thanks to James Epstein). See also *The Making of the English Working Class*, pp. 107–8.
[8] My own copy of this edition has no date.
[9] Frank Manuel has a helpful chapter on Dupuis, but does not mention Volney.

abstracted from their original impulse, and exploited as serviceable mysteries by priestcraft and by privileged orders. The text is lucid and utterly innocent of Gibbon's 'Grecian mocks'; the footnotes, with tantalising information as to the symbolism or doctrines of a score of different religions and cults, would have whetted Blake's appetite – and perhaps contributed to the dramatis personae of the prophetic books. Moreover, the narrative of the book carries the reader forward on a wave of enthusiasm, not to a politic wisdom of the world, but to the vision of a 'New Age' in which men will shed their warring religions and attain brotherhood in clear-eyed self-knowledge. Mystery, priestcraft and kingcraft will fall together. For Volney's message was also revolutionary: the error of the Declaration of Rights was that Liberty was allowed to precede Equality. Equality must be the basis upon which Liberty is founded.

The argument of Plate 11 of the *Marriage of Heaven and Hell* is close to the argument of Volney:

The ancient Poets animated all sensible objects with Gods or Geniuses, calling them by the names and adorning them with the properties of woods, rivers, mountains, lakes, cities, nations, and whatever their enlarged & numerous senses could perceive.
And particularly they studied the genius of each city & country. placing it under its mental deity.
Till a system was formed, which some took advantage of & enslav'd the vulgar by attempting to realize or abstract the mental deities from their object; thus began Priesthood.
Choosing forms of worship from poetic tales.
And at length they pronounced that the Gods had ordered such things.
Thus men forgot that All deities reside in the human breast.

In certain chapters of *The Ruins* it is difficult *not* to encounter these ideas. Thus in Chapter xxii on the 'Origin and Genealogy of Religious Ideas', Volney describes how man in his 'original state' 'animated with his understanding and his passions the great agents of nature . . . and substituting a fantastic to a real world, he constituted for himself beings of opinion, to the terror of his mind and the torment of his race':

Thus the ideas of God and religion sprung, like all others, from physical objects, and were in the understanding of man, the produce of his sensations, his wants, the circumstances of his life. . .

Hence the Divinity 'was originally as various and manifold as the forms under which he seemed to act; each being was a power, a genius. . .' (xxii, sect. 1) The idea in Blake's second paragraph (the 'genius of each city & country' placed 'under its mental deity') is implicit throughout Volney's argument, although never expressed quite as explicitly as this.[10]

The third paragraph is crucial: here Blake argues that thus 'a system was formed' which some made use of to enslave the vulgar 'by attempting *to realize or abstract the mental deities from their object*; thus began Priesthood' (my emphasis). Again, this idea is central to the structure of Volney's argument: in Chapter xxii, section 3, Volney describes how there were established 'in the very bosom of states sacrilegious corporations of hypocritical and deceitful men who arrogated to themselves every kind of power; and priests . . . instituted under the name of religion, an empire of mystery, which to this very hour has proved ruinous to the nations of mankind'.[11] The attributes of God (Volney argues) are *'abstractions* of the knowledge of nature' (my emphasis), 'the idea of whose conduct is suggested by the experience of a despotic government' (Ch. xxii):

Thus the Deity, after having been originally considered as the sensible and various actions of meteors and the elements . . . became at last *a chimerical and abstract being*: a scholastic subtlety of substance without form, of body without figure; a true delirium of the mind beyond the power of reason at all to comprehend. (Ch. xxii, section 8, my emphasis)

Volney's *Ruins*, after its appearance in Paris in 1791, quickly came to English notice. It has sometimes been supposed that Blake could not have seen it while writing *The Marriage of Heaven and Hell*, and this is a difficult textual question. It is generally agreed that the Marriage may have been started in 1790 and concluded, with the 'Song of Liberty', in 1793, and most of the work is attributed to the earlier part of this span, 1790 to 1791. And David Erdman,

[10] Thus xxii, sect. 3: 'every family, every nation, in the spirit of its worship adopted a particular star or constellation for its patron . . . the names of the animal stars having . . . been conferred on nations, countries, mountains, and rivers, those objects were also taken for gods. . .' The 'medley of geographical, historical, and mythological beings' which thus arose is central to Volney's argument and the theme of, e.g., Chapter xxi, 'The Problem of Religious Contradiction'.

[11] See also Chapter xxiii, 'The End of All Religion the Same', with its denunciation of priesthood: 'they had invented ceremonies of worship to attract the reverence of the people, calling themselves the mediators and interpreters of the Gods with the sole view of assuming all his power [cf. Blake; "And at length they pronounced that the Gods had orderd such things"] . . . always aiming at influence, for their own exclusive advantage. . .'

using the signature of a change in the mode in which Blake engraved his 'g', puts Plate 11 in the earlier part.[12] But at the same time the dating of the English translation of Volney is frequently mistaken – sometimes as late as 1795. However, a long review of the French edition appeared in Johnson's *Analytical Review* in January 1792, with extensive extracts.[13] The review concluded 'we understand that a translation of this work is in the press'.[14] And the translation was indeed published before the end of 1792, by Joseph Johnson, the publisher who was at that time employing Blake as an engraver.[15] It cannot be shown conclusively that Blake could or could not have seen an English version of Volney before writing Plate Eleven; and indeed as a visitor to Johnson's shop he could have seen manuscript or proof versions of the book before its due publication date.

But if Blake is drawing upon Volney (as seems probable) he is not merely repeating Volney.[16] He has assimilated his concepts, while giving to them a novel and characteristic twist. First, Blake's argument is extraordinarily compact: he has made the argument wholly his own. Second, Blake has introduced a new agent, unexamined in Volney's account – 'the ancient Poets'. For Volney's account stems from the limitations of the understanding of primitive men, whereas Blake sees the myth-making faculties of the 'ancient Poets' as deliberate and creative ('particularly they studied...'). Priesthood – a system to enslave the vulgar – by abstracting mental deities from their object makes 'poetic tales' into 'forms of worship': the Moral Law. This seemingly small reorganisation of Volney's sequence has profound consequences; since for Volney, the 'New Age' dawns with the over-throw of Priesthood and of Mystery, and the New Age is the Age of Reason; but for Blake, while it dawns in exactly the same way, it is the age in which the 'true man', the Eternal Man of Poetic Genius, reasserts his humanity. Third, Blake, in his own argument, has rejected certain of Volney's assumptions, and in particular two: (1) that all

---

[12] D.V. Erdman, 'Dating Blake's Script: the "g" hypothesis', *Blake Newsletter*, June 1969.

[13] *Analytical Review*, Vol. XII, pp. 26–38.

[14] But it was not listed as published until the second half of 1792: *ibid.*, Vol. XIV, p. 331. It was reviewed in the *Critical Review*, December 1792.

[15] The 1792 volume is scarce, and the only copy I know is in the collection of the Library Company of Philadelphia. My thanks to Professor Leslie Chard and Camilla Townsend for help in locating it.

[16] As Rigby affirms (above, p. 199, note 6), Volney's is a 'rationalist apocalpyse' and, as both Marilyn Butler and Jon Mee also point out, Blake will have repudiated this deification of Reason: Butler, pp. 44–5, and Mee, pp. 138–40.

the past achievements of human civilisation (and, it is implied, the greater achievements of the future) have been founded on enlightened self-interest or on 'self love . . . the parent of all that genius has effected';[17] (2) 'that man receives no ideas but through the medium of his senses'.[18] The first principle directly contradicted 'The Divine Image'; the second Blake had been at pains to refute in his illuminated plates of 1788. The plate 'ALL RELIGIONS are ONE' ('The Voice of one crying in the Wilderness') had declared, as its fifth principle, 'The Religions of all Nations are derived from each Nation's different reception of the Poetic Genius which is every where call'd the Spirit of Prophecy': and he had concluded that the source of all religions is 'the true Man . . . he being the Poetic Genius' (E1–3).

Thus Blake's particular, and intellectually structured antinomian development had prepared him to meet the moment of deist or atheist thought represented by Volney's *Ruins* in an affirmative way: but it had also prepared him to reorganise this thought: 'Thus men forgot that All deities reside in the human breast.' For Plate 11 in the *Marriage* is only a temporary resting-point before the full statement of 'The Human Abstract':[19]

> Pity would be no more,
> If we did not make somebody Poor:
> And Mercy no more could be,
> If all were as happy as we;
>
> And mutual fear brings peace;
> Till the selfish loves increase.
> Then Cruelty knits a snare,
> And spreads his baits with care.
>
> He sits down with holy fears,
> And waters the ground with tears:
> Then Humility takes its root
> Underneath its foot.

---

[17] See esp. Ch. VII.
[18] See esp. Ch. XXII.
[19] The argument of this chapter – the deist–antinomian conjunction and quarrel – need not stand or fall on the hypothesis of Volney's influence. Many of his ideas were already around – e.g., R.P. Knight, p. 176: 'men naturally attribute their own passions and inclinations to the objects of their adoration; and as God made Man in his own image, so Man returns the favour, and makes God in his' – while others Blake was quite capable of thinking out for himself. But the hypothesis of Volney neatly illustrates the question at issue.

> Soon spreads the dismal shade
> Of Mystery over his head;
> And the Catterpillar and Fly,
> Feed on the Mystery.
>
> And it bears the fruit of Deceit,
> Ruddy and sweet to eat;
> And the Raven his nest has made
> In its thickest shade.
>
> And Gods of the earth and sea,
> Sought thro' Nature to find this Tree
> But their search was all in vain:
> There grows one in the Human Brain.

That this poem is intended as a direct 'contrary' to 'The Divine Image' is manifest: the title of the Notebook draft is 'The Human Image', and the poem, in its first six lines, picks up, ironically, 'Pity', 'Mercy', 'peace' and 'loves'. And if 'The Divine Image' is the hinge upon which the *Innocence* songs turns, we should expect to find a similar significance for *Experience* in this. But it is difficult to see how any reader could find 'The Human Abstract' to be a 'satire' upon the former poem.[20] It represents, as clearly as any of the 'paired' songs, a 'contrary state', neither one of which need cancel or satirise the other: and in the most simplified terms, the one is about the source of 'good', the other about the source and the origin of 'evil'. Nor is it a plain opposite, a mere negation of the first. Blake had tried this, in the early (but rejected) contrary, *A* (as opposed to *The*) 'Divine Image':

> Cruelty has a Human Heart
> And Jealousy a Human Face
> Terror, the Human Form Divine
> And Secrecy, the Human Dress
>
> The Human Dress, is forged Iron
> The Human Form, a fiery Forge.
> The Human Face, a Furnace seal'd
> The Human Heart, its hungry Gorge.

This is a straight negative: but, even so, not one which must cancel out the earlier poem. The source of 'evil' is human, but the human

---

[20] E.D. Hirsch suggests this in his (usually helpful) *Innocence and Experience* (Yale, 1964), pp. 265–70.

form remains 'divine' since this 'evil' is projected as 'A Divine Image' of a jealous wrathful God (or Satan). Vice is self-consuming, 'hell' is the furnace of this self-consumption.[21]

But such a negation dissatisfied Blake. It states a contrary, but it offers no explanation for it. Page 107 of The Notebook shows him making two false starts before finding his way into 'The Human Image'–

> How came pride in Man
> From Mary it began
> How Contempt & Scorn

This was scratched out and followed with another opening:

> What a world is Man
> His Earth

–deleted again. Since we can be sure that 'pride' was for Blake, at this time, a virtue, the first opening suggests a poem contrasting the origin of 'The Divine Image' in Mary and of a 'human image' of 'contempt and scorn' for man's own divine humanity within man's own false consciousness. No one should ever attempt to re-write Blake, but one can suggest that he was leading on to some such contrast as:

> How Contempt & Scorn
> From Reason it was Born

But such an opposition (Mary/Reason) was a false opposition, and, moreover, one that Blake in 1792 would have thought too easily to be taken in a comforting way by orthodox Christians like Mr Pratt. The next beginning ('What a World is Man/His Earth') suggests that he was trying for an image which would suggest the common soil of both the 'divine' and the 'human', and that the image of the tree had already been decided upon. But why should the same human soil nurture two opposing trees? It was at this point that the final organisation of the poem presented itself to him. It looks as if he then wrote an advanced draft straight through.

---

[21] There is no cancelling-out of concepts here: Thomas Tomkinson who might have provided a 'text' for 'The Divine Image' (above, p. 160) also provides the contrary text: the devil 'is no where to be found but in Man': *A System of Religion*, 1729, p. 35. Thus also Reeve: 'thy Body shall be thy Hell, and thy Spirit shall be thy Devil that shall torment thee to Eternity'. Thus also Blake on Lavater: 'hell is the being shut up in the possession of corporeal desires...' (E579).

In one sense the poem starts, somewhat cryptically, with a conclusion written into the commencement:

> Pity could be no more
> If there was nobody poor–

And then, to emphasise the meaning, he struck out the second line
and wrote above it the final version:

> If we did not make somebody poor

The thought returns directly to the already-completed 'The Clod &
the Pebble': one kind of 'love'–

> . . . for another gives its ease,
> And builds a Heaven in Hells despair.

The other kind–

> . . . seeketh only Self to please,
> To bind another to its delight;
> Joys in anothers loss of ease,
> And builds a Hell in Heavens despite.

But the clod and the pebble simply offer to each other contrary
states. And Blake's actual point of entry was given to him by the
notebook poem (never used in the *Songs*) 'I heard an Angel singing':

> I heard an Angel singing
> When the day was springing
> Mercy Pity Peace
> Is the worlds release
>
> Thus he sang all day
> Over the new mown hay
> Till the sun went down
> And haycocks looked brown
>
> I heard a Devil curse
> Over the heath & the furze
> Mercy could be no more
> If there was nobody poor
>
> And pity no more could be
> If all were as happy as we
> At his curse the sun went down
> And the heavens gave a frown

> Down pourd the heavy rain
> Over the new reapd grain
> And Miseries increase
> Is Mercy Pity Peace.

Blake had tinkered a good deal with the final verse, and, in one variant, the final couplet had been:

> And by distress increase
> Mercy Pity Peace (N114)

The thought is the same as that in *Jerusalem*, Chapter 2, where 'the Oppressors of Albion in every City & Village. . .'–

> . . . compell the Poor to live upon a crust of bread by soft mild
>   arts:
> They reduce the Man to want: then give with pomp & ceremony.
> The praise of Jehovah is chaunted from lips of hunger & thirst.
> (E191)

This 'Angel' is not just a hypocrite: Mercy, Pity, Peace *could* be 'the worlds release': about these 'virtues of delight' Blake was never cynical. And this 'Devil' is not a devil of energy or of antinomian wisdom (as in *The Marriage of Heaven and Hell*): he is a real devil and no doubt Gibbon would have found him to be a man 'of polished manners and liberal education . . . conversant with the precepts of philosophy'. (The recurrent and central experience behind this, of dearth and high prices – real or manipulated – followed belatedly by a little inadequate display of benevolence and charity, need not be documented.) The poem is about class society, and in an area central to the eighteenth century: the 'paternalist' conscience of an agrarian capitalist class.

So all this was tipped in to the first quatrain of 'The Human Abstract': we start with a class society, and this is emphasised by the revision of the second line – we make others poor. The 'peace' of class society is founded only on an equilibrium of 'mutual fear', within which the 'selfish loves' increase. But this self-love only increases: it has been present from the start and is, in a sense, the unexplained source from which the whole process of the poem is generated. What is interesting is that while much of the rest of the poem follows Volney's analysis of process, Blake insists upon turning upside-down the central value of Volney's deism by which self-love, if duly enlightened, will generate all civilised values. But while Blake emphatically rejects this, he takes from Volney something of the very notion of class antagonism. For in a crucial chapter of *The Ruins* (often to be republished as a leaflet by subsequent reformers) Volney has a vision of an immense assembly (indistinctly located in France) in which the people and the privileged class separate from each other and question each other's credentials. On the one hand, there is an immense concourse of 'labourers, artisans, tradesmen, and every profession useful to society'; on the other hand a much smaller group of 'priests, courtiers, public accountants . . . &c'. The people regard the privileged class with astonishment: 'We toil, and you enjoy; we produce, and you dissipate; wealth flows from us, and you absorb it.' One can never be certain when dealing with ideas and images so widely dispersed, but Volney's vision appears to contribute to Blake's Plate 16 in *The Marriage of Heaven and Hell*: 'These two classes of men [the "Prolific" and the "Devourer"] are always upon earth, & they should be enemies; whoever tries to reconcile them seeks to destroy existence.'[22]

Perhaps Blake was seeking to put more into the first quatrain of 'The Human Abstract' than four lines could bear. By contrast, the next four quatrains have a leisurely development. The Tree of Mystery grows slowly, and it grows very much as Volney had argued and as Blake had agreed in Plate 11 of *The Marriage*. In chapter xii of *The Ruins*, Volney and the mysterious 'Genius' who is enlightening him have a distant global vision of desperate human warfare (Russian, Mussulman, Tartar) in which all parties call upon the aid of divine power for their cause. At length the 'Genius' can contain himself no longer and bursts out:

Hear these men, and you would imagine that God is a being capricious and mutable; that now he loves, and now he hates . . . that he spreads snares for men, and delights in the fatal effects of imprudence . . . that he . . . is to be appeased only by servility like a savage tyrant. I now completely understand *what is the deceit of mankind, who have pretended that God made man in his own image, and who have really made God in theirs*; who have ascribed to him their weakness, their errors, and their vices; and . . . surprised at the contradictory nature of their own assertions, have attempted to cloak it with hypocritical humility, and the pretended impot-

---

[22] Volney, Ch. xv, 'The New Age'; Blake, E39. Blake again uses Volney's vision, but departs from his conclusion, in: 'But the Prolific would cease to be Prolific unless the Devourer as a sea recieved the excess of his delights.'

ence of human reason, calling the delirium of their own understanding the sacred mysteries of heaven. (My emphasis)

Here we have the 'snares', the 'hypocritical humility', the inversion of the values of 'Christian Forbearance' (as Blake first entitled the Song of Experience, 'A Poison Tree') so that they are seen to be the chains of oppression imposed by an interested priesthood. The Tree of Mystery is certainly that of priestcraft and of State Religion: the Caterpillar and Fly are certainly priestly parasites:[23] and the Raven has the same precise areas of definition combined with imprecise, evocative symbolism: he may be Rome, or the Genius of Mystery, or Death, or Bishop Watson of Llandaff, or God hiding in the Tree waiting for Adam to eat the fruit, or the Prophet of a Prohibitive, Negating Moral Law (as he is in the 'Song of Liberty')[24] – and, more probably, he is intended to suggest all of these at once. The 'fruit of Deceit' was being more exactly defined in another of Blake's (unused) notebook drafts, 'How to know Love from Deceit'. As opposed to joyous and unconfined 'Love', which 'breaks all chains from every mind' Deceit is confined to 'secresy': it is first thought of as 'Modest prudish & confind' and then revised to 'Lawful cautious & refind':

> To every thing but interest blind
> And forges fetters for the mind.   (N106–7)

This poem provides the essential link which binds 'The Human Abstract' into 'London', with its 'mind-forg'd manacles'. But with the 'fruit of Deceit' we are also linked to 'A Poison Tree', and we have further joined the symbolism of the Tree of Mystery with that of the Fall. That kind of critic who is given to collapsing into a kind of academic supercelestial blur whenever confronted with the antique symbolism of the Fall, the Creation or the Resurrection, tends to abandon Blake's poem at this point and go off into a

---

[23] Cf. Proverb of Hell: 'As the catterpiller chooses the fairest leaves to lay her eggs on, so the priest lays his curse on the fairest joys.' But it requires very little reading in the pamphlets of radicalism and Dissent in the 1790s to find caterpillars and flies abounding: or, indeed, Trees of Mystery: for example, Henry Yorke, *Thoughts on Civil Government* (1794), 'The Clergy have planted their power in the fertile soil of Superstition, which has been watered and manured by the Ignorance, Poverty, and Fears of Men.'

[24] 'Let the Priests of the Raven of dawn, no longer in deadly black. with hoarse note curse the sons of joy . . . Nor pale religious letchery call that virginity, that wishes but acts not!' E44. Once again, a sampling of pamphlet and sermon material of the 1790s provides a profusion of reference: it is not necessary to trace such universal symbols back to neo-Platonist or to hermetic sources.

different (and irrelevant) essay in exegesis, in which the 'natural-
ism' of the poem's development is denied, and in which every
'snare', 'tear', 'shade' or priestly parasite is squeezed for the last
drop of possible mythic association. Plainly reversing the actual
movement of the poem, in which the Tree of Mystery grows up
out of self-interest in class society, we must translate it into some
Christian orthodoxy in which the Fall (the 'fruit of Deceit') is read
back into the commencement. And nothing has bothered this kind
of critic more than the symbolism of trees.

Blake's poem (we recall) concludes:

> The Gods of the earth and sea,
> Sought thro' Nature to find this Tree
> But their search was all in vain:
> There grows one in the Human Brain.

Aha! says this kind of critic. If the Tree of Mystery doesn't grow
in 'Nature' then we can't accept the poem's apparent naturalistic
development: all that must be the symbolism of something altogether more mystic and Otherwards. And the confusion is compounded by the supposition that Blake was at the same time
making a scholarly in-joke about the Upas Tree, a 'mysterious
poison plant which appeared constantly in the literature of his
time' but which 'no one stated that he himself had actually seen'.[25]

As it happens, Blake had, as we have seen (above, p. 142),
recently read a very detailed and naturalistic account, purportedly
at first hand from a Dutch traveller and medical man, of the Upas

[25] John Beer, *Blake's Humanism*, p. 73. I don't intend to suggest that Mr Beer is the kind of
critic at whom I've been making faces. If an example must be given, I have to say that
I find Miss Raine's chapter on 'The Ancient Trees' (*Blake and Tradition*, II, pp. 32–52)
one of the least helpful and most confusing sections of a book which (along with other
confusions and irrelevancies) offers genuine insights and discoveries.

[26] N.P. Foerfch's 'Natural History of the Bohon-Upas, or Poison Tree of the Island of Java'
had been serialised in the *New Magazine of Heaven and Hell*, 1790. The author claimed to
have interviewed condemned criminals who had been offered the alternative of execution
or of obtaining the poison of the tree, and who had succeeded in doing the latter. But
the failure rate was very high. The tree lay in the midst of ten or more miles of barren
land, in which all life was polluted by its miasmas: even birds, crossing this territory, fell
dead from the sky. A criminal might succeed in obtaining the poison only if he had the
good fortune, during two or three days of difficult journey over ground littered by skel-
etons, of having the wind blowing always away from the tree. The tree itself was growing
in a solitary state, except for some little trees or suckers around it. Along with much
other circumstantial detail, Dr Foerfch claimed to have witnessed state executions effected
by this poison, and to have experimented on his own account on domestic animals. The
Swedenborgian magazine published the account to demonstrate the 'intimate connection

Tree in Java.[26] But neither the Tree of Mystery in 'The Human Abstract' nor 'A Poison Tree' owe very much to this Upas Tree: Blake's trees both bear poisoned fruit, whereas the virulence of the Upas Tree lies in its bark and in its effluvia.[27] It is best with these to regard each tree as *a tree for that poem*, defined in its own terms.

But for a Tree of Mystery Blake didn't have to rely upon texts from Paracelsus or Boehme: he could have taken them from ten hundred places in previous literature, or from the common vocabulary of radical Dissent, or from Gibbon's accounts of the sacred groves of the ancient Germans,[28] or from accounts of Druid rites,[29] or from his own shaping imagination or, indeed, from Volney, who has several trees, as well as dragons, serpents, Orphic eggs, Mithraic caves, ravens and lions, in his text and notes.

What he could have taken less easily, except from antinomian or rationalist sources, was the notion of a tree of *mystery*, coincident with priesthood. I have suggested already (above, pp. 200–1) that when composing Plate 11 in *The Marriage* he may have been conversant with this notion in Volney. A separate caste of astronomers &c arose, which 'assumed to themselves exclusive privileges', and under their authority:

subsisting between the spiritual and natural worlds': Dr Foerfch provided evidence that 'the influences of Hell are as visible in the vegetable productions of certain parts of this globe' as in wild beasts. The Poison-Tree of Java may be called 'the *Tree of Death*, originating in *Hell*'. I don't think the Upas Tree played a very important part in Blake's imagination, but Foerfch offered a wonderful bunch of images. His tree turns up in a deleted line of the Notebook poem on Fayette, 'Let the Brothels of Paris be opened' (N99):

> But our good Queen quite grows to the ground
> There is just such a tree at Java found (*del.*)
> And a great many suckers grow all around

It is interesting also that the plate of 'A Poison Tree' in *Songs of Experience* (see Illus. 14) shows *not* an apple-tree (as in the poem) but a tree in a barren landscape which conforms very much to the mental image called up in my own mind by reading Dr Foerfch: a dead criminal, who has failed to get the poison, lies beneath the tree. For various attributions of the Upas Tree imagery in Blake, see Geoffrey Grigson, *The Harp of Aelus* (1948), ch. v; John Adlard, *The Sports of Cruelty* (1972), p. 45; Glen, p. 193.
[27] Foerfch's account of the Upas Tree may have contributed more to, e.g., the imagery of the Tree of Mystery in *Vala*, Night VIIa.
[28] Chapter IX: 'The only temples in Germany were dark and ancient groves . . . Their secret doom, the imagined residence of an invisible power, by presenting no distinct object of fear or worship, impressed the mind with a still deeper sense of religious horror; and the priests . . . had been taught by experience the use of every artifice that could preserve and fortify impressions so well suited to their own interest.'
[29] See Jon Mee, *Dangerous Enthusiasm*, pp. 7, 97–103.

. . . the progress of knowledge, it is true, was hastened, but by the mystery that accompanied it, the people, plunged daily in the thickest darkness, became more superstitious and more slavish. . .

From this caste came priesthoods who 'instituted under the name of religion, *an empire of mystery*. . .' (XXII, sect. 3, my emphasis). And what Blake is doing, in the final quatrain of 'The Human Abstract', is both to appropriate deist analysis and to reorganise it in exactly the same way as he had done in Plate 11 of *The Marriage*.

Let us place this quatrain side by side with the conclusion to that passage:

Till a system was formed, which some took advantage of & enslav'd the vulgar by attempting to realize or abstract the mental deities from their object; thus began Priesthood.
Choosing forms of worship from poetic tales.
And at length they pronounced that the Gods had ordered such things.
Thus men forgot that All deities reside in the human breast.

An inattentive reading leads some to suppose that the final line is saying much the same as the final line of the poem: 'There grows one in the Human Brain.' This leads us to a somewhat complacent rationalist orthodoxy, that 'good' and 'evil' both arise from man, without much further explanation of process. And Blake, when he writes that 'the Gods of the earth and sea' sought in vain through Nature for this Tree, is then making only a whimsical joke.

True, Blake *is* making that sort of joke, but it has a finer edge of irony. For 'the human breast' and 'the Human Brain' are not the same thing. Men forgot that all deities reside in the breast; the poetic genius of the 'true man' (and in this respect Blake is still not far distant from the Swedenborgians) achieves its insights in the first place through the *affections*. Nor was this poetic capacity to attribute qualities and to animate these into deities in any sense (until abused) a faculty encouraging mystery; if the Gods were imaginary, the truths of imagination were always more real to Blake than the natural observations of the senses; or, in a more contemporary definition, Blake considered that human creativity was grounded upon his poetic, mythogenic faculties, and that man lives in a world of his own creation (our 'culture') and not in 'nature'. Hence the old, poetically imagined Gods 'animated' by man from 'the earth and sea' had a perfect right to go on their rather ironic search for this new Tree. But these Gods do not (*pace* Miss Raine and her disciples) discover that the Tree of Mystery is yet one more (rather dreary and repetitive) symbol of 'nature' or of 'matter'. It is exactly in 'Nature' that they *can't* find the Tree. It grows in the human brain (and not breast). And hence the care which Blake put into revising the poem's title. In 'The Divine Image' we are given in fact an image of actual human virtue; in 'The Human Abstract' we are given an image of an imaginary God of deceit and mystery. But Blake means to insist that this God is created, not by the poetic faculty of imagination, but by the abstracting faculties of the reason. If he had not thought this through for himself, the notion of abstraction as barren and self-deluding could have come to him from many sources.[30] But he could certainly have been reminded of this propensity at several points in Volney: 'that God whose attributes are abstractions of the knowledge of nature' (Ch. xxii); 'the Deity . . . became at last a chimerical and abstract being: a scholastic subtlety of substance without form' (xxii, sect. 8); and:

. . .the understanding, at liberty to disengage itself from the wants of nature, must have risen to the complicated art of comparing ideas, digesting reasonings, and seizing upon abstract similitudes. (Ch. xxii)

We can now resume our argument. Blake had been habituated, whether in his Swedenborgian phase or before, to the way of thinking in 'correspondences' and in inversions. He took from the deists, and perhaps from Volney in particular, an enormous amount: in the case under examination he has taken a full-blown naturalistic analysis of the process by which religious mystery and priestcraft grow up. But, in the very moment of taking it, he has twisted it in such a way that it remains ambiguous. The twist is of two kinds: Volney (and mechanistic psychology generally, however sophisticated, from Hartley through Priestley to Bentham or Godwin) still saw 'self-love', in whatever form, as the basic sociological motor, for good or ill. Once self-love had been enlightened by philosophy, and mystery had been dispersed, men would see that brotherhood and equality were in their evident interest. But Blake, even in his most revolutionary temper, did not think that this kind of equation

---

[30] D.G. Gillham, *Blake's Contrary States*, p. 65, usefully recalls the introduction to Berkeley's *Principles of Human Knowledge*: 'the fine and subtile net of abstract ideas, which has so miserably perplexed and entangled the minds of men'.

would be easy. Indeed, he may have doubted this most of all at
those times when he was most sanguine about revolutionary possibilities: for brotherhood was (for him) not a matter of interest
but of love. Hence while Volney starts his analysis with self-love
giving rise to primitive societies and to civilised values (and only
subsequently becoming entangled with mystery) Blake commences
his at a point where self-love has already alienated man from man
in class society, and mystery arises from the increase of 'selfish
loves'. The second twist lies in the description of the process of
this alienation. For in Volney the process by which men have fash-
ioned the false consciousness of religious mystery is described,
repeatedly, as a 'chain of ideas' or 'a chain of reasoning'.[31] It is
scarcely possible not to see the ironic glint which must have come
into Blake's eye. For he was familiar with the imagery of other
kinds of 'fetters', 'links' and 'chains'. And in 'The Human
Abstract' (one notices) the process of maturing false consciousness
is not that of rationality but of mystification and alienating values:
'mutual fear', 'Cruelty', 'holy fears', 'Humility' and 'Deceit' which,
we recall, is itself 'to every thing but interest blind/And chains &
fetters every mind' (N106). And yet the source of Blake's chain of
values is 'in the Human Brain'. What the reason does is to
rationalise ('spreads his baits with care'), legitimate and ultimately
mystify, self-interest; moreover, in 'the fruit of Deceit', it perpetu-
ates itself. Reason, if based on self-love produces its opposite,
Mystery.

It must follow from this that if we look forward to a 'remedy',
to man's liberation from false consciousness, we must expect to
find different answers in Volney and in Blake. As indeed we do.
Volney's vision, as we have seen, is a 'New Age' of triumphant
rationality; in the light of a new self-knowledge mystery (and the
resultant alienation of nation from nation) will be dispersed; 'the
people' simply dismiss the 'privileged class' and its priestly apologists as unnecessary parasites. Blake does not offer his 'New Age'
in the *Songs of Experience*, although it is clear (from the 'Introduction' and from 'Earth's Answer') that if it should come it must be
an affirmation not of reason but of wrath and love. He had suggested it a little more plainly in the 'Song of Liberty' at the end of
The Marriage, and it is clear enough from this that any vision of his

---

[31] See, e.g., Ch. XXII, sect. 1 and sect. 8.

would be likely to take prophetic and apocalyptic form: the 'son of fire'–

Spurning the clouds written with curses, stamps the stony law to dust,
loosing the eternal horses from the dens of night, crying
Empire is no more! and now the lion & wolf shall cease. (E44)

But the new Jerusalem cannot be seen only as the driving out of self-love by affirmative love: it must also be seen as the reappropriation by man of his own humanity, by expelling the abstract, quantitative, ratiocinative power (Locke's reason founded upon the senses), and by reassuming the imaginative or poetic genius of the ancients who had 'animated' the first Gods of the earth and sea.

Blake was not concerned to argue with Volney or the deists whether these Gods were 'imaginary' or not. He was happy, at least until 1795, to co-exist with atheists and deists (of the Volney, but not of the Gibbon or Godwin stamp). But Blake's point, even in 1792–3, was different. The human world was a world of culture; 'imaginary' or not, anything created in the world of culture *was real*. The deists, with a mechanical and naturalistic psychology, placed an excessive emphasis upon material interest, whereas Blake, while appropriating some of their arguments, placed a full emphasis upon affective and imaginative 'culture' – an emphasis which became after 1795, as events in the world around him became increasingly confusing, discouraging or ominous, more and more extreme and idiosyncratic. With no alternative psychology to hand he set himself the impossible labours of the prophetic books, seeking to construct a syncretic mythology which would reorganise the myths of all past culture into a new structure. For once animated by the imagination, once released into culture and myth, those old Gods went on eternally, unless they were slain by the imagination or hammered by it into new forms and myths. As he grew older he became increasingly provoked by any levity towards the creatures of imagination. As he told Crabb Robinson, when he came across the lines in *The Excursion*:

Jehovah – with his thunder, and the choir
Of shouting Angels, and the empyreal thrones,
I pass them, unalarmed. . .

they made him ill for weeks with a bowel complaint. But earlier, in *Jerusalem*, we can detect that old argument with the deists rumbling on:

And this is the manner of the Sons of Albion in their strength
They take the Two Contraries which are called Qualities, with
     which
Every Substance is clothed, they name them Good & Evil
From them they make an Abstract, which is a Negation
Not only of the Substance from which it is derived
A murderer of its own Body: but also a murderer
Of every Divine Member: it is the Reasoning Power
An Abstract objecting power, that Negatives every thing
This is the Spectre of Man: the Holy Reasoning Power,
And in its Holiness is closed the Abomination of Desolation

Therefore Los stands in London building Golgonooza
Compelling his Spectre to labours mighty; trembling in fear
The Sceptre weeps, but Los unmovd by tears or threats remains

'I must Create a System, or be enslav'd by another Mans
'I will not Reason & Compare: my business is to Create'
                                                    (E151)

If Blake in these prophetic books moved away from deism, and
ultimately into sharp antagonism to rationalism in the assertion of
his own 'everlasting gospel', it is not very helpful to argue that he
was moving towards (or back to) anything recognisable as Christianity, orthodox or heterodox. For if he had been doing so he
would have had no need to labour at the creation of his own mythic
system. And he pursues unremittingly, through all the shifting
emanations of his curiously static and repetitive narratives, the
problem of man's self-alienation from his own true imaginative
identity, and of his aspiration to the ultimate New Age or Jerusalem which is co-terminous with the overthrow of Mystery and the
reassumption of undivided humanity. Thus, in the First Book of
Milton, Los announces the 'Last Vintage' in terms reminiscent of
the Enlightenment:

And Los stood & cried to the Labourers of the Vintage in voice of
     awe:
'Fellow Labourers! The Great Vintage & Harvest is now upon
     Earth
'The whole extent of the Globe is explored: Every scatterd Atom
'Of Human Intellect now is flocking to the sound of the Trumpet.
'All the Wisdom which was hidden in caves & dens from ancient
'Time; is now sought out from Animal & Vegetable & Mineral
'The Awakener is come. outstretch'd over Europe! the Vision of
   God is fulfilled

'The Ancient Man upon the Rock of Albion Awakes,
'He listens to the sounds of War astonishd & ashamed;
'He sees his Children mock at Faith and deny Providence.'

(E120–1)

The vision is fulfilled, the awakening has come: but it signals not the Age of Reason but the necessary dispersal of Mystery before the re-awakening of the faith of the Ancient Man. And so, after winding our way through eight nights of *Vala*, we come, in Night the Ninth, to the ultimate triumphant irony. It is Urizen himself, who, in such a voice as Volney's, cries: 'Times are Ended!', and who prepares for the final Vintage and threshing of the nations. The same reasoning power which abstracted mental deities from their object and which created Mystery has now pierced through Mystery, understood its own limitations, and is ready to destroy its own creations. Once rid of the fear of death and the hope of immortality, humankind sheds its alienation from nature. Once rid of self-mystification, humankind reassumes imaginative existence:

> The Expanding Eyes of Man behold the depths of wondrous worlds
> One Earth one sea beneath nor Erring Globes wander but Stars
> Of fire rise up nightly from the Ocean & one Sun
> Each morning like a New born Man issues with songs & joy
> Calling the Plowman to his Labour & the Shepherd to his rest
> He walks upon the Eternal Mountains raising his heavenly voice,
> Conversing with the Animal forms of wisdom night & day
> That risen from the Sea of fire renewd walk oer the Earth. . .

(E391)

But this renewed life of imagination and faith is certainly not one to be comprised in any Christian – or, for that matter, neo-Platonist – doctrine:

> Attempting to be more than Man We become less said Luvah
> As he arose from the bright feast drunk with the wine of ages
> His crown of thorns fell from his head he hung his living Lyre
> Behind the seat of the Eternal Man & took his way. . .

(E388)

This is later: but the old deist–antinomian discussion is still being argued out. And Luvah (who is sometimes Christ) may allow us to return, finally, to the question of Blake's trees. For the Tree which the Gods sought in the final verse of 'The Human Abstract' is certainly the Tree of Mystery, but it may also be allowed to suggest the Cross upon which the Christ of the gospel of forgiveness (or the human virtues of 'The Divine Image') was crucified. It is, anyway, the same tree. And the tree in 'A Poison Tree', while naturalistic in its symbolic evolution, may also be allowed to suggest the Fall,[32] just as the fruit of the Tree of Mystery, which is 'ruddy and sweet to eat' suggests the same. And both Trees must be central to *Songs of Experience* which are, exactly, songs of the 'wisdom' gained by man when he lost innocence through the Fall. But Blake's notion of the Fall is very different from any warranted by Christian doctrine or by Miss Raine's 'Tradition'. For we can now see how three of the *Songs* are intimately related. 'A Poison Tree' (if we read it in the sense that 'I' could be God and his 'foe' could be Adam) shows 'a very Cruel Being' spreading a deliberate bait before man. In the Tree of Mystery of 'The Human Abstract' we see the triumph of the prohibitive God of the Moral Law, the fruit of whose Tree continually entices man to the perpetual renewal of his own Fall. The Fall from innocence into this kind of experience – the moralising of contrary 'Qualities' or impulses into an 'Abstract' of Good and Evil – extends outwards throughout the *Songs of Experience* and pollutes both parental and sexual love. 'Thou shalt not' is writ over the door, and 'Priests in black gowns' are binding 'my joys & desires'. But we can also relate this to 'London'. For if 'The Human Abstract' shows the generation of the prohibitive Tree of Mystery whose fruit continually regenerates man's Fall, so 'London' (seen as hell) shows the condition of the Fallen, who

---

[32] Miss Raine (II, pp. 38–9) helpfully draws attention to two passages of Boehme, which imply a criticism of God for deliberately planting within the Garden of Eden a tree 'pleasant to the eye and to be desired' within which was hidden 'the Wrath of the Anger of God'. Boehme asks 'Reason says, *Why* did God suffer this Tree to grow, seeing Man should not eat of it? Did he not bring it forth for the *Fall* of Man? And must it not needs be the *Cause* of Man's Destruction?' In the same way Blake hid his unspoken wrath within his tree and 'sunned it with smiles', encouraging his foe to his own destruction. If we wish to read the 'I' of the poem as God, and the 'foe' as Adam in the Garden of Eden, then we must say that Blake (if he read Boehme's rhetorical question) answered 'yes, God did deliberately plan and cause Adam's destruction, and in a deceitful way'. Such a conclusion is perfectly consonant with Blake's explicit statement in later life: 'Thinking as I do that the Creator of this world is a very Cruel Being & being a Worshipper of Christ I cannot help saying the Son O how unlike the Father. First God Almighty comes with a Thump on the Head. Then Jesus Christ comes with a balm to heal it.' This 'Thump' is fairly clearly the contrivance of the Fall, since this sentence immediately follows upon: 'Angels are happier than Men & Devils because they are not always Prying after Good & Evil in one Another & eating the Tree of Knowledge for Satans Gratification' (*A Vision of the Last Judgement*, E555). Thus if we accept Miss Raine's helpful suggestion, it helps us to the view that the God who planted the tree and who threw Adam out of Eden was in fact Satan – a view which neither Miss Raine nor Boehme would endorse.

lie within the empire of property, self-interest, state religion and Mystery.

For 'London' bears exactly the same kind of fraternal but transformed relationship to Painite political radicalism as 'The Human Abstract' bears to deism or atheism. In these songs Blake is not quarrelling with either: he is both accepting their thought and turning it to a new account. Blake is not likely to have changed his view very markedly between writing these poems and 1799, when he wrote to Dr Trusler. Blake had been commissioned by Trusler to prepare a design of 'Malevolence' (see Illus. 15):

A Father, taking leave of his Wife & Child, Is watch'd by Two Fiends incarnate, with intention that when his back is turned they will murder the mother & her infant. If this is not Malevolence with a vengeance, I have never seen it on Earth. . .

Trusler rejected the design. Blake's 'Fancy' did not 'accord . . . with my Intentions': he had different views on 'Moral Painting' which should 'follow the Nature' of 'This World'. In reply Blake sought to defend his design against 'a mistaken' criticism,

which is, That I have supposed Malevolence without a Cause. Is not Merit in one a Cause of Envy in another, & Serenity & Happiness & Beauty a Cause of Malevolence? But Want of Money & the Distress of A Thief can never be alledged as the Cause of his Thieving, for many honest people endure greater hardships with Fortitude. We must therefore seek the Cause elsewhere than in want of Money, for that is the Miser's passion, not the Thief's.[33]

We have noted that 'The Human Abstract' appears to emerge with the 'Cause' unexplained, and prior to the poem, just as Dr Trusler complained of his Malevolence. Or, rather, the 'cause' lies in class-society, in which contraries have become polarised, and the pity of one feeds on the misery of the other. It is in this context that 'the selfish loves increase'. But self-love on its own, in its 'innocent' state, is not the ultimate cause of 'sin'. It is a 'contrary' to affirmative love, 'necessary to Human existence'. 'From these contraries spring what the religious call Good & Evil.' In *Jerusalem* the cause is described in a metaphysical sense, as a matter of

---

[33] *The Letters of William Blake*, ed. Geoffrey Keynes (1968), pp. 28–31. Blake's point is not, of course, that money doesn't matter: he probably already saw it as double-sided, as in the 'Laocoon' (E272), where Money is both 'The Great Satan' and 'the lifes blood of Poor Families'.

naming, of moralising, of thinking about necessary contraries in an abstract way:

> They take the Two Contraries which are called Qualities, with
>   which
> Every Substance is clothed, they name them Good & Evil
> From them they make an Abstract, which is a Negation
> Not only of the Substance from which it is derived
> A murderer of its own Body: but also a murderer
> Of every Divine Member: it is the Reasoning Power. . .
>
>   (E151)

This is so close to 'The Human Abstract' that one easily over-looks the fact that it is itself more abstract and indefinite than the earlier poem. What Blake is saying in the *Songs* (and also commun-icating with much greater poetic immediacy) is that one does not need to find a Cause for primary human impulses or instincts: both love and self-love exist beyond any question of Cause, and are necessary to human existence. Such impulses or instincts cannot be rationalised or moralised. They become 'innocent' or Fallen according to context, and the societal context is exactly that in which the contentment of one is the misery of another. It is this context which pollutes innocence, generates negations and turns contraries into opposites: 'Prisons are built with stones of Law, Brothels with bricks of Religion', and 'Bring out number weight & measure in a year of dearth.' It is within the context of 'dearth' and of social antagonism that the 'selfish loves increase': and it is in exactly the same soil that Empire and Mystery take root.

This is why the structural analysis which was offered of the symbolism of 'London' is important. The cause of man's Fall into this hell is, at one and the same time, its context in the clearly articulated imagery of the buying and selling of infancy, affections, life and love.[34] Commercialism, class society, activates contraries and turns them into self-bound antagonism: 'Is not Merit in one a Cause of Envy in another. . .?' 'The Human Abstract' shows Mystery arising from this soil, while 'London', in its symbolic structural organisation, shows the soil itself. To simplify (if we return to Dr Trusler) an environmentalist psychology following the Nature of 'This World' – let us say the sophisticated pain–pleasure

---

[34] We recall that the notebook lines 'There souls of men are bought & sold' which gave Blake his idea for the final verse of 'London' were at first intended as a final verse to 'The Human Abstract' – see above, p. 187.

associationism of Godwin – would have supposed that Want of Money 'caused' theft, and that if thieves had more money the cause would cease. Blake did not think so since he might have found the 'cause' in envy or self-love plus a context in which the wealth of one man inflamed the envy of another. At a less simple level, Blake insists that the Fall is made up of primary impulses (which, being primary and 'necessary', it is pointless or mystifying to describe as 'good' and 'evil') operating within a particular context which we could describe as class-culture. And it follows (although this is not argued in the *Songs*) that the abolition of this culture, by revolution, will not abolish the impulses. And all within that culture, oppressors and oppressed, bear its 'marks of weakness' and its 'mind forg'd manacles'.

Hence Blake, however close he is to the Painites, will not dispense with 'The Divine Image' or the 'Everlasting Gospel'. Just as with deism or atheism, he can agree with the analysis but still require, at the end of it, a utopian leap. The Fall is not cancelled out by abolishing the context, even if that context *is* the Fall. For humankind can't live context-less and a new context will grow up. There must be some Redemption, the creation of a new context in which not the 'selfish loves' but brotherhood will increase. But Blake could see no way to derive such an affirmation of love from naturalistic psychology, which was, at its very root, derivative from self-interest. Hence he must, even when in his most 'Jacobin' and revolutionary temper, hold fast to the Everlasting Gospel of his older antinomian faith. To create the New Jerusalem something must be brought in from outside the rationalist system, and that something could only be found in the non-rational image of Jesus, in the affirmatives of Mercy, Pity, Peace and Love.

CHAPTER 13

Conclusion

At this point we might recall the earlier arguments in this study. For if, as I have suggested, Blake had been deeply influenced by the tradition defined as Muggletonian, no symbolism would have imprinted itself more upon his mind than that of the Tree and of the Fall as being the emblem not of disobedience nor of sexuality but of the Knowledge of Good and Evil: 'That devil . . . that tempts men and women to all unrighteousness, it is man's spirit of unclean reason, and cursed imagination.' Thus Reeve and Muggleton (above, p. 94), and thus also Thomas Tomkinson: 'the tree of knowledge was not a natural tree; if it had, it could not have operated such venom in all mankind. . .' It must therefore have been the 'devil', or 'reason', a character very close to Blake's 'Human Abstract'.[1] In one sense, this Tree was taken to stand for Knowledge, and in the subsequent Muggletonian tradition could either encourage mere obscurantism, or could support a defence of the imagination and the affections against the 'reason' of the polite culture of a ruling-class. In another sense, the Tree was taken to stand for the Knowledge of Good and Evil: that is, the Moral Law of tablets and commandments as opposed to the gospel of forgiveness of sins, moralism as opposed to love, or, as Muggleton had it in his onslaught on George Fox, the Reason of Pilate which 'delivered up the Just One to be crucified by reasonable Men. . .'[2] And this same Muggletonian symbolism of Tree and Fall also (in the doctrine of man's 'two natures') offered a dramatic forecast of the inversions of *The Marriage of Heaven and Hell*, for 'the *Tree* of which Eve eat, called the *Tree of Knowledge of Good and Evil*, was her being overcome by the glorious Appearance the Devil made in the form of an Angel of Light. . .'[3] Hence the devil, seducing Eve

---

[1] *Truth's Triumph* (1823), p. 101.
[2] *A Looking-Glass for George Fox* (1656), p. 62.   [3] *Observations*, 1735, p. 8.

and transmuting himself in her womb, enters human nature (through Cain), and manifests himself in the abstracting and moralising faculties of 'reason'.[4]

And even if we dispense with a Muggletonian hypothesis, much the same symbolism could have come by way of Boehme. Thus:

Natural Reason without the Light of God seeth only to natural Image-likeness, . . . and frameth in itself the Divine Being or Essence, as if that were just such a Thing. From whence is come Strife amongst the Learned in Reason, & so that Men strive & dispute about God . . . where each of them holdeth his Imagination for Divine & will have his own Image which he hath framed in the Imagination of his Reason to be honoured for God: whereas yet it is only a natural Image of Reason.[5]

Thus just as Tomkinson's notion of virtues found only in men prepares us for 'The Divine Image' so the Muggletonian or Behmenist Tree prepares us for both 'The Human Abstract' and 'A Poison Tree'. In suggesting this I am not suggesting that Blake, in this or in any other case, took a symbol or a doctrine ready-made and used it in its original meaning. Just as he could borrow from, but transform, Volney, so he took this symbolism of Tree and Serpent and turned it to new uses. Moreover, we should never expect to find Blake employing a symbol consistently, in *exactly* the same way: we should rather think of his central symbols as a point of junction at which alternative, but closely related, meanings coincide. Thus he is using the same Tree in later life in alternative ways. In 'A Vision of the Last Judgement' (1810) the 'Tree of Knowledge' is one of officious moralising – 'always Prying after Good & Evil in one Another'; in 'For the Sexes: the Gates of Paradise' (*c.*1818) it was 'Rational Truth Root of Evil & Good'; in his conversation with Crabb Robinson it was Education (above, p. 87); in the late 'Laocoon' the symbol comprises still that emphasis upon man's self-division and self-alienation arising from self-love in class society with which 'The Human Abstract' commences:

> Good & Evil are
> Riches & Poverty a Tree of Mystery
> propagating Generation& Death

But Blake is now becoming wilful and somewhat cranky: a

[4] *Ibid.*, p. 10; *Principles*, 1735, p. 16; Tomkinson, *A System of Religion*, 1729, pp. 36–7, 87ff.
[5] Jacob Behmen, *Works* (1754), IV, pp. 167–8.

symbol can mean whatever he decides it means at any moment. 'SCIENCE' is also 'the Tree of DEATH'. 'ART is the Tree of LIFE.' Jesus and his apostles and disciples 'were all Artists'. 'The whole Business of Man Is The Arts & All Things Common' (i.e. in the simultaneous destruction of both 'Science' and of 'Riches & Poverty'). 'The outward Ceremony is Antichrist': so also is Science. 'HEBREW ART is called SIN by the Deist SCIENCE.' And 'Money, which is The Great Satan or Reason the Root of Good & Evil In The Accusation of Sin' (E270–2). In the even later Annotations to Thornton still more meanings are swept in: 'The Greek & Roman Classics is the Antichrist.' 'Christ & his Apostles were Illiterate Men . . . Caiphas Pilate & Herod were Learned.'[6]

It is splendid knockabout stuff. It is more than that – each insight probes, inverts, checks us in our tracks, turns the polite world of culture around. Such aphorisms remind us that Blake remained something of a revolutionary to the end. And also something of a Muggletonian. But we would be wrong to sit down and try to knit all these into a system: in doing so we are performing the tasks of Urizen and seeking to impose a boundary or 'ratio' upon the insights. These insights are all interrelated, certainly; they cross and inter-cross, and arise from a common nexus. But they are never worked through again with the rigour employed in the *Songs*. And the nexus from which they arise is not one of systematic philosophy nor of a particular intellectual or metaphysical 'tradition'. It is a nexus of attitude, stance, attack – the stance of the radical anti-hegemony of the antinomian tradition.

This, finally, explains one contradiction which baffles Blake studies. Where one scholar, adopting a biographical approach, can demonstrate evolution (perhaps not always of an ascendant kind) in Blake's thought, another scholar can, with equal force, demonstrate consistency and fixity of symbol and of meaning. I have suggested that the consistency is founded upon an unbroken sequence of preoccupation and of symbolism which stems from antinomianism. This endures through Swedenborgian and deist influences: and persists through the Lambeth Books to the major prophetic works to the end of Blake's life. The signatures of this consistency are to be found in a stance rejecting the polite culture; in such evidences as the symbolism of the Tree, which may fluctuate through Reason to the Moral Law to Mystery to Education to Money to Science, and the more obscure symbolism of the Serpent; and in the affirmation of the 'Everlasting Gospel': 'The Gospel is Forgiveness of Sins & has No Moral Precepts these belong to Plato & Seneca & Nero' (E608).

Few themes return more consistently than his hostility to the Moral Law. It is rehearsed frequently in the Lambeth Books, for example in *The Book of Urizen* (1794) (see Illus. 16) where Urizen writes in 'the Book/Of eternal brass'–

> One curse, one weight, one measure
> One King, one God, one Law. (E71)

(Many critics find this Book to be Blake's ironic version of the Book of Genesis for his 'Bible of Hell'). The theme is found repeatedly in Blake's paintings and illuminations. His patron, Thomas Butts, was evidently sympathetic to the theme,[7] and it was for Butts that Blake painted 'God Writing upon the Tables of the Covenant' (Illus. 17), 'The Blasphemer' (Illus. 18) and 'The Woman Taken in Adultery' (Illus. 19), as well as 'The Beast of Revelation' (Illus. 20). The theme is present in *Milton* and *Vala* and ever-present in his last prophetic book, *Jerusalem*, as when Albion is shown in chapter 2–

> Cold snows drifted around him: ice coverd his loins around
> He sat by Tyburns brook, and underneath his heel, shot up!
> A deadly Tree, he nam'd it Moral Virtue, and the Law
> Of God who dwells in Chaos hidden from the human sight. (E172)

But–

> No individual can keep these Laws, for they are death
> To every energy of man, and forbid the springs of life. . .

The same theme recurs in the prologue to *For the Sexes: the Gates of Paradise* (1818 or earlier):

> Jehovahs fingers wrote the Law
> Then Wept! then rose in Zeal & Awe
> And the Dead Corpse from Sinais heat
> Buried beneath his Mercy Seat.
> O Christians, Christians! tell me Why
> You rear it on your Altars high. (E256)

---

[7] Butts was a chief clerk in the office of the Commissary General of Musters: see G.E. Bentley, 'Thomas Butts, White Collar Maecenae', *PMLA*, 71, pp. 1052–66. He was rumoured to be a Swedenborgian, but nothing definite is known of his religion.

This remains the dominant trope throughout *The Everlasting Gospel* (*c.*1818): thus when the women taken in adultery is brought before Jesus–

> He laid His hand on Moses Law
> The Ancient Heavens in Silent Awe
> Writ with Curses from Pole to Pole
> All away began to roll   (E512)

And when in his very last year (1827) at the age of seventy Blake annotated with fury Dr Thornton's *New Translation of the Lord's Prayer*, it was still the submissive obeisance to 'law' which drew his savage commentary:

Lawful Bread Bought with Lawful Money & a Lawful heaven seen thro' a Lawful Telescope by means of Lawful Window Light   The Holy Ghost [& whatever] cannot be Taxed is Unlawful & Witchcraft.
Spirits are Lawful but not Ghosts especially Royal Gin is Lawful Spirit
No Smuggling real British Spirit & Truth (E658)

As always Blake's visionary spiritualism combines with a combative polemic against the 'Beast' of the State.

Blake was not a hurrah-revolutionary, as he is sometimes represented, nor was he a premature practitioner of Marxist dialectic.[8] But he was not isolated in his employment of the vocabulary of the 'New Jerusalem'. In the millenarian effervescence in London throughout the 1790s and into the next decade, this vocabulary was ever-present.[9] Not only Richard Brothers and Joanna Southcott were fully involved in the rhetoric,[10] but many other minor prophets and pamphleteers like William Huntington.[11] The Universalists, who emerged in the Swedenborgian nexus, were saturated with the vocabulary of the millennium, and might possibly have caught Blake's notice.[12] Their prophet, Elhanan Winchester, republished in 1792 a translation of Siegvolk's *The Everlasting*

---

[8] See David Punter, 'Blake, Marxism and Dialectic', *Literature and History*, No. 6, Autumn 1977.

[9] See Morton D. Paley, *The Continuing City: William Blake's Jerusalem* (Oxford, 1986), chapter 3.

[10] M. D. Paley, 'William Blake, The Prince of the Hebrews, and The Woman Clothed with the Sun'; J.F.C. Harrison, Part II, pp. 80–5.

[11] See, e.g., W. Huntington, *Key to the Hieroglyphical Print of the Church of God in her Fivefold State including the Holy Jerusalem*, &c (1808).

[12] There is, however, no evidence that Blake was interested in the (very loose and sloppy) Universalists or in Winchester, and I find Michael Ferber's description of Blake as a 'Holy Ghost Universalist' (*The Social Vision of William Blake*, pp. 190–1) to be misleading.

Gospel, and by 1794 the Universalists had their own hymn-book in which the New Jerusalem was announced:

> Its jasper walls so great and high,
> How glorious to behold!
> Four-square doth this great city lie.
> Its streets are purest gold.

And Winchester himself had published in the previous year a poem in twelve books, of which Book IX described the Millennium:

> Our sons shall be as plants grown up in youth,
> Beautiful, cheerful, gay, strong, innocent,
> Pleasant, wise, affable, sensible, good.
> Our daughters like to precious corner-stones,
> Polish'd, as if for palaces design'd.
> Fair, lovely, gentle, kind, polite, sincere,
> Virtuous, modest, humble, prudent, meek,
> Form'd to delight and cultivate mankind.[13]

Even the epic-prophetic mode appears to have been sufficiently familiar to a light-hearted London audience for it to have been adopted as an acceptable form of satire.[14]

To cite such anaemic comparisons as those of Winchester is to draw attention not to the typicality but to the untypicality of Blake. Among Winchester's prophecies were the personal coming of Christ; the resurrection of the saints; the conversion of the Jews; a final great war after which Satan was to be bound in the abyss for 1,000 years; then the millennium; then Satan loosed again and again overthrown; then the New Jerusalem and a general restoration.[15] All this was to happen independently of human agency, whereas Blake's 'Jerusalem' was to be built by strenuous intellectual, imaginative and artistic labours: 'to Labour in Knowledge is to Build up Jerusalem' (E230). The essential utopian leap for Blake was to brotherhood, the return to universal man. It is possible to trace in Blake's thought a lingering gnostic myth, by which an

---

[13] E. Winchester, *The Universalists Hymn Book* (1794); E. Winchester, *The Process and Empire of Christ* (1793). It is fair to state that W. Blake does *not* appear in the list of subscribers to the latter.

[14] See *The Revelation in Six Chapters* (1805), Brit. Lib. T1123(1), a jest, in messianic form, upon the supporters of Sir Francis Burdett; e.g., 'The Daughters of Albion waved their snow-white handkerchiefs/They joined in the shout of the populace, and exclaimed, "Francis for Ever!"'

[15] Elhanan Winchester, *A Course of Lectures on the Prophecies that Remain to be Fulfilled* (1789).

original Unity fell into division and ever since has sought to return
to the One once more:[16]

> ... Man subsists by Brotherhood & Universal Love
> We fall on one anothers necks more closely we embrace
> Not for ourselves but for the Eternal family we live
> Man liveth not by Self alone but in his brothers face
> Each shall behold the Eternal Father & love & joy abound
>
> (E387)

Blake did not achieve any full synthesis of the antinomian and
the rationalist. How could he, since the antinomian premised a
non-rational affirmative? There was, rather, an incandescence in
his art in which the incompatible traditions met – tried to marry –
argued as contraries – were held in a polarised tension. If one
may be wrong to look for a coherent intellectual system, there are
certainly constellations of related attitudes and images – connected
insights – but at the moment when we attempt a rational exegesis
we are imposing bounds on these insights. Certainly there are
places where Blake denies the values of rationality, but one can
also see why, to preserve the 'divine vision', he had to do so. For
within the prevailing naturalistic psychology of the time there was
no way to derive, no place into which to insert, the central antinomian affirmatives of *Thou Shalt*: Thou Shalt Love, or Thou Shalt
Forgive. Blake's unique image of Christ, simultaneously humanist
and antinomian ('Jesus was all virtue and acted from impulse, not
from rules') could be, in the available philosophy, derived only
from the inspiration of a 'madman'. It is exactly the absence of
such an affirmative in the complacent doctrine of 'benevolence' to
be found in the Godwinian circle which alienated Wordsworth and
Coleridge. One might add that these affirmatives cannot be easily
derived from materialist thought today. That is why every realis-
ation of these values (such as Blake's) is a plank in the floor upon
which the future must walk.

The busy perfectionists and benevolent rationalists of 1791–6
nearly all ended up, by the later 1800s, as disenchanted men.
Human nature, they decided, had let them down and proved stubborn in resistance to enlightenment. But William Blake, by denying
even in the *Songs of Experience* a supreme societal value to rational-

---

[16] See Ferber's helpful chapter on brotherhood in *The Social Vision of William Blake*; and, on
Gnostic and neo-Platonist myths of Unity, M.H. Abrams, *Natural Supernaturalism* (New
York, 1971), pp. 143–63.

ity, did not suffer from the same kind of disenchantment. His vision had been not into the rational government *of* man but into the liberation of an unrealised potential, an alternative nature, within man: a nature masked by circumstance, repressed by the Moral Law, concealed by Mystery and self-defeated by the other nature of 'self-love'. It was the intensity of this vision, which derived from sources far older than the Enlightenment, which made it impossible for Blake to fall into the courses of apostasy. When he drew apart from the deists and when the revolutionary fires burned low in the early 1800s, Blake had his own way of 'keeping the divine vision in time of trouble'. This way had been prepared long before by the Ranters and the Diggers in their defeat, who had retired from activist strife to Gerard Winstanley's 'kingdom within, which moth and rust does not corrupt'. And so Blake also took the characteristic antinomian retreat into more esoteric ways, handing on to the initiates 'The Everlasting Gospel'. There is obscurity and perhaps even some oddity in this. But there is never the least sign of submission to 'Satan's Kingdom'. Never, on any page of Blake, is there the least complicity with the kingdom of the Beast.

Index